NIGHT WATCH

Recent Titles by David C. Taylor

The Michael Cassidy Series

NIGHT LIFE
NIGHT WORK
NIGHT WATCH *

* available from Severn House

NIGHT WATCH

David C. Taylor

Severn House Large Print
London & New York

This first large print edition published 2019
in Great Britain and the USA by
SEVERN HOUSE PUBLISHERS LTD of
Eardley House, 4 Uxbridge Street, London W8 7SY.
First world regular print edition published 2019 by
Severn House Publishers Ltd.

British Library Cataloguing in Publication Data
A CIP catalogue record for this title is available from the British Library.

ISBN-13: 9780727892256

Severn House Publishers support the Forest Stewardship Council™
[FSC™], the leading international forest certification organisation. All
our titles that are printed on FSC certified paper carry the FSC logo.

FSC
www.fsc.org   FSC® C013056
MIX
Paper from
responsible sources

Typeset by Palimpsest Book Production Ltd.,
Falkirk, Stirlingshire, Scotland.
Printed and bound in Great Britain by
T J International, Padstow, Cornwall.

For Priscilla, Susannah, and Jennifer, as always, with love.

'For the powerful, crimes are those others commit.'

Noam Chomsky

For my friends at Severn House, Kate, Carl, Natasha, and Emma. Thank you for your warm welcome and your meticulous work in improving the novel. And thank you to my wonderful agent Lisa Gallagher, without whom I would be adrift.

One

September in New York and the first cold night of fall signaled to the city that 1956 was slipping to its end. The crisp, clear air made the lights in the great apartment buildings around Central Park glitter like diamonds. The horses harnessed to carriages at the curb on Columbus Circle huffed smoke from their nostrils as they stood heads down, their backs covered with plaid blankets, and waited for the night-time romantics who wanted to ride through the park bundled under lap robes in private darkness. The shrill wail of a police car siren rose in the west. The horses watched the car pass on 59th Street headed east toward Fifth Avenue, lights flashing. They dropped their heads again to eat hay strewn in the gutter by their drivers. They had been raised on concrete and were used to sirens. In a city of eight million there was always an emergency – someone trapped in an elevator, a restaurant kitchen fire, a domestic dispute, a liquor store stick-up, a body leaking blood across the sidewalk.

Limousines and yellow Checker cabs waited outside the Plaza Hotel for the late-dinner crowd from the Oak Room, for the serious drinkers in the Oak Bar, for the fans listening to Julie Wilson's second set in the Persian Room, and for the debutantes and their dates dancing to Lester Lanin's band in the second-floor ballroom.

1

Uniformed limo drivers clustered near a new Rolls-Royce Silver Cloud parked in front of the big metal awning at the hotel entrance. The car's stately elegance made the nearby Cadillac limos look like dowdy country cousins. The drivers smoked cigarettes and argued the eternals: sports, women, and money.

Shortly after midnight the hotel doorman swept open the bronze-framed doors and three couples came out. The chauffeur for the Rolls flicked his cigarette out into the street and opened the back door to the limousine as the couples descended the wide stairs. They were men and women in their mid-forties, prosperous, well fleshed, dressed for the evening. The men wore suits, dark wool overcoats, and cashmere scarves. Two of them wore fedoras. The third, proud of his thick chestnut hair, went hatless. The women wore long dresses in jewel colors – ruby, sapphire, and emerald – and matching silk-covered high heels, lustrous dark mink coats, and chic hats pinned to their hair.

The couples clustered around the open door of the limousine for their goodbyes, cheek kisses for the women, handshakes for the men. The hatless man accompanied his handshakes with short bows. Two of the couples got into the car. The chauffeur closed the door and went around to the driver's seat. The hatless man and his wife waved as the car pulled away from the curb at a dignified speed. She tucked her arm in his and said, 'Shall we walk?'

'Yes. Why not? A beautiful night. Shall we stop at Rumpelmayer's for *café mit schlag*?'

2

'A good idea.'

'And then through the park for a bit.' There was a tease in his voice.

'The park at night? Is that wise?'

'Have no fear. I will protect you from all the wild animals.'

She laughed. 'Oh, then, of course. We go.' It was the first small slip of her otherwise impeccable, lightly accented English.

'We'll go. Or, let's go,' he corrected with a smile.

She jabbed him with an elbow, 'All right, Mr Know-It-All, let's go.' She was a small, dark-haired woman, as bright and quick as a starling. Her face was a little too sharp to be fashionably pretty. She had eyes the color of blue ice, a scientist's eyes, coolly analytical and intelligent. Her name was Magda Brandt. It had been *von Brandt*, but her husband, Karl, who walked at her side, had dropped the *von* in deference to the democratic spirit of the country in which they now lived. She missed its designation of aristocracy, but there was no point in arguing with Karl when he made up his mind. Not that they often argued. They shared so much: work, politics, a love of music (Wagner, Brahms and, of course, Beethoven), sexual appetites, and secrets – quite a number of secrets, some of them so dangerous they did not talk about them at all except occasionally in bed when they were looking for a sharper edge.

Karl Brandt was over six feet tall and two hundred pounds. He had a handsome, square-jawed face, warm brown eyes, and thick, wavy

3

hair combed back and parted high on the right side. It was a face that gave away little beyond good fellowship and charm. He had a ready smile and a deep, easy laugh. Women were attracted to him. Men wanted his friendship and approval. He was a man who was sure that he had never put a foot wrong and never would.

They walked west along Central Park South discussing the evening. The Oak Room food was very good, but it did not in any way measure up to Horcher's in Berlin. The creamed spinach at Horcher's, that was something no one could duplicate. Perhaps it was the pinch of nutmeg, just enough to whisper on your tongue. Still, goodbye to Horcher's and all that. There was nothing to be gained by looking to the past and to the world lost. Their future was here in America, which had come through the late, unfortunate war unscathed. Of course it had lost soldiers, but people were easily replaced. Its mainland cities stood untouched. Its industries had prospered turning out the machinery of war, and it was now by far the richest, most powerful country on earth. The opportunities for the Brandts were unlimited.

'Do you trust Harry Gallien?' Magda asked. Gallien was the owner of the Rolls limousine and had been their host that evening.

'Yes, I do. He understands the importance of our work, and he understands how much money can be made from the private applications after our present contract is over.'

'I do not trust a man with a soft handshake. And his hands are damp. I don't like that.'

4

'He is going to make us very rich some day, damp hands or dry. Be nice to him, Magda.'

'Gallien is not a Jewish name, is it?'

'No. I believe it's French, but the family has been in America for generations.'

'Ah, the French, a nation of shopkeepers, a thumb on the scale, water in the wine: slippery people. Well, you'll need a very strong contract. Best get a good Jew lawyer.'

They stopped to look in through the lightly steamed window of Rumpelmayer's, the café in the Hotel St Moritz. 'Too many people,' Magda said. 'Let's go home.' They walked on toward Columbus Circle.

The Greek's hotdog cart was in its usual spot in the curve of the park wall at Columbus Circle. Leon Dudek did not know if the burly man who owned the cart really was Greek, but that was what people called him. Leon Dudek usually ate something around midnight. If he had no passengers he would ease himself down from his carriage seat, pat his horse on the rump, and limp from where he was parked to the cart at the Circle. As he went, he would decide what he wanted on his dog. Sometimes he would have onions and relish, but no mustard. Sometimes he would refuse the relish and add ketchup. Sometimes sauerkraut. On his wilder nights he would have an Italian sausage with the works, which came from his mouth as *ze verks*. Tonight he waited patiently while two young men in tuxedos bought four hot dogs with all the trimmings and carried them to their debutante dates

5

waiting on a park bench nearby. The girls wore full-skirted evening dresses under their fur capes, pearl necklaces and matching earrings, and orchid corsages, now beginning to wilt, pinned high near their breasts. To Dudek they looked fresh and beautiful, unspoiled, heart-breakingly innocent. His Anna would be their age if she had lived, but she and her mother, Rachel, had died within days of each other nearly twelve years ago, a week in which his life ended but left him living. He had often thought of suicide so he could be with them again, but he understood that to give up life that they had fought so hard to hold would dishonor them, and so he went on.

Leon took a bite of his hotdog and turned back toward his carriage.

Karl and Magda Brandt crossed Central Park South. They stopped under a streetlight near a horse-drawn cab parked along the curb. Karl took a cigarette from his silver case. He offered one to Magda, but she declined with a gesture of her gloved hand. He lit his with a gold lighter and returned the case to his pocket.

'You!'

The shout turned them.

A man limped toward them from Columbus Circle. The hotdog he held dripped ketchup and mustard unnoticed. He was dressed in a worn canvas coat, wool pants, scuffed boots, and his body twisted as if his spine had been wrenched and never set straight. His left foot dragged. His face was shadowed by an old fedora. 'You, wait!'

6

'Come,' Karl said, and took Magda's arm. He was not going to end a pleasant evening with one of New York's mad beggars. Why didn't the police do something about them so that good people could go about their lives unmolested? He and Magda turned into the park.

Leon Dudek watched the couple walk away. Was it them? How many times in the last ten years had he thought he had seen one of them? Six? Seven? There was the shoemaker near St Marks Place. That was a mistake, the police summoned, and then all the fuss. Then last month there was the man from the bakery he had followed around the Lower East Side for a week as he tried to work up the courage to confront him. He was sure about the baker, but he needed to have him admit it, needed to hear him confess. It was only by thinking of Anna and Rachel that he had been able to force himself into the man's store on an afternoon when there were no other customers. He took a loaf of rye bread he did not want, and his hands trembled when he gave the money. *Say something. Make him speak. You will know his voice. You heard it many times. You will know it. Make him speak.* 'What is your name?' His voice was a croak and he coughed to clear it.

'Tony Pellini.' The baker smiled.

This wasn't the voice, but a voice could change, couldn't it? 'Do you know me?' he asked.

'Nah. Should I?'

'You have never seen me before?'

'Don't think so. I know most of our customers, but not all. What's up?'

7

He wanted to reach out and smash him, beat him, crush him, as if he could smash all the things that had been done to him and to his loved ones. The baker saw the flare in his eyes, and reared back from the counter and put his hands up in defense. 'Hey, what the hell?' Leon read his fear and was ashamed that he had caused it, because no matter how much he wanted him to be one of them, he knew he wasn't. He turned and blundered out of the store leaving the loaf of rye by the register.

Leon watched the elegant couple walk into the park. The incident with the baker had shaken him. The baker had been the latest of a number of people he had confronted, all of them innocent, none of them the monsters he looked for, and yet these two walking away . . . Were they the same ones he had seen in August? That brief glimpse on that hot day when the horse got sick and he had started for the stable early. Once again there was something about them that struck an awful chord in him. He was angry at his uncertainty and his fear. *Follow them. Go look. If you're wrong, an apology is a simple thing. If you are right . . . What then? They have friends. They are people with money and power. What are you? Who are you?* He put his hand in his pocket and touched the bone-handled clasp knife he carried. He went into the park as quickly as his limp would let him.

Magda stole a drag from Karl's cigarette and passed it back as they walked on a path lighted by street lamps. 'Darling, are you worried about the blind trials?'

He shook his head. 'No. I'm sure they'll go well.'

'Are we still going to choose the subjects randomly?'

'Yes. The variables will be age and body weight.'

'But the doses remain the same.'

'As we discussed.'

'You don't think we need more in-house trials before we go out?'

'There's pressure from above for results. We need to move along.'

'There are risks.'

'Of course. That's the nature of scientific experiments.' He flicked the cigarette away and it hit a bench in a burst of sparks.

She read his impatience. 'Do you mind my asking?'

'Of course not.'

'Sometimes I think you would prefer it if I was a good housewife like Jane Gallien. You could go off to work and come back to the well-run apartment, the hot dinner, and the adoring wife.' There was a mocking note in her voice.

They stopped under a streetlight. The river rush of traffic on Central Park West was muted by the trees. 'I have all those things and a brilliant scientific partner. I am a very lucky man. We are very lucky people.' He pulled her close and kissed her. For a moment she held back, but then, as always, she gave in and kissed him back and put her arms around his waist. 'I'll tell you what,' he said, 'we'll do a few more in-house trials before we go out, if that's what you want.'

'Who will the first be?'

'Someone we've used before. That way we have the early trial as a baseline and we can note the variations of response. Okay? Satisfied?'

She kissed him again in thanks.

'You! You there!'

They broke apart, startled, and found that the bum had followed them into the park.

Karl moved in front of Magda to shelter her. 'Go away. We have nothing for you.'

'I know you.' Leon Dudek limped forward. He was sure now. He could not be mistaken. They were unchanged, as if the war had left no marks. 'I know you. Do you know me? Do you? I was one of them, but I lived.' He gripped the knife in his pocket hard enough to hurt his hand.

'Go away, I said. Not a dime. Not a penny.' The man was under the streetlamp now, and when the light fell on his face Karl Brandt's eyes widened in surprise. Karl heard Magda take in a breath. She recognized him too. What was his name? Leon something. It came to him suddenly.

'You know me,' Leon said. 'Look at me. You know me. Here I am. I lived so I could find you. For the others. For my daughter. For my wife. For the ones who died. I am witness.'

Karl felt Magda shift away behind him. 'You're making a mistake. I've never seen you before in my life. I don't know who you are, but if you don't leave us alone, I will call for the police.' When the man took his hand out of his pocket, he held a knife. The blade was closed, but it would only take a second to open it. Karl and Magda had always feared this moment might

10

arrive, and now it was here. How had this one survived? How had he made it to America? It seemed ridiculous that trash like this could make them stumble.

Magda appeared from the darkness behind the man. She had discarded her shoes and was moving quietly. *Whatever she is doing, I must keep him looking at me*, Karl thought. *He must not see her.* 'Who the hell do you think you are yelling at me like this?' He used his best command voice, one that had cowed subordinates for years. 'I've told you, you have the wrong man. I've never seen you before in my life. Go away. Go away! Are you an idiot?' Karl took a step forward.

Leon hesitated. The doctor was a big man, and he looked fit, and Leon was weak and broken. The idea that the man might get away made him want to weep. He fumbled with the knife, and finally managed to open it.

Magda was close now. She could smell him: horse and sweat. She removed the pin that held her hat to her hair. The pin was four inches long and slightly flattened like a blade. It was topped by a large fake pearl that gave her a good grip. She examined the back of the man's head. It had been a long time since she had studied anatomy, but she had a fine, retentive mind. She saw the spot she was looking for, above the dirty collar of the man's jacket. She drove the pin hard up into the hollow at the base of the man's skull. She twisted the steel and probed. The man stiffened. The steel blade in his brain locked his legs. He tried to turn but could not. 'Hold him,' she commanded.

Karl grabbed the man's wrists and squeezed.

Magda pulled the pin out, and the man sagged a bit and whimpered. She stabbed the pin back in at a different angle. The man bleated and jerked, and the knife fell from his hand. 'Hold him tight.'

Karl hugged the man, pinning his arms. The man's breath was thick with onions and decay. His eyes were wide and staring. His mouth stretched in agony, and his body shuddered and twitched as Magda twisted the steel in his brain. Karl noted the parchment of the man's skin, the broken veins in his nose, the gray stubble on his cheeks. He looked past the man to Magda. Her brow was furrowed with concentration. She held the tip of her tongue between her teeth, the way she did when she was working out a knotty problem.

Magda pulled the pin out and jabbed it in again. Leon Dudek bent backward like a bow, and his face strained toward the sky. He quivered as if electrified. The pin cut something fatal. His head slumped onto Karl's shoulder and Karl let him down onto the pavement and crouched to feel his neck for a pulse. 'He's dead.' He stood up. 'Well done, darling.' He kicked the body lightly. 'What did you use?'

'My hat pin.'

'I wouldn't have known where to go in with it. I've forgotten so much since medical school. You're a wonder.' He took her in his arms. She could feel their hearts racing together, and he felt the heat rise in both of them. 'We better go.'

'I have to find my shoes, and my hat fell when

12

I took out the pin. You should take his wallet. They'll think it's a robbery.' She stood on tiptoes to kiss him.

In the glow from the streetlamp her eyes were bright, and to Karl she looked beautiful.

Two

When Cassidy woke up, he was on his back on the living room floor, naked, confused, and in pain. The table near the big chair by the window was on its side, and its lamp lay shattered nearby. The dream had driven him here. He tried to remember it: a suffocating blackness like visible doom. Something was coming for him, something that wanted him dead. He ran down a dark corridor, and whatever it was followed him. It drew closer. There was a door at the end of the corridor. Reach the door, and he was safe. He yanked the door open. Ahead was another dark corridor, and the thing that wanted him waited at the end. He turned back, but the door was closed behind him, and it would not open, and the thing in the darkness was getting closer.

He had had the same dream three times in the last month. The repetition troubled him, because ever since his childhood some of his dreams had turned out to be prophetic. He would dream of a man he had never seen before and would then meet that man a few days later. He would dream of a room he had never entered, and a week later

13

would be in that room. Sometimes the dreams carried awful weight. When he was sixteen, he had dreamed of his mother's suicide and had come home in the afternoon from a friend's house to find her dead in her room exactly as he had dreamed it. Should he have known? Could he have saved her? He still carried that like ice in his heart.

When he rubbed his leg, he felt the stickiness of blood. 'Ah, shit,' he groaned.

The overhead light came on.

'What the hell, Michael?' Rhonda Raskin crossed the living room and knelt beside him. 'Are you all right? Hey, you're bleeding. What happened?'

'Sleep walking. I guess I hit the table.'

'Let me get something for your leg.'

'It's all right. I'll get up.'

'You're going to drip blood on the rug. Let me get something.'

'The rug's had blood on it before.'

She helped him to his feet and he limped to the kitchen. He sat on a stool next to the black walnut counter that separated the kitchen from the living room while she got a box of Band-Aids from the drawer next to the stove. She was a tall, slim woman about his age. She had a narrow, intelligent face made striking by huge, dark eyes. Her black hair was tousled from bed. She wore his bathrobe with the sleeves rolled high.

She took a large patch from the box and handed it to him to strip off the paper. 'We better wash that first,' she said. 'Do you have any alcohol?'

14

'There's a bottle of gin there.'

'Good as anything, I guess.' She sloshed gin on a paper towel and scrubbed the wound.

'Ow! Easy.'

'Baby.' She threw the bloody paper away, took the Band-Aid, and pressed it down over the wound. 'I think you'll live.' She went back into the kitchen and put coffee grounds and water in the percolator and set it on a burner. 'So?'

'Sleep walking. It happens.' He did not talk about prophetic dreams to anyone. He had tried once with his younger sister, Leah, just after their mother died, but she had covered her ears and told him to stop, she did not want to hear it. She understood what a horror it was to dream about your mother's death and to have the dream come true.

'I know it happens,' Rhonda said. 'It happened the last time I was here too.' She looked down at herself and pulled the robe tighter. 'Jesus, what do I look like? Something the cat dragged in.'

'The cat's got great taste.'

She looked at him skeptically. 'I'll be back in a minute. Here, put this on.' She took off the robe and handed it to him and went back toward the bedroom with the slightly knock-kneed walk of a naked woman who knows she's being watched. Cassidy stood up and took the robe. He had a narrow waist and broad shoulders. He stood a bit under six feet tall and weighed a hundred seventy-five pounds. His back was scarred as if scourged by whips – shrapnel wounds from a German mortar during the war.

15

He put on the robe, scrubbed his face with a hand to chase the last heaviness of sleep, and combed his unruly black hair back from his face with his fingers. He lit a cigarette from the pack of Luckies on the counter while he waited for the coffee to perk.

Rhonda was a reporter for the *New York Post*. They had had a thing a few years back that started hot and flamed out badly. They lost touch. He heard she got married; heard it didn't last. He ran into her at a rooftop party in Brooklyn in May on one of those impossibly perfect spring evenings. The full moon hung over the city. The air was light and soft and perfumed, a triumph of trees and flowers over gasoline, diesel, and smoke. An evening full of promise where everyone was smart and beautiful, and life would go on forever. Romance was inevitable.

They started seeing each other again once or twice a week. They discovered that they still liked each other, liked the talk, and the laughter, and the sex. They began carefully this time, no promises, no expectations, a day at a time, a week. He did not think about whether it would grow or die. It was here now, and that was enough.

She had a bitter, funny view of the world. Her explanation of the failed marriage – he wanted her to quit her job, stay home, and do what girls do. 'He wanted a cleaner, whiter wash, and dinner on the table at seven, and I didn't.'

The day was just starting to brighten the windows that overlooked the Westside Highway past the roofs of the piers, to the dark flow of

16

the river and the glint of gold where the rising sun touched the tops of the tallest buildings in Hoboken across the Hudson from Greenwich Village. Cassidy's apartment was on the top floor of a five-story building. He had bought it with money his mother had left him. The big living room had exposed brick walls and tall windows. The kitchen was separated from the living room by the counter where he sat. A short hall led to a large bedroom and a bathroom. The furniture was simple and comfortable, and most of the paintings that decorated the walls were from Village artists, many of whom he knew. A mahogany-cased TV stood against one wall next to the cabinet that held his stereo and his collection of jazz records.

When Rhonda came back, her hair was combed, her makeup was fresh, and she was dressed in a light-colored tweed suit that showed off her legs. She poured coffee for both of them and leaned on the counter and studied his face. 'Are you all right? I mean really? This sleep walking thing is a little bit weird, you know.'

'Don't worry about it. It happens. Then it stops.'

She studied him, started to say something, and then stopped and shrugged. 'Okay. But you know, Michael, there are people who talk to other people about the things that are bothering them.'

'Don't believe it. It's just a rumor put out by the shrinks to drum up trade.' Rhonda was not the first woman who complained that Cassidy hid his thoughts. What was he going to tell her: that

17

he had woken up a week ago crouched in a corner of the living room, his service revolver in his hands, the hammer back, a trigger pull away from killing his easy chair? He had had no idea of how he had gotten there or what part of the dream he was going to kill, but it scared him.

'Okay, baby.' Rhonda patted him on the cheek. 'What the hell? I've always had a weakness for the slightly bent, and you sure fill that slot. I'm going to work. Intrepid girl reporter hot on the trail of breaking news: are hemlines up this year, or down? What does the New York housewife think about the convenience of frozen TV dinners for the family? Catch the hard-hitting scoops in the *Post*.' Like most women reporters, Rhonda was assigned soft stories that were meant to appeal to women, and she chafed under the restrictions. 'Are you working anything juicy?'

'A drug thing in Hell's Kitchen, a couple of stick-ups around Times Square. A woman over on 8th and 51st shot her husband six times while he was watching television and then called us.'

'Justifiable homicide.'

'How do you know?'

'Her husband? What else could it be?' she said as she picked up her purse from the counter. 'Will you call me if you get something?'

'You know I will. When do I see you again?'

'I've got a charity thing at the Metropolitan Museum tonight. Friday?'

'I've got tickets to the fights.'

'Call me. We'll figure it out.' She kissed him lightly so as not to smear her lipstick and walked

18

to the door. She must have known he was watching, because she twitched her hips once before the door closed behind her, and Cassidy went into the day with a lighter heart.

Cassidy stood on the platform in the 14th Street subway station in the crowd of commuters for the next train that would take them uptown to their daily grinds.

He was unaware of the man who studied him from a few paces away.

The man wore a duffel coat with a deep hood that obscured his face. He had picked up Cassidy on Hudson Street and had followed him to the 14th Street subway station for the third day in a row. He had followed Cassidy through the city a number of times and had made notes of where he went and whom he met. He was good at that kind of work, and he was sure that Cassidy had no idea that he had a shadow. He had been trained to take his time for an operation like this, but now he wanted to get it done. He had denied himself the pleasure of watching Cassidy die for long enough. Why not kill him today?

The press behind Cassidy grew denser as more people arrived and pushed into the back of the crowd. He was hemmed in on both sides, and he could feel the bulk of a fat man just behind him. He turned his head and caught the man's eye, and the man shrugged an apology for the intimacy. Cassidy's toes touched the yellow warning grid a couple of feet from the drop-off edge of the platform. A distant iron whine, a vibration, a waft of stale metallic air pushed up the tunnel. The train would arrive in under a minute.

The man who shadowed Cassidy pressed against the broad back of the fat man. The fat man inched forward to relieve the pressure. That pushed Cassidy a short step onto the yellow warning grid. Cassidy leaned back against the man's bulk. The man said, 'Sorry,' and tried to edge backward, but the pressure against his back was implacable.

The blast of air grew stronger. The steel wheels shrilled on the tracks and the couplings between cars rattled and banged as the train ran hard for the station. Cassidy could see the light on the lead car down the tunnel. Twenty seconds until it arrived.

People around Cassidy shuffled forward a little in anticipation of the train. The pressure on Cassidy's back pushed him toward the platform edge. Cassidy tried to dig his shoes into the warning grid, but he could get no grip. 'Hey, give me some room. Back up. Back up.' Jesus Christ, what was going on behind him? Didn't they get it?

'Sorry. Sorry. I can't.' There was panic in the fat man's voice. 'Back up,' he yelled at whoever was behind him. 'Please back up. Give us some room. You have to give us some room.'

Cassidy's shadow pressed harder into the fat man's back, forcing him to take a small step forward. Cassidy felt himself pushed to the edge of the platform. He tried to move sideways but there was no place to go. He leaned back hard, but gained nothing. His heart hammered in his

20

chest. The front car was closing fast. He pushed back as hard as he could. The fat man grunted, but he could not give way. Cassidy felt himself tip forward.

Three

The pressure on Cassidy's back went away, and he lurched back a foot. The train slammed into the station with a squeal of brakes and the crash of couplings. The train stopped. The doors opened. The surge of people behind him pushed Cassidy into the car.

The man in the duffel coat watched the train grind into motion, pick up speed, and disappear into the tunnel. That was close. Cassidy alive one moment and then dead the next. There was no pleasure in that. Too fast. Cassidy would not even have known he was dying. He should know it was coming for a long time. He should know why. He should have to think about it. That's where the terror lies: thinking about death, knowing it's coming, knowing there's nothing you can do about it. That's what he wanted for Cassidy. Not some flick of the switch from light to dark. Where was the joy in that? He almost fucked the whole thing up out of impatience. *Get a hold of yourself. Take your time.* This was supposed to be fun. He went up the stairs and out into daylight.

* * *

Cassidy carried two cups of coffee from the corner diner up the stairs to the squad room and put one down on his partner's desk.

'Thanks,' Tony Orso said. 'Hey, what's with you? You look kind of weird.'

'I'm never taking the fucking subway again. I almost got pushed under the train at 14th Street.'

'You were standing in the front row?'

'Yeah.'

'You grew up here. You should know better. Don't be standing in the front row at rush hour. If you do, you deserve what you get.'

'Thanks. That was comforting.'

Orso unfolded a piece of paper on his desk and smoothed it out with his thumb.

'What've you got?' Cassidy took the lid off his coffee and took a sip. He lit a cigarette and tossed the pack on his desk.

Orso held up the paper to show a Regent 7 prefix, an Upper East Side phone number. 'I was down at Winky's for the game last night. There's a broad at the table. I'm thinking, what the hell, easy pickings. I've never known a broad could play poker worth a damn. Someone says her name's Amy Something. I don't catch the last name right then. Anyway, the usual crowd, Petey Blue, Al Costanza, Bill Parnell, Frankie What-the-Fuck owns that grind house on 41st, and a couple of others in and out of the game. But she's there the whole time. After a few hands I think, holy shit, Tony, watch your ass. This one's good. If they're all like this one, I don't want to see another. She can play. And she's got no tells I can see. She's having a good time, laughing,

22

talking, giving guys the needle, having a drink. None of it means a thing. She picks up her hand, looks at it, gives you nothing. Sometimes she smiles, sometimes not, also doesn't mean a thing. Same if she's got a full house or a busted flush. Cool, very cool. A couple of hours in she's cleaned three guys out, and I'm just holding my own, maybe a hundred up, not much of it her money. And I can play the game. You know I can play.'

'Yes, you can.' Cassidy's tried the coffee again.

'Right. So I'm watching her, trying to get a read, but it's hard, man. Then right at the end, I'm holding a pair of nines, pair of threes. She's raising and people are dropping out, and it's her and me, heads up, and there's I don't know what, maybe a grand in the pot. I don't know what she's got, but the way she's been playing all night it's got to be stronger than mine, but goddamn it. Enough. So I call. She lays down a pair of deuces. She was bluffing. She builds the whole night to this bluff. I show her mine. She gives me a little smile, like she knew. A couple of minutes later I'm out in the bar having a couple of pops, she comes out and stands beside me. I ask her if she wants a drink. She says, no, then slides this paper over, says call me, and goes. She's wearing trousers, and when she walks away, it's something to watch. Like two puppies fighting in a sack.'

'What do you think that was all about?'

'I don't know. My manly charm, maybe. I ask Winky who is she. He says she's a professor, mathematics, physics, something like that, over

23

at NYU down in the Square there. Last name is Parson. Amy Parson.'

'What are you going to do?'

'I'm going to call her. I could use a little more education.' He folded the paper carefully and put it in his shirt pocket.

'Is the Lieutenant in?'

'Waiting on you,' Orso said it without heat, just the tip of a needle. Orso stood up and lifted his jacket from the chair back. He was a big man, well over six feet tall and two hundred pounds. He had sloping shoulders and long arms, and a big belly, and while he might have carried a few extra pounds, he was immensely strong and quick. 'They found a stiff up in the park this morning, up near Columbus Circle.'

'Something for us?' They crossed the squad room. The only other detective in the room was at a desk in the corner using two fingers to punish an ancient typewriter.

'Nah. No signs of violence. Heart attack or something. They'll know when they do the cut.'

'Who was he?'

'Don't know. No ID. One of those night-time bottom feeders in the park must have found the body. Took his wallet, made a few bucks.'

Cassidy rapped on the pebbled glass of Lt Tanner's door and pushed in without waiting for an invitation.

'Nice of you two to join us,' Lt Tanner said as Cassidy and Orso entered.

'Sorry, Boss.'

Tanner waved his cigar stub to dismiss the apology. Recently Tanner had taken to waxing

24

his bald head, and the overhead bulbs made it glow. Tanner had a heavyweight's shoulders and chest, and the legs of a lightweight. When he was on his feet he looked like he could fall over at a touch. It was an illusion. He had been a tough street cop, and a Marine Corps Captain in the Pacific war, but he was insufficiently political to advance far in the police department, a situation that did not seem to bother him much.

Detectives Bonner and Newly were in chairs near the desk. 'The Pig and the Nig,' as they were known, though never to their faces. Alfie Bonner was an old-fashioned street cop. He was built like a tank, five feet nine inches tall and two hundred twenty pounds. He looked like he'd been put together from leftovers by someone who wasn't paying attention to the task: mismatched eyes, one blue, one hazel, looked out of a square head that held a small nose, a thick-lipped mouth, and white hair buzzed short. He knew every punk, stick-up guy, pickpocket, bunco artist, and hooker who worked Times Square and the Stem. He believed a judiciously applied nightstick taught clearer lessons than a couple of months in jail on Rikers. More than one tough guy left town nursing broken bones. He was also a full-service despiser, his disdain for all races not his own was democratic. No one could figure out how his partner, Clive Newly, escaped it. Newly was a tall, calm Negro officer, one of the few of his race who had made detective. He lived with prejudice, but hated nobody as far as Cassidy could tell, and he went about his business quietly and dispassionately.

25

If Bonner heard you disrespect Newly, he'd bust your mouth.

The four detectives nodded to each other. Orso took a seat next to Newly. Cassidy leaned against the windowsill and lit another Lucky Strike.

'Okay,' Tanner said. 'The guy we want is due to make his rounds. If he sticks to the pattern, he'll go up to that apartment on Forty-eighth around noon. We don't know if he steps on the heroin up there, packages it, or what, but he's usually there for about an hour. The apartment's in the name of a Bridey Halloran – one arrest for soliciting, one arrest for kiting checks. No convictions. Popovic's standing by in case you need a fifth, which you probably do, but I'm not going to tell you how to make it work.'

'I thought the plan was to follow the asshole up to his wholesaler,' Orso said. 'We bust this guy, another asshole's going to pop up to sell the junk.'

'The plan changed. It came down from the captain.' He got no encouragement from the men in front of him, but he went on. 'It may come as a surprise to you, but the police department runs on money like everything else in this world. The department budget is a pie. Every precinct, every division, wants the biggest piece of the pie possible. The East Side precincts get big slices 'cause that's where the rich people live, and the money gets what the money wants. A precinct like the Eighteenth has to show we should have more by showing we're doing more. This guy's been peddling horse to the neighborhood for months, but now we're going to do

26

something about it, because it so happens that Councilman Franzi's son was over here a couple of nights ago to see a show, and while he's here, he buys some smack, OD's in the Automat men's room, and now he's over at Mount Sinai. We get this guy and the councilman's going to be very grateful when the budget process begins. So get out there and bring home the asshole, 'cause that's bringing home the bacon.'

Hell's Kitchen ran from 34th Street North to 59th, and from Eighth Avenue West to the Hudson River piers. It was a traditionally Irish neighborhood of tenements restricted to a height of six stories. The neighborhood was host to dingy bars, greasy spoons, grind houses, hot-sheet hotels, and small businesses always on the verge of failure. Its residents were poor, and poverty bred crime. The cops of the 18th were urged to keep that crime west of Eighth Avenue so as not impede the flow of money into the Broadway theaters and restaurants, but it was like shoveling against the tide.

'Fucking Micks,' Bonner said, 'they live like pigs.' He lay between Cassidy and Orso against the sloping roof parapet of a five-story tenement on West 48th Street. Across the street and below them a man walked out of a brownstone with a bag of garbage. He stopped at the top of the stoop and heaved the bag toward a row of battered topless garbage cans that waited by the curb. The bag missed and split open on the street, spewing garbage. 'Pigs,' Bonner repeated in case they missed the point.

Bonner slid back from the parapet so he could not be seen from the street when he stood up. 'Fucking waste of time, is my thought. Who the hell cares whether these people kill themselves with heroin. Good riddance.'

'You're a true humanitarian,' Orso said. 'Alfie Bonner, the friend of man.'

Bonner grinned and gave him the finger.

A brassy bell clanged below them in the street. 'Is that him?' Orso asked.

Cassidy ducked back to the parapet. Below him a battered green van pulled to the curb in front of a fire hydrant. Its bell rang again and again. Women began to come out of the nearby brownstones carrying knives wrapped in newspaper. The bell stopped. The van's back doors crashed open. Moments later the men on the roof heard the whir of a pedal-operated grindstone, and the whisper of a steel blade across the grit.

Twenty minutes later the women were gone and the grindstone was quiet, and the only noise was the rush of city traffic, the blare of horns, distant sirens. The doors of the van clashed shut, but the engine did not start. Cassidy looked over the parapet in time to see the back of a man disappear into the brownstone next door. 'Jesus, he's big.'

'What do you mean, big?' Orso asked.

'I mean big. He looked huge. Have you ever seen him, Bonner?'

'Nope. So he's big, so what? You whack him a few times, he'll get small.'

Cassidy pulled back from the parapet and stood. 'Newly and Popovic?'

28

'They're in the basement across the street. They'll give him a minute or two and then come in, block the stairs.'

'Let's go.'

The three men stepped across the low wall that separated one brownstone roof from the other, and walked to the metal door that led to the stairs. Someone had hammered the lock out of the door long ago, and it was held almost shut by a tight loop of clothesline tied to the inside doorknob and something on the inside jamb. Bonner slid the blade of a folding knife into the gap, cut the rope, and pushed the door open. They exchanged glances. This was the last easy step. After this, no matter what they had planned, nothing was sure.

The landing inside the door was strewn with empty beer bottles and cigarette butts. The stairwell was dim and smelled of cooking, bad drains, and tobacco smoke. Somewhere below them a door slammed and steps clattered down toward the bottom floor.

'Third floor, front apartment,' Bonner said and led them down. They went quietly and paused at the fourth-floor landing to listen. A radio played behind an apartment door. The hall toilet flushed. The door opened, and a man came out buttoning his fly. He stopped when he saw them standing at the bottom of the stairs, dropped his eyes, hurried to his apartment, and disappeared inside. The lock clicked shut. The safety chain rattled into place. Three dangerous men standing together in a group. Whatever hell that was, he did not want to know.

A nod from Bonner, and they went down.

The third floor. Bare wood, worn and buckled, and dingy gray walls. Three doors peeling paint on either side of the hall. The apartment they wanted was at the front of the building on the right side. Downstairs the front door opened and closed. Cassidy looked down the stairwell. Clive Newly looked up at him and waved.

'Let's go,' Bonner said with a tight grin, the action already jacking him up. He slipped his .38 from his holster and held it down by his leg. Orso pulled his gun and winked at Cassidy. Cassidy left his under his arm.

They moved down the hall walking as quietly as possible. Bonner stopped short of the door. Cassidy went past him to the other side. Orso took a position facing the door. There were two locks, both of them new and shiny. Cassidy raised his hand to knock. A piece of furniture screeched across a floor and crashed against a wall inside the apartment. It was followed by an explosive grunt of effort and then another. A woman screamed.

Orso took two fast steps forward and stamped his foot into the door next to the latch. Wood ripped. Orso hit it again, and the door blew open, and Cassidy and Bonner went through fast with Orso close behind. The living room was sparsely furnished with a ratty old sofa covered by a blanket, a couple of mismatched wooden chairs, a card table holding a brass balance scale. Bonner through the kitchen door first with Cassidy on his heels as the woman shrieked again.

'Police! Police!' they shouted as they went in.

Cassidy got a quick look from a weird angle past Bonner's bulk. A peroxide-blonde woman was on her back on the kitchen table, which was slammed up against the wall. Her dress was bunched around her waist, and her knees were up and splayed, and it was clear from the expression on her face that she had not been shrieking in pain. The knife sharpener's trousers and underwear were puddled around his ankles. He was between her legs and when he jerked around toward them as they charged the room, his dick stuck up in front of him. He was a huge man, bigger than Orso, legs like tree trunks, and a vast chest and shoulders that strained his shirt. He lunged toward a table under the window where a leather roll lay open displaying an array of knives. The pants around his ankles tripped him, and his lunge turned into a hop as he tried to stay upright. Bonner drove into him, and they both crashed down in a tangle and began to thrash on the floor, each struggling for advantage. The knives slid around the floor under them. The woman was now screaming in earnest. Orso yelled at her to shut up and tried to kick the knife sharpener in the head. He missed, and his plant foot landed on one of the blades. He skated for a moment, his arms windmilling for balance, and then lost it crashed down. His gun went off when he hit the floor and blew plaster out of the ceiling.

The woman stopped screaming, and when Cassidy turned to find out why, she was coming at him with a cast-iron skillet raised to take off his head. He half blocked the blow with his arm

31

and the skillet came down on the meat of his shoulder, and his arm went numb. She kicked him, but she was barefoot, and it hurt her more than him. She raised the skillet again. 'Cut it out,' he said, but her eyes were crazed. Her lips were drawn back from her teeth, and she was wild to crush his skull.

Behind him Bonner was yelling, 'Watch the knife! Watch the knife!'

Cassidy circled away from the woman. 'Put it down. Put it down.' But she was going to put it down on his head if she could. When she swung, he blocked her arm with his left and punched her in the gut with his right. She dropped the skillet, wrapped her arms over her stomach, took a couple of steps backward, and then sat down on the floor. She bent over and gasped for breath that would not come.

Cassidy turned to help Bonner and Orso. The knife sharpener stood up. Bonner rode him like a cat on a dog's back. He had lost his gun, and he hammered the man's face and neck with his fist. It didn't bother the man much. The knife sharpener reared backward and slammed Bonner into the wall but could not shake him off. Bonner crooked his arm around the man's thick neck in a chokehold. The big man had a knife in his right hand, and he stabbed back over his shoulder, but Bonner saw it coming and ducked his head to the other side. Orso stepped up and hit the man on the head with the butt of his .38. Blood spurted from his scalp, and the man slashed at Orso, who stumbled back. Cassidy kicked the man in the back of his knee, and the leg buckled and he went down with Bonner still riding him. Orso drew a spring-loaded sap from his back pocket and hit the man twice. He sighed and went slack. Bonner dug his pistol out from under the radiator where it had skittered. He got to his feet and looked down at the half-naked unconscious man. 'Son of a bitch was strong.' He kicked him once in the side.

'Leave him alone,' the woman said in a strangled voice. 'Leave him alone, you bastard.'

'Hey, Bonner,' Orso said, giddy with adrenaline. 'Did you get a load of the dick on the bastard. I don't think he was trying to stab you. I think he was trying to fuck you.'

Bonner whirled on him, mad-eyed, and took a threatening step forward. Orso braced.

Footsteps pounded down the hall, and Newly and Popovic charged through the door with guns drawn. 'Everything okay?' Newly asked. 'We heard a shot.'

'Yeah,' Bonner said. 'Orso killed the ceiling.' And the two of them howled with laughter.

Evening light filtered through the grime-smeared windows of the squad room. The afternoon was lost to writing arrest reports: a pound of heroin found in the apartment; ten pounds of powdered milk, a favored cutting agent; the brass scale in the living room; a box of glassine envelopes for street doses; a twelve-gauge shotgun sawed off at the barrel and stock; and a diaper box filled with fives, tens, and twenties adding up to $7,805.00, which had been counted twice, sealed, and carried to the evidence room, where,

33

with luck, it would remain untouched until the trial.

Cassidy finished typing his report and sealed it in a brown envelope and put it in Tanner's inbox. Orso was still working on his shots-fired report. Bonner and Newly had taken the knife sharpener, whose name was Connor Finn, and his lady friend, Bridey Halloran, downtown for the arraignment that would begin their grind through the system.

The phone on Cassidy's desk rang. He picked it up on the third ring. 'Eighteenth Precinct. Cassidy speaking.'

'Al Skinner, here, Mike.' Skinner was a medical examiner in the Bellevue morgue. 'That stiff they picked up in the park this morning? Thought it might be natural causes? It wasn't. I found blood on his collar, so I took a closer look. Someone stuck something in there at the base of the skull, an ice pick maybe.'

'When are you doing the cut?'

'Tomorrow some time.'

'Thanks, Al.' He hung up. Orso looked over from his desk. 'The guy they found in the park, it's a homicide.'

Four

Cassidy ate a hamburger at the bar at the White Horse and then walked home. The phone rang as he came through the apartment door. He

34

caught it on the third ring. 'Hello.' No answer. He shifted the receiver from ear to ear while he pulled off his coat and threw it on a chair. 'Hello.'

'Interesting time in the subway station this morning.' The voice was slightly muffled.

'What?'

'It looked like it was all over there for a moment. Headlines: *Police Detective Michael Cassidy killed by subway train.*'

'Who is this? Orso? Stop fucking around.' He could hear traffic sounds in the background.

'Were you scared? Inches away from death. You must have been scared. Did it feel inevitable? The push toward the edge of the platform. Nothing you could do. Death coming up the track. It's almost like a metaphor of our lives. Death starts out distant, out of sight, out of hearing. Then you hear it, a whisper on the rails. It gets closer and closer. You hear it. You see it. And then it's there. Poetry.'

Not Orso. Orso didn't deal in metaphors. And this was someone who had been there. Someone who made it happen? Not the fat man. The fat man had been scared. Someone behind him had been pushing.

'Do I know you? What's the beef?'

'Everything will become clear before it's over. Don't worry.'

Where was he now? Somewhere close. The phone had rung as he came into the apartment. Was that chance, or had the man seen him enter the building? 'Why don't you come over to my apartment? We can talk about this. I'll give you a drink.'

'Not tonight. We'll meet before this is over. And I'll be there to watch you die. I'm looking forward to that.'

'What did I do to you?' Traffic noise again at the other end of the line.

'All will be explained in good time.'

A car horn honked twice, both on the phone and out the window at the same time – the telephone booth on Greenwich two blocks away. 'Hey, let me get a cigarette from the bedroom. Don't go away. We have things to talk about. I won't be long.'

He let the receiver dangle and bolted for the door. He took the stairs two at a time, and went out into the street with his gun in his hand. It took thirty seconds to run the two blocks to Greenwich. The phone booth's door was open. The light was off. Cassidy touched the receiver. It was still warm. There was nobody on the street. He stepped into the booth and closed the door. The light came on. He took the receiver off the hook with his thumb and forefinger and angled it toward the light. There were no prints on the black plastic. The receiver had been wiped clean.

'What do you mean he said he was going to kill you?' Orso asked. They were having breakfast in a diner in Times Square.

'That's what he said. He said he was the guy trying to push me on to the tracks yesterday.'

'The fat guy?'

'No. He was pushing the fat guy. Pretty smart. I never got a look at him that way.'

'You got any idea who he might be?'

'I've been going over in my mind who we've put away over the last few years, and who might be getting out of cement now, but no one pops up.'

'I'll do the same. Most of the assholes we hook think a couple of years in the joint is the price of doing business. And if they did want to clip you, they'd just do it. There wouldn't be any warning. Chances are it's some sicko who's just pulling your chain and doesn't mean it. Odds are you'll never hear from him again, but don't sit with your back to any doors.'

When Cassidy pushed through the door to the Bellevue morgue, he was met by the familiar damp heat, the odor of chemicals mixed with the sweet smell of corruption, an odor that got into his nose and clothing and stayed with him for hours. Supplies spilled out of boxes in the corridor, evidence of the chronic shortage of storage in the morgue. The city charter dictated that any violent or suspicious death would bring you to these rooms, including death 'while in apparent good health,' whatever the hell that meant. Three sheet-covered bodies waited on gurneys against the white-tiled wall outside an autopsy room. From the shapes, two of them were men, and one was a woman. If you thought death was dignified and poetic, a trip to the morgue would reorder your mind.

Al Skinner looked up when Cassidy came into the autopsy room. The assistant medical examiner was sitting on a dissecting table with his legs dangling while he smoked a cigarette and leafed through a furniture catalog. 'Hey, Cassidy. How're you doing?' He was a wiry dark-haired man in his thirties, who looked at the world with ironic cheerfulness in defiance of his work.

The room smelled like a meat locker. The tools of Skinner's trade lay on the table: an electric saw to remove the top of the skull, a tin tray of scalpels, a plastic-handled soup ladle used to scoop fluid from the body cavities, and wooden-handled brush cutters from a gardening store to chop ribs.

'My guy?' Today the atmosphere in the dead house was unbearably heavy. Today he felt like the odds were stacked in favor of his ending up here with his brain on his chest.

'Come on. I'll show you.'

Cassidy followed him down the corridor to a bank of body drawers. Skinner studied tags until he found the one he wanted, and then pulled out the drawer.

'John Doe,' Skinner said. 'A not well-nourished male in his fifties, maybe late forties. The guy saw a lot of life before he got dead.'

The man lay face up in the drawer. A sheet covered him to his shoulders. His flesh was yellow and shiny like wax. It had gone slack in death, and the bones of his face stood out. His eyes were open. They were glassy and opaque with all the light gone from them.

'Help me roll him,' Skinner said. Cassidy got his hands under the corpse's shoulders and on Skinner's nod they rolled him to his stomach. He was not a big man, but death made him dense and loose. One arm flopped over the side of the

38

drawer. Cassidy lifted it back to lie alongside the body.

'Here,' Skinner said. 'Take a look.' His finger pointed to a place at the base of the John Doe's skull that he had shaved clean. 'I don't know what he got stuck with, an ice pick maybe, except the entry looks a little flatter than a pick would make.' There were three dark-rimmed punctures in the shaved patch. 'Some sort of really thin blade. You could stick a guy there and give him a headache, or leave him half paralyzed, leave him twitching, but to kill him you've got to be very lucky, or you've got to know anatomy. Whoever did this put it in, took it out, stuck it back in, pulled it out and did it again until he got it done. And see these?' He touched two puckered scars on the man's back. 'Shot in the back twice. Years ago.' His finger traced two old ropey scars, one near the man's spine, and the other down the calf of one leg. 'And these. It looks to me,' Skinner said, 'like someone operated on him with a machete.'

'What kind of operations?'

'No idea. I might know more after the cut. Oh, and two of them killed this guy last night, I'm pretty sure. Help me roll him back. I'll show you.'

When the body lay face up again, Skinner lifted one of the arms. 'See there? See the bruising on his wrists? I think someone stood in front of him and held him real tight while the other guy did the blade work. Before I forget.' He lifted the dead man's left arm and pointed to a tattoo of numbers in dark ink on the forearm. 'Do you know what this is?'

'Yeah. It's a prisoner number. The guy was in a Nazi concentration camp.'

'The poor bastard lived through that and got taken out in Central Park for a couple of bucks in his wallet. That is the shits. One other thing: his clothes smelled like horse.'

Everything found on the dead man was in a brown paper envelope in a drawer of a gray metal desk in Skinner's office. Cassidy emptied the envelope onto a table under the window. He found a bone-handled clasp knife, four sugar cubes wrapped in a paper napkin, two carrots, a plastic change purse containing forty-two cents and three subway tokens, and a cellophane envelope that held a faded, torn piece of a photograph showing a young woman with an old-fashioned hair-do holding a baby and smiling shyly at the camera. The cellophane was meant to protect the photograph, but the paper had been rubbed by age and handling to the softness of tissue.

'No wallet?' Cassidy asked as he slid the dead man's possessions back into the brown envelope.

'Nah. Maybe it was kids did it. I've been reading about these juvenile delinquent gangs, they'll stick someone for looking at them wrong.'

'You said the guy might know anatomy.'

'Or might have gotten lucky. A kid with some homemade blade, maybe.'

'I don't think so. A mugger goes into the park, he's prepared. He's got a knife, a gun, or if there are two of them, they're going to strong arm someone. This feels improvised, like they suddenly decided to kill him, and they did it with what they had at hand.'

40

'The knife, was it in the dead guy's pocket?'
'Nah. On the ground near him.'
'Was everything else still in his pockets?'
'Yes.'
'So they weren't trying to rob him. They would have checked his pockets for more cash. They took the wallet to make it look like a robbery. Was the knife open?'
'Open. No blood on the blade.'
'So either he was going for them, or they were going for him. Maybe he knew them or they knew him. They killed him because they knew each other.'
'Fucking Sherlock Cassidy,' Skinner said with a grin.
'Fuck you. Tell me where they found the body.'

Cassidy stood on the path a hundred feet inside Central Park and studied the black-and-white crime scene photographs Al Skinner had given him. They had been taken in early morning light when the shadows were still long. The dead man lay on his stomach with his head turned to one side. His eyes stared, and his mouth was open. One leg was bent and one rigidly straight. His left arm was trapped beneath his body, and the other stretched out toward a park bench at the side of the path. The knife lay open on the ground a few feet from the outstretched hand. He put the photographs back in the envelope and quartered the area carefully, occasionally crouching down to examine something that drew his eye. There wasn't a lot to see. Ants crawled on the few blots of blood where the dead man's head

41

had rested. There was a dark patch on the pavement where his bladder had let go, not much to mark a man's passage from life to death.

Cassidy hefted the evidence envelope and felt the shape of the carrots and the sugar cubes in the bottom. He walked back out to Central Park South to where the carriages parked near Columbus Circle. Four of the drivers listened to *Backstage Wife* on a transistor radio propped on the park wall as Mary Noble struggled to decide whether to tell her husband, the Broadway star Bob Noble, that she was pregnant. One of the drivers noticed him coming and stepped out before the others saw him. 'You looking for a ride around the park, sir? I'm your man.'

Cassidy showed him his badge. 'Do you know if any of the drivers went missing last night?' He dumped the carrots and sugar into his palm. 'We had a dead man in the park this morning. No ID, but he was carrying these. I figured they were treats for one of the horses.'

'Must have been Leon,' one of the drivers said. 'Jerry Gross took his own cab in and came back past the Circle on his way home. He seen Leon's was still here at two in the morning. No Leon. He took the cab in, figured Leon had gotten sick or something.'

'Is Jerry here?'

'Nope. He won't be on till four. Four to midnight.'

'Were any of you working last night? Any of you see Leon?'

They shook their heads. 'We mostly work days.'

42

'Leon what? What's his last name?'

The four men shook their heads. 'Dombek, something like that. He kind of kept to himself. Rusty Siler might know more. He spent time with him.'

'Where's Rusty now?'

'He's got customers in the park. They've been out an hour. He ought to be back any time.'

'Thank you.' He turned away.

'Hey, so what happened with Leon? He get mugged or something?'

'We don't know yet. We're still looking at it.'

Cassidy sat on a bench next to the park's stone wall and lit a Lucky Strike. The sun was high, and warm enough to take the edge off the September air. The traffic was heavy on Central Park South, the rush of cars, honking horns, the wheeze of bus brakes, a siren, a chattering jackhammer, the sounds of a city alive with energy and purpose, unaware and uncaring that the energy had been minutely diminished by the death of one hansom cab driver.

A carriage came out of the park. The horse clip-clopped at a fast walk and pulled into the curb at the back end of the line of carriages waiting for fares. The driver opened the carriage door and helped his passengers down. They were an elderly couple and two young girls, grandparents and granddaughters, Cassidy guessed. The man paid the driver. They all shook his hand and then walked off toward Columbus Circle.

When Cassidy approached, the driver was feeding a carrot to the horse. The driver was maybe an inch over five feet tall, but he had powerful hands that belonged to a bigger man. Some of his fingers were crooked and one of his cheekbones had been broken and repaired flatter than the other and it gave his face an unbalanced look. Life had run at him hard and fast and he hadn't always been able to get out of its way.

'Are you Rusty Siler?'

'Yup.'

'I need to talk to you about Leon, last name's like Dombek, one of the guys down there said.' Cassidy showed him his ID and badge.

'Dudek, Leon Dudek. A cop? I wouldn't have made you for the law. Come on up into the cab, Detective. We can sit comfortable.' His voice had a cowboy twang.

Cassidy followed him into the carriage and they faced each other on the leather seats.

'What happened to Leon?' Siler pulled the makings from his shirt pocket and rolled a cigarette with quick, deft fingers.

'Someone killed him last night in the park.'

'Robbery?'

'Could be. His wallet was missing. What else did you hear?'

'Not much.' Siler flicked a kitchen match with his thumbnail and lit his cigarette. 'He bought a hotdog from the Greek sometime after midnight. That was the last any of the other drivers saw him.'

'The Greek?'

'Owns a hotdog cart. Usually sets up in the late afternoon. Sticks around till one in the morning. A lot of the drivers eat his dogs.'

44

'His name?'

'Don't know. Just, the Greek.'

'What can you tell me about Dudek? Did he have any beefs with any of the other drivers?'

'Leon? Nah. He was a real gentle guy. Never pushed himself on anyone. Kept to himself. Worked up here maybe four years, but I don't think anyone really got to know him. He said he liked being outside, liked the park. He didn't know horses, I can tell you that. I mean he was willing to learn, and old Jesse, the horse Leon had most days, he knew more than Leon did about the job, so it was never really a problem.'

'Did Dudek have any family?'

'I don't think so. He never said.'

'Where did he live?'

'The Lower East Side. Somewhere in the Alphabets, but I don't know the address. I guess it'd be on his license.'

'We didn't find a license. Someone stole his wallet.'

'His hack license. It'd be on his carriage.' He gestured toward a leatherette folder pinned to the back of the driver's seat that held his license and a small photo. 'I hear Jerry Gross took it back to the stable last night. It should be there still.'

The stable was a four-story brick building far west on 38th Street. Cassidy found a round, cheerful woman sitting on an apple box out front in the sun smoking a large cigar. She wore blue jeans, rubber boots, and a ratty black sweater over a man's yellow shirt. She looked him over

45

carefully as he got out of the cab and walked toward her. 'Cop?' She asked, looking up at him.

'Michael Cassidy, detective with the 18th.' He showed her his badge.

'Louisa Espinosa.' She stood up to shake hands. 'Leon, huh?'

'Yes.'

'A shame, a nice guy like him. What happened, heart attack?'

'No. It looks like someone stabbed him.'

'*Madre de Dios*. What's wrong with people?'

She led him inside and up a wide concrete ramp to an office in the rear of the building. The walls were covered with black-and-white photographs of horses and carriages dating back a century, and out-of-date calendars from feed stores and brewers. Wooden pegs held harnesses and bridles, and there was a pile of horse blankets in one corner. Louisa's desk was strewn with papers held down by thick china coffee mugs. 'Pull up a pew,' she said and waved at one of the two wooden armchairs as she went around the desk. The desk chair groaned and tilted as she settled into it. 'Now what can I do you for? Anything I can to help. Leon was a sweet man.'

'What can you tell me about him?'

'Not much.' She shook her head. 'The man's been working here four years just about. You think you know him, but push comes to shove, you don't know much. "Hello, Leon, how are you doing?" A little talk about the horse or the carriage, the weather, the business. That's about it. Of course his English wasn't so hot. I think that embarrassed him.'

'Do you know where he was from?'

'Poland, I think. Yeah, Poland. He said that once.'

'Do you know anyone who might have had a beef with him?'

'With Leon? No, no. He was a sweetheart. Nobody had an unkind word for him. Why? You think he knew the guy who did it?'

'People usually do. Do you have an address for him?'

'Absolutely.'

She got up and found a copy of Leon Dudek's license application in a tall wooden file cabinet. A black-and-white ID photograph was stapled to one corner. Dudek's address was off Avenue B on the Lower East Side.

Cassidy did not get down to the Lower East Side that day. Dudek was dead, and the living required his attention. Two men robbed a grocery store on Eighth Avenue. One of them hit the clerk with a milk bottle and fractured his skull. A Puerto Rican teenage gang, the Zombies, and an Irish one, the Vikings, rumbled in a vacant lot off Tenth Avenue. The weapons of choice were switch blades, chains, and clubs, but one inventive lad brought a zip gun made from a section of radio antenna broken off a Chevy Bel Air and cut to length for the barrel, a crudely carved wooden handle, a tack, a powerful rubber band, tape to hold the thing together, and a .22 long rifle cartridge. The result was a fifteen-year-old Zombie with a bullet in his spine and no feeling in his legs. By the time the day was

47

done it was too late to go down to where Leon Dudek lived.

Cassidy was due for a rotation to the night watch after the weekend, so he handed Dudek's address off to a detective named Foley, who listened to what Cassidy had learned about the dead man and then dropped the piece of paper into the top drawer of his desk, said, 'I'll get to it when I've got a minute,' and went back to the hunting magazine he'd been reading.

Five

Costigan's Irish pub offered a dim, religious light for the comfort of serious drinkers, and it did not distract them by serving any food except for pretzels, nuts, and popcorn in wooden bowls – salty snacks that encouraged another round.

The three men in the high-backed wooden booth along the wall might have been out-of-town businessmen closing an evening on the town, but they weren't.

'One more round?' Spencer Shaw suggested. 'My turn.' Shaw was thirty-six years old, a lean six-footer, with hair the color of straw and the tan of a man who had spent his summer on boats. Bushy russet eyebrows shaded his blue eyes, and if he let his beard grow it came in the same darker color. A thin white scar ran from the corner of his right eye down over his cheek-bone, and one of his front teeth was slightly

48

skewed. He had a habit of fiddling with the gold signet ring on the little finger of his left hand. He had the genial air of a golden retriever until you looked at him closely and realized the dog might bite. 'John, you'll have another, won't you?'

John Hoffman was a dark-haired, bulky six-footer about the same age as Spencer Shaw. He had a broad, flat face and dark eyes, and a slow, calm way of contemplating even the simplest question. 'Sure. Why not? Company money.'

'Paul? Another?'

'Nobody drinks without me.' Paul Williger was a few years older than the other men, and he was the only one at the table who wore a wedding ring. His brown hair was thinly strewn on his skull. His face and midsection were beginning to show the softness of a man who spent too much time sitting down. His eyes behind his horn-rimmed glasses were pale blue and anxious. He pushed his glass forward. 'Old Overholt, two cubes.'

'I don't know how the hell you can drink that stuff,' Shaw said as he pushed out of the booth. He picked up the three glasses and carried them to the bar. The bartender found three clean glasses, made the drinks, and slid them back across the bar to Shaw.

'Scotch, scotch, rye. I put a swizzle stick in the rye so you'd know which was which. You got 'em, or you want me to carry 'em over?'

'I've got them,' Shaw said. He pushed a five dollar bill across the bar and said, 'Keep the change.'

'Thanks.' The bartender turned away and did not see Shaw take a small glass tube from his pocket. Shaw checked to see that no one was watching and then allowed a drop of colorless fluid to fall into the glass of rye. He stirred it with the swizzle stick and carried the drinks back to the table.

'Hold on,' Paul Williger said. He put a hand to a lamp post on the corner of Broadway and Forty-sixth to steady himself. 'Whoa. Maybe that last one wasn't such a good idea.'

Hoffman and Shaw exchanged a look.

'Are you all right, Paul?' Shaw asked.

'I don't know. One too many.' Then, 'Jesus . . . The lights.'

Times Square was ablaze in neon signs for Pepsi Cola, Bond Two Trouser Suits, Canadian Club, Fly TWA, Admiral Television, the endless pour of neon nuts from the giant Planter's Peanuts bag at the intersection of Broadway and Seventh Avenue. As Williger watched, the lights melted and ran. The hole that blew the smoke rings for the Camel cigarettes man roared, and the smoke was as hard as concrete. The cars on the street were bright-eyed monsters with chrome teeth, and he could hear the raw squawks of laughter from people a block away. He put his hands to his ears to block the noise, but it came through his flesh like water through paper. The plate glass of an appliance store flexed and bulged. 'Paul,' Shaw said again. 'Are you all right?' His voice sounded like metal.

'Not me,' Williger said. 'Not me. You weren't

50

supposed to do it to me.' The sound of his own voice oozed in his head. 'We agreed. Not after the last time. Not me.'

'Easy, Paul. It's okay. We're going to get you back to the hotel. It's okay.' Hoffman gave Shaw a worried look and put his arm around Williger's waist. 'Come on, Paul. We're going back to the hotel.' But Williger clung to the lamppost, the only anchor in his world. 'Paul, it's okay. You're going to be fine. Let's go to the hotel.'

'Not me. Not me. Not me. Not me. Not me. Not me. It wasn't supposed to be me. Not again. Not me. They promised.' Williger began to weep, and his tears were hot beads on his cheeks.

People on the sidewalk looked at them curiously and kept moving. Someone's night had gone sideways, but it was not their business. Shaw pried at Williger's fingers to loosen his grip on the lamppost. His voice was harsh with impatience. 'We're all on the list, Paul. That's what we agreed to. I got through it. You can get through it. Come on. Get a grip. Tomorrow you'll be back on top.'

Shaw's anger pierced Williger's brain like hot pins. He put his hands up again to block the noise. Hoffman took advantage of the moment to turn him away from the lamppost. Shaw took his other arm, and they moved him along the sidewalk. He closed his eyes against the melting lights, but they came through his eyelids and through his skull, and swarmed his brain.

'Step down,' Hoffman said.

Williger opened his eyes and saw that they were at the curb to cross the street. The car

51

monsters, eyes glaring, chrome teeth bared, crouched in a row at the intersection. Williger pulled back, but Hoffman and Shaw urged him across and he did not have the strength to resist.

The Hotel Astor lobby was quiet. The two uniformed clerks behind the reception desk watched Hoffman and Shaw maneuver Williger to the elevators. The older clerk raised an eyebrow to the younger, and they went back to their paperwork. Another overserved guest being helped to bed by friends.

Paul Williger's room was on the sixth floor overlooking Broadway. Shaw's was through a connecting door, and Hoffman's was down the hall. They shucked Williger out of his overcoat and sat him in an easy chair. He sat tipped forward at the waist with his hands on his knees and his eyes closed.

Shaw drew up a straight chair from the desk and sat with his knees almost touching Williger's. He took a pen and a notebook from his jacket and opened it to a blank page. They were supposed to take notes, though he did not have much hope for something useful tonight. Williger was too far gone. 'Paul, how do you feel now?'

No answer.

He flipped the pages of his notebook until he found a list of questions. 'Paul, is your name Paul Andrew Williger?'

No answer.

'Do you work for the US Government?'

Silence.

'Do you have a son named Matthew and a daughter named Helen?'

Williger knew Shaw was talking to him, but he could not understand what he was saying over the interior noise in his body. His blood sang through his veins and arteries, liquids gurgled in his guts, and his breath rasped in and out, in and out. The noise was horrifying. It sounded like his body was eating itself.

'Do you know who I am?' Shaw asked.

Silence.

Shaw glanced at Hoffman and shrugged. 'Get me a cold towel, will you?'

Hoffman brought a wet towel from the bathroom, and Shaw pressed it to Williger's forehead and cheeks, but it brought no change in Williger's blank expression.

'What do you think?' Hoffman asked.

'I've seen some weird reactions, but nothing like this. He's not answering questions. I mean, what the hell good is it if he won't answer questions? The whole point is answering questions.' Shaw sighed in frustration. 'Paul, can you hear me? Nod if you can hear me.'

No response.

'It should have been me,' Hoffman said. 'I told you I was ready.'

'I know, and I appreciate your volunteering, but that's not the point. They want sequential and cumulative data. Williger took it a week ago. They wanted to know his reaction to a second protocol.'

'Well, they aren't going to love the result. I should call it in, find out what they want us to do.'

'Sure. Go ahead. We can wait it out, transport

53

him, call Dr Ambrose, whatever they want.'
Hoffman nodded and went through the connecting
door.

Shaw stood up and put his hand on Williger's
arm. The muscle was rigid, tensed to the limit.
'Paul, take it easy. It's okay. Everything's all
right. Relax. You're with friends. It's going to
be fine. Sit tight.'

No response.

Six

Cassidy hated the night watch. The worst in
people seeped out during the night. They did
things they would not do in daylight, as if darkness could hide their actions: children were
thrown against the wall for not finishing dinner,
women were beaten for changing the channel,
rapists and muggers, stick-up artists, the perverted,
and the weird, they all slid out of the shadows
looking for prey. Cassidy remembered the *Life*
magazine photographs of zebras and antelope
gathered around a waterhole at night. The flash
revealed the glowing eyes of predators waiting
in the bushes – New York City after midnight.

Night watch played hell with his system.
Nearly two weeks on, and Cassidy still was not
used to it. Sleep, difficult to find in normal times,
was thrown out of whack. He was hungry at odd
times, fought sleep on the job with too much
coffee that turned his stomach sour, went home

54

in morning light, fell exhausted into bed as Rhonda rose for her day, and waited for sleep that would not come. After the second irritable early morning exchange, Rhonda told him she would see him again when his schedule changed back to day. One night to go, then the weekend, and back to day shift just as he was getting used to night.

A uniformed sergeant named Flannigan came up from the desk downstairs. 'Hey, Cassidy, a guy went out the window over at the Astor. Splat. The beat cop called it in.'

Cassidy woke Orso from his nap on a cot in the locker room, and a squad car dropped them on Broadway in front of the hotel where two other squad cars were already nosed to the curb. They pushed their way through the rubberneckers who discussed the event in whispers as if the dead man might be offended by noise. Patrolmen had blocked off a patch of sidewalk north of the lobby doors where the body lay. Cassidy crouched beside the corpse. He guessed that the man was in his late thirties. He lay on his back. He wore a dark suit and white shirt, and his tie was pulled down a couple of inches. His head was flattened at the back where it had struck the sidewalk, and his eyes bulged from the impact. His mouth was open. His legs were bent and broken. Blood leaked from under his head and pooled on the concrete where the neon lights of Times Square turned it black. There were pieces of glass and window frame around the body, and the shade from the man's room, pulled to the end of its roller, lay six feet away.

Cassidy stood as Orso approached. 'The night manager heard him hit. He's over there with Scalabrine,' Orso said. A small man in a dark uniform with a few discreet touches of gold braid stood near the entrance with a big uniformed cop whose white hair showed from under his hat.

'How're you doing, Tony, Detective Cassidy?' Scalabrine and Orso knew each other from the old neighborhood, but he was leery of Cassidy who had a reputation in the house of being unpredictable, a guy who didn't run the normal tracks. Cassidy had done him a favor a couple of years before and had never asked for payback, and that was a little weird according to the customs of the tribe. Cassidy had also thrown a Vice cop named Franklin out a third-story window for beating up a whore, and then about a year later threw him out another window. That was big weird. Best to walk wide around him, Scalabrine thought. 'Detectives, this is Joe Pickering. He's the night manager. He heard the guy hit.'

Pickering was a thin, neat man whose blonde hair was parted in the middle. He had alert eyes, and an air of self-control. He was a man who was used to solving other people's problems. He waited calmly for the questions he knew would come.

'Tell me what happened from your point of view,' Cassidy said.

'At two o'clock I like to make a round of the lobby to be sure that everything is in its place, no cigarettes burning in the ashtrays, stationery put away at the desks if someone has been writing there, check to see that the doors to the restaurant are locked, that kind of thing. I was near the front door when I heard the impact.'

'You knew what it was?'

'I've worked in hotels for thirty-two years. It is an unfortunate reality that people occasionally use our facilities to end their lives. I suspect they do it to avoid – what shall I say? – to avoid the untidy aspects of doing it in their own homes. I have, over the years in different establishments, been on duty when six men and one woman jumped to their deaths. I did not hear them all, but I heard three. I knew immediately what this was.'

'What did you do?'

'I ran outside. He was lying as you see him now. He was alive, I think, but only for a moment. I heard him breathe, and then,' he shrugged, 'he stopped. One breath, maybe two.'

'Did he try to say anything?'

'No. I called John Jacobi, the night doorman, to stand with him and keep people away while I went to find Officer Scalabrine, who I had seen pass the hotel. Then I came back to wait for you.'

'Where is Mr Jacobi?'

'I'm afraid he was rather undone by this. I sent him to the staff dining room to wait in case you wanted to speak to him.'

'Thank you. Do you recognize him? I assume he was a guest of the hotel.'

'Mr Williger. Paul Williger, room 603.'

'You knew him. What can you tell me about him?'

'I never saw him before half an hour ago, but as you can see, he took the window shade and glass with him when he jumped. He must have come from a high floor. I simply looked up until I found the broken window with no shade and then checked the register.'

'Mr Pickering, can you let us into Mr Williger's room?' Cassidy asked.

'Of course. I'll get the passkey from my office.'

They rode up to the sixth floor in the peculiar silence elevators provoke.

Pickering opened the door to room 603 and stood back to let Cassidy and Orso pass. 'If you don't need me, Officers, I'll go back to the desk.'

Cold night air and street noise came in through the broken window. The sheer curtains fluttered in the draft. Cassidy took in the small suitcase on a stand near the closet, the impression on the bed where someone had lain without removing the spread, the glass of water on a table next to an easy chair, and the desk chair drawn up in front of the larger chair. He noticed a towel on the floor by the chairs and when he touched it, he discovered it was wet.

'Mike,' Orso was looking through the open connecting door to the next room. When Cassidy stepped over, Orso pushed the door wide. A man sat on an easy chair near the window. He looked at the two cops standing in the door but did not get up. For a moment he looked startled though he must have heard them come into the room next door. He pushed his blond hair back from his forehead with his left hand and stubbed out a burning cigarette in the ashtray with his right.

A copy of *Time* magazine lay open on his lap. The place adjoining Williger's room was a small suite. It consisted of a bedroom, a living room with two easy chairs, a sofa, coffee table, and writing desk.

Cassidy stepped into the room. 'Sir, my name is Michael Cassidy. I'm a detective with the Eighteenth Precinct. This is Detective Orso. Please identify yourself.' Both men held their badge folders where the man could see them.

'Spencer Shaw.' Shaw leaned forward to read the IDs. He looked up from Cassidy's to study Cassidy's face with interest.

'I'd like to see some identification,' Cassidy said.

Shaw stood up, and took a wallet from his hip pocket. He extracted a driver's license and handed it to Cassidy. Shaw's address was in Chevy Chase, Maryland, a suburb of Washington, DC. Cassidy handed it back. 'Mr Shaw, did you know the man who occupied the adjoining room?'

'Yes.'

Cassidy waited. Some people gushed when speaking to a cop. Others, reticent in the face of authority, waited for the questions. 'What was your connection to him?'

'We worked together.'

'What kind of work?'

'Paul was a chemist.'

'And you?'

'No, I'm not a chemist.' Orso prowled the room, and every once in a while Shaw's eyes would search him out and then come back to Cassidy. He did not seem concerned, just observant.

59

'Did you and Mr Williger spend the evening together?'

'Yes.' Shaw twisted the gold signet ring on his little finger.

'Please tell me what you did.'

'We worked until about eight o'clock. We had dinner. We walked for a while. We stopped in a bar and had a nightcap. We came back to the hotel sometime after midnight.' An evening stripped to its basic components.

'Just the two of you?'

'Yes.'

'Where did you have dinner?'

'The German place on Fifty-sixth off Seventh.'

'The Hofbrau?'

'That's it.'

'And the nightcap? Where was that?'

'One of those Irish places off Seventh in the Forties. We were walking back here.'

'The Shamrock?'

'I don't know what the name was. We stopped so I could light a cigarette. We realized that we were standing in front of a bar. Paul said, "Let's go have a nightcap," so we went in.'

'Did Mr Williger have a lot to drink during the evening?'

'No. A couple of drinks before dinner. A beer with. A couple of drinks when we stopped on the way to the hotel. Normal.'

'Not drunk enough to fall out the window?'

'No.'

'What happened after you came back here?'

'Paul wasn't feeling well. He had a headache. He said he thought he'd turn in. I came in here to

60

read. I must have dozed off. I guess what woke me was the crash when he went out the window. I ran into his room, and . . .' He hesitated as if reliving the moment. 'And he was gone. I came back in here and called the desk to tell them what had happened, and I called the police.'

Orso went back into the dead man's room.

'How well did you know Mr Williger?'

'We've worked together for more than a year. I've met his family. We're colleagues more than friends, but we have spent quite a lot of time together because of the work.'

'Had he been depressed, any problems at home you know about, any financial problems?'

Shaw took a pack of Pall Malls from the coffee table and offered one to Cassidy. Cassidy took it and lit their cigarettes with his Zippo. Shaw blew a plume of smoke at the ceiling. 'Paul had been having some problems, emotional problems.' His voice was low as if he was reluctant to discuss the dead man's personal life with a stranger.

'What kind of problems?'

'Depression. Over the past few months he was often late with work, and he confessed to me that sometimes he couldn't make himself move, couldn't get started. People at work were beginning to worry about it. He's a good scientist, but he's been having trouble keeping his nose to the grindstone.'

'Who did he work for?'

'The Department of the Army.'

'Doing what?'

'Research on biochemical compounds.'

'I don't know what that means.'

'I'm afraid I can't tell you any more. I'm not allowed to discuss the work with people who are not cleared.'

'Secret work?'

'Yes.'

'But you're not a chemist.'

'No.'

'What exactly do you do, Mr Shaw.'

'I facilitate things.' Shaw didn't seem to care what Cassidy wanted. He was only going to give him what he wanted to give.

The phone rang in the next room, and Cassidy heard Orso answer it. 'Do you work in New York, you and Mr Williger?'

Shaw hesitated and then decided the answer could do no harm. 'Sometimes we find space in the city in a government building or lab, but mostly we work at Fort Dix, out in New Jersey.'

'Do you live here in the hotel?'

'Sometimes when I'm in New York.'

'Does Mr Williger?'

'He occasionally takes a room when we have to work late and plan to start early the next day.'

'Where does he live?'

'Scarsdale. Westchester County. Sometimes it's not worth getting on the train if he has to be back in the morning.'

Orso appeared in the door to Williger's room. 'There's a Dr Ambrose coming up. He says that he was treating Williger.'

'I called him,' Shaw said.

'You said you called the desk and the police.'

'Yes. I did. Then I called Dr Ambrose. I thought he should know. He saw Paul yesterday.'

'What was he treating him for?'

'Depression.'

Cassidy waited for more, but there was no more. He followed Orso back into Williger's room. 'What do you think?' he asked.

'No note that I could find, but most of them don't leave one. Why the hell didn't he open the window?'

'I don't know. Maybe he lay there on the bed thinking about it, got up, and *wham!* out he went. Maybe he thought if he took the time to open it he wouldn't go.'

They searched the room quickly. An overcoat and a tweed jacket hung in the closet. There was nothing in the bureau drawers. A change of shirt, underwear, and socks in the suitcase. A leather shaving kit was on a shelf in the bathroom. There was a toothbrush in the holder above the sink. It was wet. He brushed his teeth, no simpler part of the daily routine, and then lay down on the bed. What the hell happened between the toothbrush and the window? Cassidy wondered. What was in his head that was so horrible that he could not go on? *Jesus, I never want to get to that place*, he thought.

A firm rap of knuckles on the door.

Orso opened it as Cassidy came out of the bathroom.

'I'm Ambrose,' the man in the doorway announced. He entered the room as if he owned it. He trailed strong body odor. He was a medium-height heavyweight with a broad chest and a

63

belly that threatened the threadbare dark blue cardigan buttoned over a red flannel shirt. He wore shapeless corduroy trousers and laced leather boots. He had a close-cropped, dark beard so thick that it hid his mouth, and his hair was thick, curly, and touched with gray. Cassidy thought he looked like one of the many poets and painters who live in the Village, but his eyes marked him as something else. They were so dark that the cornea and the iris blended to one color. They were not the eyes of a dreamer.

He looked at Orso and Cassidy, took them in, recorded them, and then brushed past them to stand looking out of the shattered window. After a while he turned around. 'I am Dr Sebastian Ambrose. Paul Williger was my patient. Who are you?'

'Detective Orso, Detective Cassidy. Eighteenth Precinct,' Orso said.

'Where's Spencer Shaw?'

'In the next room.'

Ambrose nodded abruptly and went through the connecting door.

'Asshole,' Cassidy said.

'Yeah, I could see you liked him from the jump,' Orso said. 'What's that all about?'

'I don't know. The moment he came in it was like fingernails on a blackboard.'

'Hate at first sight?'

'It saves time.'

Low voices came from the other room. Moments later Ambrose reappeared. He screwed a cigarette into a long ebony holder and lit it with a silver lighter. 'I'm taking Mr Shaw back

64

to my place and giving him a sedative.' There was no room for argument.

'What were you treating Paul Williger for?' Cassidy asked.

'Depression.'

'Are you a psychiatrist?'

'Yes.'

'Was he suicidal?'

Ambrose drew on the cigarette and blew smoke through his nose. 'I'm not at liberty to discuss my patient's case with anyone. Doctor–patient confidentiality.' His tone suggested Cassidy should fuck off. He scratched his head vigorously with his free hand, and dandruff drifted like snow. He looked across the room at the shattered window again. 'How do you feel when you confront your failures, Detective Cassidy?'

'They happen so seldom I'm usually relieved to discover I'm fallible. It indicates humanity.'

Ambrose looked at him hard, and his brow furrowed for a moment. 'That kind of remark usually indicates great insecurity.'

'I appreciate your professional opinion. Send your bill to the precinct.'

It bounced off. 'Let's go, Spencer,' Ambrose called toward the open door. Spencer Shaw appeared from the other room wearing an overcoat.

'We need Mr Shaw to come to the stationhouse with us,' Cassidy said.

'Mr Shaw has undergone a serious trauma. He needs a sedative and rest.'

'I'll have a Department doctor examine him when we get to the house. A man jumped, fell, or was pushed from a window in this room, and we need Mr Shaw to come make a report while the events are still fresh in his mind.'

'Pushed?' Ambrose said, and raised a skeptical eyebrow.

'At this point we rule nothing out.'

'Are you suggesting that Mr Shaw pushed him out the window?'

'No. For all I know the chambermaid did it, because she found him lying on the bed with his shoes on, but we still need Mr Shaw to come make his report. It won't take long, and we'll make sure Mr Shaw is comfortable and cared for.'

'Over my protest as his doctor.' Ambrose did not like being checked, and his voice was thick with anger.

'Noted. If you'd like to come with him, you may.'

Shaw watched their hostility with amusement.

'Spencer, you go with them. Don't worry about a thing,' Ambrose said, and patted Shaw on the shoulder, 'I'll take care of this.'

It almost sounded like a threat.

There was no doctor at the stationhouse to examine Shaw, but he showed no signs of suffering or unease. Cassidy gave Shaw a cup of over-stewed coffee from the pot on the hotplate in the squad room and showed him to an unoccupied desk where he could write his report. Most people were nervous when they talked to the cops at a crime scene. Shaw and Ambrose both displayed unusual arrogance. What made them feel so safe?

66

The usual night-time noises rose from downstairs at the booking desk: a couple of drunks shouted at each other until someone told them to shut the fuck up; someone howled as if possessed by demons; a crash as something hard was thrown or kicked. This was where people washed up when their night took a wrong turn near Times Square. Anger and anguish were the common harmonies.

Cassidy smoked and thought about Paul Williger lying in his room at the Astor and then getting up and throwing himself through the window. How fast would he have to be going to blast through the window and frame? Williger, from the looks of him, weighed about a hundred seventy-five pounds, a lot of weight to throw against glass and wood. Was it enough? What were the physics? What was he thinking when he went out? Jesus, how does a man do that?

'Cassidy,' a uniformed patrolman called from the top of the stairs. 'There's a guy to see you. Says he's a lawyer for the guy you brought in.'

'Thanks, Gerry. Let him up.'

A young man came up and stopped on the landing and looked around. He was in his twenties. He wore a well-cut charcoal gray overcoat. The pressed trousers of a pin-striped suit showed below its hem, and his shoes were polished black wingtips. A crisp white shirt and a dark striped tie showed in the vee of the overcoat. He carried a black leather briefcase. His dark blond hair was still wet from the shower. He was the poster boy for an Ivy League law school.

Cassidy raised his hand, and the young man

67

nodded and crossed to his desk. Cassidy stood to shake hands.

'Peter Gilbert. I'm an attorney with Sullivan and Cromwell.'

'Detective Michael Cassidy. I guess you're the lucky one they call in the middle of the night.'

Gilbert smiled. 'They sure don't call the senior partners. Is there something I have to sign to allow Mr Shaw to leave here?'

'No. He can go as soon as he finishes his report. If we need follow-up questions, we'll get in touch with him. Do you know Mr Shaw?'

'No, I don't. They asked me to come down and see that he was being properly treated, so here I am.'

'Standard service for all the firm's clients?'

'Oh, no. At least I've never heard that.'

'So he's an important client.'

'I wouldn't know. I'm just doing what I was asked to do.' He looked around the squad room with lively curiosity. A scream from downstairs jerked his head around.

'Are you a criminal attorney, Mr Gilbert?'

'No. I'm a tax lawyer.' He turned and put out his hand as Spencer Shaw approached. 'Mr Shaw, I'm Peter Gilbert with Sullivan and Cromwell. They asked me to come down and make sure you got home safely. I've got a taxi waiting.'

Spencer Shaw shook his hand. He put the yellow pad with his report on Cassidy's desk. 'That's it.'

'Okay,' Cassidy said. 'If we need more, we'll be in touch.'

'Always a pleasure to see New York's finest at work,' Shaw said, and headed for the stairs. Cassidy watched him go and wondered why Shaw acted as if the whole evening amused him, as if he had some secret that let him stand above it all.

Orso put a steaming mug on Cassidy's desk. 'Fresh pot.'

'Thanks. That might keep me awake till I get home.'

'Nice-looking suit on that kid. The overcoat's cashmere and wool. It goes one fifty at Brooks Brothers.'

'A lawyer sent to carry Shaw back to his hotel.'

'We were going to let him go anyway.'

'Maybe they just wanted to make sure.'

'Ambrose?'

'My guess.'

'Overkill.'

'Just what I was thinking. I was also thinking that Shaw didn't see it as something out of the ordinary that a tax lawyer for a big-time firm gets rousted out of bed to collect him.'

'The guy's pretty fucking calm. You don't meet many like that. I got the feeling he was laughing at us. What do you think?'

'He acts like he's got a lot of clout. I wonder where it comes from.' He noticed that Orso was freshly showered and shaved and had put on a clean shirt. 'Where are you going?'

'I thought I'd start the day with a physics lesson.'

'The professor at NYU?'

'Yeah.' He looked worried. 'Man, I don't know.'

'You don't know what?'

Orso looked sheepish. 'Do you remember a couple of years ago you were going out with that broad turned out to be a Russian spy? Dylan was her name.'

'No.'

'Okay. Okay. Remember I told you don't give her the keys to your apartment? You know what I said will happen?'

'"Soon we'd be standing up in front of some monsignor doing the till-death-do-us-part thing," I think is what you said. It didn't quite work out that way. We did the death thing before the monsignor thing.'

Dylan McCue, Russian spy, lover, who betrayed him, and who then saved his life, and was now dead somewhere in Russia, dead but not gone.

Orso was unembarrassed. 'Yeah, well, still. Good advice.'

'Did you give the professor the keys to your apartment?'

'No. She gave me the keys to hers.' Orso shrugged at life's strange turns and went down the stairs with an eager step.

Cassidy had not thought of Dylan for a long time. He had dreamed of her over and over in the months after she left New York on the Russian freighter from which he had rescued his father. It was a dream of finding her again, repeated like a loop of film in his head, but after a while he decided the dream was wishful thinking, not predictive. Soon after that, the dream stopped.

Early morning left the Times Square area nearly deserted. Daylight scattered its vampires. An occasional taxi cruised. A man hosed down the sidewalk in front of an all-night deli. A man and a woman in green aprons unloaded crates of vegetables in front of the grocery on Eighth Avenue. The neon and electric signs had been turned off. The theater marquees, now unlit, showed pale ghosts of their night-time announcements. A few cleaning crews from the theaters made their way toward the subway talking in Spanish. A newspaper delivery truck crawled Eighth while two helpers in the back threw out bundles of papers to land with thumps on the sidewalk in front of newsstands and stores. A woman in silk pajamas and slippers under a fur coat, her hair in curlers, smoked a cigarette distractedly while she waited for her dachshund to sniff out the proper place to piss. A street sweeper rumbled by, its circular brushes swishing, and left a trail of water glistening on the street. By nine the subways would be pouring out office workers hurrying to their jobs with nervy energy and the streets would be dense with traffic, but now the sky was bright, and the morning crisp, the day as yet unbruised.

God, he was tired. Home and bed and then the weekend off. But at least the night watch was over.

Seven

Spencer Shaw sat on a wooden bench and watched Sebastian Ambrose milk his goat. The doctor's brownstone was in the Village on Leroy Street and had a south-facing yard that Ambrose had turned into a miniature farm. There was a stand of corn along the east wall, and the four tomato plants staked up nearby were heavy with ripe fruit. A patch of salad greens grew in dark earth near a small tin goat shed. The goat was no more than twenty inches high at the shoulders. Her white coat was slightly soiled by the New York air. She stood placidly while Ambrose stripped her milk out into a galvanized bucket with practiced hands. 'She's a Nigerian Dwarf,' Ambrose explained. 'Six percent butter fat in the milk which makes for good cheese, but I don't do that. I just drink the milk.' His head was tucked down near the goat, so his voice was muffled. 'A glass every morning, a glass every evening, the healthiest thing you can have.' He stood up and kicked the low wooden milking stool aside, and picked up the bucket. 'Do you want a tomato? Last of the season. We'll have frost soon, and then they're done.'

'No thanks,' Spencer Shaw said.

'These are the real things, not like that crap you buy in the supermarket. They gas them to turn them red.' He pulled a tomato from one of the plants, rubbed it against his shirt to clean it, and took a bite. 'Are you sure?'

'I'm sure,' Shaw said. What made Ambrose think his shirt was cleaner than the tomato? He watched Ambrose shamble toward him. The big man wore lace-up leather boots, brown corduroy trousers worn shiny at the knees and seat, a plaid flannel shirt with a frayed collar, and a ratty blue cardigan. Bits of tomato gleamed in Ambrose's thick beard, and his hair looked like it had been groomed with an eggbeater. He stood at the bottom of the steps to the porch while he ate the tomato like an apple. He looked back over his yard with satisfaction.

'It's not easy to make a garden in New York soil. You have no idea of the poisons that accumulate here over the years. Do you know what phytoremediation is, Shaw?'

'No. Not a clue.' But he knew he was about to find out. Ambrose liked a captive audience for his lectures.

'It refers to the natural ability of certain plants to make contaminants in soils harmless. Certain plants are hyperaccumulators. They gather and degrade the toxins. I used mustard, hemp, pigweed, and stinkweed.'

The stinkweed degraded you too, pal. Shaw smiled at the thought.

'Is something funny?'

'Stinkweed's a funny word.'

Ambrose weighed him for a moment with his weird eyes, dismissed the levity, and went on. 'It took me four years, but now I have a rich, organic, non-toxic soil without the use of

73

chemical fertilizers. A triumph of nature over man's pernicious misuse of the earth.' He took a last bite of the tomato, threw the remains to the goat, and walked up past Shaw and went into the kitchen. Moments later he reappeared carrying a glass of milk. He sat on the bench next to Shaw and took a long pull at the glass and then wiped his beard with his sleeve. He searched his pockets until he found his cigarette holder and chewed it while he opened a fresh pack of Raleighs and carefully stowed the coupon in his sweater pocket before lighting up. Shaw waited. Ambrose had called him, and he would explain why when he was ready.

'Hoffman?'

'Hoffman has accepted an assignment overseas. He left for Iran yesterday morning,' Shaw said. Would it be insulting to get up and lean against the porch railing? Ambrose smelled of sweat, goat, and fried food.

'Good. Too many voices can confuse the narrative.'

'Why should there be a narrative? I made my report. We've heard nothing since. A man suffering from depression threw himself out a window. It happens.'

'There will be an autopsy.'

'Are you worried about that?' Shaw lit a cigarette and flicked the burned match into the garden.

'Not really.' Ambrose got up and retrieved the match and put it in his pocket. 'It's not something that a pathologist in a place like the police morgue is likely to identify.'

'But he might.' Stick a needle in that balloon of self-satisfaction.

'Unlikely.'

'Are you sure?'

'Are you questioning me on a scientific matter?' Ambrose turned to look at Shaw in surprise.

'You have your job, and I understand that you're the best.' Mollify the arrogant prick. 'My job is to clean up if there's any spillage. I'm good at that, but I work better if I know how big the mess is.'

Ambrose regarded him with his unsettling black eyes. Then he tilted his glass and splashed milk on the porch. 'It's that big. No more.'

'Okay. Fine. Wonderful.'

'You'll have to take Hoffman's place. We're going out with more blind trials. We need another man.'

'Sure. Love to. Should be a lot of fun.'

Ambrose examined him for sarcasm, but all he got from Shaw was a bland look and a smile. 'I did not like that detective who was in the hotel. Cassidy. An arrogant man. Are we likely to deal with him again?'

'No. Williger was a suicide. Nothing says different. There's no reason they won't sign off on it. Don't worry about him. If he becomes a problem, he's mine, not yours, part of the clean up.'

'Very well. Keep me informed. Please pull the door tight when you go. Sometimes it sticks.'

Shaw stood on the sidewalk outside Ambrose's house and finished his cigarette. A ragged bum pushed a baby carriage full of scrap iron west toward the salvage yard on Washington. Shaw turned east toward Hudson. Ambrose gave him a pain, and if it weren't for the thing he had to do about his brother, he never would have asked for assignment in New York. There was an opening in Saigon he could have. Things were happening in Saigon. He needed something, action; action was always good. Maybe the blind trials would provide a kick.

He watched a young woman in a long tight, blue skirt and a tight red sweater walk down the block toward him. How old was she, eighteen, twenty? Old enough. Guys had been screwing her in the back seats of their imaginations since she was fifteen. Someone must have told her that she looked like Marilyn Monroe, because she was sure trying, blonde hair, red lipstick, mouth a little open. She knew he was looking. She pretended not to notice. When he got close, he smiled his best smile and said, 'Hey.' She looked at him. 'Hi. Do you want to fuck?'

'What?' Shock. Her eyes went wide and her mouth dropped open. 'What!?'

'Do you want to fuck?'

'What?'

'You know, screw?' He poked his right fore-finger in demonstration through the circle made by his left thumb and forefinger. 'Do you want to screw? I've got a place nearby.'

'Go away. Go away.' Her hands were up in defense and she was backing away.

'Hey, hey, it's okay. No? That's fine. Not a problem. It's just that I'm on a tight schedule, and I thought I'd ask and save some time.' He smiled, waved, and walked away. In his experience, the odds of a yes were around fifty-fifty, a delightful discovery that had saved him a lot of time and restaurant bills. He could hear the clatter of her heels on the pavement as she took off in the other direction. Okay, then, a taxi to the Yale Club, a game of squash, and then drinks at the bar. He was bound to run into someone he knew, and the evening would move on from there.

Eight

Cassidy knocked on the pebbled glass door of Lieutenant Tanner's office and went in. 'You wanted to see me?'

'Close the door,' Tanner said. The window was wide open, and the sudden cross draft blew papers off Tanner's desk as he grabbed for them. Cassidy closed the door. The temperature in the office matched the high forties outside. Tanner wore his overcoat. He stooped to pick up the blown papers and sat back down behind his desk. He gestured toward the open window. 'I got tired of smelling my own smells in here. Fucking window hasn't been open since Prohibition. Took me half an hour to chip the paint away. Damn near popped a hernia getting the thing up.' A putty knife and an old hammer with a taped handle lay on the windowsill. 'Dr Sebastian

Ambrose? Doc of the guy who went out the window over at the Astor?'

'Yeah.'

'He says you were rude to him.'

'Oh, dear.'

'Yeah, well, he reached out to someone down at Centre Street, and they passed it on.'

'What do they want me to do, send him flowers?'

'I don't know what they want. They got the message. They passed it to me. I passed it to you. I'd say that's the end of it. The guy who jumped, Williger, they put him down for a suicide. Case closed. You don't have to see Ambrose again.'

'Who is he, Ambrose? First he sends a lawyer from a high-powered law firm in the middle of the night to make sure his friend Shaw gets back to his hotel all right, and then he dings me at Centre Street. Where does he get the juice?'

'No idea. And I don't give a shit. He's in the rearview mirror. There are other things out there that need work. That big asshole you guys busted selling smack, the knife sharpener, Connor Finn, he made bail and missed his first court date. Apparently he doesn't have faith that the system is going to come down in his favor. We'd like to get him back inside. Councilman Franzi is particularly interested in the case. His office called three times in the last twenty-four. And what about the guy who got stabbed in the head up in the park there? Leon Dudek. Where are we on that?'

78

'I've been on night watch. I gave it to Foley.'

'So talk to Foley. Find out where we are. Close the door when you go out.'

But Foley had already left the house. Leon Dudek would have to wait till tomorrow.

Cassidy walked toward Broadway. The sky was darkening toward evening, the time of day the French call 'the blue hour,' when lovers meet outside the orbits of their normal lives. Taxis dropped passengers in front of the restaurants that catered to pre-theater diners. Workers hurried home carrying bags of groceries. A group of Broadway gypsies early for the evening's call, posed with hips cocked, hands and elbows just so, and smoked cigarettes and chattered at each other near the stage door of the Mark Hellinger Theatre. They always reminded Cassidy of birds lightly connected to the earth, about to spring into the air. The theater marquee announced the hit *My Fair Lady*, starring Rex Harrison and Julie Andrews. One of the dancers did a shuffle and slide that ended with a pirouette, and the others saluted him with mocking applause. Three hookers in tight, bright dresses stilted ahead of Cassidy on stiletto heels. Just before Broadway they stopped to use the window of a restaurant as a mirror to check their makeup. A middle-aged couple at a table near the window looked at them with alarm. One of the women mimed an exaggerated kiss and made a gesture that offered a threesome, and the couple shied away as if something dangerous threatened to come through the glass into their orderly world. Laughing, the women went on.

Cassidy turned south on the Stem. The sidewalks were crowded with tourists come to the big city hoping for a thrilling brush against the sin that Broadway and Times Square promised. The Paramount Building took up the east side block between 44th Street and 43rd. The movie theater marquee advertised Alfred Hitchcock's *The Man Who Knew Too Much*, but the five teenage girls outside the theater swooned at the poster in a glass display case near the lobby door that promised Elvis Presley would be there in November in *Love Me Tender*. Cassidy went through the glass doors to the office building and rode the elevator to where his brother, Brian, had an office at ABC News.

Brian's secretary, Claire, said, 'He's expecting you, Mr Cassidy.'

Brian was a big, square-built man with an open, cheerful manner that invited confidences, useful gifts for a reporter. He had his feet up on his desk next to a framed photograph of his wife, Marcy, and their two daughters. His attention was focused on a video monitor showing a tape of an interview on the set of his news show, *Behind the Headlines*. Brian and the man he was interviewing sat in easy chairs angled toward each other and facing the camera. There was a table between them that held coffee mugs and two ashtrays. Behind them loomed a piece of electronic studio equipment Cassidy could not identify. It looked like a metal cabinet faced with dials and switches. 'Good evening,' Brian's black-and-white TV presence said looking directly at the camera. 'Welcome to *Behind the*

80

Headlines. Tonight my guest is Utah Congressman Martin Williams.' He nodded to the congressman. 'Congressman Williams, thank you for being here tonight.'

'It's my pleasure, Brian.' That stretched the truth, because Congressman Williams fidgeted in his chair and lit a cigarette even though there was one burning in the ashtray next to him. 'I've never been on television before. It's quite an experience.' A confession of his unease.

Brian turned back to the camera. His manner was calm, confiding, but grave, as if warning that important subjects were to be discussed on the program. Pay attention. 'Tonight's broadcast is part of our continuing series, *How The Government in Washington Spends Our Money.* I want to remind our viewers that the money the government spends comes from you and me, our neighbors and friends, mostly in the form of the taxes we pay. It is our government funded by our money, and we at *Behind the Headlines* believe it is important for us to look at how the process works.'

The broadcast went to a test pattern, and Brian got up and turned the TV off.

'I thought I was going to learn something there. You should have left it on,' Cassidy said.

'Watch it next month, and all will be revealed. Wednesday October tenth at eight p.m.'

'It's on a Wednesday? Are you sure?'

Brian laughed. 'Let me check with Claire.'

'I might be busy on the tenth upholding the law.'

'I'll give you the short version, without

81

commercials, over a drink.' He crossed to the bar table in the corner near the window. 'A martini?'

'Perfect,' Cassidy said. 'The congressman looked a little nervous. Did he think you were going to take him over the jumps?'

'Everybody's nervous the first time on TV. You have to keep telling them, pretend it's a conversation. Look at me when you answer. Don't look at the camera. The camera will find you. Some get it. Some don't. The good ones understand what TV is going to do for them.'

'What's that?'

'It'll take them into every home that has a television.'

'Politicians in the living room. That's going to fuck up a lot of good cocktail hours.' He accepted the martini from Brian and took a sip. 'So what's with the congressman?'

'He refused to vote for an appropriation bill, because one of the companies that would profit from it sent his re-election campaign a contribution.'

'How much?'

'What's the difference?'

'I want to know how much someone thinks a congressman goes for.'

'A thousand bucks.'

'Huh, not much more than a New York Councilman might get. You'd think a congressman would cost at least twice as much. Of course there are more of them than there are councilmen. That probably dilutes the demand.'

Brian toasted him with bourbon and laughed.

'Ah, the tough, cynical cop, but I know you, Michael. Outrage, not cynicism. Outrage drives you. And by the way, Congress has called for a select committee to look into Williams's allegation. The appropriation bill is on hold.'

'My faith in the system is restored. What was the company?'

'A medical supply company that contracts with the military. It's in my notes. Do you want me to look?'

'It wouldn't mean anything to me.'

'You said on the phone that you wanted to ask me about something.'

'What can you tell me about a law firm called Sullivan and Cromwell?'

'Why do you want to know?'

'I ran into one of their lawyers a couple of nights ago.'

'Who was that?' Brian took his empty glass and carried it to the bar.

'Peter Gilbert.'

'I don't know him.'

'But you know some of the others there?'

'I do. I went to school with some of them,' Brian said. 'How did you meet Gilbert?'

'He came to the stationhouse the other night to get a release for someone we had down there. We hadn't arrested the guy. We just asked him to come down to make a report. But it made somebody nervous, and they got Gilbert out of bed and sent him down.'

'Who was the guy you brought in?'

'His name was Shaw, Spencer Shaw. He worked with a chemist for the Department of the Army who went out a window at the Hotel Astor the other night.'

'Was it suicide, or do you think he was pushed?' Brian asked.

'It bothers me that he didn't open the window. But I don't know what goes through a man's mind at that moment. Maybe he was impatient to get it over with.'

'What did Shaw say?'

'He was in the other room. He said he didn't see anything. He heard the crash when Williger went through the window.'

'Why did someone send a lawyer to make sure a witness who saw nothing got home all right?'

'I don't know.'

Brian brought him a fresh drink and sat with his feet up on his desk. 'What do you know about Sullivan and Cromwell?'

'Nothing.'

'It might be the most powerful law firm in the country. We were going to do a piece on them about a year ago. A kind of who-pulls-the-strings-behind-the-throne thing. They *suggested* that it wouldn't be a good idea, and someone on the top floor decided there wasn't really a story there after all. They've been international power brokers since the end of the last century. They know everybody in finance, politics, the press, and everybody owes them something. They've been sitting pretty on the intersection of Washington politics and global business for seventy years. John Foster Dulles is a partner, and so is his brother, Allen.'

'The Secretary of State and the director of the

CIA? Now I know who to call when I need a lawyer.'

Cassidy lit a cigarette. 'So why are these hotshots interested in an Army chemist?'

'I don't know. But there'll be some mix of money and politics. I'm going back down to Washington. Do you want me to ask around? Maybe I could turn up something on the chemist. What's his name?'

'Paul Williger.'

'And the other guy again, the one the lawyer came to spring?'

'Spencer Shaw. If you've got time, that would be great. Don't go out of your way. It probably doesn't mean anything.'

Brian walked Cassidy down the corridor to the elevator. 'Have you seen Dad lately?'

'No,' Cassidy said. 'Not for a couple of weeks.' His relationship with his father was volatile. The affection was always there, but they banged against each other like flint and steel.

'He'd love it if you stopped by the theater and watched a run-through. He mentioned it the other day.'

'I'll try.' It was Tom Cassidy's forlorn hope that Cassidy would give up the idiocy of being a cop and come join him in the theater business.

'Okay. Be good.' Brian's forlorn hope. He squeezed Michael's shoulder affectionately and watched him into the elevator.

Cassidy ate a late dinner at the bar at Sardi's and talked with Vince Sardi about the Broadway season. *My Fair Lady* was the big hit, but Sardi

85

had high hopes for *Bells Are Ringing* and *Auntie Mame*. By the time he finished, the Broadway theaters had let out. The sidewalks were crowded. Broadway grifters and minor con artists were abroad and looking for suckers. Some of them stood in doorways and whispered offerings tinged with sin and darkness. Others glad-handed and buttonholed on the sidewalk with broad smiles designed to camouflage their greed. Some of them were vicious enough to steal a blind man's cup, but for the most part they were as harmless as lice.

Near 50th Street Cassidy spotted Benny the Dip and his sister, a cheerful, pneumatic bottle-blond named Candy, working a pair of out-of-town businessmen who had spent the evening pouring booze on their thirsts. Candy, the cannon, walked two identical little white poodles on long leashes. The dogs were well trained and managed to entangle themselves with the men. Candy apologetically tried to untangle the dogs. As the men displayed their drunken gallantry to the woman, Benny came to help and dipped both their wallets. The four people disengaged with assurances of no harm done, and the two businessmen moved off. Benny stiffened when Cassidy caught his eye. Cassidy shook his head and put out a hand. Benny shrugged and gave up both wallets.

'Jesus Christ, Cassidy.'

'Sorry, Benny. Wrong time, wrong place. How are you doing, Candy?'

'I was doing fine until a minute ago. What the hell, Cassidy, don't you ever sleep?' She said it without rancor.

'Take the rest of the night off, will you? Say hello to your mother for me when you see her.'

'We've got mouths to feed, Cassidy,' Candy complained.

'If I come back down the Stem later, I don't want to see you.'

'Okay, okay,' Benny said. He handed over the wallets. Candy gave Cassidy a sour look and followed her brother down the street with the dogs. They were the best pickpocket team in town. He could have arrested them, but Benny had a bail bondsman on call, and they'd be on the street again before Cassidy finished writing the report.

Cassidy found the businessmen standing at the foot of a stairway that led to a second-floor striptease joint discussing going up and taking a look at some poontang.

'Gentlemen, you've got to be more careful. You dropped your wallets back there down the block.'

They looked at him in surprise and tapped the pockets where their wallets should have been. Their eyes went wide. Cassidy handed over the billfolds. One of the men surreptitiously checked to see if his money was still there.

'Have fun,' Cassidy said and headed downtown.

Waiting for the light at 45th Street he looked across Broadway to the Hotel Astor. Light spilled to the sidewalk from the lobby. A uniformed doorman stood to one side of the entrance and smoked a cigarette behind a cupped hand. There were lights in rooms on some of the upper floors, but none behind the new

87

window in room 603 where Paul Williger had flown from life.

Cassidy crossed the street and headed toward the hotel entrance. The doorman ground his cigarette out under his shoe and hurried to open the door with a cheery, 'Good evening, sir. A beautiful night.'

The night clerk watched him with a professional smile as he crossed the lobby to the desk. 'Good evening, sir.'

'Evening. Is Joe Pickering on duty?'

'Yes, sir. He is. May I say who is asking for him?'

'Detective Michael Cassidy.'

The clerk turned and discreetly used a phone on a desk against the back wall. He spoke quietly for a few seconds, and then hung up and returned to Cassidy. 'Mr Pickering will be with you in a few minutes. If you'd like, you can wait here in the lobby or the bar is just to your left.'

Cassidy ordered bourbon on the rocks and took a table near the window. The waiter brought Cassidy his drink. He lit a cigarette from the second pack of the day. It tasted like burning rope. Four nuns in black habits with white headpieces sailed by looking like large dignified birds. A drunk in a plaid jacket pressed against the window and stuck out his tongue at Cassidy and then tacked away as if fighting a high wind.

Joe Pickering slipped into the chair opposite him. 'Good evening, Detective Cassidy.'

'Mr Pickering.' They shook hands across the table. 'Care for a drink?'

'Unfortunately I can't while on duty. How may I help you?'

'The man in the room next to Paul Williger's said that he called the desk and the police after Williger went out the window. Later, he mentioned that he had also called the doctor who arrived, a man named Ambrose. I was wondering if he made any other calls that might have slipped his mind.'

'Shall we go see?' Pickering stood up. 'Please bring your drink.'

Cassidy took money from his pocket as he stood.

'On the house,' Pickering said.

Cassidy dropped a dollar on the table for the waiter and followed Pickering out of the bar. The clerk lifted the desk gate as they approached, and they went through a door marked *Authorized Personnel Only* to the telephone switchboard center for the hotel. There were five night-time operators on the board. They were all middle-aged women, and they all wore earphones, and mouthpieces. They sat on swivel stools in front of the large switchboard. Three of them had knitting within easy reach, another had a paperback book with a lurid cover of a young woman in a tight sweater and a man with a gun, and the fifth had a stack of movie gossip magazines. The graveyard shift was not busy.

'Good evening, ladies,' Pickering said.

'Good evening, Mr Pickering,' they chirped and looked at Cassidy with curiosity.

Pickering disappeared around the side of the switchboard. He came back moments later carrying a large ring binder.

'September twenty-second, wasn't it?'

'Yes. About one in the morning.'

Pickering flipped pages and ran a finger down columns of figures. 'Here we are. One twenty-one, a call from 605, Mr Shaw's room to the long-distance operator. Five minutes later a call to the desk. Two minutes after that he placed a call to the police. Then five minutes later a call to a New York number. Perhaps that's the doctor's. Here, I'll write it down.' He took a fountain pen from his inside pocket and unscrewed the cap and wrote the number on a small pad he found in a drawer.

'What was the long-distance call?'

Pickering looked back at the ledger. 'It was to a number in Washington, DC. Mr Hoffman called the same number fifteen minutes later.

'Hoffman? Who's Hoffman?'

'I think he must be a colleague of Mr Shaw's and Mr Williger's. They often check in on the same days.' Pickering handed Cassidy another piece of paper with the Washington number.

'He never mentioned Hoffman. Are he and Shaw still in the hotel?'

'Let's go see.'

Hoffman had checked out fifteen minutes after Williger went out the window. Spencer Shaw checked out the next day.

Nine

In the morning, Cassidy called the DC number Shaw had called from the Astor. Someone picked up the phone on the fifth ring. 'Yes?' said a man's voice.

'This is Detective Michael Cassidy, New York Police Department. Who am I speaking to?'

There was silence on the other end. 'I'd like to speak to Spencer Shaw or John Hoffman.'

The phone hung up with a click.

Tommy Foley was reading *Field & Stream* magazine when Cassidy stopped by his desk.

'Foley, how'd you do with the Leon Dudek thing?' He offered Foley a cigarette.

'Who?' Foley took the Lucky and lit it with a kitchen match scraped on his chair arm.

'Dudek. Leon Dudek. Someone stuck a blade in his brain up in the park. I gave you his address.'

'Oh, yeah. That guy.' He put the magazine face down on the desk to hold his place. The cover painting showed a twelve-point buck in a clearing and a hunter sighting a rifle down on him from a camouflaged tree stand. 'I didn't get nowhere with that. I went down there, in the Alphabets, Lower East Side. What a crappy neighborhood. Half the people don't speak a word of English, the other half don't want to talk to a cop.'

'Did you go to the address?'

'Yeah, sure. I say, "Leon Dudek," and they nod. I say, "Where does he live?" and they all shake their heads. "Who knows him?", some turn around and walk away. Some give me the stink eye. They talk to each other in some language, sounds kind of like the German. I didn't learn much German over there during the war, enough to trade a candy bar or a pack of cigarettes for a piece of ass, but what they were talking wasn't the same.'

'Yeah, great. Good work.'

'Yeah. I figure, what the hell. They don't want me to help, I ain't going to break my balls.'

Rhonda answered her phone on the third ring. '*New York Post*, Rhonda Raskin.'

'It's me.'

'Hey, stranger. Where have you been?'

'Pining for you.'

'Liar. I am always a phone call away,' she said eagerly. 'Do you find me too eager, Michael?'

'No, I don't. How was your mother?'

'Irascible. And once again the subject came up of why I haven't married a nice Jewish doctor or lawyer. "Settle down," she says. "Stop running around." I tell her I have a job that I like. "Job, shmob," she says, I swear to god.' Some of the laughter left her voice. 'She has a real talent for making me feel like I can never measure up.'

'And yet you go back almost every week.'

'Hey, she's my mother.'

'What are you doing right now? Are you busy?'

'I've got all the information you'll ever need

on the debutante season, and I can hardly wait to plunge into writing the story. Column inches of deathless prose on organdy and hairstyles. Can my Pulitzer be far behind?'

'How's your Yiddish?'

'*Praktakli gants.*'

'That bad?'

'Practically perfect.'

'That'll have to do. Can you get away?'

'What's going on?'

'I've got to go down to the Alphabets and talk to people about a man who was murdered in Central Park. Apparently they mostly speak Yiddish.'

'Do I get the story?' Her focus was tight now.

'The murder's already been reported. Leon Dudek was the vic. He was found near Columbus Circle stabbed at the base of the skull. It got an inch in a couple of the papers.'

'Okay, but from now on, is it my story?'

'Off the record for now, but it's your story when it's time to report it.'

'Who decides on when it's time?'

'I do.'

She said nothing.

'It's either that or I find someone else to translate.'

'Okay, right.'

'You can't jump the gun on this, Rhonda. You'll have the story as soon as possible. Stories in the paper have a way of screwing up an investigation.'

'All right. All right.'

'There's a coffee shop on the corner of St

Marks Place and Third. Meet me there in half an hour.'

'That's me you see coming up the block.'

A phone rang in an apartment on the Upper East Side. Spencer Shaw rolled off the woman who said, 'Hey, what the hell?' in surprise and annoyance as he got out of bed, and padded naked toward the study. What was her name? Mary? Margie? Jesus, wouldn't it be easier if they were all named Bunny? He answered the phone on the sixth ring. Maybe that's what he'd do, start calling all of them Bunny. Keep it simple.

'Shaw here.'

The voice on the other end said, 'A Detective Michael Cassidy called the 8858 number here.'

'Uh-huh. How'd he get it?' The cool breeze through the open window dried the sweat on his skin. He watched his dick go soft.

'That's one of the things you should find out. He asked to speak to you or Hoffman.'

'Where'd he get Hoffman's name?'

'We don't know.'

'The hotel, probably. They keep records of calls. Is this about Williger?'

'Presumably. Brian Cassidy, the TV reporter brother, was down here a couple of days ago asking questions about Gallien Medical. He also called someone at the Department of the Army and wanted to know if they had a Spencer Shaw or a Paul Williger on their books. We would prefer that he not pursue his line of questioning. It's ruffling feathers.'

'So he and his cop brother are working this together from opposite sides of the street. Why are they so interested? How'd they get a hold of Gallien Medical?'

'We don't know. There are a lot of things in play here, and we do not need a reporter and a cop poking around this operation. We want the reporter discouraged. The cop's been told the Williger case is closed.'

'Okay.'

'This is not a story we want to see on *Behind the Headlines*. Clear?'

'Clear.'

There was a click as the phone at the other end returned to its cradle. He checked the clock on the desk. Almost noon. Still, plenty of time for a quickie with . . .?

He turned for the bedroom calling, 'Bunny, honey, here I come, ready or not.'

Rhonda impatiently refused coffee. 'No, thanks. Let's go.' They walked south and east toward Leon Dudek's address on East Third. She was a long-legged woman, and she matched Cassidy's pace. 'Tell me about Leon Dudek.'

'I don't know much,' Cassidy said. 'Polish, late forties, early fifties. Drove a hansom cab in the park for the last four years. I don't know what he did before that. The people at the stable didn't know him well at all. They liked him, but he wasn't someone who went out for a beer after work. The thing everybody said about him was that he was gentle, and sad.'

'Sad?'

'He was in a concentration camp during the war.'

'Oh, Jesus. And the killing? Anything about that?'

'Not much. His wallet was gone, so it might have been a robbery.'

'You're not going to get a hell of a lot from a guy driving one of those horse cabs.'

'It's New York. There are people who'll take you down for the pennies in your loafers, but I don't think it was a robbery. I think it was made to look like one. I think he knew the guys.'

'Guys?'

'According the ME at the morgue one held him and the other did the blade work.'

'How could he tell?'

'There were bruises on Dudek's arms as if someone gripped him hard there.'

The Lower East Side was traditionally an immigrants' neighborhood: Irish, Italians, Poles, Ukrainians, Germans, and Jews of all those nations had washed ashore there. The lucky and the ambitious moved up and out, and the next wave seeking the American dream took their places in the tenements and rundown apartment buildings. Rhonda stopped in front of a store offering *Friedman's Kosher Wines* and, in smaller letters, *tobacco and sundries*.

'This is where we always stopped to buy wine for Seder on the way to my grandparents' apartment. A bottle of wine, cigars for Zeyde and Dad, and a candy bar for my brother and me. But not to be eaten until after the meal. Very strict on that.'

'I didn't know your grandparents lived down here.'

'We're only scraping the surface of what you don't know about me.'

Laundry hung from the iron railings of the six-story tenements on 3rd Street and from clotheslines strung on pulleys across the airshafts. The building where Leon Dudek had lived was halfway along the block. Two women sat on wooden kitchen chairs taking the sun on the sidewalk. A third was on the fire escape above them collecting laundry from the railings and folding it into a wicker basket. They could have been sisters. They all wore formless dresses in gray or brown cotton that extended to their ankles, and earth-tone wool overcoats. Their gray heads covered with dark scarves. Their faces were lined by time, work, and worry. They were aware of Cassidy and Rhonda the moment they turned the corner. Strangers to the neighborhood were viewed with suspicion. They tracked Cassidy and Rhonda along the block and then flicked their eyes away when they stopped in front of the building.

'Good afternoon, ladies. How are you today?' Cassidy said with what he hoped was disarming charm.

The women looked back at him with flat, wary gazes.

'Is this where Leon Dudek lived?'

One of the women picked up knitting from her lap and began to shuttle the needles.

Cassidy showed them his badge. 'I'm a policeman. I'd like to speak to whoever knew Mr Dudek.'

97

The knitter said something in a language Cassidy did not understand. He picked out the word *Cossack*, which is what his father had called him when he joined the cops. Rhonda snorted in amusement.

'Is there someone in the building I could talk to? A super?'

Neither woman looked at him. The one who wasn't knitting dug in her coat pocket and found half a cigarette. She lit it with a kitchen match scraped across the pavement next to her chair. She said something to the knitting woman and then sucked greedily on the cigarette. The woman on the fire escape said something that made both the women on the sidewalk laugh shortly. The knitter replied. Whatever she said drew nods and grunts of agreement.

'Well, at least they think you're good-looking,' Rhonda said. 'But that one said, "Good-looking men are a dime a dozen and mostly not worth the price."'

'Tell them if they don't cooperate, I'll send an ugly cop down to talk to them. We've got plenty.'

Rhonda said something in Yiddish, and the women laughed.

The door to the building opened and a young man in a worker's blue coveralls, a cheap nylon windbreaker, and a cloth cap came out. When he saw Cassidy and Rhonda, he hesitated as if to go back into the building.

Cassidy's badge was still in his hand. 'Hey, buddy, I'd like to talk to you.'

The young man ducked his head and went around the women without going near Cassidy.

98

'Hey, hold on a second,' Cassidy said to him, but he walked away quickly, head down. Cassidy had a fleeting impression of a boy in his late teens or early twenties. There was something about the side of his face. Maybe a scar. 'Hey, stop. I just want to talk to you.'

The boy took off running.

'Shit.'

Cassidy went after him. The boy was quick. He dodged between parked cars and went out into the street. Brakes squealed and horns blew. The kid flew around a corner, and when Cassidy followed he found a garbage can upended and rolling toward him. Cassidy went over it like a low hurdle and stretched out, but he could not gain. The boy juked past a man pushing a rack of clothes on hangers, ignored the outraged shout of a woman with a baby carriage, yanked open the door to a diner, and disappeared inside. By the time Cassidy came through the door, the only evidence of the kid was the door bouncing back from the wall at the end of the room. Somewhere at the back another door slammed. The open door led to a storeroom. The second one was closed, and when Cassidy yanked it open, he was in time to see the boy slip through a narrow opening in a high board fence that blocked the end of the alley. It took Cassidy a few seconds to understand that he would never fit through the gap. The kid was gone.

Cassidy went back into the diner gasping for breath. Goddamn cigarettes. He used to be able to run.

The only other person in the place was the

99

counterman, a heavy black-haired man with a thick mustache. He watched Cassidy warily. One hand was under the counter holding whatever weapon he kept for comfort: knife, machete, baseball bat, gun. Cassidy showed him his badge and the man relaxed.

'Do you know the kid who just ran through here?' Cassidy asked. He sat on a counter stool to catch his breath.

'What'd he do?' The man had an Italian accent.

'He didn't do anything as far as I know.'

'Then why you chasing him?'

'I'm a cop. He ran. I chased. That's what cops do when people run. Instinct and training. Like Pavlov's dog.'

'Whose dog?'

'Never mind. Give me a coke, will you?'

'Fountain or bottle?'

'Bottle.' Cassidy slid a quarter onto the counter. The man popped the top off a Coke and slid Cassidy the bottle.

'You want a glass?'

'No, thanks. Tell me about the kid.'

'You really got no beef with him?'

'No beef. Let's start with a name.'

'That's Freddy. Maybe not his real name, but what everyone calls him, Freddy. *Pazzo*, a little crazy.'

'How so?'

'I don't know. Don't talk much. Nervous like a cat. You be talking to him, suddenly he just turn and walk away, no reason. Just, boom, gone.'

'Does he live in that building down there in

100

the middle of the block, the one where the women are talking?'

'Yeah, he coops in a place in the basement. But not just there. A couple or three other places around the neighborhood. Not regular rooms, but places. Like I hear he's got some sort of cave over there under the bridge.'

'What does he do? Does he work? Go to school?'

'School, no.' A half-laugh. 'Nah, nah. He scuffles, you know? He runs errands. You need something carried from here to there, he do that. You need help tearing something down, building something, he help if it's not too complicated. He been known to pick up stuff that fell off the back of a truck. Not telling nothing, but if you ask, he maybe could get you a carton of cigarettes without the tax stamps. The hustle. You know what I mean?'

'Yeah, I know.'

'And he ain't in trouble.'

'No.'

''Cause the reason he's a little squirrely, they say, is he was in one of them camps during the war. Them camps over there in Germany, the death camps. Spent the whole war in a death camp. Imagine, a kid, seven or eight when he went in. Come out alive but maybe a little bit off.'

'Uh-huh.'

'Could fuck up anybody from what I heard.'

Rhonda was no longer in front of Dudek's building. The woman with the knitting gestured with her head toward the front door. He went in.

The hall was dim and smelled of fried onions

101

and disinfectant. A staircase rose against one wall. The risers were worn to hollows by generations of feet. A door was open at the end of the hall. He heard Rhonda say something too quietly to understand.

'Rhonda?'

'In here, Mike.'

The apartment was shabby but neat. A small living room held a sagging sofa covered in faded chintz with a low wood table in front of it, a wooden armchair with a seat and back cushioned in brown corduroy, and a cracked leather ottoman. A cheap print of a rabbit hung above the sofa. The room smelled of furniture polish and cigarette smoke. He rapped the doorframe with his knuckles.

'Back here,' Rhonda called. 'The kitchen.'

The kitchen was a long, narrow room with a big, black stove on one wall, and a deep metal sink flanked by zinc-topped counters on the other. Rhonda sat at a small table near a window that opened on the airshaft at the back of the building. A small, gray-haired woman ironed shirts at an ironing board. A cigarette dangled from the corner of her mouth, and her head was tipped to one side so the smoke didn't get in her eyes.

'Mike, this is Mrs Tanenbaum. She's kind of the super here. Mrs Tanenbaum, this is Detective Michael Cassidy who I told you about.'

Mrs Tanenbaum nodded to Cassidy and flipped the shirt so she could iron the other side. Her cigarette ash fell to the floor.

'She has a key to Leon's apartment. As soon

102

as she's finished ironing, she'll take us up.' She looked at Cassidy to make sure he understood the priorities in this kitchen: ironing, and then homicide.

Leon Dudek's place was on the top floor of the tenement, where it would get all the heat that rose through the building in the summer, and little of the heat that rose through the radiators in the winter. Mrs Tanenbaum opened the door with a key from a ring that jangled with many other keys. She stepped back to let Cassidy and Rhonda in.

The apartment was one small room that had been chopped out of a bigger apartment next door. The only window looked out at a taller building and at the sliver of sky that showed over its roof. There were hooks along one wall near the door that held Dudek's clothes. A small chest of drawers stood against the wall just past the end of the narrow iron cot where the dead man had slept. The cot was neatly made up. Three big pillows in faded red plaid lined up against the wall to give it a semblance of a sofa. A counter held a two-burner electric hotplate. Rough wooden shelves above it held a few pots and a frying pan and a mismatched assortment of heavy china and glasses. The toilet and sink were in the corner behind a curtain. An old wooden armchair was positioned next to a standing lamp with a torn shade. A small table next to the chair held a tobacco jar and two pipes in a wooden rack and three paperback books that were not in English. It was the room of a lonely man waiting out his days.

103

'Mrs Tanenbaum, did Mr Dudek have any family in New York?'

'Family? No. They killed all his family.' Her voice was heavily accented.

'Who did?'

'The Nazis.' Her look condemned him as an idiot. 'You remember the Nazis, Detective?'

'Yes, I do.'

'Leon was in Auschwitz. So were his wife and daughter. They did not survive.'

'I see.'

'Do you? No. If you were not there, you cannot *see*.' She rolled up her sleeve to show the blunt black numbers on her arm.

'Did you know Leon?'

'In camp, no. The men and women were apart.'

'His wife or daughter?'

'No. There were many of us. Too many to know. So, no.'

Rhonda prowled the room, touching the books, looking behind the curtain that gave privacy to the toilet, running her hand along the clothes on the hooks as if she might feel something left by the dead owner.

'How long did Leon live here?'

Mrs Tanenbaum shrugged. 'Five year. Since he come to America. He in displaced person camp in Germany four, five years. Then here.'

'Did he have any enemies?'

'Yes, but he no find them.'

'I'm sorry. I don't understand.'

'Enemies. He look for enemies, but he no find them.' Again her look condemned him as an idiot.

104

Rhonda spoke to Mrs Tanenbaum in Yiddish and received a long reply.

'She says that Leon was looking for people from the camp who killed his wife and daughter. She says he was a little bit crazy about it, that he followed people on the streets and sometimes confronted them, but they were never the people he was looking for.'

'Guards?'

'I don't know,' Mrs Tanenbaum said. 'People from camp. This is all I know. He said it to me, but not so clear.'

'So he'd see someone on the streets here in New York and follow them thinking they were people from Auschwitz, but then he'd discover they weren't?'

Mrs Tanenbaum looked to Rhonda for clarity. When Rhonda finished, the old woman turned to Cassidy and nodded.

'Nazis in New York?' he asked.

'You think no Nazis in America?'

'I don't know. I never thought about it.'

'Millions of Nazis. Millions. Not all dead. Not all in Germany now. Why not New York?' She took a cigarette Cassidy offered and bent her head to his lighter for a moment. She looked at him with bright eyes through the smoke. 'Leon a little *meshuge* maybe. Chase people in street. But he was good man.'

'Did he have any friends I could talk to?'

Another shrug. 'Maybe Friedrich.'

'Who is Friedrich?'

'Live here sometimes, there sometimes. He in Auschwitz too.'

'Do they call him Freddy?'

'*Ja*. Freddy.'

'Where can I find him?'

'Sometimes here. Sometimes not. Freddy a little . . .' She tapped her temple, the universal sign of craziness.

'Okay. Thank you, Mrs Tanenbaum. You've been very helpful. I'm going to look around the apartment for a while.'

'Okay. You look. This weekend all go. Monday I rent.'

She left trailing smoke, and they could hear her slow tread down the stairs.

'On Monday when this is gone, there won't be a trace that Leon Dudek ever lived,' Rhonda said. 'One of millions.' She followed Mrs Tanenbaum downstairs leaving Cassidy to search the room.

He did not know what he was looking for or if there was anything to find, but he set about it methodically. He went through the pockets of the clothes hanging on the wall hooks, and pinched the seams and shoulder pads to see if anything might be hidden there. He checked the undersides of the furniture for anything taped there. The toilet cistern revealed nothing but the float in rusty water. He lifted the thin mattress from the bed and put it back. He checked to see if anything hung outside the single narrow window. There were no papers in the table drawer, no diary or calendar, no scrap hidden between pages of the few books saying *the butler did it*. At the end of twenty minutes he decided he was wasting his time. There was nothing to find. Leon Dudek was one of those deaths that

106

happened all the time, deaths that were only important to the person who died and that importance died with him, a death that did not leave a ripple. So why did it grind him? What did one man's death matter out of the tens of millions who had died in the war? Leon Dudek was dead and there was nothing he could do about it. Anger twisted up through him.

Cassidy sat down in the chair by the table and looked around the room. What had he missed? Where had he not looked? He lit a cigarette while he let his eyes wander the room. Sometimes you find something not by looking at it, but by letting your eyes brush by without focus.

A piece of cloth lay on the shelf next to the two-burner hotplate. He had passed over it in his search as a makeshift potholder. He got up to take a closer look. The cloth was about a foot square. It was made of faded pale coarse cotton with wide faded blue stripes and it had been worn thin and soft by use. Cassidy had seen shirts made from cloth like this on the dead and the nearly dead outside a small town in Germany in April of 1945.

The platoon rode in three Jeeps and an M9 half-track mounting a .50 caliber machinegun over the cab. Cassidy's orders were to patrol east ahead of the battalion's advance. If they met resistance they were to pull back and report. They had seen nothing of note all morning. They had driven through two small German towns, but word of their advance had cleared the streets and only occasional movement behind windows,

107

the flick of a curtain, a child's face pulled back by an adult hand, showed that people watched their passage.

The day was warm. The sun was bright in a blue, blue, cloudless sky. A narrow river ran fast with snowmelt down the center of the valley. Neat farms with whitewashed buildings occupied the flatlands along the river. The fruit trees in the orchards were in blossom, and brown-and-white cows roamed the green pastures. The war seemed far away, but it wasn't. Once when the platoon rounded a bend in the road, crows hopped away from the pecked head of a dead Wehrmacht soldier sprawled in the ditch with a bloody bandage around his neck. He was a scrawny example of the Master Race. Someone had stolen his boots but had left the shreds of filthy socks on his bony feet.

A couple of miles down the road, the wind brought them the stench of rot and death and shit. Men covered their faces with handkerchiefs wetted from their canteens. A mile farther they found the source.

A high fence topped by razor wire and pierced by a wide gate led to the concentration camp. They knew of units that had liberated other camps like this, but nothing they had been told prepared them for what was in front of them now. Human skeletons in striped rags clung to the fence and stared at the Americans with uncomprehending eyes. The camp gate was open, but none of the prisoners clustered there came out. No one dared to take the first step to test the freedom offered.

108

'Mendel,' Cassidy said. 'Tell them we're Americans. Tell them it's over. Tell them they're free.' He got out of the Jeep and waved his men out of the other vehicles.

Saul Mendel had been born in Germany, but his parents, sensing what was to come when Hitler came to power, sold their pharmacy and got the family out of the country. 'Yes, sir.' Mendel walked past Cassidy and stopped ten feet from the gate and began to speak in German. When he stopped, a murmur ran through the crowd. A woman, so emaciated she was beyond age, crumpled to the dust. Men and women in the crowd began to weep. They parted by some unspoken command as if to invite Cassidy and the platoon in.

A man attached himself to the platoon as guide. His head was like a skull, and when he smiled he showed the four teeth left in his mouth. His arms and legs were sticks. He was so thin he was nearly transparent. His name was Simon. He often reached out to touch Mendel as if to reassure himself that he was not dreaming.

There were rows and rows of low barracks on the bare, beaten earth of the camp, enough for tens of thousands of prisoners, but there seemed to be only a couple of thousand people inside the wire. 'Ask where the other people are,' Cassidy said.

Mendel listened as Simon spoke at length gesturing to the gate and then to another part of the camp. 'He says that a lot of the prisoners were forced to leave in the last few weeks when the Allies started to get close. He says the rumor *was they were being transferred to a camp called Dachau. The ones who are left were too weak to make the march. And the others are over there.'*

Simon led them past an imposing three-story building of cut stone to where bodies were stacked near the wire. There were hundreds of them, men and woman, some naked, some in the striped pajamas the living prisoners wore. They had been piled up haphazardly like discarded waste. Their arms and legs were askew like broken branches. Their skull heads lolled and their eyes stared as sightless as stones.

Some of the platoon turned away. Some could not. Cassidy knew these were sights and smells and sounds that would never leave them.

'Ask him if any of the guards are still here,' Cassidy said.

'Some of them are in the headquarters building, the big one we passed,' Mendel translated.

'Do they have weapons?'

'Yes. He thinks so.'

Cassidy deployed the platoon in front of the stone headquarters building in a show of force. Someone moved behind the windows on the first floor. Mendel went forward and demanded that the occupants of the building come out one by one with their hands up. They were to leave all weapons behind. He shouted it twice and then stepped back to join the rest of the platoon.

Prisoners gathered behind them. They waited.

'Burchard,' Cassidy said. 'Put a couple of rounds through the window to the left of the door.'

The BAR gunner sprawled in the dirt behind his weapon. He shifted the barrel, checked his aim, and squeezed off a short burst that blew the glass out of the window. Moments later, the front door opened, and a hand waved a white hand-kerchief in the gap. Mendel yelled for them to come out. The door opened, and an SS major stood there for a moment and then walked out into the open space between the building and the platoon. He was a tall, thin man with a high forehead and a bony face. He wore steel-rimmed glasses. His uniform was immaculately tailored. The trousers were tucked into polished, black boots. He held his hands at shoulder height as he came. He was followed by ten other SS officers and enlisted men. The major stopped in front of the platoon, drew himself up, and saluted crisply. 'I am Major Heinrich Weber. Who am I addressing, please?' His English was lightly accented.

'Lieutenant Michael Cassidy, US Army.'

'We are your prisoners. According to the Geneva Convention of 1929, we are to be removed from the area of combat as quickly as possible.' It sounded like a speech he had prac-ticed, but it was tinged by fear.

Someone in the crowd behind them translated. A murmur of anger ran like a wave.

'We must go now before there is trouble,' the major demanded.

'We have a medic with us. There are people here who need whatever help we can give,' Cassidy said.

'The Convention is quite clear on this matter. Prisoners are to be removed from harm's way.'

111

A hiss rose in the crowd like escaping steam, and feet shuffled on the packed dirt.

'Lieutenant,' Burchard said with warning.

Cassidy turned. The crowd of prisoners flowed forward. Some passed through the gaps between the platoon members. Some went around the ends of their line. The murmur had become a harsh noise that made the hair on the back of Cassidy's neck stand up. The SS major stepped toward Cassidy, and his men bunched in behind him. The arrogance was gone and only the fear remained.

'Do something, Lieutenant. We are your prisoners.'

'What the hell do you want me to do, shoot them? I'm not going to shoot them.'

One of the men in striped pajamas put a gentle but firm hand on Cassidy's shoulder, turned him away from the SS men, and pushed him back toward the waiting platoon as more prisoners filtered through and the crowd around the SS men grew dense.

'Mendel,' Cassidy said. 'Tell them these men are our prisoners.'

Mendel shouted in German, but no one paid attention. The prisoners moved forward. They were emaciated, bent, diseased, and dying, but there were hundreds of them. Cassidy could see over their heads to where the SS men stood, tall, uniformed, well fed, strong. He could see in their faces they knew what was coming. The major pulled a small automatic from his jacket. He pointed it uncertainly at the encircling mob, but they ignored it. When he pulled the trigger, the

112

gun made a thin, flat crack that was swallowed up by the murmur of the crowd. A man went down. The major fired again, and another prisoner folded forward and fell at his feet. The noise of the crowd grew louder and harsher until it became a howl, and they surged forward. For a moment Cassidy could still see the SS men. They began to scream as the prisoners tore at them, and then they disappeared.

Cassidy stood in the middle of Leon Dudek's room holding the piece of striped cloth that had triggered the memories. Had Dudek cut it from his own uniform? Why had he kept it? To remember? What made him think he could forget? He folded the cloth and put it in his pocket. If he left it in the room, he was afraid someone would throw it out.

As he went to the door, Cassidy noticed a small nail hammered into the wall. The wallpaper around it was discolored in a rectangle. Something had hung there, but there was nothing in the room that would have fit the discolored space.

He found Mrs Tanenbaum in her living room knitting something large and brown and asked her if Leon had had a picture of some sort hanging on the wall.

'Yes. A print by the artist Albrecht Dürer like this one.' She pointed to a small framed print of a rabbit that hung above her head. 'The Dürer – how you say, hare? – is very popular where we come from. It brings luck.'

Not to Leon Dudek.

'It's gone.'

113

She shrugged. 'Maybe he sell it. Maybe he no like it any more.'

Cassidy and Rhonda ate an early lunch at Katz's Delicatessen on the corner of Ludlow and Houston. The waiter banged down their plates of food in the traditional manner, and went away to do more important things.

Cassidy took a bite of his sandwich and spoke around the mouthful of pastrami. 'What did the ladies tell you about Leon?'

'They liked him. More than that, I think. They didn't say it exactly, but from the way they talked I think each made a pass at him, but he turned them away, nicely, apparently. They liked him very much, and part of it was that he was still so in love with his wife he couldn't think of being with someone else. They thought it was sweet, and it made them very sad.'

'What about his looking for people from the camp?'

'He had a photograph from the camp: some of the SS men and women. Beata saw it once in Leon's room. She said they were at a picnic, all of them smiling and laughing.'

'I didn't find anything like that in his room. Did he ever see one of these people?'

She drank some ice tea. 'Beata says that he thought he saw some of them in August. Because Leon was worried that the heat made his horse sick, he was going back to the stables early, and he thought he saw them near Columbus Circle.'

'Who?'

'He called them "the doctors".'

'The doctors?'

'Yes.'

'What doctors?'

Rhonda pushed her soup away. She took a cigarette from the pack near Cassidy's coffee cup and lit it. 'You know they experimented on people in the camps.' It was not really a question. 'Doctors used inmates as guinea pigs. You know that, don't you?' Her voice was tight. The words were hard to get out. 'They froze people and tried to revive them. They burned them. They cut them open without anesthetics. They used them to test new drugs. Leon was one of them.' Her voice rose. 'Doctors! Men and women who swore to first do no harm. Doctors!' She smashed the cigarette into her plate, jerked up from the table, and rushed away. She pushed open the door to the ladies room with a crash and disappeared inside leaving silence in her wake.

An elegant old woman in a dark red dress and green hat with a pheasant feather aslant smiled at Cassidy from a table nearby and reached to pat the hand of the white-haired man sitting across from her reading the *Daily News*. Sympathy for a lover's spat.

Rhonda came back as Cassidy was finishing his sandwich. 'Sorry.'

'For what?'

'For yelling, I guess.' She gripped the back of the chair hard. 'Can we get out of here now?'

'You don't want to finish your soup?'

'No.' She headed for the door walking fast.

Cassidy dropped money on the table and went

after her. When he got outside, she was headed west on Houston. He caught up to her halfway down the block. She glanced at him and kept going. Her jaw was set and she looked like she could walk through a wall.

'Are you okay?'

'No.' She kept walking as if speed would free her from what was turning her inside out. 'I had to get out of there. Half the people in there would have been dead if they had lived in Germany in 1939. Dead for no reason.' Her anguish twisted her face. 'I don't want to be Jewish. I don't want anything to do with it. I don't want to carry it. I don't want to think about it. I don't want to know.' She turned and threw herself at him, and he almost fell catching her rush. His back thumped against the wall behind him and saved him from going down. She buried her face against his shoulder and cried shuddering sobs, and he patted her back and made the soft, useless sounds men make when women cry.

After a while Rhonda's crying slowed, and he could feel her tighten in his arms. He let go and she stepped back and took a deep breath and let it out.

'Okay. I'm okay. Sorry about that.'

'Hey. It's okay. It's fine.'

'Give me your handkerchief.'

He took it from his jacket pocket and gave it her. She blew her nose and handed it back and caught a glimpse of herself in a store window.

'Oh, God, I look like hell.' She took a comb, compact, and a lipstick from her purse, and then shoved the purse at him to hold while she made

116

repairs. When she finished, she took the purse back and stowed the tools and snapped the purse shut like punctuation. 'Jesus, no wonder they keep the girl reporters away from the tough stories.'

A few passes of a comb, lipstick, and a compact's powder puff, and she was restored, at least on the outside. How did women do that?

'Why don't you stop beating yourself up.'

She looked at him for a moment and then smiled. 'Okay. A good call. Any sympathy, I'd start wailing again.' She looked at her watch. 'I've got to get back to the paper.'

'Let's get you a cab.'

They walked west toward Broadway, keeping an eye out for a cruising taxi.

'These doctors,' Cassidy said, 'did Beata and Lena believe Leon really saw them?'

'They don't know. Lena was with him when he went after a shoemaker over near St Marks Place. Leon accused him of being one of the guards who took people to the gas chambers. It turned out the man had never been out of New York State. It wasn't the first time he went after someone who turned out to be just a guy.'

'What about Freddy? What did they say about him?'

'Freddy's a very different case. Freddy went into Auschwitz when he was seven. He was there for more than four years, and he survived. Very few children survived, but Freddy did. He scares them. They think he's possessed.' She waited to see if Cassidy would laugh.

'What does that mean?' A man plagued by

117

prophetic dreams and waking nightmares holds a less skeptical view of what might or might not be real.

They stopped on the corner. A cab slowed, but Rhonda ignored it. 'Do you know what a *dybbuk* is in Jewish mythology?'

'Some sort of ghost, or monster.'

'Close enough. It's a spirit of a dead person who possesses someone living. A malicious spirit.'

'Freddy's possessed by a *dybbuk*?'

She shrugged. 'Not by a *dybbuk*. Not by something malicious. The opposite. They say *ibbur* is a positive form of possession. If I got this right, it happens when a righteous soul occupies a living person to complete an important job, or to fulfill a *mitzvah,* a religious duty of some sort that can only be done by someone living.' She waited for his reaction.

'So Freddy survived because someone who died needs him to do something.'

'Maybe not just someone. Maybe a lot of people who died at Auschwitz. That's what they say.'

'What do you think?'

She shook her head. 'I don't believe in ghosts.' She raised her hand, and a cab swerved to the curb.

'Will I see you tonight?'

'I don't think so, Mike. I'm feeling, I don't know, kind of solitary.'

She got in the taxi. He watched until the cab made a left on Broadway and disappeared downtown.

Ten

The stalker sat on a folding campstool behind the window on the fifth floor of an abandoned building on Bethune Street. He had been there since late afternoon, and now it was dark. He had a clear view over the rifle's sights to the front of Cassidy's building on Bank Street. Two carriage lamps lighted the front step, and the interior hall light shone through the arched fan of glass above the door. The rifle was an M-1 Garrand, the standard-issue rifle for the American soldier in World War Two and Korea, and he knew it well. He had calculated the distance to Cassidy's door as 296 feet, 206 feet for the block between Bethune and Bank, 15 feet each for the sidewalks, and 60 feet for the width of Bank Street. The height of the building put the distance at just over one hundred yards, and he would have to adjust for shooting down from a height. He had killed men with the rifle at three times that distance.

It was dark when Cassidy got out of the cab in front of his building on Bank Street. A few cars rolled on the elevated highway, and he could hear the sing of their tires on the pavement as he put his key in the lock of the outside door.

The first shot blew out the fanlight above his head on the right side of the door. The second blew out the fanlight on the left. Cassidy dropped to one knee, twisted the key and knob, flung the door open, and threw himself inside. A third shot ripped splinters from the stair banister in the hall. Cassidy drew his pistol, hooked the door with his foot, and pulled it close. Part of his mind registered that the gunman was using a rifle. Two shots banged into the door. It was a metal cored fire door and the bullets clanged against it but did not blow through.

The door to one of the first-floor apartments opened, and the tenant, Calvin Bull, a fifty-year-old artist, stood in the doorway, wide-eyed. A paintbrush in his hand dripped bright yellow paint on his shoe. He saw Cassidy on the floor with a gun in his hand. 'What the hell, Mike? Those were shots.'

'Get back in your apartment. Stay away from the windows. Turn off the lights.' Cassidy got to his feet, turned off the hall lights, and ran up the stairs to his apartment. He ignored the envelope someone had shoved half under the door. He moved quickly to one of the windows without turning on the lights. No one moved on the street below or in the buildings across the street. There were taller industrial buildings farther north, and the gunman could have been in any one of them. The rifle gave him plenty of range.

Cassidy pulled curtains across the windows and went into the windowless kitchen and called the Ninth Precinct on Charles Street. He identified himself and reported what had happened. While he waited for the cops to arrive, he retrieved the envelope from under the door and

120

opened it. There was one sheet of folded type-writer paper inside. It held a message printed in block letters:

PRETTY GOOD SHOOTING, HUH?
SEE YOU SOON

The cops were there for an hour. They searched the area but could not establish the gunman's location. All the likely buildings that had a view of Cassidy's front door were dark and locked for the night. They would come back in daylight to see if they could find the gunman's perch. They examined the crime scene and dug out the bullets that had gone through the fanlights to the back wall of the hallway. The detective in charge, a man named Tarbuck, took his statement, put the note in an evidence bag, and asked all the obvious questions about who might want him dead.

'You're lucky,' Tarbuck said. 'Three shots with a rifle before you got the door closed, and he missed every one. Real lucky.'

'Uh-uh,' Cassidy said. 'He missed on purpose.'

'How do you figure?'

'He wrote the note and put it under my door before I came home. He wanted me to see it. Hard to do if I was dead.'

'What the fuck?'

'He's screwing with me, whoever he is. He wants me to know he's out there. He wants me to think about it. He wants me scared.'

'Someone you put away. Guy sits in the can for a few years thinking about how unfair it was

121

that you nailed him. He gets out, he wants revenge. Someone you put away. Got to be.' He yawned wide enough to make his jaw crack. 'Sorry. Fucking night watch. I hate it. It screws up my sleep. By the time I get used to it, I'm back on days.'

'I've just been there.'

Tarbuck yawned again. 'We'll come back in the morning, do a canvass of the buildings that might have worked for him, see what we see. I'll let you know.'

They went away, and Cassidy went up to his apartment, made himself a drink. He turned the lights out in the apartment and stood back from the window and looked at the buildings to the north. Only a few of them would have given the sniper the angle he needed. He thought about who might hold enough of a grudge. Nobody came to mind.

A detective from the Ninth named Blandon called Cassidy the next day just before lunch. 'We found the building. It's on Bethune, second in from West Twelfth on the south side. Been abandoned for a while. The front door showed signs of break in. On the fifth floor there's a place a guy has a perfect view of your front door. There's crap all over the place, but someone cleaned up an area by the window. The window was open. A couple of cigarette butts on the floor, but no brass. He picked up his brass. And no prints. He was careful. The windowsill had something on it. We have a guy in the squad was a sniper in Korea. He used a beanbag for a steady rest. Says it might have left a mark like that.'

'Okay. Thanks.'

'Keep your head down.'

He called a clerk in Records and asked to have his arrest reports from the last five years sent to the station house. Maybe they would turn someone up. In the meantime there was Leon Dudek.

Eleven

A stocky welterweight was beating the crap out of a sparring partner in Ring Two when Cassidy climbed the stairs to Stillman's Gym and paid his quarter to Jack Curley who guarded the door, owl-eyed behind his steel-rimmed glasses. The man who followed Cassidy up the stairs tried to slip in without paying, but Lou Stillman, with his ex-cop's eyes, spotted the move from his perch near Ring One.

'Pay the quarter, you cheap bum,' he yelled, and the man turned back sheepishly and dug in his pocket for change.

It was late afternoon, and the gym was hot and crowded. The lights were on, as they always were, because the windows were covered with thirty years of grime, and what daylight managed to work through them arrived defeated by the struggle. If there had been an exhibition sched-uled, or if a big fight was imminent and name boxers were training, the folding chairs and the seats in the gallery would be crowded with silky women in furs and men with cashmere coats over their arms. But today was a workday at Stillman's, and the East Side and Uptown crowds gave way to trainers and managers, matchmakers from the Garden and St Nick's and the arenas in New Jersey. Most were aging palookas with lumpy faces, badges of honor won in the ring in younger days. A thin, old man with scraggly white hair and clothes he had bought when he was twenty pounds bigger muffled the receiver of a pay phone against his shoulder and called out, 'Anyone got a lightweight for a six rounder on Friday in Newark? Anybody got a lightweight for Friday at Newark?' Three men in old tweed jackets and fedoras broke from the crowd and moved toward him. Under one of the grimed windows a heavyweight with shoulders like a horse stood easy with a cigarette in the corner of his mouth while his trainer wrapped his hands. Boxers waiting their turns shadow boxed and shuffled in the narrow corridor past the rings.

Cassidy breathed in the familiar smell of sweat, coal dust, liniment, disinfectant, and tobacco as he moved through the fight mob. Some of the low hanging cigarette and cigar smoke had probably been exhaled before the war.

The former middleweight champion of the world, Rocky Graziano, broke away from a group of admirers and came toward him with his arm around the shoulders of Whitey Bimstein, his old cut man and trainer. He gave Cassidy a nod and paused and said, 'Hey, Mike. How're you doing?' A couple of young fighters nearby began to hammer speed bags in attempt to attract Graziano's notice.

'Doing fine, Champ. How are you?' He stopped to light his cigarette off Bimstein's cigar.

'Couldn't be better.'

'I hear that Paul Newman guy who's playing you in the movie's a lot prettier than you are.' A movie about Graziano called *Somebody Up There Likes Me* was due to open in December.

'Yeah? Well, he didn't get hit in the face as many times as I did.'

Bimstein laughed, and Graziano ran an affectionate hand over the older man's bald head.

'Is Terry Mack around?' Cassidy asked.

'Yeah. The other side of Ring Two with that welter,' Bimstein said. 'He thinks he's got something there. He may be right. The little fucker can punch.'

Cassidy found Terry Mack leaning with his forearms on the ring apron while he studied the sparring with educated eyes. Mack was a lean, dark-haired man with a narrow face and prominent chin that, he learned early in his career, could not take a punch. The discovery changed his dream from becoming the light heavyweight champion of the world to becoming the trainer and manager of a champion of the world, weight class not important. So far he had been disappointed, but he was an optimist. He nodded to let Cassidy know that he was aware of him, but he did not take his eyes off the fighters.

By the time Germany surrendered in the spring of 1945, Cassidy had served under eight commanding officers. Three had been wounded,

125

two killed, and the rest promoted out of the company. Terry Mack had been the company commander for the last eight weeks of the fighting, and Cassidy had been his executive officer. Mack had proved to be a brave but cautious leader who understood that the war was winding down, the Germans were defeated, and that the most important part of his job was to bring home as many of his men as he could, an attitude Cassidy applauded.

Cassidy stood beside him and watched the action in the ring.

Bimstein had called Mack's fighter 'the little fucker', so he had to be the shorter of two men, but he wasn't little. He was short and broad with wide shoulders and thick, muscled legs. His sparring partner was a tall, light-skinned Negro. Both men wore headgear. The sparring partner's ribs and stomach were mottled red, and when Mack's fighter hit him, Cassidy understood why. The punch, a right hook, sounded like someone hitting a side of beef with a baseball bat. Mack's guy hooked him again, and the sparring partner lurched sideways from the force of the blow. His hands came down, and Mack's guy hit the side of his headgear and drove him into the ropes. As the man's hands came up to protect his head, Mack's guy hit him with a left and a right to the ribs, and the sparring partner spun away toward the other side of the ring. Mack's guy went after him with short, balanced steps that took him across the canvas with surprising quickness. He walked through the sparring partner's jab and hit the man twice in his reddened belly, and all the fight went out of him. He tied up Mack's guy with his arms and leaned on him wearily. Mack rang the bell at his side, and the men broke and touched gloves. The sparring partner slipped through the ropes, eager to get away from the pain maker and lie down somewhere. Mack climbed through the ropes and crossed to where his fighter waited for him. Mack undid his gloves while he talked to him. He stepped back to demonstrate a jab, and then patted the boxer on the shoulder and held the ropes for him to make his exit easier. He walked back across the ring, climbed down, and picked up a leather jacket from a folding chair at ringside. 'What do you think?' he asked.

'He looks like he could knock down a wall,' Cassidy said.

'Yeah. He can punch. You know why I like him? He's always moving forward, and he's always busy. He crowds 'em. He drives 'em. He won't let 'em up. He gets in close, and he hits 'em. You get a fighter who wants to crowd 'em and hit 'em, you're halfway there. Now if only I could get him to learn the jab. He thinks the jab's for sissies. Jesus. You get one who can jab, but he can't punch, or he can jab, but he can't take a punch, or he punches, but he can't jab. It's always some goddamn thing. But this one, this one I believe is going someplace. This one's going up the ladder if he don't turn out to be too dumb to learn.' Cassidy offered him a cigarette and lit one for himself. 'What's up, Mike? A day off? You want to go a couple of rounds?'

127

'I want to talk to you about something.'

'My business or yours?'

'Mine. I'll buy you a drink.'

'Bet your ass you will. Maybe two.' He grinned and shrugged into his jacket. 'Let's get out of here.'

They went down the stairs and out through the big metal door to Eighth Avenue and up to the corner of Fifty-fifth and into the welcoming gloom of the Neutral Corner Bar and Grill. The walls were covered with framed photos of fights, fighters, managers, and handlers, some of the prints yellowing with age. Men who looked like they could have stepped from those photos drank and talked at the bar and at the tables on the floor. Tough men in a tough business.

Cassidy followed Terry Mack to a table against the wall. Cassidy asked the waiter for a Jack Daniels on the rocks, and Mack asked for a Jack neat with water back. When the waiter brought them, they clinked glasses and drank some liquor.

'Terry, remember at the end of the war when we were supposed to be demobilized.'

'Sure. We were stationed in Frankfurt. I haven't had a hot dog since,' he laughed.

'And then you got transferred out to some special unit the day before we were supposed to go home.'

'Yeah, because I spoke Kraut. Thanks for that, Mom. I stick around Germany while you go home to all the grateful, hero-worshipping virgins.'

'Something about de-Nazification.'

'Nah. That was some other outfit. I was

128

assigned to this unit they called Alsos. You ever hear of that?'

'No.'

'A bunch of people looking for Hitler's atomic research stuff, the scientists, the documents, records of tests, that stuff. But I was only with them a little while and then they turned me over to this other outfit that was looking for German rocket scientists, biological warfare experts, chemical warfare researchers, medical researchers, useful guys we could ship back to the States. The Russians were looking for the same people and hauling them off to Russia. I guess some people in Washington understood the Cold War had already started. It was like a fucking treasure hunt with guns.'

'What happened to the guys you shipped back here?'

'I only know about a couple or three of them. One's up at MIT. The other works for DuPont. The third turned out to be a Nazi. The deal was that anyone who was a real Nazi couldn't get clearance to come here. Of course if you wanted any kind of Kraut government job back before the war, you had to join the Nazi Party, so they were trying to figure out who was really gung-ho, and who just joined to get the job.'

'And the third guy was a real Nazi?'

'Yeah. Early party member. A real shithead.'

'So he didn't get to come.' Cassidy signaled the waiter for another round.

Mack caught Cassidy's eyes and then looked away and lit a cigarette. 'Yeah, he came. A bunch of them came anyway, party member or not.'

129

'What the hell?'

'One day, some guys show up at our billet. A couple of jokers in uniform, but with no insignia, a couple of hard men in civilian clothes, and a general to give them some heft. There's been a change. Some of the guys we rejected are needed in the States, and we can't let them fall into the hands of the Reds. There's a list of scientists they want. We're going to change their job histories, erase their party memberships. They're going to be our guys now, and we need them, so they're good guys.'

'Terry, you saw what those fuckers did.'

'That war was done. This is the new one. I get it, even if you don't. The Russians want to rule the world, just like Hitler did, and the only thing stopping them is this country. So these guys did some bad shit. If the Russians get them, they're going to do some worse shit. With us they're working for something good.'

'You really believe that?'

'Don't give me that crap. We're the good guys here. You want to compare us to the Russians? Fuck you.'

'How can I find out who they brought over?'

'I don't know. It's all classified stuff. You got a security clearance?'

Cassidy shook his head. 'Do you remember any names?'

'Uh-uh. I already told you too much. That's it. No more from me. You want to come to the gym and work out, spar a couple of rounds, I'm happy to see you, but I'm done with this. I'm not talking to you or anyone else. It gets back to me,

130

I lose my license in a second, maybe go to jail. Then what the fuck am I going to do?' He shoved back his chair and stood up.

'Terry—'

'No, Mike, that's it. No more. I don't know nothing.'

Twelve

Spencer Shaw watched while the whore picked up the target subject at the bar at P.J. Clarke's. They did not know who the man was, but they had been instructed to find someone of his apparent age, size, and demographic: six feet tall, about a hundred eighty pounds, educated, white-collar worker. The whore was a twenty-four-year-old graduate student at Columbia working her way toward a Master's degree in anthropology who had persuaded herself that her side job was fieldwork. She knew how to dress and had more class than some of the other girls they used, so they could send her into the upscale joints after targets. She called herself Maxie Lively, but that wasn't her name. She had a good body, long dark hair, an upturned nose, and an overbite that he found sexy.

Shaw watched her slip the guy the dose when he turned to the bartender to order her a drink. She reached for his pack of cigarettes on the bar, and the dose made a small splash as her hand went over his glass. You wouldn't see it unless you were looking for it. They had practiced the pass many times before they sent her out for her first assignment, and now the move was nearly invisible. There were bartenders in the city who took offense if someone slipped a mickey to a customer, and the last thing they needed was some sharp-eyed mixologist calling the cops. It wasn't a mickey she had slipped him, but that wasn't something they could explain to the local flatfoot.

Shaw was on the sidewalk when they came out of Clarke's. The guy had his hand on the whore's hip, and she was laughing at something he said. Shaw didn't think of her by her name, either her real one or the one she had made up. He liked to think of her as 'the whore.' It kept it simple and defined her place in things, and he liked that with women. What man didn't, he wondered. He watched them get into a taxi and then waved up his car and driver and followed them to the safe house on West 4th Street.

His driver, Stefan Horvath, was a Slovak, one of those people washed out of place by the tide of war and deposited in the States by a series of fortunate accidents beginning with his recruitment by an OSS agent in Yugoslavia in 1944 who was in the market for a sniper. The war had given him skills that were useful in war but frowned upon in peacetime, except in the shadows where Shaw worked. Shaw liked him because he did what he was asked to do, and he rarely spoke.

By the time the whore got the john up to the viewing room on the third floor of the safe house, the guy was feeling the drug. He stood in the middle of the room neither helping nor hindering her as she took off his clothes. He looked around with delight as if he had never before seen a room like the one he was in. There was not much to see. A machine-made oriental rug covered the floor. The wallpaper pattern was pale yellow-and-red flowers on an off-white background. The bed was covered with a red velvet spread. There were two cheap easy chairs with a table between them. The one-way window looked like a mirror to the man in the other room, and he stuck his tongue out at it and made a face.

The whore led the guy to the bed and stripped quickly. Shaw watched them critically as they screwed, but there was nothing unusual going on, so he checked to see that the tape recorder was running. The microphones that fed it were hidden in the lamps, and in the hollowed-out corners of the headboard and footboard of the bed. The idea was that the whore would talk to him after they screwed. Most men who paid to get laid knew the girl would leave quickly afterwards to maximize her time, and they had discovered that many men were flattered if the girl wanted to stay and talk. It made it almost like a date. Her job was to get the john to open up, to spill secrets, to see if the drug made him more susceptible to telling things he shouldn't tell: infidelities, sexual peculiarities, business or industrial secrets. It didn't matter what as long as he gave up information he would normally hide.

Shaw, satisfied that the equipment was working, went downstairs.

Sebastian Ambrose, and Karl and Magda Brandt were at a round table in the kitchen at the rear of the ground floor. Karl and Magda sat close to each other and faced Ambrose across the table. Karl Brandt wore a soft, dark blue flannel shirt, heavy tobacco-colored corduroy trousers, and polished half boots, the picture of a well-off man of leisure. His hammered silver cigarette case was on the table within easy reach. Magda Brandt wore high-waist gabardine trousers like those Marlene Dietrich had made popular, a dark green silk blouse, and a tweed jacket. Diamond earrings glittered when she turned her head. She wore a necklace of thin gold rounds. Her black hair was smooth and glossy. She was as neat and fashionable as Ambrose was not. Ambrose wore the same clothes Shaw had last seen him wearing in the garden behind his house, or maybe he just had multiple versions to avoid making decisions.

The three doctors had designed the experiments that took place in the house on West 4th Street. They had explained the purposes to Shaw with pride. The boundaries of chemical manipulation of the human brain would be pushed back. Breakthroughs were certain. Interrogations would become more efficient. People in the know spoke with high anticipation of mind control, of enemy operatives unmasked, re-educated, and turned back into enemy territory, but now under the control of the forces of democracy. Think of the efficiencies. Think of the lives saved by the information gained. It was a matter of national security. It was well known that the Chinese and the Russians were working overtime on mind-control experiments. The brainwashing of captured American soldiers in Korea was only the tip of that iceberg. It was understood in the corridors of power that this area would be crucial in the growing contest between the forces of freedom and democracy and those of Godless Communism. The race to understand and control the mind was thought by some to be as important as the missile race.

Karl and Magda Brandt were in charge of the chemistry. Ambrose designed the psychological applications. There were, of course, minor malfunctions, the occasional glitch. It was a new field. The chemistry was difficult. The psychology was still imprecise. But, they assured Shaw, they were very close to an optimized, controllable drug, one that would have useful, lucrative applications in the world of mental health as well as in the clandestine world. Very close.

Shaw's role was pragmatic. He was there to guard, monitor, assist, and to deal with the real-world problems that might arise. He was like the superintendent in the apartment building where he had grown up. The super was always on call by the residents to change a light bulb, fix a leaking faucet, remove a worn-out sofa, or clean up something ugly that had spilled on the floor.

Shaw detoured to the Frigidaire and took a pint of Gilbey's gin from the freezer and a lemon from a refrigerator shelf. He put the bottle and the lemon on the table at the empty seat and got a glass from the cupboard next to the sink before sitting down. The Brandts and Ambrose watched as he took a small silver-cased knife from his pocket, sliced peel from the lemon, twisted it into the glass and then filled the glass from the bottle. He raised the glass in toast. 'The premade martini. A shot of vermouth in a pint of gin, and then bang it into the freezer, a time saver for the working drinker. I should go into the business, make a fortune.' He took a sip and savored it. 'Would you care for one, Doctor? It'll put hair on your chest.'

'No, thank you.' Magda Brandt looked at him coldly. He knew she did not like him, that she found him unserious, a deadly sin to this woman, and he enjoyed poking her to see if he could make her flinch. He also wanted to fuck her, but he hadn't yet figured out how to make that happen. She was in her forties, older than the women who usually attracted him, but she was taut and fit, and there was something about her imperious disdain that attracted him.

'Doctor, how about you?' This to Ambrose, who, he noticed, had bits of food in his beard.

'I prefer wine.'

'Dr Brandt?'

'Yes, please,' Karl said. He smiled his bland smile. 'I like a martini. A civilized drink.'

'Tell me about tonight's subject,' Ambrose demanded. He was impatient with small talk unless it was his own.

Shaw took a notebook from the inside pocket of his suit jacket and flipped the pages till he found the one he wanted. 'Chris Collins, age twenty-eight, height six feet one inch, weight

136

one eighty-eight.' He looked up. 'She slipped me his wallet. This is off his driver's license. We've got his address, and he's got a business card that says he's a copywriter for an ad agency. He belongs to the New York Athletic Club. He's easy to find if we want to run him through it again.'

'What dosage?' Magda Brandt asked.

'Seven hundred mics.'

'That is too much.'

'It's what I was told.'

'Too much.' She took a cigarette from a gold case and screwed it into a short silver holder with an ebony bite.

'I don't set the dosages.'

She dismissed him with a look, and lit the cigarette with a small gold lighter.

'Sebastian,' Karl said in a mild tone stripped of all confrontation. 'We decided after Williger that we would reduce the dosage until we had a better idea of the controllable effects.'

'No,' Ambrose said. 'You suggested that course. I decided against it.' He took a sip of his wine, swished it around in his mouth and swallowed it. When he smiled, his teeth were stained with wine.

Karl was not intimidated. 'The chemistry is our responsibility. We have had a good deal of experience with experiments like this.'

'Yes, we are aware of your *experiences*,' Ambrose said. He did not like to be challenged.

'Then you would do well to listen to us,' Magda said, ignoring her husband's look of warning.

'Liked the war, did you?' Shaw asked.

137

'What?'

'I asked if you liked the war,' Shaw said and took another sip of his martini.

She stiffened. 'No, I did not like the war. What a ridiculous thing to say. Nobody liked the war.'

'All those lovely experiments with all those willing volunteers?'

'Everything we did was sanctioned by our laws.'

Shaw laughed. 'The laws of a criminal government. A bunch of madmen and deviates.' He began to sing in a surprisingly good baritone. *'Hitler only had one ball. Goering had two, but they were small. Himmler had something similar. And Goebbels had no balls at all.'* He toasted them with his martini.

Magda bristled. Karl, knowing her, tried to intercede. *'Nein, nein, liebling.* Let it go.'

She did not know how. 'The work we did saved the lives of many of our soldiers, and we treated our subjects with care and dignity. They were taken off work detail. They were fed a nutritious diet. Many of them benefitted from our experiments.'

'Right. It was a health resort. Come to sunny Auschwitz and all your troubles will go up in smoke under the gentle ministrations of Doctors Karl and Magda *Von* Brandt. The Jews were *dying* to work with you.'

'That's enough, Shaw,' Ambrose said.

But Shaw was having too much fun. 'It's the fucking hypocrisy that gets me. You loved it. You got to do things in the war you never could

138

have done otherwise. Nazi Germany was the best thing that ever happened to you.'

'We were never Nazis,' Karl Brandt said. 'Not willingly. We joined the Party because people in our position had to. There was no choice.'

'Oh, for Christ's sake. I read your files. I was one of the guys who brought you over. You and a bunch of others like you. A little rewriting, a few out and out lies, a little whitewash, and you passed muster, but I know who you are and what you did.'

The Brandts looked at him stonily.

'Ah, come on. I don't hold it against you. The war was great,' Shaw said cheerfully. 'I admit it. I loved it. Fun, fun, fun. Where else could a red-blooded American boy lie, cheat, steal, rape, pillage, and kill with the encouragement and blessings of his superiors and his government? Here's to war. I wish it had never ended.' He raised his glass.

'It hasn't,' Ambrose said. 'We just have different enemies. And that's the point. The past is past. We are allies now. We work together. This conversation is over. Shaw, if you continue, I will report you.'

Before Shaw could reply, footsteps clattered in the hall, and Maxie burst into the room. She wore a thin robe and her high heels. She gripped a clipboard, forgotten, in one hand. 'Somebody better get up there fast. Something's really gone wrong with this guy.'

Magda took the clipboard and thumbed through the pages. 'You did not complete the questions.'

Maxie was too agitated to hear her. 'Doctor, you better get up there,' she said to Ambrose. 'He's acting really strange. I haven't seen anyone like this.'

'Why did you not complete the questions?' Magda was a dog with a bone.

'He stopped talking. He just stopped. Then he began scratching himself, and he wouldn't answer me, okay? It's not my fault. He just stopped.'

Ambrose patted her on the arm. 'We'll go see. You'll come along. He knows you.'

She edged toward the wall, her shoulders hunched protectively. 'I don't know. I don't want to go back up there.'

'No, no, you have to come. Everything will be all right. Mr Shaw will be with us. He'll make sure everything is fine.'

His look said she was coming with them one way, or the other.

Ambrose looked to Karl. 'Doctor, are you coming?'

'Of course.'

Magda looked over the tops of her glasses. 'I will finish looking at the questions the girl managed to ask him. I'll follow in a minute.'

They went up the stairs to the third floor, Ambrose and Karl leading, Maxie sandwiched between them and Shaw. The thin fabric of the robe clung to her, and Shaw admired her ass as they climbed.

'What's that robe made of, Maxie, nylon or something?'

'What? I don't know.' Distracted. 'Yeah, nylon, or maybe Dacron.'

'Very nice.'

They stopped in front of a door on the third floor. 'Calm and quiet, everyone,' Ambrose said. 'No agitation. Calm and quiet. Agreed?' It wasn't really a question. 'Shaw, are you armed?'

'Yeah.' He touched his tweed jacket where the gun was holstered beneath his left arm.

'Just in case.'

Ambrose reached for the doorknob. Maxie moved behind Shaw. Karl Brandt stepped to one side. Ambrose looked at Shaw and raised his eyebrows. Shaw nodded. Ambrose opened the door.

Chris Collins, the evening's experimental subject, was crouched in a corner of the room near a standing lamp with a tasseled shade. His naked body was covered with sweat, and the light made it shine. He looked at them with unseeing eyes and scratched at himself as if insects crawled beneath his skin. Collins's shoulders and arms were striped with deep bleeding furrows from his fingernails, and he had gouged his face bloody.

'Jesus,' Shaw said in awe of the man's capacity for self-savaging.

'Interesting,' Ambrose said. 'He doesn't seem to feel any pain. Dr Brandt, have we seen that before with any of the others?'

'No. You're right; it is interesting. If the drug can mask pain, it is something we should explore. It may be another application,' Brandt said.

'What are we going to do with him,' Shaw asked. To him the end of these evenings simply presented a disposal problem. Usually it was a matter of persuading the men that it was time to leave. Yes, of course the girl was in love with him. Yes, it was wonderful that she was so interested in what he had to say. Yes, of course he could set up a date for another time. Leave a phone number. Of course she'd call. He would bundle the man downstairs and out the door and into the waiting car, and they would drive uptown and leave him on a corner a couple of blocks from wherever he lived. And that would be that.

Tonight was going to be a little more complicated.

The naked man stopped scratching. His lips drew back from his teeth, and he snarled like a dog.

'It's all right, Mr . . .' Ambrose looked to Shaw for the name.

'Collins,' Shaw said.

'Mr Collins. Everything is fine. We're here to help you. Now, I want to give you something to calm you.' He took a small pill bottle from his pocket and selected one tablet. Shaw retrieved a half-full glass of water from the bedside table. 'Mr Collins, this is meprobamate, or Miltown, as people call it. It's going to calm you down, and make you feel better.' Ambrose spoke in a soothing voice. 'All right? I'm just going to give it to you with this glass of water. I want you to swallow the pill all the way down with some water. And then you'll feel better. Okay? Here we go.' Ambrose approached Collins slowly with the glass held out in one hand and the pill in the other. As he went he bent his knees and ducked down to minimize his height, to lessen any sense

142

of threat. 'All right. Here we are. Everything's going to be just fine.'

Collins lunged forward, snarling, his teeth snapping. Ambrose jerked back, and the pill flew one way and the glass shattered on the floor. Collins crouched back in the corner and began to tear at the skin on his legs.

Ambrose pushed his glasses back up his nose and took a deep breath to calm himself. 'All right, we'll do this another way. Shaw, you and I will hold him. Maxie, you're going to feed him the Miltown.'

'Uh-uh. Not a chance. The guy's nuts. I'm out of here.' She turned for the door. Ambrose looked to Shaw for help.

'Maxie,' Shaw said, 'I know where your parents live.' She stopped and looked back at him in surprise. 'The sweet little church up the street. Dad's real-estate business. Mom's job at the library. Your brother just starting out at the bank. And I've got some wonderful photographs for them.' He glanced at the one-way mirror.

The threat registered. 'You shit.'

'Yeah, I know. You're absolutely right. Sometimes I just feel so bad about what I do. But then, you know, I think what the hell? Somebody's got to do the dirty jobs, and I like them. So come on over here and feed this guy a pill, and we can all go home.'

'Why can't the other doctor do it?'

'You've been fucking the guy. He likes you,' Shaw said. 'Just do what you're told. It'll be over in a second.'

Shaw came at Collins from one side, and

143

Ambrose from the other. 'Slowly,' Ambrose said. 'No sudden moves.'

Collins scratched at himself. His head was down, and his breath came and went in long, shuddering gasps.

Shaw met Ambrose's look. A quick nod. They moved in unison. Shaw grabbed Collins's right arm as Ambrose grabbed his left. Collins howled, and bucked against the restraint. He tried to bite Shaw, who grabbed his hair and pulled his head back hard. Collins opened his mouth. Maxie darted in and pushed the tranquilizer into Collins's mouth. His jaw snapped shut, and Maxie screamed and jerked away, blood pumping from her forefinger which was now missing its tip to the first joint.

'Oh, shit,' Ambrose said.

Maxie held the ruined finger up in front of her face, unable to look away, and screamed until she ran out of breath.

Collins jerked out of Ambrose's grip, and slammed sideways into Shaw. Shaw lost his hold on Collins who lurched for the door in a strange, disjointed run.

'Stop him,' Ambrose yelled.

Shaw bolted after the running man. By the time he got to the stairs, Collins was halfway down to the second-floor landing, where Magda Brandt, on her way up, stood in surprise, the clipboard in one hand.

'Stop him,' Shaw yelled.

Magda pressed back against the wall, her hands up in defense, and as Collins hurtled by, she stuck out a foot and tripped him. Collins stumbled across the landing, lost his balance, and pitched off the top step in a dive. When his head hit the newel post at the bottom of the stairs, the impact shook the house.

Shaw went down the stairs fast and turned Collins over. He felt for a pulse, but there was no need. Collins's head lay at an awful angle. His neck was broken. He was dead.

Magda Brandt looked down at Shaw without expression from the second-floor landing. Ambrose and Karl appeared above her on the third floor. Ambrose had his arm around Maxie. He had bound her wounded finger with a piece of cloth. She leaned against him and sobbed as he guided her down the stairs.

Thirteen

A cold, gray afternoon darkened toward an evening that promised rain. A breeze swirled dead leaves against the park wall as Cassidy walked toward the hotdog cart at Columbus Circle. A woman in a stained tan raincoat and wool cap over dirty gray hair walked away from the cart in high-top Converse basketball sneakers cut open at the toes to accommodate her sore feet. She was eating a large pretzel. The brown paper bag she carried was spotted with grease. The Greek watched Cassidy approach and waited for him to order. Cassidy showed him his badge.

The Greek looked at it without expression and

145

shrugged. 'My permit up to date. You like see?' His accent was thick. He wore a blue wool vest over a white shirt buttoned to the collar, and a brown windbreaker, all protected from food splash by a dark green apron spattered with ketchup, grease, and mustard. A battered fedora warmed his head.

'No.'

The Greek nodded in resignation. Another cop looking for a free meal. 'So, what you want? On the house. Hotdog? Sausage?'

'No, thanks. What's your name?'

'Stavros. Stavros Contomicholos.'

'Mr Contomicholos, I want to talk to you about Leon Dudek.'

'I don't know him. Who is he?'

'He's the horse cab driver who was killed in the park.'

'Oh, sure, sure. A nice man. Always, hello, how are you, please and thank you. Very polite. Hotdog man. Sometimes mustard, sometimes ketchup and onions. Sometimes this, sometimes that. Maybe once a month a sausage. Nice man.'

'Did you see him the night he was killed?'

'Sure. Like always.' Contomicholos adjusted the gas under his griddle and shoved a tangle of onions to a cooler space. He rolled six hotdogs over so they would cook evenly and put two sausages in the warmer to stay hot while he talked. 'Midnight he comes for a hotdog. Mustard and ketchup that. No drink. He almost never have a drink.'

'Did you see him talk to anyone? Was there someone waiting at his cab?'

146

'I hear him shout, "Hey, you," something like that. I look. A man and woman. I think he shout at them.'

'Did they say anything back?'

'I don't think so. He shout again. They go into park. He go after them, maybe. Maybe just go in park. I don't know.'

'What did the man and woman look like?'

'Big man, small woman.'

Cassidy waited. 'Anything else?'

Contomicholos shrugged. 'No. Big man, small woman.'

'How old were they?'

The Greek shrugged again. 'No young. No old.'

'What was the man wearing?'

Contomicholos checked the bun warmer while he thought. 'Overcoat.'

Cassidy waited.

'No hat. He no wear a hat.'

Most men wore hats. 'What about the woman?'

The Greek nodded. 'Sure. She wear a hat. Little hat.'

'What else?'

'Overcoat. Mink, maybe. Expensive.'

'Did you ever see them before?' Cassidy offered him a cigarette and took one for himself. The Greek lit them both with a match struck on the griddle.

'Thank you. Maybe I see them. Maybe no. I think I see them before, but . . .' He shrugged again. 'Maybe rich people look the same.'

'How do you know they were rich?'

Contomicholos smiled. 'Good clothes. Mink.

147

And the rich walk like they own everything. The poor man is like this' – he hunched his shoulders and stooped – 'the rich man, like this' – he threw his shoulders back, stood tall, raised his chin, and puffed out his chest – 'yah?'

A city garbage truck pulled to the curb. The driver and the can thrower got out and approached the cart. The Greek saw them coming.

'Anymore?' he asked Cassidy.

'No.' Cassidy passed him a business card. 'If you think of anything more, or if you see them again, give me a call.'

'Sure.' He tucked the card in his jacket pocket and turned toward his customers.

By the time Cassidy left the stationhouse at the end of the day, the rain had started – a cold, steady rain that dripped from the buildings and awnings and ran deep in the gutters. People hurried, heads down, under umbrellas. The weather matched Cassidy's mood. The Dudek investigation was going nowhere. The search for the heroin dealer Connor Finn and his girlfriend was just as wet, but a little luck swung Cassidy's way when a cab stopped to let three people out in front of Schubert Theatre. He sank gratefully into the back seat and gave the cabbie the address of the *New York Post*. When they got to the *Post* building, Cassidy told the driver to keep the meter running. He'd be right back.

'Hey, man,' the driver looked back from the front seat. 'The only way to hold a cab in this weather is with a gun. Somebody's going to get in and tell me where to go.'

Cassidy opened his jacket and showed him the .38 under his arm.

It wasn't enough to throw a New York cabbie. 'Good enough. Anyone gets in, I'll hold him here till you come out and shoot him.'

Cassidy went into the large, echoing lobby and called Rhonda from the bank of pay phones near the elevators. She said she needed ten more minutes, so he bought a fresh pack of Luckies and the *New York Times* from the newsstand in the lobby and sat on a marble bench under good light while he read.

Egypt and their new friends from the Soviet Union rejected the idea of international operation of the Suez Canal, and the US Secretary of State John Foster Dulles rejected Egyptian Foreign Minister Dr Mahmoud Fawzi's assertion that the US had refused to support the building of the Aswan Dam in retaliation for Egypt's close ties with the Soviets.

Cases against communists led the Supreme Court's list of upcoming hearings.

An Army veteran of the Korean War named Harold Green was indicted for shooting and killing three fellow workers at a trucking firm in the Bronx. His lawyer claimed diminished capacity. Mr Green, the lawyer said, had been brainwashed by the Chinese while a prisoner of war in Korea.

Rhonda was putting on her coat as she came out of the elevator. He stood to kiss her and threw the paper in a wastebasket.

'Reading the *New York Times* in the *Post* building is worth your life.'

'I like living out on the edge.'

149

She took his arm and they went out and made a run for it through the rain to the taxi.

The driver dropped them at a small Italian restaurant on Bleecker Street called Aldo's. Because of the weather, the place was only half full and the owner, Aldo, a small, happy man with the energy of a cricket, was delighted to see them. He led them to a table by itself near the window, presented the menus with a flourish, and leaned close with an air of conspiracy to announce, 'The *saltimbocca* is sublime tonight, sublime. And I bring you two martinis. So good to see you, Mr Cassidy, Miss Rhonda.' He went off clapping his hands as if to start a band. He was back in a minute with their drinks, which he had had the barman start the moment he saw them enter.

The first clear, cold sip. 'God, that's good,' Rhonda said. 'It makes the rest of the day insignificant.'

'A bad day?'

'No. A good one. Just a little frustrating. I spent the day in the library looking for stories on Nazis coming to America.'

'Find any?'

'One, a couple of column inches in 1950 in the *Boston Globe* about a rocket scientist working at Fort Devens in Massachusetts who turned out to be a Nazi. He was deported in 1951 after an immigration hearing. I talked to people at the paper here, and a couple of them remember a story we did from around then, on someone like the guy up in Massachusetts. I'll chase it down in the next few days.'

Aldo arrived with two more martinis and took

150

their orders, the *saltimbocca* for Rhonda, which made him beam, and veal Milanese for Cassidy, which got him a nod of approval. Cassidy ordered a bottle of Barolo, which got him a nod and a smile, and Aldo went away humming.

'I spoke to a guy I was in the Army with. They kept him in Germany after the shooting was over because he spoke German. He was supposed to help round up scientists of different kinds who people thought would be useful over here.'

'What kind of scientists?'

'All kinds. Rocket scientists, chemical warfare, biological warfare, I don't know what else.'

She put her glass down and watched him intently. 'And?'

'They started off with orders that no committed Nazis were to be included. The way he described it, it became a race between them and the Reds, and the orders changed. Useful scientists got their records expunged, got new papers, new histories, and were shipped over here.'

'Nazis?'

'Nazis.'

'Here in New York?'

'Maybe. I don't know. He didn't know. But here in the country, so why not New York?'

'So maybe Leon Dudek did see someone he knew, someone from Auschwitz.'

'Maybe. But he thought the baker was one of them, and he wasn't, and there were a couple of other mistakes like that.'

'Someone killed him.'

'It could have been a mugging. His wallet was missing.'

151

'Michael, what the hell? The guy told you there are Nazis here. What are you saying, that you don't believe him? I want to talk to him.'

'He won't talk to you.'

'How do you know?'

'He said he wasn't going to talk about this stuff anymore. He says it's classified. He signed some sort of secrecy thing. He doesn't want to get in trouble.'

'I can persuade him. Ask him if he'll talk to me for five minutes.'

'He said no.'

'Jesus Christ, Michael, we're talking about mass murderers, people who helped kill millions of people.'

'I'm not giving this guy up. There have to be a lot of other people who know about this. You'll have to find them.'

'But you've got this guy. Come on.'

'I can't.'

'What the hell?'

'He's a big reason I got through the end of the war alive. I owe him.'

She started to say something and then stopped. 'Okay Okay. But I'm going to get this story. It's my story. If I break this . . .' She shook her head at what it could mean.

'If what he says is true, then this was a government operation. It's classified. They are not going to like anyone poking around.'

'Sure. Sure.' She grinned at him and clinked his glass with hers. 'Michael, you just handed me my future.'

'Just don't jump the gun on this. I'm still

looking for whoever killed Dudek. If he turns out to be some Nazi, you'll be the first to know. But don't get ahead of me on this.'

'I heard you. I heard you. I'll just do some background stuff, research, and get ready.'

The rain had stopped by the time they finished dinner, and they walked home in a city that felt washed clean. Occasional cars swished past on the wet streets, and the few people they passed nodded in greeting as if they all shared something rare and wonderful.

The walk along the last blocks of Bank Street to his building quieted Rhonda, as it often did. This part of the Village was little traveled, and many of the blocks were industrial and unpeopled at night. The darkness seemed denser, and it spooked her. 'I want a big glass of cognac when we get home,' she said.

'You said you don't sleep when you have cognac.'

'So we'll stay up.' She jabbed him with an elbow, and her eyes were shining.

Cassidy found his keys, and they went in through the front door bumping hips and laughing.

The stalker watched from the darkness of a deep doorway across the street. He hadn't counted on the girl being with Cassidy. He had hoped to have a conversation with him tonight, to clear up the confusion, to bring it all out into the open. It would have to wait. It didn't matter. A few more days wouldn't change anything.

Cassidy and Rhonda stopped to kiss at the fourth-floor landing and then went up to the top floor in a rush of anticipation. A large florist's delivery stood on the mat in front of Cassidy's door. All they could see was the curve of the black vase. The flowers were shrouded in white paper. An envelope with Cassidy's name on it was pinned to the paper. Cassidy pushed Rhonda up against the door and kissed her while he fumbled the key blind into the lock. The door swung open, and they half stumbled, half fell into the apartment still locked in the kiss. Cassidy heeled the door shut and went to work on the buttons on Rhonda's blouse.

Rhonda broke the kiss. 'Michael, what about the flowers?'

'What flowers?'

'Michael . . .'

He pulled the blouse out from the waistband of her skirt. 'They'll be fine till morning. They're in water.' He reached up her back to undo her bra.

'At least bring them inside.'

'Women,' Cassidy said, 'have no sense of priorities.' He opened the door, swept the vase in, and pushed it out of the way. He kicked the door shut, picked up Rhonda, and carried her in laughing protest to the bedroom.

Fourteen

Rhonda got up at first light. She kissed Cassidy awake enough to tell him she was going home to change before she went to work. He grunted

154

and turned over and the alarm clock woke him an hour later. He padded naked into the kitchen and started the coffee. As he headed back toward the shower, he noticed the vase by the front door. When he pulled the envelope, the covering of paper came off. There were six white lilies in the black vase. They were tied with a large black bow. It was a funeral arrangement. He ripped open the envelope. The card read:

SO SORRY TO HEAR OF YOUR
APPROACHING DEATH.

Cassidy threw the flowers in the trash and dumped the vase in the garbage can hard enough to break it. This son of a bitch was beginning to get on his nerves.

The man in the flower store on Hudson looked at the card and nodded. 'Yep, that's what they wanted. Some sort of joke, I guess. Bad taste in my opinion, but what the hell, the customer is always right. Right?'

'Can you describe him?' Cassidy asked.

'Never saw him. A letter through the slot some time during the day when I was busy. Instructions, address, and twenty bucks. Never saw him.'

Clips of the archived stories from the *New York Post* were kept in dusty brown envelopes on shelves in the paper's morgue. The morgue was overseen by an equally dusty, gray-haired dragon named Tuttle, her first name known only to history and the payroll department, who sat behind the wooden counter in a worn,

155

rump-sprung upholstered chair and knitted something long and shapeless and brown. When you presented your requests, Tuttle would look at them suspiciously and then yell for Ralph, who would appear from a small office behind her desk. Ralph was stooped and bald, with a monk's fringe of white hair. One leg dragged a bit, and the house rumor was that he had been wounded in the First World War by a shell that had left him with a vague but cheerful manner in contrast to Tuttle's. Ralph would take the request slip and disappear into the rows of shelves with the invariable promise of 'Back in a minute. *Tout de suite*,' which sometimes proved true.

Rhonda sat at a long wooden table and looked through the clips Ralph brought. By late afternoon, the dust was in her nose and lungs, and her fingers were black with printer's ink. One story held her interest. It had been written in October of 1953 under the byline of William Long. She did not recognize the name.

She spent ten minutes in the ladies' room trying to get the old ink off her and the dust out of her, gave up and took the elevator to the newsroom. The people at the desks near hers did not know William Long, but the Metro Editor, who had been at the paper for years said, 'Sure, Bill Long. A good reporter. Left the paper a few years back, I don't remember why. Some beef with somebody about something. The last I heard he was working in his family's business. Check with Stan Nagosy in sports. They were pals.'

* * *

156

Rhonda's taxi took her through the financial district. The Stock Exchange, the brokerage houses, and the banks were closed, and the streets were empty-lighted canyons. The moneymen had gone home and the money slept or did whatever it did when no one was watching. She got out at Front Street and Beekman and walked the last block to South Street. The Fulton Fish Market came awake late in the evening, and now it was running full blast. Loaded trucks whined away from the market in low gear. Growling forklifts carrying stacked wooden boxes rumbled and rocked over the wet cobblestones. Gulls wheeled and squalled in the air and landed heavily to tear at fish guts discarded in the gutter. Men in rubber boots and bloodstained overalls shouted prices and come-ons at buyers in overcoats and fedoras. The air smelled of fish, and diesel, and the sea. Sometimes when a workman turned and the light hit just right, the fish scales on his clothes glinted like sequins.

Two men with long knives were filleting big tunas on wooden tables at the entrance to one of the market houses. Rhonda stopped to watch the long blades slide in along the spines, the dark red meat revealed as the men lifted the fillets away. One of the men stopped to light a cigarette and to take an admiring look at Rhonda. 'Can I help you, Miss?'

'I'm looking for William Long.'

'Bill? Two stalls up. Where the van's parked.'

A young man with an Elvis pompadour, a cigarette dangling from the corner of his mouth, and the sullen look of someone with better things to

157

do was shoving boxes of fish into a dark green panel truck with a silver swordfish painted on the side below *Long and Sons Fresh Fish* in silver script.

'Is Bill Long here?' Rhonda asked.

The young man loaded the last box, slammed the doors, and turned to look her up and down. 'Yeah. In the back.'

She could feel his eyes on her as she went into the stall past the trays of fish on crushed ice and into a back area stacked with empty fish boxes. Two men were gutting fish at a knife-scarred wooden table with blood grooves along its sides. The tall, thin man who looked up at her had curly gray hair and the broken-veined face of a drinker.

'Can I help you?'

'I'm looking for Bill Long.'

The younger man, a newer version of the older man opposite, said, 'That's me.' He slit the belly of a large fish, jerked out the guts and gills, and tossed them in a metal bucket at his feet. The fish went onto ice on a shallow wooden tray next to the bodies of two others. They shone silver under the harsh overhead lights in metal shades.

'My name's Rhonda Raskin. I work for the *New York Post*. I wanted to ask you about a story you wrote in 1953.'

'Oh, yeah? What story was that? I wrote a lot of stories in 1953. I was a story writing maniac in 1953.' He grinned at her, pulled another fish over, inserted the point of his knife in its anus, and sliced it open to the gills with one rip.

'It was about a German scientist who was

brought over to work for Wernher Von Braun on the rocket program in Huntsville, Alabama. The guy turned out to be a Nazi war criminal. Hans Muller.'

Bill Long put down the knife, and his face clenched. 'Yeah, yeah. I know his name. But who are you, really?' The man on the other side of the table stopped working.

'Rhonda Raskin. I told you.'

'Why do you want to talk about that story?' His eyes were suspicious.

'I wanted to know why you didn't follow up. That story was just the beginning. It begged for follow up, but there was none. I couldn't find another story on it in the morgue. Why not?'

'Who sent you?'

'Nobody sent me. I work for the *Post*, just like you did. Call Stan Nagosy if you don't believe me.'

'Yeah? So what do you care?'

'Easy, Billy,' the older man said.

'Sure, Dad. I'll take it easy.'

'I think what you found was the tip of the iceberg,' Rhonda said. 'I think there are a lot more Nazis working here. I want to know about it. I want to write about it.'

'Yeah?'

'Yeah.'

He studied her for a moment. 'Let's you and me go have a drink.'

'Billy,' his father's warning voice.

'It's okay, Dad. It's okay. What's your name again?'

'Rhonda Raskin.'

159

'Okay, Rhonda. You're buying.'

They walked to a bar on Front Street. It was a dingy joint with a low ceiling and sawdust and peanut shells on the floor and an odor of fish competing with the smell of stale beer and cigarette smoke. A tired-looking sailfish hung on a wall near the door. Its blue had faded, its silver belly was dull, its sail drooped, and the tip of its bill had broken off. Men stood shoulder to shoulder at the bar, but few of the tables were occupied.

'What are you drinking,' Bill Long asked.

'A shot and a Knick.'

He nodded approval and waited.

'Right,' she said, and dug a five dollar bill from her pocket.

'Expense account,' he said.

'Maybe.'

'Hey, if you haven't learned to fiddle your expense account, you're no newspaper man. Table in the corner. I'll be right there.'

She watched him move to the bar. He seemed a cheerful man except when she mentioned the Nazi story. He hadn't liked that.

She took a chair with her back to the angle so she could see the whole barroom and lit a cigarette. Her feet and back hurt, and her eyes were gritty from too little sleep, too much coffee. All she really wanted to do was go home, take a hot bath, crawl into bed, and pull the covers up. *Perfect*, she thought, *you've got a story that could change your life, and you want to go home and cuddle with your teddy bear. They say women can't cut it, and you sure ain't going to help the cause by giving up easily.*

160

Bill Long carried their drinks to the table, and put them down carefully. 'Don't want to spill a precious drop.' He took her change from his breast pocket and passed it across the table. 'I left Sammy a bit of a tip. Hope you don't mind.'

'No. Of course not.'

Long pulled out the chair and sat with a sigh of relief. 'Feels good to sit for a while. Been on my feet all day. Either the floors are getting harder, or I'm getting older.'

'Just what I was thinking.'

'Well, the hell with it. Life goes on.' He raised his shot glass to her, 'First of the day,' and took a sip and then a swallow of beer. He took another sip of whiskey and chased it with beer. 'Okay. What've we got?'

Rhonda told him about Leon Dudek and his search for Nazis in the city.

When she finished, Long shrugged. 'Dudek sounds a little screwy. Of course he has every right to be after what he went through He didn't leave you much to work with.'

'Do you think he was right?'

'Well, he may not have been right about the guys he went after, but he wasn't wrong about there being Nazis in the city.' He shook a couple of cigarettes out of a pack of Camels and lit hers first.

'A lot?'

'I don't know about a lot, but some. I just don't know what the hell people are thinking. We fight them for years. We're told that they're the worst of the worst, the end of civilization

161

and freedom if they win, and then when it's over, the same guys who've been telling us that stuff start bringing them over here to work for us.' He shook his head at the idiocy of the world. 'My brother didn't make it back. Killed at Anzio. Then I discover this Nazi son of a bitch is here living high on the hog working for the government on rocket development. I think, well, it's a mistake. He covered his tracks in Germany, and they don't know who they've got working for them. I do a little digging and find out he was on the list of bad guys.'

'What did he do?' Rhonda tasted the whiskey. It had a rawness to it that she liked.

'He was an engineer who helped design the V-1 and V-2 rockets. He ran a factory for the Krauts building parts for them. They used slave labor from the concentration camps. They figure more than fifteen thousand prisoners died of starvation on his watch. He fed them just enough to keep them alive for a while, and when they died, they brought in more. Muller rented the prisoners for pennies a day from the SS who ran the camps. Every week he would select two men and a woman and have them hung from a beam near the entrance to the factory as examples against disobedience.' Bill's grin was awful.

The cigarette, forgotten, burned Rhonda's fingers. Startled, she flicked it to the floor.

'At the time I figured that maybe he forged some papers, took someone else's name, something. Arrogant prick, excuse my French, told me that he was here legit, and that I could go piss up a rope. So I wrote the story, identified

162

him, said what he had done over there. A couple of the wire services picked it up, and pretty soon he disappeared back to Germany. Like they say in the movie, the government was "shocked, shocked" to discover there were Nazis working here.'

A waitress stopped near the table. 'You and your friend want another, Billy?'

Long raised his eyebrows in question, and Rhonda nodded. The waitress took the empty glasses and went away.

'You never wrote a follow-up story.'

'No.'

The waitress arrived with their drinks, took Rhonda's money and went away.

'Why not?'

Long looked uncomfortable. He fiddled with his shot glass and took a sip. Then he sighed and shrugged. 'A few days after the story ran, a couple of guys came to see me. Not at the paper. They picked me up on the street when I left to go home. Very polite. Very firm. Put me in a car and took me to a house up in the Village. Sat me down and told me how it was. Muller was going back to Germany. The story was dead. No follow-up necessary. I wanted to be a good American, didn't I? I didn't want to help the Ruskies by undermining our military preparedness, did I? I asked if Muller was the only one. "Sure," they said, "he's the only one." But they didn't give a shit if I believed them or not, because the next day they showed me who had the power, me or them. A bunch of city inspectors showed up at Dad's stall over there and closed him down. This violation and that violation, closed until further notice. The next day he got a summons from the IRS to go over his taxes back five years. A couple of FBI agents show up at my brother's widow's place of work to ask her about an organization she belonged to in college that had ties to the Communist Party.'

'I get it,' Rhonda said.

'Yeah, I got it too. And you know what the final straw was?'

'No, what?'

'My editor never asked for a follow-up. It was a good story, maybe the beginning of a really big story, but no one asked me to go on with it. Maybe someone talked to them. I don't know. Maybe they just didn't see it the way I saw it, but they were done. Okay, so was I. Sometimes you just can't fight City Hall.'

'Who were the men who talked to you? Were they FBI? Did they show you IDs?'

'They didn't show me anything, but they didn't have to. They had that look, that fuck-you arrogance, pardon my French, of guys with a lot of clout behind them. You could tell.'

'Where was the house in the Village where they took you?'

Long took a sip of his drink and watched her for a moment over the rim of the glass. He shook his head. 'Jesus, you've got the bug, don't you? You want the story and the hell with everything else. The reason I didn't push on it, the reason I quit, is that I cared about everything else more than the story. Once I knew that, I knew I was

164

going to be a mediocre reporter. I'd rather sell fish.'

'Do you remember the address?'

He shook his head again. 'Lady, forget it. I'm not telling you. I don't want them coming back at me and mine.'

'They wouldn't know. I don't give up my sources.'

'They'd know.'

'How would they know? They've probably taken plenty of people to that house. Why would they pick you to come back at three years later?'

'I don't know how, but they'd know. I'm not risking it.'

'Bill—'

'No. Forget it.' He shoved his chair back and stood up fast.

'Give me something. Anything. A hint, a name, something.'

'I can't. I've got to protect me and mine. Thanks for the drinks. Nice meeting you.' He got up and walked away.

'Shit.' She stubbed out her cigarette, left money on the table for the waitress and went out into the night.

Rhonda's story in the *Post* came out three days later in time to pull a cloud over Magda and Karl Brandt's early lunch at Rumpelmayer's in the Hotel St Moritz. Magda had ordered the jellied tomato bouillon and then the filet of flounder grille St Germain. Karl preferred the sea food cocktail and the prime ribs of beef au jus. She asked for a half bottle of the Paul

Ruinart champagne, and he would have a half of the St Moritz special reserve Claret. They would decide on dessert later, something with whipped cream for her, chocolate for him, Rumpelmayer's specialties.

Karl picked up the newspaper from the sill of the window that looked out across 59th Street at Central Park and toward the horse-drawn carriages that parked along the curb. They did not usually read the *Post*, because, Magda said, 'It is not a paper of any culture,' but it was there, so he took a look.

He found Rhonda's story on page six.

It was a 'think piece' and was set off from the hard news in a box with wavy black borders. The facts were few: Leon Dudek, a survivor of Auschwitz and the horrors of the Holocaust, had been stabbed to death in Central Park by parties unknown on a Tuesday morning sometime just after midnight. Two people had been involved, one who held him, and another who stabbed him in the base of the brain. No witnesses had yet come forward. Dudek's wallet had been stolen, but that, the writer suggested, might have been a ruse to cover the real reason for the murder. Leon Dudek, she wrote, had lost his family to the Nazi death camp, and he used his free hours to search for former members of the Nazi Party who had managed to escape justice and who might have come to live in New York. She had statistical information on the membership rolls of the Nazi Party, more than eight million members at its peak, and quotes from historians at Columbia and NYU who claimed that most

166

of those members survived, since few party members went to the front lines. She referred to a story in a Chicago newspaper from six years before that reported the arrest of a former SS officer who had been working in that city running a highly successful import–export under an alias. He had been unmasked by a former inmate of Sachsenhausen concentration camp as a commander of the SS contingent there. The article speculated that Dudek, too, might have run across one of his former persecutors. A source who preferred to remain unnamed, who worked with the US Government programs in Germany immediately after the war to recruit German scientists and technicians, indicated that a number of recruits had their war records white-washed to meet the criteria for entrance to the States. This was confirmed in at least one instance by a story found in the *Post* archives from 1953 concerning a German rocket scientist who had been unmasked as a war criminal. Given the number of Party survivors and the chaos of the refugee resettlement programs after the war, it was likely, she concluded, that there were Nazis living among us as our neighbors and coworkers. It was possible that it was Leon Dudek's bad luck that he confronted two of them. The New York Police, she wrote, had not ruled out that possibility.

Magda Brandt had started to say something soon after Karl picked up the paper, but she saw that whatever story he was reading had his full attention. When he finished, he folded the paper so that the story was now the front page, tapped it with his forefinger and handed it to her. He said nothing while she read. When she finished, she folded the story back into the middle and put the paper on the chair next to her and looked around to see if anyone was within earshot.

'Should we worry?' she asked.

'I don't see why. Did you notice the byline? Rhonda Raskin. Typical Jew provocation, a few facts held together with innuendo and unsupported supposition.'

'It says the police are not ruling out a connection to someone like us.'

'They did not rule out a connection to a Hottentot assassination squad either.'

'Be serious, Karl.'

'I am being serious. There were no witnesses. We left no physical evidence. How could anyone possibly connect us to a piece of trash like that?'

'Someone else from the camp, from the medical compound?'

'No. The experiments are dead. They were dead before we were evacuated from the camp. You know that. You watched it done.'

The men and women lined up at the edge of the pit. The SS machine gun teams. The gunfire and the bodies toppling forward. The SS officers with pistols standing at the edge and firing down into the bodies.

'Perhaps the clean-up squads were not as efficient as they should have been. It was a time of confusion. The Russians were close, hours away, as I remember. Perhaps one of them lived.'

'Well, he's dead now,' Karl said.

'Should we mention it to our employers?'

168

He thought for a moment and then shook his head. 'No. Let's not disturb them. It would make them worry unnecessarily. They will protect us as long as our value to them is greater than the problems we cause. They have a lot to protect. It's not just us, you know.'

'If this Jew reporter were to die—'

'It would only draw more interest in the story. Let's wait and see. If there is no follow-up we can stop worrying.'

'Are you sure?'

'Yes.' He left no room for discussion. 'Ahh, lunch,' he said, and smiled as waiters arrived bearing their first courses.

Cassidy sat at a long wooden table across the squad room from the stairs. The wall above the table was covered with WANTED posters, and announcements of new departmental regulations that no one ever read. He had a stack of arrest records in manila folders on his left. He would pull one in front of him, glance at the crime, the name, the mug shot, close it, and pass it to the right. The pile on the left was much smaller than the one on the right, and he had not seen one person he thought might be his stalker.

A phone rang in the squad room. Newly answered it. 'Cassidy. A guy on line three for you.'

Cassidy got up and went to his desk and picked up the receiver. 'Cassidy here.'

'You fucked me, Cassidy.' Terry Mack's voice, raw with rage. 'They're going to find me, and they're going to take my license and Christ knows what else.'

'Easy, Terry. Easy. What are you talking about?'

'I'm talking about the story, you son of a bitch.'

'What story?'

'The *Post*. Page eight.'

'What the hell were you thinking?' were Cassidy's first words when Rhonda entered the apartment. 'I said no story until I gave you the go-ahead.' He came around the kitchen island and faced her.

She looked at him without saying anything, her fingers working the buttons of her coat.

'I got a call from my guy telling me I fucked him.' His anger had been building since Terry Mack's call. 'I said you couldn't use him.'

'I said "a source." I didn't name him. I don't have his name.'

'I gave him my word.'

She said nothing. Her fingers stopped undoing her coat buttons.

'You agreed.'

'Yes.'

'What the hell happened?'

'It was too important to sit on.'

'More important than a murder investigation?'

'People have a right to know that these people are out there among them.'

'You don't know that they're out there. Leon Dudek accused people of being Nazis who'd never been out of New York.'

'But what if he was right about others? Statistics

170

are in his favor. We know that former Nazis have been caught in the States and sent back to Germany. We know the government recruited war criminals and changed their records.'

'It's not about Dudek being right. It's about you getting a story. You getting a byline.' His anger was pushing him out onto thin ice, but he could not stop the slide. 'We had a deal.'

'This was more important.'

'More important than finding who killed Dudek?'

'You said yourself that finding them was unlikely. No witnesses. No physical evidence.'

'My case. My choice. Not yours.' He stepped closer to her.

She did not step back. 'I'm sick and tired of waiting to get permission from men to do something I do well. Leon's dead, and there are people in this city who may have killed tens of thousands more like him. People need to know it. That's why I wrote it.'

'Bullshit. You wrote it to get your name on a story that wasn't about Mamie Eisenhower's dresses or the Debutante of the Year.'

For a moment, nothing, and then her hand moved fast and cracked across his face. She spun around and went out the door, leaving it to bang against the inner wall. He could hear her footsteps clatter fast down the stairs.

Fifteen

In the dream he ran down a corridor chased by something he could not see. The corridor was familiar but he did not know where he was. The doors had no knobs and could not be opened. Every time he turned a corner in the corridor, what chased him was now in front of him, and he would turn and run in another direction. When he turned the next corner, the thing would be ahead of him again, and he would turn and run. At the end of the corridor was an open doorway framing darkness. If he could reach it, he'd be safe. The thing was closing in. Could he reach the safety of the doorway? The thing was closer. And then he was at the doorway. He hurled himself through it with relief.

He began to fall and fall.

He woke up gasping.

The phone rang while Cassidy was eating breakfast standing at the kitchen counter. There was no one he wanted to talk to. It rang again. Rhonda calling? Unlikely. It rang again and again and again. He picked up the receiver. 'Hello.'

'Michael, it's Marcy,' his sister-in-law said.

'Hi. What's up?'

'Have you heard from Brian?'

'No. Should I have? What's up?' He finished the last of his coffee and lit a cigarette.

'He's in Washington. He's been there a lot

172

these last weeks. He went down again a couple of days ago, and I haven't heard from him.' He heard the worry in her voice.

'He's probably busy, Marcy. You know Brian. He gets focused on something, and he forgets to eat.'

'He doesn't forget to call home. Every evening when he's away, every evening and every morning. He calls before the girls go to bed, and he calls before they go to school. It doesn't matter where he is or what he's doing.'

'Is he staying at Aunt Kay's?'

'Yes. I was going to call her, but I thought I'd call you first.'

'I'll call her, and I'll call you back.' Brian thought being late for an appointment was a mortal sin, and if he said he would call you at a certain time, he would. Missing two calls to Marcy and the girls was way out of character.

He found his address book, poured another cup of coffee, and called his Aunt Kay Lockridge in Georgetown. The phone was answered on the third ring by her butler, 'Mrs Lockridge's residence.'

'Mr Farrington, it's Michael Cassidy.'

'Mr Cassidy, how nice to hear your voice.'

'Is my aunt available?'

'I'm sure she is for you. If you'll hold for a moment, I will find her.'

Cassidy drank coffee and lit another cigarette while he waited.

'Michael, it's Kay. How are you?'

'I'm fine, thank you. I just had a call from Marcy, who is worried that she hasn't heard from Brian since he went down to DC yesterday.'

173

'I'm a bit worried too. We were supposed to have dinner last night, but he never showed up, and he didn't call. That's very unlike him.'

'Did he say where he was going?'

'No. Just that he had a couple of appointments. I think one of them was on the Hill, but I don't know whom he was meeting. He didn't come home last night.'

'Oh.'

'I thought maybe he spent the night with a friend.' There was a hesitation in her voice.

'A friend?'

'You know.'

'I don't think so. Not Brian, steadfast and true.'

'You make that sound like a character fault. In a way I was hoping it might be a woman. It would be the least of many evils. He said something peculiar to me when he stopped by to drop off his bag.'

'What?'

'He thought he might have been followed from the train station. He stopped along the way to do some errands, and he thought he saw the same man a couple of times when he came out of stores. Then he laughed it off. He said he was spending too much time with you, and the cop was rubbing off.'

'A description of the man?'

'No. And by the time he left the house he had me convinced that it was just a coincidence.'

'Aunt Kay, I'm coming down. I can catch the two o'clock.'

'Michael, now you've got me worried.'

174

'No, no. I have a few days off. And if I come down, he'll show up. That's how it works.'

'All right.' She did not sound convinced.

What if his stalker had decided to add Brian to his target list? That scared him.

Kay Lockridge's house in Georgetown was a big, brick Federal set back from a street lined with mature shade trees still in full foliage. Apparently, Aunt Kay had not yet given the leaves permission to fall. Limousines crowded the semicircular drive and street curbs. Cassidy's cab left him at the front door. He rang the bell, and moments later the door was opened by a portly, round-faced Negro in a black suit, white shirt, black bowtie, and white cotton gloves. His neutral servant's expression lightened when he recognized Cassidy.

'Detective Cassidy, welcome. How nice to see you.' His voice sang with a Jamaican lilt.

'How are you Mr Farrington?'

'I'm fine, sir. Thank you for asking.' He held the door wide to let Cassidy into the coolness of the front hall with its black-and-white marble floor and the grand staircase that curved up to the second floor. The big living room beyond was full of people, and the murmur of their cocktail party chatter, the clink of ice in glasses, occasional bursts of laughter came out to the hall.

'Has my brother shown up?'

'No, sir. We haven't seen him since yesterday. Mrs Lockridge put you in the blue room as usual. Shall I take you up?' He reached for Cassidy's overnight bag.

'Thank you. I'll find my way.'

'As you wish, sir. Please ring if you need anything.' His shoes made little sound on the marble floor as he went off toward the kitchen area. Sam Farrington had run Kay Lockridge's houses in Washington, Maine, Colorado, and London for thirty years with a perfect blend of deference, taste, and iron will.

Kay was Cassidy's mother's older sister. She had been married for fifteen years to Frank Lockridge, a two-term senator from Montana who had been Franklin Roosevelt's ambassador to Siam, and his personal envoy to China and Japan before the war. Lockridge had died in a plane crash in England during the war while on a diplomatic mission for the president. He left Kay his mining fortune, which made her, rumor had it, the richest women in Washington. She had beauty, money, and brains. That combination and a deep interest in how the machinery of government worked had made her, over the years, a powerful force behind the scenes in the capitol. Parties at her house in Georgetown were the most sought-after invitations in the city. She knew where the bodies were buried and who dug the holes. She gave money to both parties and refused to swear loyalty to either. There were those who said that if she had been a man, she would have made a fine president.

Cassidy carried his bag up two flights to the room he used when he came to visit Aunt Kay. He unpacked the few things he had brought. He washed his hands of train grime in the bathroom and checked himself in the mirror. Washington

176

was a formal town, and he had dressed accordingly in a charcoal gray J. Press suit with a faint red pinstripe, a blue buttoned-down shirt, and a dark paisley tie. He would blend in with the people downstairs if he remembered to hold his tongue.

Cassidy went down to his brother's room on the second floor. Afternoon light slanted in through the big windows and threw long shadows on the thick rug. The room was neat. The bed was made. The closet door was closed. The desk chair was pushed in tight. Brian habitually scattered change on the bureau when he undressed for the night and usually forgot to put it back in his pocket in the morning. It had been gathered into a small brass bowl. The ashtrays and wastebasket were empty. The pad on the desk was squared in the middle of the leather edge blotter below a narrow silver tray that held two fountain pens and two sharp pencils. A maid would have cleaned the room soon after Brian went out. She had left it neat and orderly for his return.

Why did the stillness and order of the room put Cassidy on edge?

He used the phone on the desk to call Brian's secretary, Claire, at ABC in New York and caught her as she was about to leave for the day.

'No, Mr Cassidy, he hasn't called. He said he'd be back in the office on Monday. Is there anything I can help you with?'

'Do you know who he was seeing in Washington?'

'I don't. He made his own appointments for the trip. He likes to do that when he's unsure of

177

his schedule. That way he can change things on the fly if he needs to without going through me.'

'Is there anything on his desk calendar?'

'Let me look. Could you hold a minute?' The phone went dead for a minute until she came back on. 'Mr Cassidy?'

'Yes, Claire.'

'There's nothing on the calendar for this week, just his train down and back on Friday.'

'Thank you.'

'Is everything all right?'

'Yes. Everything's fine.' He hung up and lit a cigarette. If everything was so fine, why was his skin so fucking tight?

He went downstairs to the party.

An election year drives the losers from the halls of power and the winners take their places. But an election year makes little difference to the power brokers and insiders who make up a small, permanent class of Washington Mandarins whose influence is constant no matter which party was on top. They are the pundits, the super lawyers, the influence peddlers, the strategists, people with the money, or connections who could bend legislation or policy. Many of them were in Kay Lockridge's living room drinking her booze, grazing through her hors d'oeuvres, and basking in the glow of power and privilege that reached critical mass in gatherings like this.

Cassidy got a martini from a bar near the door and moved into the crowd looking for his aunt. It was a large, light-filled room that looked out through French doors to a wide porch and a well-tended formal garden. The furniture was

178

expensive, solid, and comfortable. A brightly colored Joan Miró painting shared a wall with a still life by Marc Chagall. On the opposite wall was a large abstract by Jackson Pollock, who had died the past summer in a car accident on Long Island just as his reputation as an artist soared. Antique tables held silver-framed portraits of family members, but there were none of the vanity photographs so popular in Washington houses showing the owner with men of power. Kay Lockridge did not need to remind people who she was.

He spotted Kay near the fireplace talking to a tall, square-jawed, silver-haired man he recognized as Sherman Adams, Eisenhower's White House chief of staff. Kay saw him at the same time, raised her eyebrows in recognition of his presence and with a small shake of her head, signaled that he was not to interrupt. He turned away and scanned the crowd for a familiar face, and there were some, but they were only familiar from the newspapers and magazines: Sam Rayburn, the speaker of the house, Walter Lippmann, the political writer and journalist, General Omar Bradley, Washington Redskins quarterback Eddie Le Baron, New York Governor Averell Harriman, Washington Senators third baseman Eddie Yost, and a couple of other faces he could not put names to.

For a while he circulated through the room. The talk was about the coming elections or the situation in Europe, Hungary on the edge of rebellion, the hope for a relaxing of tension now that Krushchev had consolidated power in Russia

179

and had denounced Stalin's purges. After a while, he got another martini and went out onto the porch that overlooked the garden.

There was a grouping of high-backed rattan chairs on the porch. They reminded Cassidy of the black-and-white movies he watched as a boy of British colonials in linen suits sitting around in chairs like these on their plantation verandas, drinking scotch and soda and waiting for the natives to attack out of the jungle. He took refuge in one of them.

He was halfway through the martini when someone came out and sat in another of the rattan chairs. The man leaned forward to put an iced bowl of caviar and a tall drink on the low glass-topped table that separated his chair from Cassidy's. Cassidy recognized Allen Dulles, the director of the CIA. He looked at Cassidy through round, wire-rimmed glasses. Cassidy returned the inspection. Dulles was a handsome, stocky man about six feet tall and in his early sixties. He had a big square head and heavy chin. His clipped mustache did not extend past the corners of his mouth. He wore a conservative gray suit, a white shirt, and a green-and-yellow-striped tie. He studied Cassidy with the bland regard of a man who is sure of his high place in the world and then dipped two fingers into the bowl and carried a gob of caviar to his mouth.

Cassidy disliked him on sight.

There was something in Cassidy's blood, passed from his Russian father, that recoiled from the lordling, the man on the horse with the whip and the power. Allen Dulles was such a man. He was the head of the CIA. His brother, John Foster Dulles, was the secretary of state, as their uncle and their grandfather had been. It was said, Aunt Kay had told him, that the brothers formed their own foreign policy and then told Eisenhower only what they wanted him to know so that he saw the world through their eyes. Their grandfather, John Foster, had been the first US secretary of state to engineer the overthrow of the government of a sovereign nation. The brothers followed the path he cut.

Dulles raised his glass. 'Cheers.' He took a sip. 'Ahh, that's good. Hello, I'm Allen Dulles. I don't think we've met.' He had a gift of instant affability. 'Do you mind if I join you out here? I can stand about fifteen minutes of that chatter, and then I want to scream.' He leaned over to offer his right hand.

Cassidy shook his hand. 'Michael Cassidy.'

'Sure. Kay's nephew. You're the New York policeman, aren't you?'

'Yes, I am.'

'Good for you. The world would be a better place if more men with your background would do what you're doing. It can be unpleasant work, but we leave too much of it to unpleasant people.' He spoke with the winning, open sincerity of a practiced liar. 'Have some caviar. It's Iranian beluga. The Shah sends it to Kay and I steal as much as I can when I know it's here.' He took a pipe from his jacket pocket, stuffed it with tobacco, and lit it with a kitchen match struck on the bottom of the table. He flicked the burned

181

match out into the garden. Dulles dipped his fingers back into the caviar and ate another scoop. 'What are you in DC for, Michael? Business or pleasure?'

'I came to see my brother.'

'Brian, isn't it? He's a journalist of some kind. Wait . . . I know. He's with one of the television networks.'

'Yes. ABC.'

'What's he working on?' Dulles had the honed curiosity of a long-time spy. Secrets were his currency and a source of his power.

'He didn't say.' Cassidy's instinct was to tell this man nothing.

'Where is he?'

'Out doing what he does.'

'You haven't spoken to him?'

'No.'

'I see.' Dulles took a pull on his drink. 'How long have you been a cop? Do you mind my asking?'

'I joined in 1947.'

'After college?'

'Six months at Columbia. I dropped out.'

'College doesn't really matter.' He waved a hand dismissively. 'You learned more on the street than any classroom could have taught you. Do you like being a cop?'

'I do.'

'Why?'

There was something about the scrutiny and the questions that chafed Cassidy, like something scratching along the outside of the house looking for a way in.

'An early fixation on Bulldog Drummond and Sam Spade, I guess.'

'It was a serious question.'

'I don't have a better answer.'

'We're looking for good men with a variety of experiences that would be useful in our work.'

'The CIA? No, thank you. I like the simplicity of my job. The crimes are usually clear, and the bad guys are usually identifiable.'

'I can offer you bigger bad guys. We're at war to preserve our way of life. Unless we hold the line, the Communists will destroy everything we stand for. There is nothing simpler than that.' He was a man armored against doubt.

'I'm sure you'll do fine without me.'

A look of annoyance crossed Dulles's face. 'You don't like me, do you?' It was a ploy, an accusation that demanded a courteous denial, and then, by some peculiar chemistry of polite society, Dulles would have gained the moral high ground.

'No, not much,' Cassidy said.

'Why not?'

'I don't like people who tip the table so everything slides down to their end.'

Dulles looked at him with cold eyes. He was used to greater deference. He tapped his pipe out to gain a moment.

High heels clicked on the porch flagstones, and Kay Lockridge walked past them to lean on the porch rail. She was a tall, slim, regal woman in her sixties. Her hair was dramatically white. She and Cassidy's mother had a similar beauty that

183

had passed on in a different form to his sister, Leah. She wore her late husband's thin gold watch on a leather band on her left wrist, a necklace of flat gold links and matching earrings, and a dark green Chanel suit. She took in Dulles looming over Cassidy.

'Hmmm, I get a strong whiff of burning testosterone. Have you two been at each other?'

'Not at all,' Dulles said. 'We've been having a very interesting discussion.'

'That's what I love about spies,' Kay said. 'They lie instinctively and believably. The good ones do, anyway,' Kay said cheerfully. 'Allen, you're staying for dinner, aren't you? I learned something on the Hill this afternoon I'd like to discuss with you.'

'I can't tonight, Kay. Something's come up. Tomorrow for lunch?'

'Tomorrow.' She accepted his kiss on the cheek, and then turned as Cassidy rose to kiss her. She smelled faintly of the same perfume his mother used to wear. 'Have you heard from Brian,' she asked.

'No. Not yet.'

'Kay, I have to go,' Dulles said.

'I'll walk you out.' She put an affectionate hand on his arm. Allen Dulles was married, but he had a reputation as an extracurricular cocksman, and in Cassidy's family it was understood that he and Kay Lockridge had a longstanding, on-again-off-again affair.

Dulles kissed her on the cheek at the front door, and patted her on the hip. 'I'll call you in the morning.'

She turned back into the house as he walked down the stone path to the waiting Cadillac.

Cassidy was smoking a cigarette when she came back out to the porch.

'Are you going to tell me?' Kay asked.

'There's nothing to tell.'

'Were you rude to him?'

'Yes.'

'Any particular reason?'

'Not really. Sometimes you meet someone who's like fingernails on a blackboard to you.'

'You don't want him as an enemy, Michael.'

'He's got the whole world to run. He's much too busy to worry about a lowly New York cop.'

As the Cadillac rolled toward the street Allen Dulles leaned forward from the back seat to give the driver an address in McLean and then slid the dividing window shut for privacy. He took the telephone receiver out of the polished wooden box built into his armrest and dialed a number. Spencer Shaw answered the phone on the third ring. Dulles did not bother to identify himself. The people he called were expected to know his voice. 'Is he responding?'

'We're in the process.'

'What has he told you?'

'Very little so far. We're trying different doses.' The safe house he was in was similar to the one in the Village in New York. It was single-family house in a seedier part of town where neighbors would pay little attention to comings and goings. Shaw was in a room on the second floor. He could see Brian Cassidy in the next room through

185

the one-way viewing window. Brian sat in a wooden chair in the center of the room. His arms were strapped to the chair's arms, a new precaution since the unfortunate events in the Village safe house. His head lolled back, and his eyes were closed. As Shaw watched, Magda Brandt swabbed his arm with alcohol-soaked cotton and then gave him an injection. Karl Brandt smoked a cigarette in a short black holder as he leaned against the windowsill and watched.

'His brother is here,' Dulles said into the phone.

'Is that a problem?'

'That would be one of the lines of questioning. What do they know? How did they penetrate the operation? What's the cop's part in it?'

'We'll ask.'

'I want both these men neutralized.'

'Neutralized,' Shaw said. 'Permanently?'

A look of irritation crossed Dulles's face. 'I don't believe there's any need for that at the moment. I want less noise, not more.'

'You're the boss.'

Kay took Michael to dinner at Rive Gauche, a small French restaurant in Georgetown. The owner guided them to a corner booth, and the waiter brought their drinks, took their dinner orders and went away.

'What did Brian talk to you about yesterday before he went out?' Cassidy asked.

'Not much. He said he was working on something to do with the influence of money on the legislative process. It's a story that every generation of newsman discovers.' Kay leaned toward

186

Cassidy so he could light her cigarette. 'Money and politics have always gone together. Sometimes the money influence is heavy, and sometimes it's just grease for the wheels. I remember Frank telling me that if you can't take a man's money, eat his food and drink his liquor, and then vote against his interests, you have no business being in politics.'

'Can many people do that?'

'No. Not many.'

Dinner arrived, and they ate in silence for a while.

'Michael,' Kay said, 'don't worry about Brian. He's a big boy, and he's a well-respected journalist. He's busy chasing a story. He'll be home when we get there.'

But he wasn't home when they got there. He had not called, and he wasn't there the next morning.

Sixteen

The dream was the same: running from something he could not see. Corridors branched, and when he turned a corner, the thing would be in front of him. If he turned back, it was there waiting for him. Darkness at the end. Something waiting there to kill him. Cassidy awoke. He was naked on the floor in the corner of a room with his back pressed hard against the join of walls. What room? Where was he? His .38 was in his hand pointed at the door. The hammer was back, and his finger was on the trigger, about three pounds of pull away from killing whoever came through the door. Dawn light came through the window. He could see the outline of a bed, and a desk against the wall opposite. He was in Brian's room.

No one came through the door. The house slept.

Cassidy eased the hammer back down and put the gun on the bed. He went into the bathroom and splashed it on his face trying to drive away the remnants of the dream that still scraped his brain. Splinters of the nightmare were with him, but he could not recapture the details. He turned on the shower and stepped in. The cold water was a shock, and the dread of the dream died to a prick of unease. He knew there was a man out there threatening to kill him: the guy on the subway platform, the one with the rifle. Who was he? Maybe next time the dream would show him a face.

He wrapped a towel around his waist and went back into the bedroom and turned on the lights. The pad was still centered in the middle of the desk. The top page was blank. He picked up the pad and tilted it toward the light. Brian had written on the top page and had then torn it off, but the pressure of the pen had left indentations on the page below. Cassidy found a pencil and swept the lead lightly back and forth across the paper until the ghosts of the writing from the missing page appeared. It was a phone number.

Cassidy pulled the phone over and dialed. It rang six times at the other end and was answered with a click. The taped voice of an answering machine announced that he had gotten the congressional office of Representative Martin Williams of Utah, the offices were closed, and normal office hours began at nine o'clock.

Williams was the congressman Brian had interviewed for returning a campaign contribution.

At nine o'clock Cassidy was in a phone booth at an intersection of two echoing corridors in the Congressional Office Building listening to the phone ring. The voice that answered grated with impatience. 'DCPD. Logan speaking.'

'Is Sam Watkins on duty?'

'Yeah, I just saw him come in. Who wants him?'

'Michael Cassidy.'

'Hold.' The receiver clunked on a desk and the man shouted Watkins's name.

Moments late the receiver was picked up.

'Yeah.'

'Sam, it's Mike Cassidy.'

'Hey, Mike. What's up? You in town?'

'Yes. I need some help, Sam.'

'Shoot.'

'Do you remember my brother, Brian?'

'Sure.'

'He was down here working on an assignment, and he went missing the day before yesterday. He was due to meet our aunt for dinner. He didn't make it. No one's heard from him or seen him since.'

'Yeah, well, you know, a guy's down here on his own, out of his regular orbit, so to speak. Maybe he meets someone in a bar. Maybe he

189

finds some place else to sleep. It happens. Besides, you know how it works – they want a guy to be missing forty-eight hours minimum before they start throwing manpower at it.'

'Do you have time to call around, hospitals, other squads?'

Watkins hesitated. 'Okay. Does he still look pretty much the same? A bit over six, a couple of hundred pounds, sandy hair. Just in case he got mugged or something, lost his ID.'

'Yes. A scar at the corner of his right eye about an inch long. And he's had his appendix out.'

'Where can I reach you?'

'I'm up on the Hill to see someone. I'll call you.'

'You got it.'

'Thanks, Sam. I owe you.'

'I'll collect. Your father got a play on?'

'Next month.'

'Tickets?'

'Sure.'

'And a blow job by some big Broadway actress. Not Ethel Merman. Gwen Verdon, maybe. Jesus, those legs.'

'Sam, even God can't get you that.'

'Then what's he good for? Call me.'

Congressman Martin Williams's office was a meager space that befitted a freshman congressman with no accrued power. There was a small reception area with worn leather chairs, a leather sofa and a secretary's desk, a small side room not much bigger than a closet for two congressional aides sitting opposite each other at two small metal desks pushed together, and a closed door

190

that led to the congressman's office. The two aides were arguing about something in low, intense voices when Cassidy walked in. The secretary looked up at him with the cheery smile designed to welcome constituents.

'Good morning, sir. May I help you?'

'My name's Michael Cassidy.' He slid his identification across the desk to her. 'I don't have an appointment, but I was hoping to get a few minutes with the congressman before his day got too busy.'

'I'm sorry, but the congressman won't be in today.'

'Is there any way I can contact him? Maybe he has some time.'

'I'm afraid he's gone home for a few days.'

'Do you have the address?'

'Oh. I mean he's gone to Utah to talk to his constituents. He feels he should stay in touch as much as possible, so he goes out there once a month while Congress is in session. He'll be back Monday. Is there anything I can do to help?'

'My brother, Brian Cassidy, either called him or came by to see him.'

'Yes. That's why the name was familiar. He was here for about an hour.'

'Do you know what they talked about?'

'No. They were in Congressman Williams's office.'

'How about the guys in there? Do you think they might know something?'

'Jeremy? Excuse me, Jeremy.' The two young men stopped arguing and turned to look at her. 'This is Mr Cassidy. He's a policeman. His

191

brother was in with the congressman yesterday. He wants to know what they were talking about. Mr Cassidy, this is Jeremy Hauser and Andy Steadman. They're the congressman's aides.'

The two young men came out of their closet and shook hands with Cassidy. Hauser was tall, thin, dark, and studious, with horn-rimmed glasses and thinning hair. Steadman was fair and stockier, and he carried himself with an assurance Hauser did not have.

'We don't usually talk about what goes on in the congressman's office without his say so,' Steadman said.

'My brother's gone missing. I'm trying to find out where he was, who he met, what he talked about.'

The two young men looked at each other. 'We don't know what they said,' Steadman said. 'We weren't in his office. But he asked us to bring in whatever research we had on who had lobbied him over the last eighteen months and who had contributed to his coming re-election campaign.'

'I'd like to look at the material.'

'I'm sorry, Detective, but we couldn't do that without Congressman Williams's permission.'

'Okay. Can you tell me this, were there any obvious overlaps, people who contributed and also lobbied?'

The two aides exchanged a look. Steadman shook his head and smiled apologetically. 'I'm sorry.'

'Do any of you have any idea where my brother was headed after he left here.'

Neither one knew anything about Brian's movements, and after a few more questions, they went back to their desk. Cassidy offered the secretary a cigarette, but she refused it. 'I don't smoke.'

'How did Brian seem to you? Agitated? Nervous?'

'No, I don't think so. Do you think he might have gotten sick or something?'

'I don't know. He hasn't been seen by anyone I know since he was here.'

'Jeez, I'm sorry. I mean, if my sister was missing, I'd be worried sick.' She twisted the pencil in her hand and looked toward the small office where the two aides were again in heated conversation. 'If I tell you something, you won't tell anyone, will you?'

'No. I promise.'

She lowered her voice. 'When he called for his appointment, he asked how long it would take to walk here from K Street.'

'K Street?'

'Yes.'

'Did he mention who he was seeing there?'

She glanced at the two aides in their office. 'Jeremy and Andrew take everything so seriously. Every little thing that goes on in the office is super secret. The government might fall, or something, if anyone knew what the congressman had for breakfast.'

Cassidy waited while she worked up to telling him what she wanted him to know.

'There's a company on K Street that contributed to the Congressman's re-election campaign, and Congressman Williams gave the money back, because he thought there was a conflict of interest. He's very strict about things like that.'

'A medical company? Brian mentioned that.'

'Gallien Medical. I could give you the address, but you have to promise not to tell.'

'And you think my brother saw him.'

'I heard him say he had just come from there when I took him into the congressman's office.'

A silver Rolls-Royce was parked in front of a six-story granite block building on K Street where the taxi dropped Cassidy. The brass-bound elevator carried Cassidy up to the fifth floor. Gallien Medical was identified by gold script on a pebbled-glass door. The waiting room was furnished with aggressively modern pieces. There were abstract art prints on the walls framed in chrome, and the chrome standing lamps looked like industrial accidents. The receptionist sat behind a desk with no straight lines. The top was an off-center oval of blond wood, and the thin ebony legs were bowed. The receptionist was a striking blond woman wearing a steel-gray suit with broad shoulder pads and lapels cut on a radical bias and a light gray blouse made of metallic cloth. The three pins on her jacket looked like silver shrapnel. The buttons were jagged red Bakelite shards. She wore glasses with heavy black round rims. 'May I help you?' she asked in a cool voice reserved for people who appeared without an appointment.

'I'd like to speak to Mr Gallien.'

'And you are?'

'Michael Cassidy.' He slipped the leather folder from his pocket and showed her his badge and ID. 'My brother, Brian Cassidy, had an appointment with Mr Gallien yesterday. He's gone missing, and I'm trying to trace his movements. I'd appreciate a minute of Mr Gallien's time.'

The receptionist looked at Cassidy with bright blue eyes that missed no details. 'He's quite busy today, but I'll go ask him. I'll just be a minute.' She got up and went through the door to the inner office.

Cassidy cocked a hip on the edge of the desk. The furnishings and the receptionist announced that this company was on the cutting edge of tomorrow. If you wanted to buy into the future, Gallien Medical was selling it today.

The receptionist came back out. 'Mr Gallien will see you now.'

Harry Gallien had a round head, bald and shiny, and a round, symmetrical face, a tubular neck, a rounded chest and belly with no discernible waist. It was hard to tell his age, but Cassidy guessed he was in his forties. He wore a beautiful dark blue silk suit hand tailored to disguise the peculiarities of his body, a cream-colored shirt with gold-and-sapphire cufflinks, and a bright yellow-and-red Countess Mara tie. He smiled at Cassidy in welcome, and offered a soft, damp hand across the desk. Cassidy took it and then gave it back. Gallien waved Cassidy to a chrome-and-leather armchair.

A lot more money had been spent to furnish Gallien's office than the outer room. Abstract oil paintings rather than prints filled the frames on

195

the walls. The desk was a massive amoeba slab of steel. A strangely shaped ebony table held expensive liquor bottles. The air was faintly perfumed.

'Tell me what I can do for you, Mr Cassidy. A cop. I don't think I've ever met a real policeman before.' His eyes twinkled.

'You must lead an exemplary life.'

'What? Oh, yes. I see. Never met a cop. Never been arrested. I see. I see. Very good. No. Not even a traffic ticket.' He let out a warm chuckle. He was, apparently, a man of great good humor.

'I think my brother came to see you.'

'Yes. Brian Cassidy. A very interesting man. And charming. I watch his show religiously.'

'Would you tell me what you talked about?'

'Sure. Absolutely. He wanted to ask me about a donation I had made to a congressman's campaign for re-election.'

'Congressman Martin Williams.'

'Of Utah. Exactly.'

'What did Brian want to know?'

'He was interested in why the congressman sent the check back.'

'Why did he?'

'Congressman Williams is a man of high principle, and he was afraid that taking my check might in some way suggest that he might be influenced in his vote on a question in front of the House.'

'A question concerning Gallien Medical?'

'Yes. Congressman Williams is on a subcommittee of the House Appropriations Committee. Do you know what the Appropriations Committee

196

does? Simply put, it decides on how much money will be spent by the government and who gets what.'

'How much was the check for?'

'A thousand dollars.' Gallien waited for a reaction.

'The price of a pretty good used car.' Cassidy took out a pack of Luckies and offered it across the desk. Gallien shook his head and pushed a crystal ashtray closer while Cassidy lit his cigarette. 'Was that all Brian wanted?'

'He wanted to know whether Gallien Medical made contributions to other congressmen or senators. Of course, we do. We are very much interested in the legislative process, and we want to help the process wherever we can.'

'Has anyone else ever sent a check back?'

Gallien smiled. 'No. These men understand that I'm not trying to buy their votes, I'm just supporting men who see the roles of government and business the way I do. That's the joy of democracy. You have the freedom to support the people you want to support.'

'Did Brian ask you for the names of other senators or congressmen you've contributed to?'

'He did.'

'Did you give him the names?'

'I did not.'

'Why not?'

'It wasn't any of his business.'

'What does Gallien Medical do for the government?'

'Research and development in the medical field. We have laboratories and manufacturing plants in Delaware. Were you in the war, Mr Cassidy?'

'I was.'

'Wounded?'

'Yes.'

'Gallien Medical supplied the sulfa drugs that stopped infection, the plasma, the morphine, the bandages; pretty much anything that kept you alive, we supplied.'

'Thank you for that.'

Gallien waved it away. 'Oh, we're proud to have helped save young American lives. Proud. And I have to say, we made a dandy profit doing it. That's the American way, what I call enlightened self-interest. Since the war things have been a bit sparser, a bit tighter. But we're working on some research that we hope will have applications for the military and in the wider civilian world.'

'And you'd like the government to fund that.'

'America runs on business, Mr Cassidy. What's good for business is good for America. The war was a terrible thing, but business thrived during it, and we came out of it as the most powerful nation on the planet, economically and militarily. We were a rather small company in 1940, but we are now one of the leading medical supply companies in the country. The war and its aftermath proved that business and government are joined like Siamese twins. They cannot be separated. And that's a good thing, because, as we all know, we're now at war with people who want to destroy us. We must be strong going forward.'

'Did he mention any other appointments he had that day?'

'No, he didn't. I like your brother. He's a straight shooter. I could tell that immediately. As I said, I watch his show and enjoy it immensely. He doesn't always get it right, but who does?'

Cassidy stood up. 'Thank you for your time.'

'Not at all. It was my pleasure.' Gallien stood. 'I'm sure you'll find that he ran into a friend or something and just lost track of the time.' Again he offered his soft, damp hand. Cassidy shook it and returned it again. There was something about the texture and feel of the hand that made him want to wipe his own on his jacket. He turned to go.

'This is America's time, Mr Cassidy. America is going to thrive, and Gallien Medical is going to thrive with it.'

He left Gallien's office and walked down the stairs rather than wait for the elevator. By the time he got to the bottom, he realized he liked the way Harry Gallien decorated his office, including the decorative secretary, but he did not like Harry Gallien much at all.

Seventeen

Cassidy came out of the building onto K Street and stopped to light a cigarette. A big man in a leather jacket was at the curb admiring the interior of the Rolls-Royce. Cassidy was at a

199

dead end. Brian's trail was twenty-four hours cold. He had nowhere to go unless Sam Watkins had found something from the DC police. He found a phone booth on the corner, put a coin in the slot, and dialed. A man picked up on the fourth ring. 'Sanderson, DCPD. Your dime, start talking.'

'Is Sam Watkins there?'

'No, he ain't.'

'Do you know where I can reach him?'

'No, I don't. He caught a squeal and went out of here like his ass was on fire. Wait a minute. Wait a minute. Are you Cassidy?'

'Yes.'

'He said if you called, it looks like your brother's over at Sibley Memorial.'

When Cassidy came out of the booth, the man in the leather jacket was still inspecting the Rolls. Cassidy hailed a cab and told the driver to take him to Sibley Memorial. He looked out the window as they drove through the city and tried to keep his mind blank about what had put his brother in the hospital. He would know soon enough.

Brian was asleep in the hospital's open ward on the second floor. There was a bruise under his left eye, and his stubbled face was drawn, pale, and slack. He looked older than his years, diminished and weakened. Brian had always been the calm center in the family, unruffled, unbreakable. Cassidy had never seen him like this. The ward doctor's name was Rowe. He read Cassidy's dismay and put a comforting hand on his arm

200

and said, 'There's nothing organically wrong that we can find. A few scrapes and bruises. We gave him a sedative, because he was terribly confused and anxious when they brought him in. They're doing the blood work now. It might tell us something more.'

'Who brought him in?'

'A police car. They found him wandering over near Rock Creek Park. One of the cops recognized him from TV, that program he does once a week, what is it? *Behind the Headlines.* Detective Cassidy, does your brother tend to drink to excess?' Rowe fiddled with the stethoscope around his neck while he talked.

'No. He's a social drinker. I haven't seen him really drunk for years. Why?'

'He was staggering, incoherent, and there was a strong smell of liquor about him.'

'Did he say where he'd been?'

'He said nothing we could understand. As I said, he was incoherent. Babbling. Occasionally throwing his arms around, not violently, but out of control and yelling. Once he jumped up while a nurse was drawing blood, and ran for the door. The orderlies had to restrain him.'

'Maybe there's something in his clothes that would tell us where'd he'd been, a matchbook from a bar, a receipt.'

'He wasn't wearing any clothes.'

'What?'

'He was naked. I'm sorry, I thought someone would have told you.'

The police report was clipped to a carbon copy of the hospital intake report. Two cops in a patrol

201

car had found Brian wandering naked at the western edge of Rock Creek Park. He had been unable to identify himself or to explain what had happened to him. He smelled of alcohol. He had been admitted to the hospital at 12:24 am. The hospital intake report outlined the procedures that had been followed and noted that blood had been drawn and sent to the lab. Dr Rowe said it might be a couple of hours before Brian awoke, but that Cassidy was not to worry. Then he went off to make rounds.

Cassidy got a handful of change from the gift shop and called Marcy from a booth in the front lobby. He caught her as she was about to leave to pick up the girls from school. He told her what had happened and then listened to silence until he thought the phone was dead. 'Marcy?'

'I'm trying to take it in. Is he all right? Should I come? I can get Leah to take the girls, and I could be there by this evening. God, drunk? He doesn't get drunk. And naked? Michael, what the hell happened? This isn't Brian.' She was trying to sound calm, but a spike of anxiety rose in her voice.

'Marcy, he's asleep. I'll be here when he wakes up, and he can tell me what happened. The doctor says there is nothing really wrong with him, but he wants to keep him overnight. When he's ready to go, he and I will catch a train home. There's no need for you to come down. I'll call you when he wakes up and let you know.'

'Are you sure?'

'It's up to you, but I'm here, and there's nothing to do.'

'All right. Call me, though. Please. Call me when he's awake.'

'The moment he's up.'

Cassidy called Kay at home and told her what had happened. She said, 'I'll be there as soon as I can.' Cassidy went back upstairs. He pulled a chair close to Brian's bed and sat where he could reach his brother's hand where it lay on the cotton blanket. Brian's chest rose and fell slowly with his breaths. Some color had come back into his face, but he still looked pale and drawn. What the hell had happened? Marcy was right; this was not how Brian behaved. Brian was the one who pulled Cassidy and their sister Leah back from the drop. What drove him off the rails?

Cassidy dozed.

He was awakened by a hand on his shoulder, and lurched back into consciousness.

Kay Lockridge stood by his chair. 'I canceled my appointments.'

He rubbed his face. 'I fell asleep.'

'Yes. How is he?'

Brian had turned over on his side, the first movement Cassidy had seen. Maybe it was a sign that he was throwing off the sedative.

'I don't know. The doctor said he should wake up soon, but that he might be disoriented when he does.' He found another chair and pulled it next to the bed.

Kay sat down and looked at Brian without expression for a moment and then sighed. 'Have you seen the paper today?'

'No.'

She had it folded in her lap and now she handed it to him. It was turned to the front page of the Metro section. There was a photograph above the fold. It showed Brian caught in the sudden glare of a camera flash. He was naked, crouched near bushes, staring terrified at the camera with black eyes like a wild animal. The story below the photograph reported that the prominent ABC Television reporter, Brian Cassidy, was found wandering near Rock Creek Park by a police patrol. The officers reported the subject was naked, dazed, and incoherent, and he smelled of alcohol. He was taken to a local hospital where he was sedated and kept for observation.

'Jesus. What the hell was he doing way out there? How the hell did he get there like that? Naked.' He stared at the photograph.

'I don't get the paper delivered to the house,' Kay said. 'It goes to the office. I don't read the paper at breakfast. It's too early in the day to let that crap intrude. Somebody left it on the front step. It was folded open to the Metro section. Someone was taking the trouble to make sure I saw it. I've made enemies over the years. In this town if you don't have enemies, you've never taken a stand on anything. Someone wanted to make sure my day started off badly. It won't hurt me. It'll be a little bit embarrassing, because people will delight in talking to me about it, but it's terrible for Brian. A man in his business depends on his reputation. Who's going to believe reports from a drunk?'

Cassidy put the paper down. 'Brian doesn't get drunk.'

204

'Oh, Michael, I know you love him and respect him, but everyone can stumble at some point.'

'Not like this.'

Kay held up her hand to forestall any argument. 'Do you have a cigarette?'

He gave her one and lit it, and then picked up the paper again. Something about the photo of Brian. He went through the paper, stopping at the photographs in the first section and the Metro section and checking them against Brian's. 'Kay, there's no credit on the photo of Brian.'

'What? I don't understand.'

'Every other news photograph has the photographer's name on it. The credit. Brian's doesn't.'

'Is that important?'

'I don't know, but why is it different? That might be important. Do you have any friends on the *Post*? I want to talk to the reporter who wrote the story.'

'I can make that happen.'

The reporter's name was Dan O'Malley. He agreed to meet Cassidy at a tavern in Foggy Bottom, but he did not sound happy about it. The tavern was a low brick building on a bank above the river. The barroom had big windows that looked out at the water. The bartender looked up from the Mickey Spillane paperback he was reading and pointed Cassidy toward his only customer, who leaned against the far end of the bar.

O'Malley was a big Irishman of middle age. His tweed jacket and charcoal flannel trousers were nearly as rumpled as his shirt. A well-used

205

fedora lay on the bar like an exhausted animal next to a nearly empty mug of beer and a pack of Chesterfields. He straightened as Cassidy approached, and held out his hand.

'Cassidy, I'm Dan O'Malley.' He was a few inches over six feet tall and more than a few pounds over two hundred, and his hand swallowed Cassidy's. 'What do they call you, Michael or Mike?'

'I'll answer to either.'

'Good on you. How about a beer?'

'Why not?'

'Tim,' O'Malley called to bartender, 'how about a couple of suds down here?' The bartender put down his book and went to rummage in a cooler. 'Michael Cassidy, New York cop, brother of Brian Cassidy of ABC and the recent nocturnal ramble.' He was a guy who had covered much of man's foolishness for the edification of people drinking their breakfast coffee, and his amusement shined through. 'Nephew of Kay Lockridge. That woman's got more juice in this town than Minute Maid. I get a call, Mr Phil Graham wonders if I have time to speak to him up in the publisher's office. That's a bit like the Pope wondering if the parish priest can spare him a minute over in the Vatican. So off I go to the *sanctum sanctorum*, and Mr Graham, with whom I've only exchanged a couple of words at a Christmas party a few years back, asks if it would be too much trouble for me to meet Michael Cassidy, New York cop. And here I am. He also suggested that maybe we'd hold off on a follow-up on the story on Mr Cassidy's wayward brother. That kind of chaps my ass, but it's his paper.'

The bartender slid Cassidy a mug and then punched a church key through the tops of two pale yellow cans of Old Georgetown beer and passed them over as the foam started from the holes. O'Malley poured his mug full, took a sip, wiped foam from his lip with his tweed sleeve, and sighed. 'Ahhh, that's good. Lots of things are going to shit, but that is good. What did you want to see me about?'

'The story on Brian – what happened, did the cops tip you?'

For a moment O'Malley weighed how to answer. 'I did speak to the cops.'

Cassidy's ear was tuned to the minor evasions of people being questioned. 'You talked to them after you knew there was a story.'

O'Malley took a long pull of beer and watched Cassidy with his bright and realistic eyes. 'They confirmed that they had brought your brother to the hospital. Drunk and disoriented. Naked too, which makes it a better story, what with the photo and all. He's a well-known man, and people love to see someone tumble from a height.'

'The photographer just happened to be driving by Rock Creek Park at midnight when my brother stumbled out of the bushes. And he recognized him in the dark and fortunately had his camera by his side.'

'Coincidences happen all the time. Some of them are news.'

'I'd like to speak to him.'

'The photographer? No.'

207

'Why not?'

'I can't identify a source to a cop.'

'What's he the source of?'

'The photograph, and he was eye witness to the arrest.'

'I'm not going to tell anyone.'

'The photographer would know. It would get around quick that I couldn't be trusted. Once that happens, I might as well get out of the news business and sell insurance, maybe drive a bus, because no one would talk to me in confidence anymore.'

'I get it. Reputation counts. How about this photographer? My guess is he's a freelancer.' From O'Malley's expression, he was right. 'Is he reliable?'

A hesitation. 'It's not quite the same as with a reporter. He's taking pictures. He's not trying to get behind the scenes. He's getting the front of the scenes, if you see what I mean. He doesn't need someone's trust. He just needs them to turn around. He makes his rep by how good his photos are.'

'He gets his credit on the photos so people know he shot them.'

'Right.'

'So why didn't he put a credit on this one?'

O'Malley stiffened. 'What?'

'He didn't put his name on the photograph. Why not?'

'Sure, he did.'

Cassidy took the photo he had torn from the paper out of his pocket and slid it across to O'Malley, who peered at it closely and said,

'Maybe the composing room forgot to put it on.'

'Sure. And he forgot to check if the photo made the paper, and he didn't care enough about the credit to call you and raise hell.'

O'Malley pushed the piece of paper aside. 'Okay. So what does that mean? It doesn't change the story.'

'Did this guy say he called the cops to come get Brian?'

'No. The cops were there before he got back in his car.'

'Do you know why?'

'Why?' Curiosity showing.

'Because they got an anonymous tip that there was a crazy drunk tearing it up at the park,' Cassidy said. 'The tipster told them exactly where Brian was.'

'And?'

'Someone set him up. Someone took him out there and dumped him. And someone called your photographer to document it.'

'Why?'

'I don't know. Maybe someone didn't like the story Brian was chasing.'

'What was the story?'

'I don't think I can tell you that. You guide me. If I knew of a story you were working on, would you want me to tell another reporter?'

'No.'

'I think the photographer was part of the setup. That's why he didn't take the credit. He didn't want anyone coming after him, and he figured he could trust you not to ID him to someone like me.'

209

'Could be. But there could have been other reasons he didn't take it.'

'Like what?'

O'Malley did not answer.

'I need to talk to him.' Cassidy drank beer while O'Malley thought about it.

'I can't do it. Even if you're right, it doesn't change what I can do. He's a source. If he didn't want his name on this, then I have to respect that.'

'Call him and ask him why he left his name off the photo.'

'Why would I do that?'

'Because you're a reporter. You're curious. It's part of the story, you just didn't know that when you wrote it.'

'You think I'm that easy?'

'Hell, yes. Reporters want to know what they missed.'

O'Malley put the mug down unfinished, and stood up. 'You're an asshole,' he said with a grin, and walked to the phone booth at the back of the room pulling change from his pocket. He closed the door and the light came on. He spread his change on the shelf below the phone, selected a dime, and called a number. Cassidy watched and drank his beer. The first call only lasted a few seconds. The next went longer. The third went on for a while, and the longer it went the more animated O'Malley became behind the glass. He slapped the receiver back into its cradle, crashed open the door, scooped up what remained of the change, and came back to the bar. He picked up his mug and finished it fast. 'He's not talking.'

'Why not?'

'He's scared.'

'Who's he scared of?'

'He's not talking about that.'

'You know him. You know the town. What's your best guess?'

O'Malley thought about it. 'Where are we?'

'DC.'

'Right. You know what DC's the center of?'

'Government.'

'Half right. Power. You know who power attracts?' He did not wait for an answer. 'Some good people, sure. But it also attracts a lot of nasty people. This guy we're talking about, he knows a lot of those nasty people.'

'Which ones?'

'I don't know for sure. Maybe all of them.'

'That's not much. Can't you give me anything more?'

'Nope.'

'Okay. Thanks. And thanks for the beer.'

'Whoa, whoa. You took me away from my daily search for truth. You're buying. And if anything comes of this, I'd like to hear about it.'

'I'll give you a call.' Cassidy shook hands with O'Malley and put five bucks on the bar. As he walked out, O'Malley was calling for another beer.

What had he learned? Kay's guess that someone was trying to screw with Brian's reputation fit with what O'Malley hinted at, that Brian had stumbled onto something people with power wanted to conceal. Brian was chasing a story on how money influenced voting in Congress. Kay said that was an old story, but that didn't mean today's players wanted it in the papers. It didn't seem like enough. There must be something he wasn't seeing.

Cassidy headed up the block for the corner in hopes of finding a cab. He was thinking about what O'Malley had told him, and barely noticed the boxy white GMC delivery van parked at the curb. The hood was up. A man leaned on the fender and reached in to fiddle with something on the engine.

Something about the man. A leather jacket.

Outside the Gallien Medical building on K Street?

He started to turn. The man in the leather jacket slammed into him from behind. Another man charged him from the mouth of the alley opposite. The big man wrapped him up, pinning his arms, and then leaned back, lifting Cassidy's feet off the ground so he had no traction. The smaller one bent to make a grab for his legs. Cassidy kicked him in the neck hard enough to drive him back. He jerked his head back into the bigger man's face and drew a grunt of surprise and pain, but the man did not loosen his grip. Cassidy lunged backward and rammed him into the side of a van. The metal side boomed like a gong. The man grunted at the impact. His grip loosened, Cassidy broke free, stumbled, and went down on one knee. The big man tried to kick him in the stomach. Cassidy leaned away from the kick. He got a hand under the man's heel, and used the kick's momentum to drive his leg high. The man's other leg flew out from under him, and he went down on his back. His head cracked against the sidewalk. The back doors of the van flew open, and another man jumped out. The one Cassidy had kicked was on his feet now, and as Cassidy tried to get up, the two men swarmed him and dragged him into the back of the van where a third man waited.

'Get it into him. Get it into him!' one of them yelled.

The man in the van fumbled a hypodermic needle out of a hard leather case as the two other men tried to wrestle Cassidy to the floor.

'Hold him. Hold him, goddamn it.' He jabbed the hypodermic toward Cassidy's exposed neck. Cassidy stamped a foot against the wall of the van and drove himself and the two men holding him against the opposite wall. He heard the breath rush out of one of them. It smelled of garlic and peppermint.

'Hold the fucker. Goddamn it, keep him still.'

The needle scared him. What the hell was in the hypodermic? Nothing good. An elbow came out of nowhere and hit him on the temple, and for a moment his world went gray. His legs buckled, and the man in front of him took the opportunity to pin them. He tried for another head butt on the man behind, but he ducked away and punched Cassidy in the kidneys. Cassidy bladed his fingers and stabbed back over his shoulder, searching for eyes, but the man saw it and turned his head, and Cassidy's nails ripped his cheek.

The man behind tried for a chokehold, but Cassidy tucked his chin down tight, and the man's arm barred across his face, mashing his lips into his teeth.

'Hold his legs still. I'm going there. Hold them.' The needle man came in at a crouch, the hypodermic held like a dagger, with his thumb on the plunger. Staying back as far as he could, he reached out with his free hand and touched Cassidy's thigh, feeling for the spot he wanted. 'Hold him. Here we go.'

Cassidy opened his mouth wide, and the arm barred across it went in, giving him a taste of cloth, the slickness of nylon sleeve. Cassidy bit down as hard as he could and felt the radius bone break under his teeth. The man screamed and jerked his arm out and went to his knees behind Cassidy. The hypodermic holder drove the needle toward Cassidy's thigh. Cassidy got his left hand out. The point of the needle entered his palm and went out the back. The man thumbed the plunger, and a spray of clear liquid blew from the end. Cassidy jerked the needle out and backhanded the man breaking his nose. The man fell backward. Cassidy grabbed the man on his legs by the throat with his wounded hand and hit him twice in the face. The man rolled off his legs, and Cassidy dragged his gun from under his arm and hit him with the barrel, and the man sagged back against the van wall.

He kicked the back doors open and slid out onto the street. The big guy who had hit his head was on all fours trying to get up. He reached a tentative hand for Cassidy's ankle, and Cassidy bent and swatted him with the gun, and he collapsed on his side.

Two men and a woman walking past took a wide path around them, looking at them wide-eyed. One of the men said, 'Hey, what's going on here,' in an uncertain voice.

'Nothing,' Cassidy said. 'Just one of those family disagreements.'

They kept going, looking back over their shoulders every once in a while. He could hear the woman's voice raised in protest and knew they would call the cops from the first pay phone they found. He didn't have time for the cops. He took a moment to search the downed man's pockets. He found twelve dollars in bills and some change, a key ring with three keys, a ballpoint pen, and two mints wrapped in foil. No wallet. No ID. He suspected that the men in the van would be just as anonymous. The two men and the woman went into the bar. Looking for a phone. Time to go.

A couple of blocks later the world began to turn weird.

The red of the traffic light that held Cassidy at the curb oozed from its lens and ran down the pole. The pole undulated and then went rigid again. Cassidy felt tightness in his chest and a strange alertness. His senses fired hard: the smell of diesel from a passing bus was thick and oily, the rub of tires on the pavement sandpapered his ears, a pigeon flying in slow motion overhead revealed every feather and a bright dark eye, the click of heels on the pavement as the people around him surged across the street was the rattle of a snare drum while he stood rooted, unable to move his feet. He looked down at his

215

left hand and saw the angry red spot where the needle stabbed. He turned his hand over. The exit was a bead of dried blood. The veins on the back of his hand were blue, thick with blood, and when he flexed his hand, they writhed like snakes under the skin and little bursts of color flew from his fingertips like drops of light.

What the hell? The needle driven through his palm, the spray of liquid on his pants as the thumb drove the plunger. Some of that shit was in his blood. What was it? Was it killing him? Were they still coming after him? Were they here already?

He whirled around. People on the sidewalk looked at him curiously. Some of them shied away.

A police siren rose in the distance. *Get away from here. Move. Move.*

The light changed again, and he crossed the street feeling as if he was walking through chest-deep water. Two blocks later he came to a small park dense with trees. He followed a curving path into the middle of the park and found a bench in a turnout that was nearly hidden by the bushes around it. He sat down on the bench and tried to slow his breathing.

It's going to be okay. This will pass. There's not much in you. It just needs time. Breathe – in – out – in – out. He looked at his watch. Was the second hand moving at all? He shook his wrist and looked again. Had it moved? Breathe. For a moment he stood outside himself and watched himself sitting on the bench, head down, hands on his knees, and then he was back inside,

216

watching the ants that went busily about their business in the dirt at his feet. He could see into their world. The cracks in the pavement were canyons; the grains they carried were as big as boulders.

A uniformed cop went by walking fast. He did not look through the narrow gap in the bushes to where Cassidy sat, but if he knew the place, he might be back to check it. Time to move again.

Cassidy wandered without direction to the Mall and into the protective herd of tourists who thronged there, and then up past the Smithsonian, and toward the White House. The cops would be thick on the ground there, so he turned away. He walked side streets and stopped at a small diner with no other customers. The counterman brought him a cup of coffee and went back to his conversation with the cook through the service window. In an hour his head had cleared of everything but a lingering sense of dread.

Who tried to take him? What did they want? What was in the hypodermic? The man in the leather jacket had been outside Gallien's office. Had they picked him up there, or had they followed him from the Congressional Office Building? Or from Aunt Kay's? They had to be the same crew that snatched Brian. But why had they come after him? Brian was working a story about money in DC. It had nothing to do with anything Cassidy was working on.

He hailed a cab to take him back to the hospital. He thought about Brian's missing hours from when he left Congressman Martin's office until

217

he was picked up at Rock Creek Park. Where had he been? Who had he seen and talked to? The key to what happened was in that blank space of time. When Brian woke up, they would reconstruct his day, and then Cassidy would take it from there.

Eighteen

When Brian woke up, he remembered almost nothing of the day before. He vaguely remembered the meeting with Harry Gallien, but the details were gone. He remembered being at Congressman Williams's office but nothing of what was said there. He did not know where he went after he left Gallien's office. 'But a lot of that stuff will be in my notes.'

When Cassidy told him there were no notes, no clothes, that he had been found naked and disoriented, Brian looked at him without comprehension and then lay back on the pillows and closed his eyes. 'Tell me.'

He told him what he knew.

'Naked? I was naked? Jesus, what happened to my clothes? My notebook, everything is in my notebook.' His eyes opened for a moment and then closed again, and his face twisted with pain and embarrassment. 'What happened to me?'

'You were set up.' Cassidy told him about the photographer's refusal of credit in the paper and Cassidy's meeting with O'Malley.

218

Brian opened his eyes. 'He was right. He couldn't give up a source.'

'The photographer was part of the setup.'

'Still, O'Malley couldn't give him up. I have to know who they were. We have to find them. I have to know what happened.' His voice was full of pain.

'We will,' Cassidy said, and wondered if he believed it himself.

Brian called Marcy, and Cassidy left the room to give them privacy. He called Sam Watkins at the DCPD from a booth near the elevators, but Watkins had nothing new to report. Dispatch had gotten an anonymous call reporting a crazy man at Rock Creek Park. The patrol car was in the neighborhood. They hadn't seen anyone but Brian.

Kay brought clothes from the house, and over the doctor's protest, they checked Brian out of the hospital. Kay insisted they use her car and driver. They dropped her at her office near the Hill, but they did not go home. Instead they drove to the Congressional Office Building. Brian and Cassidy got out of the car and went up the steps to the front door. They turned and walked down the steps, duplicating Brian's departure from Williams's office. Brian stopped at the bottom.

'Where did you go from here?' Cassidy asked.

'I don't know.'

'Can you remember if you turned right or left?'

Brian looked first one way, then the other. 'I don't know. Left? Maybe. No. Right? Jesus, Mike, I don't know. Maybe right.' He sounded lost and scared.

'It was lunch time when you left. Maybe you went someplace to eat.'

'But where?'

The driver took them past the restaurants nearest to the Congressional Office Building. It was mid-afternoon and the day was warm and bright, and the sidewalks were crowded with people enjoying the weather. Brian stared out the window. Every time they passed a restaurant he leaned toward the window in hope. Sometimes he asked the driver to slow down as he examined the front of a building, and then he would shake his head, and they would go on. Once he put his hand on Cassidy's arm and squeezed, and Cassidy said, 'Hold on,' and the driver stopped the car opposite a French bistro. Brian relaxed his grip on Cassidy's arm. 'No. No. I was there a couple of months ago for lunch with Aunt Kay.'

'Are you sure? We can go in and see.'

'No. No. It's no fucking good. It's like something just wiped part of my brain clean.' He slapped the door in frustration.

'It's okay,' Cassidy said. 'It'll come back. The doctor said it'll come back.'

'The doctor said it *might* come back. *Might.*'

Cassidy asked the driver to take them to Rock Creek Park. He smoked cigarettes and left Brian to his troubled silence until they got there.

The driver pulled over at the intersection of Broad Branch Road and Ridge Road where a stone bridge crossed Broad Branch stream, a narrow rill of thin autumn water over mossy stones. The breeze kicked up dry fallen leaves and swirled them across the pavement.

220

Brian stood uncertainly on the bridge. 'This is where I was?'

'According to the police report, you were against that stand of trees by the side of the road. The photo pretty much shows that, which means you didn't move much between when the guy took the shot and when the cops arrived. Do you want to see it?'

'No. Maybe later. I'm not ready for that. Jesus.'

'Whenever you want.'

Brian turned a full circle to take in the landscape, the leafless trees stark against the bright sky, the underbrush, the stone walls of the bridge, the shallow stream, the road with its few passing cars.

'Anything?'

'No.' He turned again. 'Maybe if I took off all my clothes.'

Cassidy saw the hint of a smile tug his brother's mouth and thought, *Thank god, he's coming back.* But Brian's expression turned bleak again. 'If I had to swear, I'd swear I was never here before. No inkling. No hint.' He blew out a breath in frustration. 'Why here?'

'At that time of night there's very little traffic, so whoever brought you could pull across the bridge and no one on the main road would know they were there. They had to get you out of your clothes. They wouldn't have chanced driving here with you naked, unless you were in the trunk. But even if you were, they still had to get you out and set up for the photographer. They needed privacy.'

'And the setting makes it look worse somehow,

221

doesn't it, wilder, more out of control? The trees, the bushes, the fucking wild man of Borneo . . . Let's get out of here.'

'He doesn't know anything. The whole thing looks like a coincidence,' Spencer Shaw said.

'I don't like coincidences. I don't believe in them.' Allen Dulles dug around in his pipe bowl with the blade of a small silver pocket-knife and tapped the char out into an ashtray. 'Coincidences are for people who don't have the imagination for a complex understanding of events.' He looked at Shaw over his wire-rimmed glasses to see if he got the point. It was the same look Shaw's father used to give him when once again he failed to measure up.

Shaw had been summoned to meet Allen Dulles at the Alibi Club on I Street. The club was housed in a shabby three-story building a few blocks from the White House and was so secretive and exclusive that few knew about it, and those who did could not decide which of the two buildings was the seat of Washington power. Presidents came and went, but the fifty members of the Alibi were there until death.

They were in the dining room on the first floor, a room that might have been lifted from a tavern in the mid-1800s. Shaw had been led there by a thin, gray, silent servant, who seemed to have no more substance than a ghost and who had disappeared without a word through a door at the back of the room to be heard no more. A table that could seat thirty crowded the room. The walls were covered with photographs of

222

club members from the last seventy years, oil paintings and water colors (some good, some very bad), a few stuffed heads of dead animals with staring glass eyes, propaganda posters from both world wars, and framed letters from Presidents, princes, and foreign dignitaries. Shaw had time to examine them while Dulles kept him waiting half an hour, a wait that was meant to remind him of his place. In mild defiance, Shaw made himself a large scotch on the rocks from the bar table in a corner. Dulles raised his eyes at the liberty when he came in, but said nothing.

Shaw took a long pull on the drink and waited for Dulles to go on.

'What've you got?,' Dulles asked. He tamped tobacco into the pipe with his thumb and lit it.

Shaw opened a small notebook. 'The snatch team tagged him from Gallien Medical on K Street to Williams's office on the Hill. They picked him up in a removal van after his meeting there. No muss, no fuss. They were at the safe house twenty minutes later.' He looked up from the notebook. 'Do you want to hear about dosages?' It was always safer to omit nothing without permission.

'Just the results and conclusions.' Dulles went to the bar and made himself a drink.

Shaw glanced at the notes, though he knew what was written there. 'The doctors conclude that Brian Cassidy knows nothing of the operation. His interest in Gallien was caused only by Congressman Williams returning Gallien's campaign contribution. He is doing a segment on his television program on the influence of

223

money on the legislative process. Williams is the only Congressman he could find who rejected a contribution. Brian Cassidy has no interest and no understanding of anything that Gallien Medical does.'

'They're sure?'

'Yes. Actually, they were quite excited. They feel that Brian Cassidy's willingness to openly answer any question they asked was a breakthrough.'

'What will he remember?'

'Nothing. A brain wipe. That day's gone from his memory as if they'd used a scalpel. It was my idea to dump him out by Rock Creek naked and stinking of booze. Nobody's going to believe a word the guy says after that no matter what.'

'And the doctors are sure they got everything?'

'Positive.'

Dulles looked at him without expression. 'What happened with the brother, the cop?'

Shit. 'The snatch team fucked it up. The guy was good. We didn't know how good. Four guys, and they couldn't take him. Lorburg's got a concussion. Sanchez has a broken arm. The fucking cop bit through his arm bone.'

'What does he know?'

'According to his brother, nothing. He wasn't sure Williger was a suicide, but the cops have closed the case. It's over. He knows nothing about the operation.'

Dulles studied him while he thought about it. 'All right.' Dulles swallowed the rest of his drink, put the glass on the bar, and left the room.

You're welcome. Any time. Glad to be of

service. What a prick. Shaw finished his drink and looked around the room to see if there was something worth stealing, a little trophy, a little screw you. He put the bottle of scotch in his pocket and left the club.

Kay Lockridge's car delivered Brian and Cassidy to Union station in the late morning over her protests that Brian needed more rest, and they caught the noon train for New York. Brian spent the ride leaning against the window and staring out blankly. A spark in him had been stamped out, and Cassidy wondered if it would ever reignite. Whatever had happened to him had cracked his understanding of who he was. He was sinking.

Marcy met them at Penn Station. She offered Cassidy a brave smile and hugged Brian tight. He kissed the top of her head, and they walked through the great, echoing marble lobby with their arms around each other. Cassidy turned down their offer to join them at home for a late lunch, and put them in a cab. He walked down through the garment district for fifteen minutes to stretch his legs, and then waved down a taxi and went home.

The apartment was full of stale air and silence. His coffee cup and plate were still in the sink. There were no lipsticked cigarette butts in the ashtrays. The clothes he had left on the chair in the bedroom were as he had left them, and the bed was unmade, a laziness Rhonda rejected. She had not been here since he left. What did he expect?

He called the *New York Post*, but she was not at her desk, and no one had seen her in the last couple of hours. He tried her apartment, and left a message with the answering service that he was home.

Nineteen

Mid-afternoon, and the low angle of the sun turned the river silver. The Fulton Fish Market was not yet awake. The metal shutters were up on the fish stalls and shops where trucks maneuvered on the cobblestones to deliver ice. Gulls, bright white in the sunlight, flicked and swooped overhead or stood on wharf pilings and building roof peaks.

Rhonda, following directions, found the *Amy Lou*, a Grand Banks trawler tied up to a pier near the foot of the Brooklyn Bridge. She was a high-bowed, broad-beamed, wooden boat battered and scarred by wind and weather. The rails were splintered in places, and the cabin superstructure needed paint. Tires roped to the side as fenders squeaked and groaned with the rub against the pier.

Rhonda stepped through the open gate in the trawler's rail and was suddenly reminded that she lived at the edge of the living sea. She went from solid, unmoving pavement to a tar-seamed wooden deck that was alive under her feet from the river surge. She had to clutch the rail for

226

balance in her high heels. The air smelled of fish and salt. Nets lay in piles near the stern, and the trawl booms slatted and banged in the wind against the slack of their tie downs. Bill Long stepped out onto the bridge wing and called to her and pointed to a metal stairway that led to the bridge. She climbed it, hobbled by her skirt, annoyed and a little embarrassed that she felt so out of place.

'How are you?' Bill Long asked. 'You found me okay. That's great.' He sipped from a thick china mug of coffee. 'Do you want some coffee?'

'No, thanks, I'm fine.'

'Meet Jug Cousins. He owns the boat.' He waved his mug at a man standing just inside the bridge door.

'The bank and I own the boat.' He was a thick, powerful man in his mid-forties. He wore blue jeans tucked into rubber boots, a worn and stained canvas jacket over a plaid wool shirt, and a black wool watch cap. He had dark eyes, and a dense, closely cropped beard beginning to show strands of gray. He shook hands with Rhonda, and then nodded to Bill Long. 'I'll see you when you bring the truck for the fish.' He disappeared down an interior companionway.

'A good fisherman. It's in his blood. Fifth generation. He could find cod in a mud puddle.'

'You said you wanted to talk,' Rhonda said.

'Yep.' Long offered Rhonda a cigarette and lit one for himself when she refused. He leaned against the rail of the bridge wing while he sorted his thoughts. 'I've been thinking about what you said the other night, what we talked

227

about. The government bringing Nazis into New York City. What kind of country are we? I was in that war. They did really awful things to people. I mean, I get that we're at war with the Reds, but why do we need these guys? We've got the best scientific minds in the world. It's nuts. We don't need them. It's just wrong.' He sucked hard on his cigarette. 'I started thinking about it after that drink with you, started thinking about those guys who came and put pressure on my dad, came and threatened my brother's widow because of the story I wrote. He gave his life for this country, goddamn it, and they came and pushed her around. That is not who we are. That is not what Americans do.' He shook his head at the thought.

'Okay,' Rhonda said. Somewhere in the boat a clock struck the bells of the hour.

'I don't want to get you in trouble,' Long said. He flipped the dregs of his coffee from the mug overboard.

'No. There won't be any trouble.'

'I don't know. The guys who picked me up sure looked like trouble to me. I'll tell you flat out, Rhonda, they scared me. I mean, I was halfway out the door at the *Post* anyway. I don't know what I said to you the other night, but that's the truth. I was probably going to quit in a few months anyway, but they made it easier.' He flicked his cigarette away. His face twisted in disgust. 'I kind of hate to think they made me run. Anyway, I don't remember exactly the number of the house they took me to. I was pretty nervous in that car, not knowing what

228

was going to happen. But I'm pretty sure I remember the block.'

Long walked Rhonda to Water Street and hailed her a cab. He held the door while she got in. He started to close the door, and then stopped and leaned down so he could see her. 'Hey, uh, listen, I don't know, but would you like to have dinner or something one of these days?'

She hesitated for a moment. 'Yes. That would be nice.'

'Great. Great. Okay. I'll call you.' He grinned and shut the door and slapped the cab roof to send it on its way.

Bill Long could not remember the exact address of the house where he had been taken. He knew it was on West 4th Street north of Bank Street and south of Eighth Avenue, because when they let him go, he walked north to Eighth to find a cab. The house, he was sure, was brick, but that did not narrow Rhonda's search by much, because many of the houses on West 4th were brick. Some of them were well kept with window trim and doors shiny with new paint. Others showed crumbling stoops, peeling doors, bare wood beginning to crack and separate on windowsills, glazing chipping from the window mullions. Would a government agency maintain its house, or would it let things slide? What face would it offer the street to hide what went on inside?

Rhonda wore a large 'I LIKE IKE' button and a rosette that said *VOLUNTEER*, which she bought at a five-and-dime on Seventh Avenue.

She carried a clipboard of old Census Bureau forms and a yellow legal pad covered with indecipherable notes. A row of cheap fountain pens was clipped to the breast pocket of her overcoat next to the rosette. She had pulled her hair back in a severe bun and scrubbed her face clean of makeup. She was now a serious-minded volunteer for the Eisenhower Re-election Committee intent on getting out the vote. There were lights on in most of the houses on the street. People were home from work, preparing dinner, reading the evening paper, chivvying the children to do their homework. Some windows glowed with the blue light of a television. It was the time of day when people were, for the most part, relaxed, open to a few innocuous questions about the political campaign.

Rhonda began ringing doorbells at the corner of Bank and West 4th on the east side of the street, because Bill Long was sure the house they had taken him to was on that side. Sometimes the door was opened by the man of the house, sometimes by the woman, sometimes by a child. People were happy to answer her questions. Yes, they were going to vote for Ike. They thought he was doing a good job. Yes, they knew where their polling place was. Three houses were staunch Adlai Stevenson supporters. And at one an irascible old man with wild eyes and hair, and a prophet's beard told her he would never vote for that fascist bastard Eisenhower, he was voting for Eric Hass of the Socialist Labor Party, and she was to get the hell off his stoop.

She did not know exactly what she was looking

for, but she thought she would know it when she saw it: a house full of grim men in trench coats, maybe, and government-issued furniture. The thought made her smile. And what would she do if she found it? Fear clenched her chest for a moment. Well, keep one foot out the door, and get ready to run. No, don't be silly. She was an inoffensive volunteer for Ike. No one would give her a second thought.

Her feet hurt, and her face felt stiff from smiling, and she was beginning to resign herself to the fact that whatever house Long had been in was no longer used by the men who took him. She had probably already been in it, the door opened by a boy in a red flannel bathrobe, or a woman in a house dress, the men and their secrets long gone.

She stepped out into the street and counted the houses up the block. Six to go. And then what if nothing shows up? Another dead end.

She straightened her coat, tugged her hair tight, put on her volunteer face, and climbed the stoop to the sixth house in from the corner.

Karl Brandt unwound the bandage from Maxie's finger and exposed the ragged, bitten wound. She sucked in her breath as the last piece of gauze pulled off. 'It hurts.'

Brandt turned her hand to the light that hung over the kitchen table at the back of the safe house. 'Of course it hurts,' Brandt said. 'When the body is insulted like this, there is always pain. But it looks much better. You are well on your way to health now.' He smiled encouragingly,

231

but at the same time he saw Magda's pursed lips and the small shake of her head. She had seen what he had seen: the wound was an angry color, pus leaked from under the partial scab, and a red line of infection ran up the back of Maxie's hand. The finger needed to be properly treated, and they did not have the facilities for that. She needed a hospital.

'I think I should go see a doctor,' Maxie said.

Brandt smiled and patted her good hand. 'Maxie, Magda and I are doctors. We are doing what any doctor would do. If you go to someone else there will be questions. Questions and explanations. This would not be good.'

Spencer Shaw leaned against the wall near the sink smoking a cigarette and occasionally sipping his premixed martini. He watched the byplay at the table and said nothing. There was no reason to interfere as long as the doctors controlled the situation.

Maxie turned her hand in the light. 'It's infected, isn't it? I can tell. I'm not an idiot. It's infected, and someone has to do something.'

'Maxie,' Magda said, 'it may be a little infected, but we have a new antibiotic, tetracycline, which is stronger than the penicillin you have been taking, and we will start you on a course of that today. I'm quite sure this will take care of the problem.'

'I want to see a real doctor.'

Magda smiled through her annoyance. 'We are real doctors, I promise you. We will take care of you.'

Shaw stubbed out his cigarette. 'I think the best

232

thing is for you to stay here in the house until you're okay. The doctors can keep an eye on you, make sure everything's going right.'

'Bullshit. I'm not staying here with these creeps.'

'Maxie, don't be a pain in the ass. Do what you're told, and everything will work out fine.'

She heard the warning note in his voice, but she had enough courage left for one more protest. 'I want to go to a real hospital. They can come with me, but I want a real hospital.'

'Maxie, don't push it.' The knife in his voice made her look down at the table.

Magda patted her hand again in conciliation. 'Maxie, let's start with the tetracycline, and then we'll clean the wound again. You'll see, everything will be fine,' she lied.

The doorbell rang.

'Expecting anyone?' Shaw asked. The Brandts shook their heads. Maxie did not respond. 'I'll get it,' Shaw said, and left the room carrying his glass.

Rhonda heard footsteps approaching the door. A safety chain rattled off, and a lock clicked, and the door opened and a man stood in the gap. He was about six feet tall and had hair the color of straw and eyebrows that were nearly red. He carried a martini glass and looked at her with the casual cheer of a man who has decided the world is a comedy. 'Hello, hello,' he said. 'Honey, whatever you're selling, I'm buying.'

She offered a slight smile. 'I'm selling Dwight D. Eisenhower for President in November.'

'And I'm buying. I like Ike.'

She looked down at her clipboard as if to check the questions she was supposed to ask. 'How many other voters are there in the house?'

'I'm the only one.' He took a sip of his martini.

She wrote something on the yellow pad. 'Are you the owner of the house?'

'No. I rent.' He took another sip of the martini while watching her over the rim of the glass. She looked up in time to see something change in his eyes. When he took the glass away, his smile was wider. 'How about a drink? I make a great martini, and as much as you like Ike, it's got to be pretty goddamn dull work volunteering. You need a pick me up.'

The cop's girlfriend. Cassidy's goddamn girlfriend. She was with him the other night when I followed them home. What the hell is she doing here?

'No, thanks. I can't, really. I'm not allowed.' A smile of apology. 'How long have you lived here?'

'A couple of years.'

She doesn't know who I am. Or she's awfully good and isn't showing it. What the hell is she doing here? What's she after? Did the cop send her? How did he know about the place? Is she a cop? No. The NYPD doesn't hire women who look like this. Get her inside. Give her some of the stuff. Ask her.

'Look, I know you've got more questions, why don't you come inside so I can shut the door and keep the cold out and the warmth in. Otherwise I vote for Stevenson.' He offered a hand.

'All right. I do have a few more questions.' It would be good to get out of the cold for a moment, and then on to the last five houses. She stepped in, and Spencer Shaw closed the door behind her. She checked her list. 'Do you think that Ike was right to keep Richard Nixon as his vice-president?'

'Tricky Dick? I don't know. He could have done worse, I guess. Could've done better. What do you think?'

She shook her head and ticked off the question. 'What is the most important problem Ike faces in the second term?' There was almost no furniture in the parlor off the hall. What there was looked shabby and mismatched as if it had been put there as stage dressing.

'The Reds. No question. Let me get you that drink.'

There was something dark under his smiling, genial exterior. Suddenly she felt hemmed in by the shadowed hall. Rhonda took a half-step back, smiling to soften any offense. 'I really can't. I've got blocks to go still. But thanks.' She heard voices coming from somewhere at the back of the house. But he had said he was alone.

'Stick around. One drink.'

'I really do have to go.' She opened the door. He put his hand on it to stop it from opening wide.

'One drink. What's the harm?'

'I don't want a drink.' She pulled at the door, but he held it so she could not move it.

'Please.'

'I think you should stay.' He took her arm and

235

pulled her away from the door. She tried to jerk away, but he was too strong. 'Let me go.'

'Yeah, sure. In a minute.'

Fear made her heart stumble. She swung the clipboard at his head. He blocked it easily. 'Come on, honey, don't do that. It's going to be okay. I just have a few questions to ask you.' He dragged her further from the door. She fought him, but he was too strong. She hit him with the clipboard again. 'You bitch. Cut it out.' He slapped her hard. Her sight dimmed, and her head rang.

Somewhere at the back of the house a piece of furniture crashed. It was followed by a man's shout of alarm and a woman's cry of anger. Shaw turned in time to see Maxie burst out of the back hall. Her wounded hand trailed gauze like a pennant. Shaw released Rhonda and turned with his arms spread to stop her.

Rhonda kicked Shaw in the back of his left knee. The leg crumpled, and as he lurched to one side, the girl with the half-bandaged hand cannoned into him, and they both crashed against the wall and went down in a tangle with girl on top. She tried to crawl over him, but he grabbed her by the leg. She yelled and kicked, but she could not get loose.

Rhonda threw a look at the door, at escape. But she couldn't leave the girl. She ran back down the hall and took the girl's hand to pull her free. The girl screamed and pulled her wounded hand away, and Shaw yanked her back and put a hand on her chest to push himself up. Rhonda ran. She jerked open the front door and half fell, half jumped down the steps. She caught a heel and went down on the sidewalk, ripping a stocking and skinning her knee. She pulled herself up by the wrought-iron fence at the base of the stoop and took off in a hobbling, high-heeled run, sure that the man would be after her. At the corner, she had the courage to look back. The man limped out the front door and stood at the top of the stoop looking for her. She flattened herself in a doorway, and after a moment, the man turned and went back inside and closed the door.

Rhonda hurried east on Jane Street and north on Greenwich Avenue to put distance between herself and the house on West 4th. Every time she looked back, she expected to see the man with the straw-colored hair, but he was never there. She finally made herself stop at a phone booth at Jackson Square Park. She looked up the number of the police station on Charles Street, but the phone was busy. She hung up and waited while she counted to thirty. She tried again. Busy. Again. Busy. Again. Busy. She had to do something. The woman in the house was in trouble. She looked for a cab, but every one she saw had fares.

It took ten minutes walking fast to get to the Ninth Precinct station house. She went in through the big, stone-columned doorway looking for help.

She found chaos.

A man in the rough work clothes of a long-shoreman lay groaning in pain on the tile floor while a uniformed cop tried to staunch the bleeding wound in his side using a handful of toilet paper as a compress. The desk sergeant

237

shouted into a phone for ambulances, and five cops carrying shotguns stampeded past Rhonda and out the door. Cops behind a partially shut door to a back room shouted to each other the way men do in crisis.

Rhonda pushed her way to the desk, but the desk sergeant waved her away as he yelled into the phone, 'We've got two cops down, and the fucker's barricaded himself in the storeroom. Send me everybody you've got.'

Rhonda tried again.

'Beat it, lady,' the sergeant barked. 'I don't have time.'

A gray-haired uniformed cop took her arm and, not unkindly, moved her away from the desk. 'Miss, you're going to have to come back later. There's been a shooting at a bar over on Washington. We've got a couple of officers hurt, and the man's locked himself in with a gun and some hostages.' The cop led her toward the door. He had a drinker's belly, broken veins in his cheeks and nose, and the sad eyes of a man disappointed by life.

Rhonda stopped and pulled free of his weak grasp. 'A man in a house on West Fourth tried to kidnap me. And he already had another woman in the house, and she's hurt.'

'Uh-huh. Well, that's not good.' He looked around at the chaos. 'Why don't we find a place where you can sit down, and I'll get you a pad, and you can write it all down?'

'Sure. Great. I'll write it. You'll read it and then pass it off to someone else to read, and by that time that woman might be dead.'

He held up a hand in protest. 'Look, lady, you don't understand, we've got a situation here. I can't be running off. Somebody's got to be here in case something comes up.'

'Something has come up. I'm the something. Don't you get it? Someone tried to drag me into a house by force. He already had a woman in there, and she is hurt. What more do you need?'

'Have we got a problem, here?' A man in a tan gabardine coat and a fedora had stopped near them. The shiny skin of a burn scar covered his left cheek and chin and pulled that corner of his mouth up in a permanent crooked smile.

'Lieutenant, this lady's reporting a guy who she said tried to attack her over on West Fourth. She says he may have another gal in the house and she may be hurt.'

'He did attack me, and he does have another woman in the house, and she is hurt. I was lucky to get away.' She raised her skirt enough so the lieutenant could see her skinned knee. He looked from her to the gray-haired cop.

'We're just trying to figure out what's best to do,' the older man said.

'Best go take a look, don't you think, Seeley?' The lieutenant's voice was mild, but the command was unmistakable.

'Yes, sir,' relieved that someone else had made a decision.

The lieutenant touched his hat brim with a forefinger and went out the door with two men in shirtsleeves carrying fire axes.

Rhonda said, 'Let's go,' to Seeley, and left without waiting to see if he followed. Her knee

239

had begun to stiffen, but she walked fast, and after a couple of blocks she could hear Seeley puffing to keep up.

'Jesus, lady, take it easy. Let me catch my breath for a second.' He stopped and bent over with his hands on his knees. 'I'm eleven days away from thirty years in, eleven days from my retirement, and you're going to kill me.'

'That girl in the house may already be dead.'

'So what good is it going to do her if I'm dead out here?'

Rhonda checked her impatience. 'All right. Tell me when.'

When his breath slowed, he nodded to her and they set off again. Rhonda slowed her pace, but he was half a block behind when she stopped at the bottom of the stoop of the house on West Fourth. The windows of the front rooms were dark, and no lights showed in the higher floors of the house. The carriage lights on either side of the door were unlit. Seeley arrived, puffing, and stood with her at the bottom of the stoop.

'It don't look like anyone's home,' he said. 'No lights.'

'They might be in the rooms at the back.'

'Waiting for the cops to arrive?' He saw her look, and held up a hand and said, 'Okay, okay. I'll go see. You hang back.'

He trudged up the steps to the front door. After a moment, Rhonda followed. Seeley looked over at her for a moment but said nothing. He loosened the gun in his holster and then took a deep breath and stabbed the bell push with a thick finger. A bell bonged somewhere deep in the house. They waited. No footsteps approached down the hall. Seeley stabbed the bell again. No one came to the door.

Seeley, relieved, said, 'Okay, then, no one here,' and moved for the stairs. Rhonda reached over and turned the doorknob, and the door swung open to the dark front hall. Seeley hesitated for a moment until the demand of the open door became clear, then he drew his gun.

The gun in his hand changed something in him, recalled who he had been at some younger moment when the uniform had fit. With one arm he barred Rhonda from going in, pushed open the door with his foot, and followed the gun into the house. Traffic noise from Eighth Avenue came to her: a bus wheezed to a stop at a corner, horns blared, a car door slammed, a loose manhole cover banged up and down as a car rolled over it. A car passed behind her on West Fourth, the radio playing through an open window.

The hall light clicked on. Through the open door she could see Seeley pressed against the wall at the base of the stairs, his gun pointed down the hall toward the back of the house. He waved her back when she stepped through the door, but she ignored him. He slapped a hand at her, urging her to get out, but she did not retreat. He shook his head and went down the narrow hall toward the kitchen with his gun out in front.

She waited where she was. Her heart tripped in her chest, and she found it hard to get full breaths. She strained for sounds from in the house. Was there anyone upstairs? Where was

241

Seeley? All she could hear were city noises through the open door. Should she close it? She looked out to the lighted houses across the street, to life going on normally and knew she did not have the courage to shut herself away from that. Where was Seeley?

A metallic crash at the back of the house was followed by a curse. Footsteps started toward her. She edged toward the open door. A light came on down the hall, and Seeley appeared holstering his gun. 'Nobody back there. I think they've gone.'

'What happened? I heard something fall.'

'I knocked a pot off the stove in the dark.'

'What about upstairs?'

'There's a phone in the kitchen. I'm going to call the stationhouse and see if they've got anyone to send for backup. I don't think there's anyone up there, but I'm not going up those stairs alone.'

She followed him back toward the kitchen. A ball of bloody gauze lay against the baseboard. 'That's from the woman I saw,' Rhonda said. 'There was something wrong with her hand. It was bleeding.'

Seeley picked up the phone on the wall near the kitchen door and dialed. Rhonda surveyed the kitchen. The pot Seeley had hit lay on the floor near the stove. There were a few glasses and plates on shelves above the sink, and an empty bottle of wine on the counter. The sink held four dirty glasses. She opened the refrigerator and found a piece of cheese wrapped in waxed paper, a partial bottle of milk, and some bottles of

Coca-Cola. The freezer held two ice trays and a bottle of Gilbey's gin. No one lived here. They camped out.

'Seeley, here. I'm at that house the woman said someone tried to grab her.' He shifted the phone to his other hand. 'Yeah, she's with me. No, so far nobody, but I only cleared the first floor. There are a couple more floors, but I'm going to need some backup.' He listened. 'Yeah, fine. I'll hold tight.' He hung up the phone. 'They're sending a couple of guys over. We'll wait for them.'

Detective Osgood was a stocky, balding man whose maroon wool suit pants showed below the hem of a gray tweed overcoat. When he took off his fedora he revealed an iron-gray brush-cut and ears that stuck out like side-view mirrors. Seeley introduced him to Rhonda and told him about her encounter with the blond man and the woman with the wounded hand. He gave her a brief handshake and a sour look. The patrolman with him was a beefy blond kid with bright blue eyes who looked like he had wandered in off the farm. His name was Warshak, and he greeted Rhonda with a bashful bob of his head.

'Okay, lady,' Osgood said, 'you stay down here while we check out the rest of the joint.'

'Not a chance,' Rhonda said. 'I'm going with you.' She held up a hand to stop Osgood's protest. 'What am I supposed to do if they come back, scream girlishly and hope one of you gets down here before someone slits my throat? I'll stay back. I won't touch anything. I won't speak. But I'm not staying down here alone.' She was

243

scared, but more than that she wanted to see the rest of the house. She wanted to know what went on here, and she could not know that standing in the front hall.

Osgood thought about it for a moment and then nodded. 'Okay, but if one of us tells you to do something, do it fast.'

Osgood found the stairwell light switch. The three men unholstered their guns. Osgood nodded and led them up the stairs. Warshak followed. Seeley went third, and Rhonda trailed. The beds in the three bedrooms on the second floor had been used. The beds were unmade. The ashtrays on the bedside tables were full of butts. In one room there was a dark red lipstick on some of the butts, in another the lipstick was a paler shade.

'Two different women,' Rhonda said. Osgood nodded and led them to the third floor. The three doors off the hall were open. One led to a bathroom. Osgood gestured to Warshak who reached in with one hand and turned on the light and then poked his head and gun into the room. He retreated a moment later shaking his head. Seeley cleared another room.

'You want to stay out here, Miss,' Osgood said. He led the men into the back bedroom. Rhonda stood back from the door and watched.

The big bed was a wreckage of sheets and pillow, and a red bedspread was crumpled on the floor. There were two cheap easy chairs with a table between them. Sheer white curtains were drawn across the windows whose panes were painted black.

Osgood crouched down to inspect the rug near the windows. 'Blood over here.'

Rhonda started to enter, but Seeley held up a hand to stop her. 'Uh-uh. Crime scene.' She retreated to the hall.

'More over here,' Warshak said. He was bent over in a corner of the room. Rhonda glanced at the door to the other room and wondered what Seeley might have missed with his cursory inspection. She pushed open the door, turned on the light, and went in.

Osgood led the two uniformed cops out into the hall. 'Where'd the broad go?' he asked.

'I'm right here,' Rhonda said from the doorway of the other room. 'You might want to take a look at this.' She stepped aside and the men crowded past her.

'Oh, yeah,' Osgood said when he saw the one-way window into the big bedroom. He moved in for a closer look. He shook his head. 'Yeah, okay. That's what's what.'

'What?' Rhonda asked.

'A cathouse,' Osgood said. 'You know, like prostitutes.'

'I know what a cathouse is,' Rhonda said.

'Some guys like to watch,' Seeley said and then coughed to cover his embarrassment.

'You're lucky you got out, lady,' Osgood said. 'You could've ended up in a bad situation here. These guys'll take a woman, feed her drugs till she's addicted, then turn her out to make money.'

'What happens next?' Rhonda asked.

'We'll turn it over to Vice. They'll try to track

who owns the joint, who rented it. They'll check their snitches. Maybe they'll get lucky.'

'You don't sound very confident.'

Osgood shrugged. 'It is what it is. People who run these places, they know how to move fast and how to cover their tracks. Chances are they'll be back in business by next week, if not sooner.'

'What about the woman? She was trying to get out.'

'Yeah. Well, good luck to her.'

'That's it?' She could not keep the anger from her voice.

'Hey, we'll do our best, but what are we going to do? They're gone. She went with them. You come back to the house and we'll take descriptions, get a sketch artist in. Maybe someone in Vice will recognize them.' He did not sound hopeful.

Twenty

Cassidy had breakfast at a brand new diner on Eighth. It was a Buck Rogers dream of curved aluminum, big, slanted windows, Formica-topped tables in weird shapes, and waitresses in high-waisted slacks, ruffled white shirts with black bowties, and funny little hats that looked like fezzes. To pay for all that the joint charged an exorbitant buck twenty-five for a plate of ham and eggs, toast and potatoes, but they threw in the coffee for free.

246

The front page of the *Post* was taken up with the shooting at a bar on the waterfront. Witnesses reported that an argument about football became a shoving match, a fistfight, and then gunplay. The shooter barricaded himself in the men's room. The cops were called to talk the guy out. The shooter fired shots through the door. The cops broke down the door and shot him sixteen times. Cassidy figured the cops got bored with talk that was getting them nowhere and were pissed off at the shots through the door. The thing ended the way it was headed the moment the gun came out of the guy's pocket to support his point that Charlie Conerly was too old to be playing quarterback for the New York Giants.

On page eight, Cassidy found a story under Rhonda's byline describing the house on West Fourth, the attempt by the man to keep her there, the young woman with the wounded hand who tried to flee, and Rhonda's return to the house with cops from the Ninth, the same precinct that was involved with the shooting at the bar. A busy day for the Ninth. She wrote about the search of the house and the discovery of the viewing room next to the upstairs bedroom, and the cop's conclusion that the place had been used as a whorehouse. A good story, concisely written with just enough flare and color to pop it up above the rest of the gray prose on the page.

Orso was in the squad room when Cassidy arrived. He had his elbows on his desk, and his hands supported his head as he pored over a book open in front of him.

247

'What are you reading?' Cassidy asked.

Orso shut the book with a look of relief and shoved it in a desk drawer. 'Physics.'

'What?'

'I don't know anything about physics. I can't talk to Amy about what she does.'

'Oh, boy.'

'Yeah, I know. I know. But what am I going to do? I'm that far gone. I went over to the high school yesterday and found my old science teacher, Mr Root. He gave me the book. Basic physics text. I thought he'd laugh his ass off, but he just gave me the book and patted me on the shoulder, and said he admired me. Fucking guy never gave me higher than a C minus when I was in his class.'

The phone rang on Cassidy's desk. Nothing much good ever came through that phone. He let it go while he lit a cigarette and picked it up on the fourth ring. 'Cassidy.'

'Al Skinner, Mike. I've got another one of those guys with that stuff in him.'

'What guy? What stuff?'

'The guy who went out the window over at the Astor. He had stuff in him. You didn't read the report?'

'What report?'

'I sent it over, what? A week ago, ten days ago at least.'

'I was on night watch. Night watch screws everything up. Let me see if someone put it in my desk. Hold on.' He put the phone down and went through the drawers in his desk and found a manila envelope with his name on the front in

248

Skinner's scrawl. 'I got it. What am I looking for?'

'Second page, down near the bottom. A note after the toxicology report.'

Cassidy ran his finger down the page. 'Okay, I got it. "Unidentified chemical compound evident in decedent's blood." So what is it?'

'Hey, it says unidentified, because I don't know what it is.'

'But you will.'

There was silence on the other end of the phone for a moment. 'Jesus, Cassidy. I sent it down to the FBI lab. They'll let me know in a month, if I'm lucky. But, like I said at the top, I've got another stiff with the same stuff in him. And a couple of other things make him interesting . . .' Skinner waited.

'Okay. What?'

'He had his underpants on backward.'

'Sure. Why not? What else?'

'I found someone's fingertip in his stomach.'

The fingertip lay in a Petri dish of formaldehyde on a small metal stand near the morgue table where the dead man's body lay. The meat of the fingertip was grayish, and it was raggedly cut at the base.

'You can see the flesh is little degraded by the stomach's gastric juices,' Skinner indicated with the point of a scalpel. The fingernail polish was still bright red.

'Cause of death,' Cassidy asked.

'Broken neck.'

They turned their attention to the body on the

249

table. The dead man's head was bent to one side at an ugly angle. His eyes were open in the stone stare of the dead.

'Where'd they find him?'

'The bottom of the stairs at the Fourteenth Street subway station. It was supposed to look like he fell down the stairs, but we didn't believe it.' Skinner raised a finger to begin a count. 'One, he was on his back there, but the blood had pooled in the front 'cause wherever he died, he lay on his stomach for a while.' Another finger up. 'And his underpants were on backward, so someone dressed him in a hurry.' Another finger. 'And if he took a dive there, the abrasions on his forehead would be full of dirt and concrete dust. What he's got are mahogany splinters. There's no wood on that stairway. I mean, what do they think we are over here, idiots? Jesus, that chaps my ass.'

'Somebody hit him with a piece of wood?' Orso asked. He had been impatient since they arrived at the morgue, and he checked his watch for the fifth time.

'I don't know. Maybe Mantle could lean on a bat hard enough to put a man's head at that angle. I think he took a header from up high someplace, and slammed his head into the door or the wood paneling at the bottom with all his two hundred pounds behind him. Something like that. And, by the way, he had just gotten laid, 'cause there was spermicide from some broad's diaphragm all over his dick.'

'The girl with the missing fingertip,' Orso suggested.

'Sure. Why not?' Skinner said. 'Bring her in, and we'll see if the tip fits.'

'When did it happen?' Cassidy lit a cigarette off the butt of the one he was smoking, a futile attempt to block out the heavy smell of the morgue.

'They found him the beginning of last week. He was in a drawer here till I had time to do the cut.'

'Any identification?'

'No, but he's an uptown guy. The suit he was wearing is better than anything I've got hanging in the closet. There's the mark on his wrist from a watch, and on his pinky finger on the right hand from a ring. They took those. Robbery?'

'Or they would identify him,' Cassidy said. 'Let's go take a look.'

The dead man's clothes hung in a locker near Skinner's office. The suit was a gray flannel with a chalk stripe. The shirt was yellow broadcloth, and the tie was a predominantly maroon-and-yellow paisley. The shoes were dark wingtips. All the clothes came from J. Press. A laundry mark was stamped into the waistband of the suit pants. Cassidy copied it into his notebook, while Orso went through the pockets of the jacket. He found nothing.

When they finished, they found Skinner in his office rattling a typewriter. A full skeleton hung from the ceiling behind his desk. Its teeth clenched a large cigar, and one of its bone hands held a martini glass with an olive glued into it.

'Tell me about this chemical you found,' Cassidy said.

251

'Like I said, I don't know what it is, but it shows up in this guy's blood and it was in the blood of that Williger guy who went out the window at the Astor. I sent it down to Quantico to the FBI lab. Don't hold your breath on getting a result.'

'You can't tell us anything about it?'

'You bring me someone who's got some arsenic in him, cyanide, even curare, I'll tell you in a second, but this one is beyond even my vast knowledge.'

'What about the fingertip?' Orso asked, and glanced at his watch again.

'Female. Mid-twenties. Well nourished. Smoker. Give me a little time, I can probably tell you the name of the nail polish. He bit it off her. I found some skin particles between his teeth. First time I've seen that one. I had a guy in here once had someone's ear in his stomach, a broad with a piece of a guy's dick, but this is the first fingertip.'

Cassidy and Orso went out onto First Avenue, grateful to be out of the heavy smell of the morgue. 'What do you think?' Orso asked.

'This opens up the Williger case again. We're going to have to look at that as a possible homicide. If we can ID this guy maybe we'll find a connection to Williger – work, friendship, family. See if we can figure out how they both have the same chemicals in their bodies. Have you heard of any new drugs out there?'

'No. Same old: horse, reefer, cocaine. They say there are still some opium dens down in Chinatown, but no white cop's going to find

252

them. Is that what you think it is, someone's putting out a new drug, and both these guys found it?'

'I don't know.' He took a sip of coffee and lit a cigarette. 'What's the name of that detective up in the Nineteenth who keeps a book of laundry and dry cleaner marks? Finley?'

'No. Uh, it's like that. Uh, Fernly. Jack Fernly.'

'Right. I'm going to give him a call, see if he can help us out with the dead guy's laundry mark.'

'Sure. Hey, Mike, how about I take off for a while? I told Amy maybe I could break away for lunch.' He threw it away, but Cassidy could see that he wanted to go.

'Sure. Go ahead. I'll catch you later. If anything's happening, I'll leave a message at the desk.'

'Okay, thanks.' Orso was relieved. 'I'll make it up to you.'

'After your physics lesson, call around to the emergency rooms. See if a woman came in missing a fingertip.'

Orso gave him the finger and said, 'Okay.' He hailed a cab and got in without looking back. Cassidy envied him. The man was in love, and Cassidy wasn't, and hadn't been since Dylan died two years ago.

Detective Jack Fernly had an office the size of a large closet off the main squad room in the Nineteenth Precinct on Lexington Avenue at 67th Street. It was just big enough to hold a desk and desk chair, two filing cabinets, and a visitor's

253

chair with a standing ashtray next to it. Fernly was a pudgy man with limp colorless hair who looked at the world with inquisitive blue eyes through horn-rimmed glasses. He had been an ineffectual street cop who had found his calling as the encyclopedic memory of the precinct. He remembered faces, aliases, obscure evidentiary facts, tenuous connections between crimes and criminals, dates, the minutiae of cold cases, and what he didn't remember he could find in his file cabinets. A smart precinct commander had taken him off the street and made him a one-man research bureau available to any cop who needed his skills.

Fernly studied the laundry mark Cassidy had copied from the dead man's suit. He pushed it aside, closed his eyes, and tipped back in his chair for a moment. 'Triple A Cleaners on Lex and 78th. The west side of the street right next to a flower shop.'

Cassidy shook his head in admiration. 'Amazing.'

Fernly grinned. 'An easy one. Bring me something hard the next time.'

'Thanks, Jack.'

Fernly waved away the thanks and went back to the book he had been reading when Cassidy arrived.

Triple A Cleaners was where Fernly had said it would be, on Lexington sandwiched between a flower shop and a locksmith. A bell tinkled over the door when Cassidy went in. It was a narrow room with a counter that ran from wall to wall ten feet inside the door. Behind it clean clothes in plastic bags hung from metal racks, and blue boxes of freshly laundered shirts waited on shelves for pick up. The place smelled of steam, and cleaning chemicals. A well-used, black Singer sewing machine on a treadle table waited under the street window.

A woman came out from the back room and stood behind the counter. Her gray hair was pulled back and pinned. She wore a black dress with an elaborate silver clip at the throat. She looked at Cassidy with the distant politeness of someone who faces many strangers during her workday. 'May I help you?'

He showed her his badge and a Polaroid photograph of the dead man Skinner had taken at the morgue. 'Do you know this man? Apparently he's had cleaning done here.'

She picked up the photograph to examine it. She turned it to the light to see better, and then looked up at Cassidy. 'Yes. This is Mr Collins. Has he been in an accident?'

'Do you have an address for him?'

'Yes. We offer pickup and delivery. It's convenient for people who work, and they don't mind paying a little extra.'

'May I have it?'

'Of course. Of course.' She went to a wooden file box at the end of the counter and thumbed through the index cards in the box until she found the one she wanted. Cassidy wrote down the address, thanked her, and went out into the street.

Collins lived in a one-bedroom apartment on the seventh floor of a building on 76th Street

255

between Lexington and Third. The building superintendent let Cassidy in with a passkey and then stood in the doorway and watched while Cassidy explored. A leather sofa and a matching leather chair were placed to view the big wood boxed television. A wood-cased record player was next to the TV. Framed travel posters from Paris decorated the walls. The bed in the bedroom was unmade, and there were dishes in the sink in the kitchen – marks of bachelor life. A dish on the desk held some business cards with Collins's name and the company he worked for on them. Cassidy picked one up and put it in his pocket. There was no sign of a struggle. Chris Collins had left his apartment one morning for a day at work not knowing that he would never see it again.

The advertising firm of Batten Barton Durstein & Osborn took up much of 383 Madison Avenue. A receptionist directed Cassidy to an office on the eighth floor. The walls in the corridor outside the elevator were decorated with ad posters for agency clients. Bright-eyed, leggy women smoked Lucky Strikes. An auburn-haired beauty with glossy, parted lips offered Revlon's Fabulous Futurama permanent lipstick, while near her a dark-haired beauty suggested that you could *Look lovely all day long with Revlon's Love-pat*. There were colored photographs of Chrysler's line of new cars for the year, and a small TV embedded in the wall next to them showed a big finned, two-tone sedan running down a country road while a cheerful voice sang a riff on a Cole

Porter classic: 'It's delightful, it's delovely, it's De Soto.'

A secretary in a severe charcoal gray skirt waited to escort him down the hall. 'This way, please, Mr Cassidy.'

The tightness of her girdle and calf-length skirt hobbled her, and she took short steps on high heels that clicked on the hardwood floor. Halfway down the hall she knocked on an office door and then opened it without waiting for a reply. 'Mr Allen,' she said into the office, 'Mr Cassidy.' She opened the door wider and smiled at Cassidy again as he passed, and then closed the door behind him.

It was a big office with windows overlooking Madison Avenue. Framed ad posters decorated the walls. Leather chairs and a leather sofa were grouped around a glass-topped coffee table at one side of the room, and there were two comfortable visitors' chairs pulled up in front of the desk. A tall, thin, young man with the eager manner of a salesman came out from behind the desk with his hand extended and a smile of welcome. 'Detective Cassidy, I'm Jerry Allen. Pleased to meet you.' They shook hands.

'We don't usually get members of the Police Department up here.' He put a hip up on his desk. 'Can I get you a drink?' He waved at a wet bar in a corner of the office.

'No, thanks.'

'A little early, huh? Well, I might have a nibble.' He went to the bar and poured a couple of fingers of scotch into a glass and added ice.

'I want to talk to you about Chris Collins.'

257

'Right. That's what my secretary said. Chris didn't come in all last week, and not a word. No answer at his apartment. We were starting to get worried about him. Is anything wrong?'

Nobody expects a bad answer to that question, and Cassidy had never figured out how to deliver the news softly. It always arrived like a thrown rock. 'He's dead.' *Crap, can't you do better than that?*

'Dead? What happened?' Allen's face paled. The glass was forgotten in his hand halfway to his mouth.

'We don't know yet, but we're treating it as a homicide.'

'Jesus Christ.' He remembered the drink and took a sip.

'Did Collins use drugs?'

'Drugs? Like what, like penicillin or something?'

'No, like heroin or marijuana.'

'No. Are you kidding? Booze, sure, but that stuff, never, as far as I know.'

'Never talked about experimenting with something?'

'No.'

'There was evidence that he was with a woman that evening.'

'Oh, yeah? No surprise there. Chris was a real hound.'

'Do you have any idea who it might have been?'

Allen laughed. 'Oh, God, Chris? No. Hit and run. Hit and run. If he went out with a broad three times in a row, he got nervous.'

'Would he keep a calendar?'

258

'He might. I'll call his secretary, but half the time he liked to go out and see what he could find. He called it the urban hunt. Head out to the watering holes and see what tender little beasts came for a drink.' He laughed and shook his head in admiration. He picked up the phone and dialed. 'Marie, this is Jerry Allen. Will you take a look at Mr Collins's calendar and see if he had a date Friday evening? I'll hold.' He muffled the phone against his shoulder. 'I never knew a guy who got as much as he did.' He lifted the receiver to his ear. 'Yeah. Yeah. Okay. Thanks.' He hung up and explained, 'I've got to find a way to tell people on the team what happened. I don't want any rumors to start before I get to it. Anyway, nothing on his calendar.'

'What watering holes?'

'I don't know. It's a long list. I'll write down what I can remember.'

Chris Collins seemed to favor hotel bars. Maybe he found that traveling women were easier prospects. Here today. Gone tomorrow. No expectations. No muss, no fuss. The bartender at the Rough Rider Room in the Roosevelt recognized him from the photograph but had not seen him for a couple of weeks. He had not been in the Biltmore since two weeks before and had left alone. The bartender at Peacock Alley in the Waldorf Astoria knew him but said Collins had not been in lately. Cassidy stopped at a couple of the Irish bars from the list on Lexington and Third Avenue, but he had no luck until he went into P.J. Clarke's. It was

259

early in the evening, and the after-work crowd had not yet arrived. The bartender gave him a nod of recognition. 'You're Cassidy, right? Sometimes a Jack Daniels, sometimes a martini up. I used to work at Chumley's.'

'Rocco, right?'

'Yeah.' He reached across the bar and they shook hands.

'Good to see you.'

'What can I get you, Jack or mart?'

'Martini. Thanks.'

'Up, with a twist.' He went off to mix the drink, and Cassidy lit a cigarette and looked out the window past the end of the bar at the traffic on the avenue. Evening was coming, and the cabs and buses had their lights on. Some of the people who passed the window hurried on their way home from work, while others moved with less haste, not yet ready to face domestic obligations or empty apartments.

Rocco slid a martini onto the bar in front of Cassidy and watched while Cassidy tasted the drink and nodded his approval. Cassidy showed him the Polaroid of Chris Collins. Rocco held it up to the light near the back bar mirror.

'Yeah. Okay. Chris Something. Scotch on the rocks. Dewar's. A good guy. He looks pretty weird here. What is he, dead?'

'Yes.'

'I thought so.'

'When was he in here last?'

'Ten days, two weeks ago, something like that. Right where you are.'

'Did he have a girl with him?'

Rocco thought for a moment. 'No. I mean not with him, but . . . Anyway there was this broad next to him. A hooker, but uptown, you know? Stylish. I've seen her around. Anyway, she wasn't hustling anyone as far as I could see. I thought maybe she just came in for a drink, so I was giving her the benefit of the doubt. If she made a move I was going to run her. The bosses don't want that in here. I went down to mix a whiskey sour, when I came back they were going out the door.'

'Do you know her name?'

'No. No, I don't.' He thought for a moment. 'Hold on a second.'

He walked down the bar to where another bartender was talking to a man in a black coat and plaid hat and pulled him away. They talked for a little while, and then Rocco came back. 'Willie says her name is Roxie, or something like that. Not quite that, but something like it. Trixie, maybe.'

'What did she look like?'

'Mid-twenties, long dark brown hair, one of those little noses that kind of turns up at the end. What do you call it when their teeth kind of stick out a little bit at the top, not buck teeth, something else?'

'Overbite.'

'Yeah, that's it. I like that. There's something real sexy about that. What happened? Did she do the guy?'

'I don't know yet. Thanks, Rocco.' He left a couple of bucks on the bar and went out onto Third Avenue to look for a phone.

Madison Square Garden's Eighth Avenue marquee announced in its usual abbreviated manner: *Rgrs – Brns tnight – 7:30.* The first period was already underway when Cassidy arrived. The roar of the crowd was muffled here, but it rose and fell as the play shifted up and down the ice. A whistle blew, and the noise of the crowd fell to a murmur. Cassidy went through a portal and stopped at the top of the stairs. He looked down at the rink through the haze of cigarette smoke that permanently clouded the upper reaches of the Garden. The ice gleamed bright white under the lights. As he watched, a Bruin won the face off and flicked the puck back to Vic Stasiuk. The Bruins were in penalty, one man down, but this was a chance for a short-handed goal. Stasiuk snapped a pass to Dave Conte as he broke over the blue line. Gump Worsley skated out of the goal to cut the angle, and Conte faked a shot. Worsley went low, and Conte flipped the puck over his stick-side shoulder into the net. The Ranger crowd went quiet.

Cassidy found May Stiles in her usual seat in the front row of the center loge. Her blond hair was perfectly set. She wore a light gray tweed suit with dark red accents, a pearl necklace with matching earrings, and high heels. A mink coat was draped on the back of her seat. She looked like Madison Avenue matron, or the prosperous owner of a specialty store, which, in some ways, she was. She was a madam who ran a string of high-end hookers catering to the Upper East Side trade. She saw him when he reached the bottom of the stairs.

'Hey, Cassidy. How are you? Sit down. Sit down.' Cassidy took the empty seat next to her.

'How are you, May?'

'I'm fine. I didn't know you were a hockey fan.'

'Not really. Wanda said you'd be here.'

'It's a home game. Where else would I be? This is our year. The Stanley Cup, I swear to God.' She raised silver opera glasses to her eyes to follow the action. Andy Bathgate intercepted a Bruin pass, broke in over the blue line and fired a slap shot that hit Terry Sawchuk's glove, bounced off, and trickled into the goal. The Ranger fans erupted.

'May, I need to ask you about someone.'

'Uh-uh. I'm here for the game, Cassidy. You want to talk business, you'll have to wait for the end of the period.'

The skaters flew around the ice. The puck banged off the glass. Hip checks thudded men into the boards. The crowd noise rose and fell with the action. The horn blew, the period was over, and the skaters left the ice.

'I'll buy you a drink at the Garden Club,' Cassidy said.

'Let's go.' She slung her mink over her shoulders, and Cassidy followed her up the stairs.

The heavyweight on the door at the Garden Club said, 'Good evening, Mr Cassidy,' and waved them in. The bar was full of people having a drink before the next period. Most of them were men crowded at the bar, but there were a few women at tables with their husbands or dates.

'A martini?'

'Sure. Fine. Thanks.' Cassidy caught the bartender's eye and held up two fingers and then pointed to a table in the corner. The man nodded and waved.

May settled into a chair against the wall and took a gold cigarette case from her purse. She selected a cigarette and waited for Cassidy to light it. A waiter brought their drinks, and they clinked glasses and took the first sip. 'Chin, chin. What's up?'

'Do you know an uptown girl with a name like Roxie, Trixie, something close to that?'

'Hmmm. Why? You're out of Vice.' She took another sip of her drink.

'I need to ask her about a guy she was seen with. It's not about her. It's about the guy.' Not the whole truth, but May had been around long enough to know that.

'Roxie or Trixie. Have you got any more than that? What does she look like?'

He described her the way the bartender at Clarke's had described her.

May thought about it and shook her head. 'It doesn't ring a bell. Let me ask around. Anything else you can tell me about her?'

'She's missing the tip of one of her fingers.'

'How's that?'

'The guy bit it off.'

May winced. 'Christ.' She took a slug of her drink. 'I'm getting out of the business. Did I tell you that?'

'Not lately.' May was always getting out of the business.

'I've had it. I don't know which is worse, the

men or the girls, but I'm done. I've made money, and I've got an investment guy who's been smart with it. I'm through.'

'What are you going to do?'

'I don't know. But it's a great big world full of interesting things, and running high-class hookers is way down the list.'

The buzzer sounded to announce the next period. May finished her drink and stood up, eager to see the face off.

Cassidy left money on the table and walked her back to the top of the loge stairs. 'Call me if you hear of anything.' People pushed past them and hurried down to their seats.

'I will. Thanks for the drink.' She went down the stairs in the rush of people as the teams came out onto the ice to warm up to loud organ music.

Twenty-One

'Someone's going to be unhappy if we open this up again.' Lieutenant Tanner lit a cigarette off the butt of the one he had been smoking when Cassidy and Orso had come into his office.

'Williger and Collins both had the same chemical in their systems. The cases are connected,' Cassidy said.

'I get it,' Tanner said, 'I'm just telling you people aren't going to like it. They liked Williger as a suicide. There's something political going on. Someone cashed some chips. I don't know what it's about, but it's about something.'

'So?' Cassidy asked.

Tanner scrubbed a hand over his bald head. 'I don't know. What the fuck? Do what you do. I'll back you as far as I can.' They started toward the door. 'Hey, and when you come back, let's keep it in mind that Connor Finn is still out there. Councilman Franzi calls me every couple of days to find out why we can't find the only heroin dealer in the city bigger than King Kong. And where are you on the Dudek killing?'

'Nowhere. We need a break. I don't know where the hell it's going to come from.'

Cassidy and Orso picked up an unmarked car at the police garage and left the city on the West Side Highway. It was a cold day, under a clear blue sky. A red-and-black Moran Company tug shoved a barge upriver toward the George Washington Bridge past a gray Navy destroyer like a knife in the water headed fast downstream toward the open ocean. Cassidy drove, and Orso slouched in the passenger seat smoking cigarettes and watching the passing scene out the window.

The late Paul Williger had lived in a modest half-timbered brick house on a tree-lined street a mile from the town center of Scarsdale. The shading elms and maples were a riot of autumn colors, and the front lawns were mottled with fallen leaves. Cassidy parked at the curb behind a Buick sedan with New York plates whose metal still pinged as its engine cooled. He and Orso walked up the brick path to the front door.

266

Cassidy flicked away his cigarette and rang the doorbell. Somewhere deep inside the house the bell rang. Heels clicked on a wood floor, and moments later a handsome woman in her fifties opened the door. Her dark hair was streaked with gray. She looked at them with calm dark eyes. She wore a calf-length brown tweed skirt and a yellow cardigan over a round-collared pale blue blouse.

'Mrs Williger?' Cassidy asked.

'No. I'm Janet French. You want my daughter, Penny. They're in the living room.'

They? Who were *they*?

Janet French stepped back and opened the door wide and examined Cassidy and Orso as they entered. She led them down the hall, stopped at the arched doorway to the living room, and waved them in.

Penny Williger looked like a younger, more timid version of her mother. Her dark hair was pulled back and tied with a black ribbon, and she wore a black skirt and a black sweater over a white blouse. Mourning for her late husband.

Dr Sebastian Ambrose, unkempt in stained khakis and a flannel shirt, hair afly, sat next to her on the sofa. Spencer Shaw lounged in a chair with one leg hooked over the arm. He greeted their entrance with a sardonic grin and a two-finger salute. Seeing him again, there was something familiar about him, but Cassidy could not pin it down. Had he met him in the past before the night in Williger's room at the Astor, or did he just look like someone he knew?

'Mrs Williger, I'm Detective Michael Cassidy.

267

I spoke to you on the phone yesterday. This is my partner, Tony Orso.' Penny Williger nodded and extended a hand, and Cassidy leaned forward to shake it.

'Mrs Williger called me,' Ambrose said. 'She thought it might be a good idea if I was here for this discussion because of my relationship with Paul. Mr Shaw, offered to drive me out.'

'I want to speak to Mrs Williger alone.'

Ambrose shook his head. 'That's not going to happen. Mrs Williger asked us to be here. I'm going to honor her wishes. Penny?'

'I want Dr Ambrose to stay,' she said without conviction.

Cassidy sensed that pressing the issue would get him nowhere. He pulled a chair around to face her across the narrow coffee table. Orso took a seat where he could watch everyone.

'Mrs Williger,' Cassidy said, 'I'm sorry about your husband. It must be a terrible blow.'

'Yes,' she said, and twisted her hands in her lap.

'When was the last time you spoke to your husband?'

'That evening. You know, the night he . . .' It was too hard to finish.

'Do you remember what time? Was it after dinner, or before?'

'Before. I don't know exactly what time. I was cooking dinner for the children, and they usually eat around six.' She took in a deep breath and sighed.

'How did he sound?'

'I don't know. He sounded like Paul. He

sounded tired.' She glanced at Ambrose, and he nodded encouragement.

'Did anything sound wrong? Did he sound anxious, nervous, angry?'

'No. Not really. I asked him if everything was all right, and he said yes, he was just tired.'

'Why did you ask him if everything was all right? Did he not sound all right?'

She glanced at Ambrose again. 'No, I just asked if everything was all right the way you do. You know, how are you? Is everything all right?'

'And he said everything was all right?'

'Yes.'

'And then a few hours later he jumped out the window.'

She flinched and turned her head aside. Ambrose raised his eyebrows at Cassidy's cruelty, and reached out to touch Penny Williger's arm in concern.

'Mrs Williger,' Cassidy said, 'I'm sorry for being so blunt, but you must know your husband well. You've been married for fourteen years. You say you detected no worry in his voice, no anxiety of any kind, and yet the same evening he killed himself. It's hard to believe that a man who was thinking about committing suicide wouldn't betray something to his wife.'

She shook her head and looked down at her lap. 'No. Nothing.'

'Hunh.' Skepticism in the grunt. Cassidy glanced at Orso, who read his look and his tone.

'Maybe he didn't commit suicide, Mike,' Orso

said. 'Maybe someone shoved him out the window. Shaw, here, maybe he tossed him.'

Shaw laughed.

'That's an outrageous suggestion,' Ambrose said. 'Paul Williger and Spencer Shaw were colleagues and friends.'

'What about Hoffman?' Orso said mildly.

'Who?' Ambrose covered his surprise well.

'John Hoffman,' Orso said. 'The guy in the room down the hall. The guy who came in with Paul Williger and Spencer Shaw and went up in the same elevator.'

'I don't know what you're talking about. I don't know any John Hoffman.'

'How about you, Shaw?' Orso asked.

'Never heard of the man.'

'You checked in together more than once.'

'It's a popular hotel.'

'You called the same number in Washington a few minutes after Williger went out the window.'

'Really? This Hoffman person and I did? Whose number?' He did not care if they believed him.

'We don't know whose it is, but we'll find out.'

'When you do, let me know.'

'Mrs Williger, did your husband talk about his work with you at all?' Cassidy asked.

'Sometimes. Not very much.'

'He worked for the Department of the Army. Is that right?'

'Yes.'

'At Fort Dix.'

'Yes.'

'Do you know what he did for them?'

270

'He was a biochemist.'

'Can you tell me what he was working on?'

She shook her head. 'We didn't really talk about it much. I didn't really understand it.'

'You must have talked about it enough to discover that you didn't understand it. Maybe you could tell me whatever you remember.'

She began to speak, but Ambrose held up his hand.

'Detective Cassidy, I told you before that Mr Williger's work for the Army was classified. His talking to Mrs Williger is an understandable indiscretion, but repeating anything to you would be out of bounds.'

'Mrs Williger, did Spencer Shaw come see you after your husband's death?'

'Yes, he did. He was very kind.'

'Did he tell you anything about that evening that might shed light on what happened?'

Shaw lit a cigarette and blew smoke at the ceiling, the picture of a man without worries.

'No. He said they went out for dinner, and stopped for an after-dinner drink, and then went back to the hotel, and that Paul seemed fine.'

'Not depressed?'

'No.' She looked up as if the question startled her. 'I mean, not more than he has been lately.' A quick glance at Ambrose for encouragement.

'Dr Ambrose was treating him for depression. Is that right?' Cassidy lit a cigarette.

'Yes.'

'Had that been going on for long?'

'About three months,' Ambrose volunteered. 'It started in the summer.'

271

'Did you prescribe any medications?'

'Miltown, to help with anxiety, to help him sleep.'

'Anything else? Any experimental drugs?'

'No. Experimental drugs? I don't know what you mean.'

'There were traces of a chemical compound found in his blood.'

'What chemical compound?'

'We haven't identified it yet.'

Ambrose shrugged. 'Paul was a chemist. He had access to a great many chemicals.'

'But you were just treating him with Miltown?'

'And a normal course of psychiatric evaluation and therapy. Do you understand what that means, Detective?'

'Nope.'

'Then there's not much point in discussing it. But you should know that Paul came to me once a week for therapy. We worked through his problems, and for a while I thought he was doing better. In the last few weeks, unfortunately, he seemed to be regressing. But I never thought he was a danger to himself.'

'What were those problems?'

'That falls under doctor–patient privilege.'

A board creaked in the hall as if someone had shifted weight. Maybe it was just an older house talking. Cassidy listened, but the sound did not repeat. 'Thank you, doctor. Mrs Williger, did your husband ever bring work home?'

'No, no. He wasn't allowed to do that.'

'Do you mind if I look in his desk?'

'It's in his study across the hall,' she said.

272

When Cassidy went into the hall, he saw Penny Williger's mother, Janet French, standing in the door to the kitchen. She looked at him without expression for a moment, and then turned away and disappeared. He wondered how much she had overheard.

The study was a small, dark room furnished with an old leather easy chair with a reading lamp next to it, a large wooden roll top desk, and wooden bookshelves heavy with science books. The wall over the desk held a framed Bachelor of Science degree from the University of Illinois, and graduate degrees from the University of Wisconsin and Georgia Tech. There was nothing in the desk drawers that attracted Cassidy's interest, but there wouldn't be, or Ambrose would have stopped him from looking. He went back across the hall to the living room. Shaw had gotten up to lean casually against the mantle. He tapped the ashes from his cigarette into the fireplace.

'Mrs Williger, thank you for your time. I hope that wasn't too hard on you.'

'That's all right. I know you have to ask those questions. I'm sorry I couldn't be more helpful.' She was relieved they were going.

'Dr Ambrose, I need a contact number for you.'

'Of course.' He got to his feet and drew a thick, worn wallet from his back pocket and passed over a dog-eared business card that read *Dr Sebastian Ambrose – SPring 7-4397 – Psychiatric Consultations*. There was no address, but the SPring exchange meant that his phone was in the Village.

273

'Mr Shaw, how do I get in touch with you?'

Shaw flipped his cigarette onto the stacked logs in the fireplace. 'No point, really. I'm just the chauffeur.'

'Just in case.'

Shaw smiled and shrugged. 'Call Ambrose. He usually knows how to find me.'

'It would be simpler to call you.'

Shaw shrugged. 'I move around a lot.'

'You can always leave a message for Mr Shaw at the Hotel Astor, or with me. I'll be sure he gets it.'

Shaw smiled into Cassidy's irritation, but there was no point in pushing it. It would be like a playground fight, a waste of energy for no useful result.

'Mrs Williger, was Chris Collins a colleague of your husband's?'

She shook her head in bewilderment. 'I don't know that name.'

'How about you, Ambrose? Do you know that name?'

'I don't. Who is he?' Ambrose tugged at his beard.

'Shaw?'

Shaw shook his head.

'Mrs Williger, one last question. Did your husband ever work for a company called Gallien Medical?'

'Yes. He worked there just after the war. It was his first job after graduate school.'

'How long did he work there?'

'Eight or nine years, I think. Until he went to work for the Army.'

'What did he do for them?'

'He worked in their laboratory as a research chemist.'

'Do you know what he was working on?'

'No. I wasn't much for science class at school, and Paul didn't talk much about work when he came home. We had other things to talk about.'

Penny Williger's mother, Janet French, walked them back to the front door. For a moment Cassidy thought she was going to say something. She looked back down the hall as if gauging if she could be heard from the living room. She held Cassidy's eyes for a moment and shook her head, and then closed the door behind them.

They found a diner near the Scarsdale train station and ordered hamburgers, fries, and beers.

'What do you think?' Cassidy asked. He relied on Orso's ability to read people. It was the talent that made him a lethal poker player.

Orso took a sip of his beer. 'Penny's scared. I don't know what she's scared of, but she's scared. Ambrose lied about almost everything. He's good at it, but not as good as he thinks. His pupils dilate a little when he lies. If it's a big lie he fucks with his beard. It's the kind of tell you see at the tables when a guy's bluffing a crappy hand. Penny's mother wanted to talk, but chickened out, and this guy Shaw is a piece of work. I don't think he gives a shit about any of it, but he likes playing the game, whatever the hell the game is. I'll tell you one thing, they both knew Chris Collins. And they didn't like the question about Gallien Medical.'

'After lunch we're going back to talk to the ladies without Ambrose and Shaw.'

When they drove up to the Williger house half an hour later, the Buick was gone. They walked back up the brick path and rang the bell. When Janet French opened the door, she did not seem surprised to see them. 'Penny is taking a nap. Should I wake her?'

'I don't know,' Cassidy said. 'We got the impression you wanted to talk to us. Maybe we should let her sleep.'

'Can my daughter get in trouble?'

'With us?' Cassidy asked. 'I don't see how.'

'I don't like those men. I've never liked Dr Ambrose. He's been here before with Paul, and he always gave me the creeps.' She glanced up the stairs that led to the second floor and the bedrooms. 'Come into the kitchen.' She led them down the hall and into the sunlit kitchen which looked out on a backyard that was strewn with children's things – a bicycle, a seesaw, a baseball glove left on a planter, a bat leaning nearby.

'Where are the kids?' Orso asked.

'My husband took them to the movies and an early dinner, and they're going to spend the night at our place. They need to do things, and Penny isn't up to it at the moment. They're fine when they're at school, but coming home is hard for them. May I offer you anything, tea, coffee?'

'No, thank you,' Orso said. 'We got lunch in town.'

They sat at the kitchen table near the window. The ashtray was full of cigarette butts. Some

276

were smeared with the red lipstick Janet French wore. Others carried the shade her daughter used. It was clear that the two women sat here for hours at a time, one in grief, and the other in worry.

'Penny loved Paul,' Janet French said. 'Really loved him. When they were together, it was as if nobody else existed. They've been married for fourteen years, and they were still like that. Do you know anyone like that?'

Both men shook their heads.

'I don't know how she's going to get through this. I just don't know.' She took a pack of Winstons from the windowsill and lit a cigarette with a silver lighter. 'Why would he kill himself? He loved Penny. He loved the children. He had a good job. Why would he do it? He wouldn't.'

'Did Penny call Dr Ambrose?'

'Yes. She's always been a bit of a scaredy-cat, and when you called, it made her nervous. I tried to talk her out of it, but she was afraid of doing something wrong, so she called.'

'Was Ambrose Paul's boss?'

'I think so, in some way. I never quite understood what he did.'

'Not just his shrink?'

'No. Actually, today was the first time I heard that Paul was talking to him as a psychiatrist. It was the first time I heard that Paul was depressed. He never showed it when he was around us. He always seemed pretty cheerful. At least up until sometime last month.'

'What happened then?'

'I don't know. Something changed in him. He was irritable and nervous. I don't know why.

He had trouble concentrating sometimes, and Penny said he slept badly. He had nightmares. He was just different.'

'What do you know about Paul's work?'

'He has a top-secret clearance, and he doesn't talk much about the work, but I know it excited him. I don't know much about science, but he did say they're making new chemical compounds and that they think they'll have therapeutic applications, that they'll be helpful for some health problems. I don't know which, and I don't think that's the main reason for the work.'

'Why do you say that?' Orso asked.

'Paul got tipsy one evening at our house. Our son, Tom, was there. He's younger than Penny. He was in Korea with the Marines. Paul missed the war, because of a broken eardrum, and I think it always embarrassed him a little that he didn't go. Anyway, he began saying that the Cold War wasn't going to be won with rifles and machine guns. It was going to be won by new weapons. He pointed to his head and said they were going to find ways to unlock secrets in the brain.'

'What does that mean?' Orso looked to Cassidy for a clue, but Cassidy did not know either.

'Did he explain?' Cassidy asked.

'No. Penny told him he shouldn't be talking about that, and he clammed up.'

'And that's it. That's all you ever heard.'

'Yes.'

'What did Ambrose say to Penny before we got here?' Cassidy asked.

'He said he didn't want any discussion of

Paul's work. She was to follow his lead.' She stubbed out the cigarette in the mound of butts. 'He threatened her.'

'Oh, yeah, how?' Orso asked. 'That he'd hurt her?'

'No. He just said that if she revealed anything about Paul's work, she would be in danger of losing Paul's insurance, his death benefits, and his pension. He made it clear. She wouldn't have anything to live on. And she has the boys. She's never worked. She and Paul were married right out of college. If she lost Paul's benefits . . .'

'How could Ambrose withhold Paul's insurance?'

'It was a government policy, and Dr Ambrose is quite high up.'

'In the Department of the Army.'

'Well, in a way, I guess. I mean that was what they said, but it wasn't quite true. It was a story.'

'What was the truth?' Cassidy asked.

'Paul worked for the CIA.'

Twenty-Two

There were two message slips on Cassidy's desk. One was from May, no last name, no number, May Stiles being discreet. Another was from Kay Lockridge, he was to call her at home. Cassidy found May's number in his address book and called her first. She picked up on the third ring. 'May Stiles. Your pleasure is our business.'

279

'Jesus, May, where'd you get that?'

'Cassidy? A client in advertising gave it to me. For free.'

'Worth every penny. You called.'

'I found the girl you were asking about – Maxie Lively – pretty good name for the business, huh? She used to work out of Marge Gale's house, but she went out on her own. I've got a number for you.'

Cassidy wrote it down. 'How about an address?'

'Working girls don't give out a home address. The last thing you need is some client showing up to tell you he's sure it was love after all.'

'Thanks, May.'

He hung up and dialed the long-distance operator and gave her the Lockridge number in Georgetown. Mr Farrington answered and went to find Cassidy's aunt.

'Michael, I'm dashing out, and I'm unforgivably late. I asked around about Harry Gallien, and people were not happy that I was doing so. I got some very dark looks. But here's what I found. Gallien Medical had big military contracts during the war. After the war, many of those dried up. If you want, I can send you a list of the medical supplies and equipment he sold on those contracts. All those contracts were itemized.'

'And now?'

'He does have contracts with government agencies, but they're all black.'

'Meaning?'

'There is nothing specific in the budgets as to

280

how much Gallien Medical is paid or what it is paid for. Black budgets are Intelligence related, and they are not itemized.'

'Can you ask Allen Dulles for details?'

'No, I can't.' There was no leeway in her voice. 'Michael, I really do have to run. I hope this helps. Talk soon.' Cassidy was left listening to the dial tone.

He tried the number May Stiles gave him. After six rings an answering machine picked up. He hung up. He found the squad's reverse directory propping open a window in the locker room. Maxie's number belonged to an address on East 22nd Street.

He left the precinct in late afternoon. The low autumn sun offered little warmth. Men and women hurrying home from work outnumbered the tourists on Broadway. A wind that promised winter blew from the river, and Cassidy pulled his overcoat tight and thrust his hands in its pocket. He walked the few blocks down to the building where his brother had an office at ABC News.

Brian's secretary, Claire, was not in the outer reception, and when Cassidy pushed open the door to Brian's office, he found his brother in shirtsleeves packing papers into a cardboard box. Other boxes, already sealed, were piled near the desk. 'Hey,' Brian said with an attempt at cheer, 'a friendly face. What are you doing here?' His face looked thin, and his color was bad.

'I just stopped by to see how you were.' Brian's desk no longer held the framed photos of Marcy and the girls. 'What's going on?'

'I've been suspended.' His face twisted in what might have been a grin. 'Yeah. A big meeting upstairs. All the company royalty. A lot of head-shaking sympathy, expressions of concern and support, pats on the back. Take some time. For your own good. Get checked out. Make sure everything's all right. A few months. Come back refreshed. Clean bill of health and all that. But the underlying message is that I'm an embarrassment to the network.' Cassidy could read the pain in his eyes. 'I was in the crapper up there before the meeting. Bobby Walsh and another guy were in there, and I guess they didn't know I was there. Walsh loves to pass on the office tittle-tattle. It turns out he's heard there was some pressure from Washington to knock me down a peg. The network's license is up for renewal and someone let it slip that there may be irregularities in the application.'

'And all that could go away if you're off the air.'

'Something like that.' He slammed a couple of books into the box and slapped on some tape. 'Claire can finish this in the morning. Let's get out of here before I go out the window.' It was supposed to be a joke, but it came out flat and hard.

'Easy, man.'

Brian heard the concern in his voice. 'Hey, little brother, don't worry about me. I'm the guy who looks before he leaps, and then takes the stairs. Remember?'

They agreed that they did not want to go to a bar where they might meet someone they knew, and that ruled out Sardi's and Dempsey's and the theatrical watering holes. They walked east on 44th Street and turned into a joint just west of Sixth Avenue that they had never tried. They both ordered martinis up with a twist. The waitress nodded, stuck her pencil into her hair and went away.

'The only job I ever wanted was broadcast news,' Brian said. 'I went into the booth at the radio station at Yale freshman year and thought, Jesus, I'm home. And TV was even better. Well, I guess that's the end of that.'

'You'll be back.'

'No. Not at ABC, not at NBC, not at CBS. Not unless I can do something spectacular. Maybe I can find a job at some independent somewhere, but I'm out of the big leagues. Nobody's going to touch me after this. And I don't even know what happened. I get up in the morning and I'm Brian Cassidy, respected investigative reporter for a respected news program. The next day I'm a naked drunk laughing stock.' He stopped talking while the waitress brought the drinks.

'Anything else, boys?'

'How about two more in ten minutes,' Brian said. 'The only good thing this week is that the medical report came in from Sibley. I didn't have any alcohol in my blood. There was some other stuff they haven't identified, but no alcohol.'

'What other stuff?'

'They don't know what it is. They've sent it down to the NIH to see if they can identify it.'

'Did you tell ABC?'

'Sure. But it cut no ice. The way they see it, if I wasn't drunk, I was high on something else. What the hell happened that day?'

'Someone snatched you off the street in DC,' Cassidy said. 'A team of at least three men who knew what they were doing and had done it before. One to drive, two, maybe three to subdue and load you. Probably in a van.' Brian watched him without speaking. 'Why'd it happen? They thought you knew something they didn't want you to know. They wanted to question you, and they wanted to neutralize you so that any report you made would be dismissed.'

'Report on what, for Christ's sake?'

'I don't know exactly, but it has something to do with Harry Gallien, Gallien Medical, and drug experiments the CIA is running.'

'Harry Gallien? I talked to Harry Gallien twice on the phone and once in person about political contributions. He gave a thousand bucks to Congressman Williams, and Congressman Williams gave it back. What's the big story?'

'I asked you to check on a couple of names with the Department of the Army, remember?' Brian nodded. 'The Army was just a cover. One of them used to work for Gallien. You disappeared. I came into town and started looking for you, going back over your day. The next thing I know four pros carrying no ID try to snatch me off a street in broad daylight. One of them was outside Gallien's building when I came out. They're probably the same team that took you.'

Brian took a slug of his martini. Cassidy could

284

sense his brother's brain whirring as he went back over what he had said. 'But I wasn't investigating Gallien Medical. I didn't know it had anything to do with the CIA. I was just looking for you.'

'Because I was investigating something that *is* connected to the CIA. But I didn't know it either. And since we're brothers, they thought we were working together.'

'Would the CIA really have the balls to kidnap a journalist and a New York cop off the streets of the capital?' Brian asked.

'Small risk, big gain. You don't remember what happened to you. You don't know who did it to you. If they'd gotten me, I'd have the same amnesia you have. If they have a drug that does that, they probably have a drug that makes people tell them what they want to know.'

'Those fucks. They stole from me. They stole my memory and time, my dignity. They stole my job. They upset my family. They did it like swatting a fly. What do they think we know? What makes it so goddamned important?'

'I don't know. We're missing something. We've got a dead chemical guy. What was he doing that's so secret? Chemical warfare experiments? Bio-warfare experiment? We assume that the Army is working on that stuff, and there's no reason the CIA wouldn't be involved. If they thought that's what you were onto and they wanted to back you off, they would have said you were in danger of exposing classified information and they would prosecute you if you did. It has to be something they really don't want

285

known. It's still out there, and we're going to find it.'

'We are?'

'Sure. Because that's what we do.'

Brian smiled for the first time in days.

Twenty-Three

A woman's voice on his answering machine offered Cassidy information on Leon Dudek's burial if he wanted to come. He did not recognize the voice.

In the afternoon, Cassidy got an unmarked car from the police garage, and drove to Queens.

The Machpelah Cemetery in Queens was halfway to Idlewild Airport. Cassidy parked near the elaborate cemetery office with its tower and green-tiled roof, left a POLICE placard on the dashboard, and walked through the massed gravestones of the long dead and newly dead to Leon Dudek's gravesite. The air was cold, but the sun shone out of a clear blue sky. The beauty of the day seemed to make a mockery of man's dark and solemn rituals of death.

A small gathering of people waited at Leon Dudek's grave. Stacks of pale autumn sod and a pile of dirt lay next to the harsh rectangle cut in the earth. Cassidy saw Lena and Beata, the two women stoop sitters from Dudek's apartment building. They stood with Rhonda to one side of the hole. Rhonda saw him and nodded, but there was no invitation in the gesture. The landlady, Mrs Tanenbaum, stood nearby with two older men he had never seen before. They wore heavy dark wool overcoats and stood with their hats in their hands. They could have been Leon Dudek's brothers. They were stooped, and round shouldered from years of hard labor and marginal living. Their gray hair was cropped short, and their faces were pale and hollow cheeked, and their eyes had seen too much. A rabbi stood at the end of the open grave. Metal pipes supported Leon's plain pine coffin over the hole. Two gravediggers hunkered near a granite mausoleum twenty feet away smoking cigarettes and talking in low voices.

The young man called Freddy watched from the partial concealment of a marble monument. He wore a black nylon windbreaker over shirt and a sweater. His eyes found Cassidy and then slid away.

The rabbi's service was short. He spoke in Yiddish, and his voice was strong. The mourners stood with their heads bowed, except for Freddy who stared at the coffin. At the conclusion, the gravediggers flicked their cigarettes away and were joined by four other workmen at the graveside. The workmen lifted the coffin by ropes that ran under it, and the gravediggers slid the pipes out. The workmen lowered the coffin into the grave, then pulled the ropes free, coiled them and carried them away. The gravediggers leaned on their shovels and waited while the rabbi and the mourners picked up handfuls of dirt and dropped them on the coffin.

The dirt was powdery and dry in Cassidy's hand. It fell on the coffin lid with a whisper. He dusted his hands together to brush off the last of it and turned to find Rhonda waiting for him. She wore a black dress, a black coat, and a black hat with a short, dark veil that blurred her face and left her eyes unreadable. 'Thank you for coming, Michael.'

'You're welcome.'

She looked at the others walking back toward the cemetery entrance. 'You'd think there'd be more to mark the end of a life.'

'Yes.'

'Sad.'

'I've got a car. Can I give you a ride back?'

She thought for a moment. 'I don't know. I don't think so. I don't think I like you much right now.'

'It would give me time to apologize.'

She searched his face. 'Really? Is that what you want to do?'

'I said some lousy things I had no right to say.'

'Yes, you did. Some others, I don't know. Maybe you were right.'

'Ride with me. We can talk.' He wanted this to happen.

She thought about it and then nodded. 'Okay.'

'Give me a minute. I want to speak to that Freddy guy.' But when he turned, Freddy was gone, and the gravediggers were shoveling dirt into the hole.

They went to Chumley's and ordered martinis and steaks and French fries and iceberg lettuce with Roquefort dressing and a bottle of Château Neuf-du-Pape, a splurge at eight bucks. They had talked on the drive in from Queens, and it almost felt like they had regained the ground they had lost in argument, but there was still tension, things that could not be unsaid, wounds still raw.

The night had turned colder by the time they left the restaurant. They walked up Bedford Street to Hudson and continued north. There were not many people on the streets, some late diners headed home like they were, some dedicated drinkers moving from bar to bar, club hoppers headed to the Vanguard or the Half Note, and a few of the solitarios, the lonely night-time people who swam through the city at all hours on mysterious errands.

When they turned west on Bank Street, Cassidy again had the feeling there was someone shadowing them. 'Hold on a second.' He stopped and put his foot up on a fire hydrant and re-tied a shoe that needed no re-tying, and used the moment to watch for movement from the corner of his eye. He saw nothing. They went on.

'What was that about,' Rhonda asked.

'I've got an itch that someone is following us.'

'Maybe it's just cooties.' But she took his arm for comfort and looked back along the dark street.

'I want you to do something.' He put his arm around her and leaned in and spoke softly, a romantic gesture to anyone watching. 'I want you to laugh as if I said something funny. Then we're going to turn downtown on Greenwich as if maybe we decided to go for a nightcap. When we're around the corner, I want you to laugh again and then talk as if you were telling me a story and keep walking.'

'What are you going to do?'

'I'm going to wait at the corner to see if anyone comes around it. Can you do that?'

'Sure.' She looked at him with serious eyes.

'Don't exaggerate it. Just laugh, keep walking, laugh again, tell the story. Keep walking.'

'So he thinks we're going down the block.'

'Right. If I tell you to run, do it. Don't hesitate. Don't come back. Run for Hudson Street. Run for people.'

'Michael, what are you saying?'

'Just in case.'

'Just in case of what? You're scaring me.'

'Nothing to be scared of. It's going to be fine. Do this for me, okay? Please.'

'Be careful.'

'Sure.' They were getting close to the corner. 'Now laugh.'

She laughed. It sounded strained to Cassidy's ears, but the follower would not know her laugh.

'Okay, here we go,' he said. They went around the corner. He stopped and Rhonda went on.

She looked back at him, worried. He nodded. She laughed again and began to talk in a voice just loud enough to carry. Cassidy stepped into the dark doorway of a plumbing supply store. Halfway down the block Rhonda went silent for a moment and then laughed as if responding to

290

something Cassidy said. Her voice picked up again, fading, less distinct as she walked.

Cassidy took his gun out from under his arm and waited in the darkness. He slowed his breathing to quiet it and strained to listen.

What was that? A footstep?

A vagrant pressure in the air, told him that someone had stopped at the corner. Whoever it was waited and listened like he did.

Rhonda neared the end of the block. She looked back wondering whether she should turn the corner out of sight or continue. She laughed again, and crossed the street.

Cassidy heard a scraping whisper, maybe a shoe against concrete, maybe a sleeve against a wall. A small intake of breath, and then a figure came around the corner hugging the dark shadows along the building. He knew in an instant the follower was too small to be Shaw.

Cassidy lunged from his doorway and grabbed the man by his jacket. 'Freeze. Police.' He tried to run him into the wall, but the man was incredibly quick. An elbow caught Cassidy high on the cheek and jerked his head back. Another elbow knocked the gun from his hand. A knee drove into him, missing his groin but numbing his thigh. Cassidy punched the man in the ribs and drew a gasp of pain. The man twisted hard in his grasp and he almost lost him. Stiffened fingers aimed for his eyes scraped across his forehead. He pulled the man back toward the building, hoping to pin him there, but the man stamped a leather-soled shoe down Cassidy's shin in a rip of pain, and twisted loose leaving

291

Cassidy holding his jacket, and sprinted for the corner. Cassidy went after him. As he rounded the corner, there was a loud metal clang, and a garbage can rolled toward him. He tried to dodge, caught a foot, and went down on the sidewalk skinning his hands and one knee. His assailant was a dark blur headed fast toward Hudson Street.

Cassidy hissed at the sting of the iodine Rhonda swabbed on his skinned knee.

'Don't be a baby,' Rhonda said.

Cassidy fingered the rip in the knee of the pants he held on his lap. 'I liked those pants.' He tossed them in the corner of the living room.

'Let me see your hands.' He held them out, and Rhonda swabbed iodine on the scrapes, turning his palms dark red.

'Goddamn, that stuff stings.'

'I'm going to get some ice for your face.' She went into the kitchen and opened the freezer and took some ice from the metal bowl he kept there. 'Did you see who he was?'

'It was too dark, and the whole goddamn thing was over in seconds. But I know who it was.'

'Who?' Rhonda wrapped ice cubes in a dishtowel and then smacked it against the counter until the ice broke up in the cloth. She brought it to him, and he pressed against his cheek where the man had elbowed him.

'Freddy.'

'Freddy? You mean Freddy from Leon Dudek's place? Why would he follow us?'

'I don't know, but that's the jacket he was

292

wearing at the funeral.' Rhonda picked up the iodine bottle. 'Hey, hey, enough,' he protested.

'Uh-uh,' she said. 'If those scratches on your forehead get infected it could leak inside and destroy the few brain cells you have left.'

'Is that your best bedside manner?'

'Hold still.' When she finished, she capped the iodine bottle and put it back in the drawer in the kitchen and dropped the bloodstained wash-cloth and towel in the laundry bin. 'Do you want a drink?'

'There's a bottle of Jack Daniels on the bar.'

'What are you going to do about Freddy?'

'I'm going to go ask him why he was following us.'

Rhonda brought him a glass of bourbon and one for herself, and they carried them to the window and looked out to the lights on the New Jersey shore across the dark water. A freighter was loading at the pier at the foot of Bank Street. He could see its white superstructure and black-and-red funnels above the highway. Bright loading lights illuminated the cranes that carried cargo nets full of crates up from the docks and swung them high above the decks before lowering them into the unseen holds. Cassidy took the cigarette from her hand and took a drag and gave it back to her.

'Do you ever want to get on one of those ships?' she asked. 'The hell with it. Get on and head downriver, and go wherever it's going, leave everything behind?'

'All the time. Do you want to come?' He put an arm around her waist and drew her close.

* * *

293

Freddy stood in the shadows of the elevated highway and looked up at the two people framed in the lighted window. He held his elbow tight against his ribs where the cop had hit him. It hurt when he took a deep breath. Still, it wasn't as bad as being hit with the wood batons the *Kapos* carried in the camp. He had hated them worse than the SS guards, because the *Kapos* policed their own people to gain better rations and better quarters. Jews beating Jews. Jews killing Jews. Jews herding Jews to the gas chambers. He crouched down and made himself small and tight as he often did when the memories came.

The scrape of the straight razor on the ruddy cheeks of the SS officers he shaved every morning in the little barbershop overlooking the parade ground where the prisoners waited for roll call. The snip, snip, snip of the scissors as he trimmed their hair. Below them, the prisoners in their striped shirts and pants and wooden shoes waited to be counted. Even the dead. Those who had died in the night had to be held upright by the living until the count was over. The new SS officers laughed and pointed at them while they waited for their turn in the barber chair, but after a week or so they stopped, because the standing dead were there every morning, normal, not worth commenting on.

It was the barbershop that kept Freddy alive. When he and his father and mother got off the transport train at Auschwitz, he and his mother had been sent left by the officer at the selection desk, left, to the gas chambers, while his father, a skilled barber, had been sent right, to life. But his father had clung to Freddy's arm and, holding down his fear, speaking with great calmness though his hand on Freddy's arm trembled, had explained that his eight-year-old son was a brilliant barber who had worked in his shop since the age of five. And so his mother, her eyes full of tears and fear, had been sent left, and he and his father had gone right, and he had strained to hold her in sight until she disappeared in the crowd.

Two years later, his father was dead, dragged down by fever and starvation, and Freddy was the barber for the SS officers. They would come in the morning, well fed, happy, smelling of cologne and tobacco smoke, for a shave and a trim. He was their mascot to be teased and offered treats of chocolate and tinned foods, and occasionally to be cuffed on the head or kicked if an officer was dissatisfied with his haircut. He joked and laughed with them and told them what they wanted to hear. Sometimes women came, the ones who wore their hair shorter than the fashion of the time. There was one in particular that he remembered, a small woman, quick and bright like a bird, but with cold blue eyes, who would come once a month. She came with her husband, who was called Herr Doktor *by the SS officers, and who was very proud of his thick chestnut hair, very particular about how it was to be trimmed. She would not talk to Freddy but would watch him in the mirror as he worked on her, and when he was finished, she would examine the result carefully, nod to him, and give him a*

hard candy that tasted of fruit he did not recog-
nize. The SS officers called her 'Eis' behind her
back, and while they were polite to her, there
was something about her that unsettled even
them. She and her husband worked in the medical
compound, a place from which no one returned
healthy. He wondered what she did that could
make SS men uncomfortable.

Sometimes when he shaved one of them he
thought about drawing the blade hard across the
exposed neck where the large vein pulsed under
the skin. In his mind's eye he saw the spurt of
blood and the look of fear as the man realized
he was dying. But he had never had the courage
to do it, and so he had survived.

The hard edge of the steel highway support
dug into Freddy's back and reminded him that
he was here, now, in New York City, and that the
memories were just smoke in his head. He had
learned that the cop's name was Cassidy and
that he was trying to find Leon's killer, and he
had a vague thought that if he followed Cassidy
he might discover who the killer was. But then
what? And what about the woman? She was a
Jew, a newspaper reporter. He did not know
much about her or what a newspaper reporter
did. Was she trying to find Leon's killer? He
would have to think about her and what she was
doing. He would have to study on it.

He went up the street staying in the deep
shadows along the buildings. He did not think
they would be watching from the apartment, but
the shadows were where he was comfortable.

296

Twenty-Four

Cassidy nursed a beer at a table in the White Horse and thought about Paul Williger. Chemistry tied Williger to the dead Chris Collins and to Brian's kidnapping, but there had to be more to it than that. Still, chemistry was the thread to pull on. He was wondering if it was strong enough to unravel the whole business when Spencer Shaw sat down in the chair across the table. He carried two brandy snifters and pushed one across to Cassidy. 'Hennessy, VSOP. Good. Not the best, but very good.'

Cassidy lit a cigarette and waited for Shaw to get to the point.

'We had a call from Penny Williger,' Shaw said. 'She said you went back to the house and talked to her mother after we'd left. Apparently her mother told you some tales.'

'She said that you and Ambrose and Williger were working for the CIA.'

Shaw shrugged. 'Big deal.' Then he said, 'Russell Crofoot.' He said it mildly but he watched Cassidy carefully for a reaction. 'You remember him, don't you?'

Russell Crofoot, Cassidy thought. So that was his first name. He had never known it. Sometimes he forgot that Crofoot ever lived. 'Sure. He was one of your agents in New York a couple of years ago. Rudi Apfel, the Russian KGB agent, the blackmail ring and all that. I never knew his first name.'

'And the woman, Dylan McCue, wasn't it?'

'Yes, it was.' Cassidy worked to keep his reaction to her name neutral.

'Crofoot was killed a couple of blocks from your apartment.'

'I remember. Him and another guy. Apparently they shot each other. The other guy had ID that said his name was Fraker, but the ID turned out to be a fake. We never did find out who he was. One of yours, probably. That's what everyone thought.'

'Why would two of our agents shoot each other?'

'Maybe they got their secrets mixed up.'

'The New York Police Department never solved the crime.'

'Sure, we did. Crofoot and Fraker shot each other. We never found a motive. Your office wouldn't cooperate.'

'We never believed they shot each other.' Shaw's tension showed in the bunched muscles of his jaw and a tightening at the corners of his mouth. 'Fraker had a broken neck. A bullet from Crofoot's gun hit him after he was dead. The agency thinks someone killed Fraker and then shot Crofoot with Fraker's gun. We wondered what they were doing on that block, and the only thing we could come up with that would draw them there was you. You lived nearby.'

'That's true. Crofoot knew that. Maybe he was coming to see me. We were both working the same side of the street back then. Maybe Fraker didn't want him to talk to me.' A small lie with an element of truth. They had been both after a blackmail ring tied to a Russian spying operation, but Crofoot wanted the blackmail material for his own benefit and the benefit of his masters.

'Did you see Crofoot that night?'

'No.' A bigger lie. 'According to the police report on the time of the shootings I was having dinner ten blocks away.'

'We both know how accurate those reports are.'

'You're implying I killed them. I didn't have a beef with either one. I never saw Fraker before I saw him in the morgue. Crofoot and I were fine. Why would I do it?'

'We don't have an answer to that yet.' Shaw took his empty glass and Cassidy's back to the bar for refills, and left Cassidy to think about Crofoot and Fraker and what had happened on that dark street two years ago.

At that time, he had been tormented by a recurring dream. In the dream he walked on a dark sidewalk at night and as he approached a darker place on the street, a dead man had warned him to turn back from a danger that waited. That night, as he walked home, he found himself back in the dream, dreaming and yet awake as he walked. A patch of darkness in front of him was darker than the night, and as he passed it, the dead man's warning from the dream turned him in time to see Fraker step from a dark doorway with a gun raised. They had fought, and he had killed him, broken his neck, and then Crofoot had lunged out of a car across the street firing

299

a gun as he ran toward him, and Cassidy had killed him with Fraker's gun.

Shaw came back with the drinks and sat down. 'The thing is, I don't need proof. This isn't going to a court. I know you killed him.' He took a sip of his cognac. 'Russ Crofoot was my brother. Well, my half-brother. Mother was a serial marrier. My father came right after Russell's. There were a couple more after that, but Russ was the one closest to me. He got me laid for the first time, taught me how to shoot, gave me my first cigarette, my first drink. I joined the OSS because of him. He was my brother. He was my best friend. I owe him a lot.'

'Wow,' Cassidy said. 'What a heart-warming family story.'

'I just wanted you to know why. It's not random. There's a reason behind it. You're a smart guy. You get what I'm talking about, don't you?'

'The thing on the subway platform. That was good. I admit it, that scared me,' Cassidy said. 'The gunfire didn't work as well. You could have killed me with the first shot, so by the third shot I knew it was a warning. I see why you did it. The pushing on the platform might have been just one of those unfortunate things that happens in a crowd. You had to let me know there was really a threat before you sent the flowers. I liked the lilies. That was a good touch.'

Shaw looked around to be sure there was no one within earshot. 'I don't think you're as cool as you're pretending to be. You know I'm out there. I'm going to kill you. You won't know when until it's happening. There's nothing you can do about it.'

'How will you get away with it? When I leave here, I'll call my partner, call my lieutenant, let them know.'

Shaw smiled. 'Sure. I expect that. That isn't going to make a difference.'

'How about if I shoot you now?' Cassidy put his hand under his jacket and touched his gun.

Shaw said, 'Go ahead.' He waited a moment, and then pushed back from the table. 'I understand you were offered a chance to join the agency. You should've accepted. That would have fucked me up a bit.'

So Allen Dulles told him about the offer, because nobody else knew about it. 'Fucked up how?'

'Because the agency takes care of its own. But you aren't one of us.'

'Shaw, the day you come for me, I'll kill you.'

'Sure you will. Enjoy your drink. Sleep well. See you soon.' He turned and went.

'The son of a bitch came right out and said he was going to kill you?' Orso asked.

'Yes,' Cassidy said. They were in squad room.

Orso had his feet up on his desk and was working his nails with an emery board. 'Because he thinks you killed his brother?' Orso watched Cassidy for a reaction. Cassidy knew he had never quite bought the story of how Fraker and Crofoot had killed each other not far from Cassidy's apartment. He never pushed it. He was smart enough to know that a secret shared

301

was no secret at all. Cassidy appreciated his reticence.

'I can't prove I didn't.'

'Do you believe him?'

'Shaw showed me twice that he could do it. Once on the subway platform, and then with the rifle.'

'So what are we going to do?'

'I don't know yet,' Cassidy said. 'I've got some time. He's not going to try soon. He likes the game. He wants me to think about it. Sleepless nights. Jumping at noises. Now that I know it's, it's going to be harder for him.'

'Not much harder.'

'Thanks for the boost.'

'I'm just saying.' Orso lit a cigarette. 'What makes him think he can get away with it?'

'He said something to me. He knew that Allen Dulles asked me if I wanted to join the agency. He said that if I had taken the job it would have given him a bigger problem, because the agency takes care of its own. If I'd joined, I would have been protected. But it also means that Shaw is in direct contact with Dulles. Dulles knows about the operation Shaw was running with Williger.'

'So he's got a lot of clout. Let's clip him before he gets set. I've got a throw-down gun at the house. We can make it look like self-defense.'

'Not yet. I want people to know what they're doing. I want to blow this open.'

Orso threw up his hands at Cassidy's lack of foresight. 'Jesus . . . You think about this thing with Shaw. You'll see I'm right.'

Cassidy called the Hotel Astor. Pickering, the

302

night manager, was not on duty, but the day manager was happy to check the records. Mr Shaw had checked out a few days after Mr Williger's unfortunate accident. He had left no forwarding address. Cassidy found Dr Ambrose's SPring 7 phone number on a piece of paper in his desk drawer. Ambrose would know where Shaw was living, but he would not give it up to Cassidy. He'd have to find a way to Shaw without alerting him. He needed to track him, to know his habits. It was good to know the habits of whatever's hunting you.

Orso came out of the locker room drying his hands on a paper towel. 'I'm going to take off,' Cassidy said.

Orso canned the balled-up towel in a wastebasket. 'Hey, I met a guy with Amy last night. He's a chemistry prof at NYU. A good guy, but full of himself. You know, a guy who's always the smartest one in the room. I kind of pimped him. I told him about these blood samples we had, and how nobody could identify the crap that's in them. Told him the FBI couldn't come up with a thing. He bit, man. He's sure he can identify them.'

'Call Skinner. See if he'll give us samples.'

Shaw was awake when the phone rang. He had been lying on his back in bed looking at the ceiling and thinking, the way one does when waiting for sleep that will not come. In the beginning he had been thinking about the recent past trying to decide where and when the train had begun to run off the tracks. Williger going out

303

the window, maybe. He had been going over it step by step. What if he had done this? What if he had done that? But it all came back to Cassidy, like some weird force tied them together. Some sort of cosmic shit the way Cassidy cropped up in his life, first he killed Russ Crofoot, and then he just happens to be on duty when Williger goes out the window. And his girl just happens to stumble into the house on West Fourth. It was enough to make a man a believer.

From the past he had moved on to contemplate his future. He liked the work he did, and he pretty much knew that it did not have many applications outside an intelligence agency. They didn't pay much, but on the other hand Government work had perks. If an operation went sideways, they would bail him out, change his identity, deny his existence, post him under cover to another country where the agency operated. They could make him disappear. As long as they didn't make him disappear permanently. The thought did not make him smile.

The phone's ring in the quiet of the apartment jerked him out of bed. He picked up before the third ring. 'I'm here,' he said. He did not have to ask who was calling. The son of a bitch always called at awkward hours. Maybe he didn't sleep. Maybe he just hung from the rafters by his feet like a bat.

'We're closing the lab at Fort Dix. The operation will move south to an environment we can control better. We're looking at Fort Detrick.' Shaw heard the scrape of a match and the puffing necessary to get a pipe going. 'I want you, the

304

Brandts, and Ambrose out of New York as soon as possible. Clean up the loose ends.'

Shaw hesitated, but he had to ask. 'Permanently?'

The phone at the other end cut off with a click.

Twenty-Five

The weather could not make up its mind. It snowed during the night. The next day the temperatures rose to the high forties. By mid-morning it was gone except for the piles the plows left, which were turning to gray slush. Cassidy rang the doorbell marked *Superintendent* in green ink on a scrap of cardboard at the front of the building where Leon Dudek had lived. Mrs Tanenbaum opened the door. She held a dinner plate in one hand and went back to drying it with her apron. A half-smoked cigarette drooped from the corner of her mouth. Her stance in the middle of the doorway was no invitation to enter. She looked at him without curiosity and waited for Cassidy to state his business.

'Have you seen Freddy since the funeral?'

No, she hadn't seen Freddy since the funeral. Freddy was a wild animal. No one knew where he went or what he did. The cops should leave Freddy alone. Freddy had suffered enough. He wasn't right in the head.

'When was he last here?'

'The day we buried Leon. I have not seen him since. This is not unusual. He comes, he goes.'

305

He thanked her and left.

Two Con Ed workers in soiled coveralls were eating hamburgers at a Formica-topped table in the diner on 3rd Street. Their tool belts and heavy canvas gloves rested on the extra chairs. An old man in a ragged black overcoat sat on a counter stool near the door and crumpled free saltines into his soup. Cassidy took a stool at the far end of the counter. The counterman came to take his order.

'Coffee, black. Pie?'

'Apple.'

'Any good?'

'My wife bake it this morning.' A little bit of a challenge there.

'I'll take a piece.'

The coffee came in a thick white mug, and the generous piece of pie was accompanied by a pitcher of cream. The counterman waited while Cassidy tasted the pie.

'Good,' he said. 'Very good.' He poured some of the cream on what was left.

The counterman nodded. 'Her strawberry's even better, but she do that in the spring. She don't believe that frozen crap tastes the same.'

'I'll stop back for a piece.' He took a sip of coffee. 'I was in here a few weeks ago. I chased a kid through here, never caught him.'

'Yeah. Freddy. I remember.' He pulled at his thick, black mustache.

'Have you seen him lately?'

'He in trouble this time?'

'No. I just want to ask him some questions.'

'Yeah?' A New Yorker's skepticism about cops.

306

He pulled at the mustache again. Maybe that's what he did when he was trying to make up his mind.

'Cross my heart.' Cassidy did it with forefinger across his coat. 'Have you seen him?'

'In here a couple of days ago.'

'Do you know where he's staying? I asked at the place down the street, but they say they haven't seen him.'

'Nah. He don't talk much. I don't ask him. Live and let live, know what I mean?'

'You said you thought he had a coop somewhere over near the bridge. Do you know where it is?'

'Nah. Not really. I don't know exactly. From what he sometimes say, it could be right at the bridge.' He shrugged his shoulders.

'Not in a building?'

'I don't know. Maybe. I just got the feeling. Could be wrong.'

It was a ten-minute walk to the Williamsburg Bridge. Cassidy crossed East Houston Street with its big brick and granite buildings holding printing plants and light manufacturing and skirted the vast construction area where a slum of tenements had been razed in preparation for a development to be known as the Baruch Houses. The ramps to the bridge rose to his right and the southern edge of the Baruch Houses construction site was on his left. Steam shovels took big bites out of the ground while bulldozers clanked and roared as they shoved dirt and rubble into piles on the torn land.

He dodged through the light traffic on Delancey

307

and went in under the elevated road. The passing cars and trucks roared and thumped overhead. The area under the roadways was a dumping ground. There were broken bottles, splintered lumber, wheels with no tires, tires with no wheels, a wrecked and mangled baby carriage, old refrigerators, a couple of car doors, a crumpled tricycle, a broken manhole cover, tin cans, punctured fifty-gallon drums. It was strewn haphazardly, but Cassidy was looking for a sense of order that might indicate Freddy's coop, things piled to make a cave, an abandoned car body with the windows blocked. He found nothing and kept walking toward the river.

The bridge spanned the East River like a giant's erector set. The towers in the river near the eastern and western shores were made of an interlock of steel girders that rose a hundred feet from the river to the roadway and a hundred feet above the road. The anchor tower on land on the Manhattan side rose in front of Cassidy. Unlike the river towers it was made of big stone blocks. Stone blocks left over from the construction were stacked in the shelter of the roadway. There was something built in the shadows between the stack of blocks and the tower. Cassidy, wary of getting closer, moved until he could see it clearly. It might have been a toolshed during the bridge's construction fifty years before. It was made of weathered gray boards, and was about ten feet by twelve feet, and roofed in tin. It leaned back on the tower wall as if too tired to stand by itself.

Cassidy looked for a place he could set up to watch the shack. He wanted to talk to Freddy about Leon. And he wanted to know why Freddy had been following him. Freddy was skittish. Cassidy would have to approach him gently. If he tried to muscle him, he would get nowhere, and if Freddy ran, he might not find him again.

He found what was left of a 1946 Hudson coupe in the junk under the roadway – no wheels, no windows, one door hanging by a hinge, no hood, no engine, no trunk lid, no seat – perfect. An orange crate gave him something to sit on with just enough height to see out the front to the shack door twenty yards away. Nobody could get in or out without him seeing. He settled down to wait.

There was a padlock hasp on the front door of the shack, but there was no lock through the hasp. Was there someone inside? Maybe. Maybe it meant there was nothing inside worth stealing. Impatience ate at him as it always did when he had to wait. He counted the stones piled next to the shack but lost count halfway up and had to start again . . .

He awoke with a jerk. How long had he been asleep? Now there was a padlock on the hasp on the door of the shack. He snapped his head around and caught a glimpse of Freddy as he slipped into the big construction site across Delancey. By the time Cassidy got to the gate, Freddy had disappeared.

A Master padlock secured the door to the shack under the bridge roadway. Cassidy studied the lock and then took a roll of leather from an inside pocket and opened it. He selected a flat tensioner and a small rake from the lock picks it held. He slipped the tensioner into the lock and let it dangle and then pushed in the rake until it stopped. He added pressure to the tensioner and then pulled the rake out fast. The lock clicked open.

Cassidy pulled the door open. There were no windows in the shack, but enough light came through the door so Cassidy could see a rudimentary bed of planks on cinderblocks with a mattress covered by blankets and a pillow without a case. Next to the bed was a wooden box holding three candle stubs of different heights. The top of the crate was covered with wax. A row of hooks held a few jackets and trousers. Two wooden wine boxes that rested on the plank floor below them held shirts, socks, a couple of sweatshirts and a heavy wool sweater. A pair of cracked leather lace-up boots was in the space between the two boxes. A rudimentary stove made from a five-gallon tin sat on a piece of scrap steel in the corner, and a narrow stove-pipe ran up through the roof. There was a box full of scrap lumber to feed the stove. Two small pots and a frying pan hung on nails nearby close to a small shelf of canned soups and canned beans. A bookcase of planks and bricks held a dozen or more books. Some of the covers were torn. Some had no covers at all. Three of them were westerns by Max Brand: *Outlaw's Code*, *The Rangeland Avenger*, *The Untamed*. This was Freddy's sanctuary.

A piece of cloth hung from two nails above the head of the cot. A yellow Star of David was sewn to the faded blue-and-gray-striped scrap that had been torn from a jacket worn by a prisoner at a Nazi death camp. Next to it hung a framed print of a rabbit, a twin to the Dürer print that hung in Mrs Tanenbaum's kitchen. Cassidy guessed it was the missing picture that had hung in Leon Dudek's apartment. A small triangle of dark, shiny paper protruded from the bottom of the frame.

Cassidy lifted the picture from its nail and turned it over. The cardboard backing was loose. He pulled the piece of paper clear. It was a black-and-white photograph. He carried it to the light at the door to look at it. Eight people were having a picnic in the shade of a tree in a meadow. Five men and three women. Some of the men stood, two sat on the ground near the women, who sat on a blanket next to an unpacked wicker picnic hamper. Next to it was an ice bucket with a bottle of champagne. Even in the black and white of the photograph it was clear that two of the women were blond. The third was a small, dark-haired woman with a thin, attractive face. She wore a long, full, dark skirt and a light-colored blouse with a high collar to which she had pinned an enameled-and-metal swastika. The men all wore uniforms of the SS with their death's head insignias. Everyone in the picture held a glass of champagne, and they all smiled cheerfully at the camera. A happy day for members of the master race away from the cares of work.

Someone, probably Leon Dudek, had drawn a circle with a pen around the head of the dark-haired woman and the head of one of the standing men. He was taller than the men next to him, a

311

big, good-looking man with thick hair combed back from his forehead.

Why had Dudek circled the man and woman? Because he had seen them in New York.

Cassidy put the photograph into his jacket pocket and hung the rabbit back on the wall and blew out the candles on the table. He looked around to make sure that he had not left any obvious sign of his being there. He hoped that if Freddy discovered the photo was missing, it would simply be one of those mysteries life threw at you, like the solitary sock in the laundry, the book that finally turned up under the bed.

Next to the door was a narrow board shelf nailed between the wall studs. There were three straight razors on it, the kind known as cutthroats. One had an ivory handle, two were black. Cassidy opened the ivory one. The blade was clean, shiny, and sharp. A disturbed place in the dust on the shelf showed where a fourth had lain until Freddy picked it up and put it in his pocket as he went out into the city.

Twenty-Six

'I think I've got the rest of the body that goes with the fingertip we found in that guy's stomach,' Skinner said over the phone. 'We just pulled her out of the Hudson. You want to see her, come on down.'

312

'The morgue?' Cassidy asked.

'Still on the dock. The meat wagon got into a fender bender. They're sending another, but it's going to be a while.'

'We're on our way.'

Orso came out of the can zipping up his fly. He saw Cassidy pulling his overcoat from the coat tree near the stairs. 'What's up?'

'Skinner thinks he's got the hooker who had her finger bitten off. A floater in the Hudson.'

Orso grabbed his hat and coat and followed Cassidy down the stairs.

The patrolman leaning against the squad parked at the entrance to the pier on 23rd Street came to attention and tugged the hem of his uniform jacket straight when he recognized Cassidy and Orso.

'Where's Skinner?' Orso asked.

'Out at the end of the pier, sir,' the patrolman said.

The wind off the water at the end of the pier was cold. Gulls wheeled and cried against the gray sky. The air smelled of salt and diesel. A mournful foghorn blew as a tug pulled a barge full of garbage downstream through the chop toward its ocean dumping ground. The flying bridge of a moored police launch rose just above the edge of the pier. Al Skinner and a group of men stood near the woman's body, which lay on a canvas tarp on the concrete. There were a couple of cops from the boat, and a police swimmer in a black suit made of rubber.

Skinner waved a hand in greeting. 'Cassidy, Orso.' He gestured to the other men: 'Valentine

313

and Cappelli. The guy in the condom suit is Wagner. He pulled her out.' All the men nodded in greeting. Cappelli pointed a finger at Orso and said, 'Erasmus Hall, Mrs Bishop's English class.'

Orso laughed. 'Oh, yeah. All that *Moby Dick* torture. You're Molly's cousin.'

'You leave my cousin out of it,' Cappelli said with mock severity, and both of them laughed the way men sometimes do when talking about a girl from their teens.

Cassidy and Skinner knelt by the dead woman. Her body was slack in her sodden clothing. She had lost one shoe. The other had snagged a piece of brown paper in the water that wrapped part way up her ankle. There was a piece of eggshell in her wet hair. Her clothes were stained with oil from the river, and water that ran off her had pooled to soak the canvas. Her face was pale. Her eyes were open, and blank as agates. Her mouth gaped. Nothing could have looked more dead.

Skinner pointed to the dead woman's right hand. The tip of the index finger was missing. The wound looked raw and blue. 'I saw that, I called you.'

'Cause of death?'

'I don't really know until I do the cut, but check her neck. I'm guessing strangulation.'

Cassidy bent close and saw the bruises fingers had left on the pale skin of her throat. 'How long has she been dead?'

'My guess is five days to as much as ten. The air's been cold. The water's cold and salt in this

314

part of the river. I'll know better when I get her on the table.'

'Hey, Cappelli,' Cassidy said. 'You got any idea where she might have gone in the water?'

Cappelli turned away from talking to Orso. 'Hard to know. Tide in, tide out, current, eddies. Sometimes you drop something off one of these docks you never see it again. Other times, the thing comes back two, three, four times to the same place over a period of a week.'

'Al, get me a photo I can show around,' Cassidy said.

'I'll do it before the cut. Clean her up, dry her out, a little make up, comb her hair. Pick it up this afternoon.'

The street lamps were on against the early darkness, and the stream of commuter cars on West Street followed their headlights uptown toward the Holland Tunnel, or south toward the end of Manhattan and the bridges to Brooklyn. Spencer Shaw stood in darkness beside an iron pillar under the West Side Highway across from the front of the *New York Post* building. Cars and trucks rumbled and banged across the pavement dividers overhead, and the pillar vibrated with their passage. People poured out of the building, hurrying with the cold and the wish to get home. Shaw watched for Rhonda Raskin, but she had not yet appeared.

Was the Raskin woman an enemy? Or was she just another road kill on history's highway? It didn't matter. It wasn't up to him to decide. She was interfering with the mission. She had to go.

315

His only regret was the waste of a good-looking woman. And then Cassidy. Yes, Cassidy was going to be, what? Interesting? Fun? Maybe both.

He could see his car parked between a delivery van and a street sweeper half a block away. His driver was an indistinct hump behind the wheel in the gloom under the highway. A good man, Stefan. He did not ask questions about why, only about how or when or where. If Raskin left on foot, Shaw would follow her. If she caught a ride, they'd use the car. Shaw took one of his gloves off and put his right hand in his coat pocket to touch the gun. The suppressor on the barrel made it a long, awkward shape. He also carried a gravity knife in his right pants pocket. It had a five-inch blade that released with a flick of the wrist. Different tools for different situations.

There she was.

Raskin came out onto the sidewalk and stood in the spill of light from the big lobby door. There were other people with her, three men and another woman. They were laughing about something. One of the men said something, and the other woman nodded and then said something to Raskin. She shook her head. They all began to talk to her at once. They were trying to persuade her to do something. She shook her head again. The other woman put a hand on her arm, and one of the men put his hands together in prayer and bent his legs as if he was about to get down on his knees. There was more talk, and then the Raskin woman laughed and nodded, giving in, and the group moved away

316

from the lighted door to the *Post* and turned east at the corner.

Shaw followed. As he dodged the traffic to cross the broad avenue, he heard the car start up behind him.

Raskin and her friends walked a couple of blocks to Greenwich Street and then went into a pub called the Billy Goat under a sign that showed a goat standing on its hind legs drinking from a foaming stein. Shaw stepped into a doorway across the street. He pulled his coat tight around him against the cold and lit a cigarette, resigned to wait. A minute later he saw his car cruise slowly up the block. He stepped into sight from the doorway, and Stefan went by him and into a parking space near the corner.

An hour later, Rhonda Raskin came out of the pub alone. She paused for a moment in front of the door to button her coat and light a cigarette, and then she started north with a slight wobble in her walk. That last drink on an empty stomach.

Shaw stepped out of the doorway to follow her. As he passed the car he raised a hand to the driver to wait. Raskin stopped on the corner and looked south. She was probably looking for a taxi, because the nearest subway was blocks away.

Greenwich Street was quiet. A few cars waited blocks south at a red light, but none of them showed the roof light of a cab. Shaw saw no pedestrians. Okay, wait till the cars pass. He pulled his hat down to shade his face confident that she would not recognize him until too late. He slipped the knife out of his pocket and held

317

it down by his leg. Even with the suppressor, the gun made a noise like two shingles slapping together, enough to draw someone's attention. Better the knife. She was about twenty yards away. *Just walk to her, not too fast. Too fast and she spooks.* A woman alone on a street at night, she'll spook easily. *If she moves, call her name. That'll hold her for a second or two, and then you're on her. One up under the solar plexus going for the heart. Across the throat. Into the car, and gone.* Blood on the coat, of course. That couldn't be helped. Another unsolved killing in the city. One of many. *Okay, let's go.* He did not know it, but he was smiling.

'Rhonda. Rhonda, wait up.'

A woman's voice.

Shaw stepped back into the shadows. The other woman from the *Post* was hurrying toward the corner. 'Share a cab?'

'Sure,' he heard Raskin say. 'If we can ever find one.'

They stood talking while they waited. He could not hear what they were saying, but occasionally laughter would rise. A few minutes later a cab came up the street and pulled to the curb.

Shaw waved up the car, and they followed the taxi uptown through heavier traffic flow north of Greenwich Village. The cab turned east on 22nd Street and north again on Madison. It went right on 70th and stopped opposite a building in the middle of the block between Lexington and Third. No one got out. 'Drive on by and pull over near the corner,' Shaw said.

As the car slid by the taxi, Shaw glanced

318

over with his hand up blocking his face in case she was looking in his direction. The two women were talking animatedly in the back seat. The building where the cab stopped had no doorman. There was a shallow lobby with bell pushes next to apartment numbers, and then a locked inner door leading to the elevator lobby.

Stefan pulled over next to a fire hydrant and shut off the headlights. Shaw watched over his shoulder. Rhonda Raskin got out and went into her building. Shaw opened the door. 'Keep the motor running.' He put his hand on the gun in his pocket. The cab carrying the other woman went by him and turned up Third Avenue.

Shaw could see Raskin through the glass front door. She was looking for her keys in her purse with the concentration of the slightly drunk. *Wait till she gets her key in the lock; go in fast before she can shut the door.*

She found the keys.

Shaw watched her put the key in the lock of the inner door. She put her shoulder to the door, and pushed it open.

Shaw moved quickly for the outside door. He put his gloved left hand up to shove it open. The pistol was in his right. One push, and he was in. His left hand caught the inner door just before it closed. *Step into the lobby. One in the back to drop her. One in the head to make sure.*

He started to push open the inner door.

Inside the lobby the elevator door opened and a man and a woman stepped out. They stopped to talk to Raskin. Shaw slipped the gun into his pocket, turned, and went out. When he looked back, Raskin was getting into the elevator. As the couple came out through the front door, Shaw walked quickly to the car.

'Well, shit,' Shaw said as he dropped into the front seat. 'Okay, drop me at the Boom-Boom Room. Then you can go home.'

Twenty-Seven

'Whose blood is it?' said Professor Junius Moulton – a big voice from a big man as hairy as a bear wearing a tweed jacket as big as a tent. He held up a hand to block any answer. 'Not important just now. Maybe never important. Two people, different blood types, obviously, AB positive and O negative.' He clinked two blood-filled test tubes together and peered over horn-rimmed glasses to where Orso and Amy Parson sat thigh to thigh on an old leather sofa. Amy Parson was in her late thirties. She had a broad Scandinavian face, and big, dark eyes that coolly analyzed anything that came within range. Her blond hair was held back from her high, wide forehead by a black velvet headband. She wore a pale lavender tweed suit with a skirt short enough to show off her legs. When Cassidy first met her outside the building, she examined him in a way that made him feel like a bug on a pin. But she had welcomed him with a warm smile and a firm handshake that allowed him to shake off the feeling.

Cassidy was in a matching chair across from Moulton's large wooden desk in his office on the third floor of the NYU science building. 'Dead? Probably dead, otherwise why are the police here?' He was used to holding the attention of a large classroom of students with provocative questions and half-completed ideas designed to lead the listeners on. 'So, you want to know what chemical is in the samples.' He waggled his heavy caterpillar eyebrows and waited for a response.

'Can you tell us?' Cassidy, playing along.

'Of course I can tell you.' He tapped the two glass tubes against his forehead to show where the knowledge lay. He leaned back in his desk chair, which protested with a groan, and held the test tubes high. 'D-lysergic acid diethylamide.' He waited for a reaction. He got nothing but blanks looks.

'Elucidate, Junius,' Amy said.

'Yes, yes. Of course. LSD – 25. From the fungus *ergot*, which grows on rye and other grains. First made by the Swiss chemist Albert Hofmann in, correct me if I'm wrong, 1938.'

'What's it for?' Orso asked.

'A very good question. At first there was no application, but in 1943 Hofmann took a larger dose than he intended and discovered that the drug had hallucinogenic properties. Then the pharmaceutical company Sandoz marketed it as Delysid for various psychiatric uses. 1947, I think.'

'What kind of psychiatric uses?' Cassidy asked.

'They were hoping the drug would help retrieve repressed memories, and in some cases it did.

321

For some patients it was effective for relief of anxiety or obsessional neuroses. Hard to control though.' He scratched vigorously at his scalp with both hands, and then looked at his fingernails to see if they had unearthed anything interesting. 'The big problem is that it can cause wild mood swings. Some patients got panic attacks, paranoia, thoughts of harming others, suicidal thoughts. It's difficult to know what dose to use.'

'If a man who was having mental problems – depression, say – was given too much, could it make him jump out a window?' Cassidy asked.

'Could.'

'Without opening it?'

'Could, indeed. I'm not a psychiatrist, but the disturbed mind is a powerful engine. Could drive you to almost anything.'

'Are there any antidotes? Is there something you can give someone who's having a bad time with it?' Cassidy lit a cigarette.

'There is some indication that a tranquilizer helps,' Moulton said.

'Who uses it?' Cassidy asked. 'Psychiatrists?'

'Some. Not many. . I have a question.' He thumped forward in his chair and leaned across the desk to give more weight to what he asked. 'I deduce from your questions that one of these men committed suicide. Did the other?'

'No,' Cassidy said.

'But both of them had been given LSD before they died. Do you know who gave it to them?'

'Yes.'

* * *

322

Cassidy made coffee in the kitchen, a towel around his waist, his hair still wet from the shower. Rhonda came in from the bedroom and began to rummage through the living room looking for something.

'What are you looking for?'

'My notebook. I had it last night when I got here. Now I can't find it. I swear to god the thing can move by itself. I spend half my life looking for it.'

'It's in the bedroom. I saw it last night.'

'Where?'

'I don't know. In there someplace. Try the top of my bureau.' She disappeared toward the back of the apartment. Cassidy poured himself a cup of coffee, took a couple of sips, and lit the first and best cigarette of the day.

Rhonda came back from the bedroom a minute later. 'What's this? Why do you have this? Who is she?' Her face was pale, and her intensity made her hand shake. She shoved the photograph of Maxie Lively in front of his face. He had left it with the other things from his pockets on the bureau the night before.

'She's a hooker we pulled out of the river. Someone strangled her. She's connected to that other case we're working.'

'She's the woman who was in the house on 4th Street where that guy tried to grab me.'

'What?'

'She's the woman, the one who tried to get out. He grabbed her, and that's when I ran. I swear to God. It's her.'

'Are you sure?'

'I'm sure. I'm sure.'

Cassidy dressed and bolted his coffee under the lash of Rhonda's impatience. They walked quickly to the Ninth Precinct stationhouse on Charles Street.

'Why do we have to go talk to the cops?' Rhonda asked. 'You're a cop, I know where the house is on West Fourth. Let's just go there.'

'Professional courtesy. It's not my precinct, it's theirs. You don't just come in and start rooting around someone else's territory without asking.'

The desk sergeant sent them upstairs to talk to Lieutenant Blandon, who turned out to be the cop with the burned face and the crooked smile who had sent the patrolman with Rhonda to the house on West 4th.

'Yeah, I remember,' he said. 'You and Seeley went over, but everyone was gone.'

'The woman she saw over there ended up in the river,' Cassidy said. 'Did anyone ever search the place?'

'No. Locked it up and sealed it. We were kind of busy that day – two cops shot, and that fucking guy holed up in that bar on Washington. Seeley reported there's nobody there. We figure it was a whorehouse, and now it isn't a whorehouse, so not much pressure to do anything about it. Then, you know how it is. You think you're going to get back to something, but something else comes up, pretty soon the other thing slips.'

'Do you mind if we go take a look?'

'No. Go ahead. Anything you find comes back here first, okay?'

When they arrived at the house, Rhonda hesitated on the sidewalk in front and looked up at the house. 'I'm scared.' There was no light on in the house, and the windows stared blankly at the street.

'Rhonda, you don't have to go in. Go to the diner on Hudson. I'll meet you there.'

'No. I have to.'

'You don't have to. I'm just going to go in and take a look around. I won't be more than half an hour.'

'I have to, Michael. If I don't, it's going to stay with me. I won't be able to shake it.'

'All right. Don't worry. There's no one there. They wouldn't risk coming back.'

'You're sure?'

'I'm sure. Plus, I'm here to protect you.' He flexed one arm.

'Now I feel better,' Rhonda said, and managed a smile.

They went up the steps, and Cassidy cut the police seal with his pocketknife. The new padlock on the front door opened to the key the desk sergeant at the Ninth had given him. Rhonda followed him into the front hall with her hand touching the small of his back. The front windows were curtained, and the hall was dim. Cassidy found the switch near the door and turned on the lights.

The air was dusty and stale. The house was quiet. It felt abandoned, lifeless, as if the people in their hurry to leave had sucked the vitality out with them.

'He was trying to pull me back there' – Rhonda

pointed down the hall – 'and then the woman came out, and I got away.'

'Tell me what he looked like.'

'I told you.'

'You told me, a blond guy about six-feet tall, maybe thirty-five years old. You told me how much he scared you. You told me how strong his hands were. This is where you saw him. Picture it. Remember it. Tell me again with as much detail as you can.'

She took a deep breath to gather herself. 'All right.' She left him there and went to the front door and opened it and went outside. She turned and stood as if waiting for someone to answer the door, and then came back into the front hall. Her eyes were half closed, and she was turned inward toward memory.

'Okay. He opened the door,' she said in a low voice. 'Six feet tall. Blond. Smiling, as if he was happy to see me. I told him I was canvassing for the election. He asked me in. I was going to turn around and leave, because this didn't seem like it could be the house I was looking for, Government agents, and all that. He insisted I come in.' She opened her eyes wide, and let out a breath. 'Oh, boy.' The memory twisted her.

'It's all right. Go on.'

'He grabbed my arm. Hard. I knew, then.'

'Don't think about that. Describe his face.'

'Lean. Almost bony, but good-looking. Blue eyes. His eyebrows were almost red. What do they call it, russet? He hadn't shaved that day, and his beard was coming in the same color. I remember his hair was really blond. He was

326

smiling, but there was nothing good in it. He was very strong.' She saw something in Cassidy's face. 'What?'

'He had a gold signet ring on the little finger of his left hand, and when he smiled one of his teeth was crooked.'

It startled her. 'How do you know that?'

'His name is Spencer Shaw. He works for the CIA. You were in the right house.' He had told her about Spencer Shaw, about Paul Williger going out the window of the Hotel Astor, about Chris Collins, the advertising executive who died with the same chemicals in his blood. 'Shaw must have seen you with me somewhere. He needed to know what you were doing here, what you knew. Christ, he must have been surprised when he answered the door, and there you were.'

'I didn't know anything. I thought I was in the wrong house. I was looking for the house where Bill Long was taken after he wrote about Nazi scientists being brought to the States after the war . . .' She stopped while understanding surfaced. 'Is that the connection? Nazis? They were using Nazis for something here.'

'We think they were doing experiments in mind control. Nazi scientists? Maybe.'

'What if they're the ones Leon Dudek saw?'

Cassidy shook his head. 'No. No.' It was too wild a coincidence. 'We don't know if he saw anybody.'

'What if?'

Cassidy led her past the stairs toward the back of the house. There was an empty bottle of wine on one of the kitchen counters and the bottoms of the glasses in the sink held crusts of dried red wine. A first-aid kit lay on the table. Next to it was a bottle of Mercurochrome, a roll of gauze, a roll of white surgical tape, and a pair of scissors.

'She had a bandage on her hand,' Rhonda said.

He opened the refrigerator. It held a bottle of milk with about an inch left, a piece of cheese going green, an unopened bottle of white wine, three bottles of Coca Cola, and a narrow wooden tray with low sides made of wooden slats about two inches high. He pulled it out. An inch of rubberized material filled the bottom. A dozen holes a half-inch across and a half-inch deep had been cut into the rubber. Cassidy put the tray on the table and crouched to look into the refrigerator. Broken glass glinted on the bottom shelf. He used a business card to scrape the pieces of glass to him. The glass was very thin, and the pieces were mostly splinters and specks, but there were two larger bits. One was narrow-neck sealed at the top. The other was a round piece that must have been the bottom of the broken thing. Rhonda looked over his shoulder while he put the bottom piece into one of the holes in the rubber liner of the tray.

'What was it?' she asked.

He showed her the narrow neck. 'It's a drug ampoule. People get careless when they're in a hurry.'

It took them almost an hour to examine the rest of the house. It looked the same as when Rhonda had been there with the cops.

*   *   *

328

Hours on the phone over three days led Cassidy to the dead end he suspected he would find. Records from the phone company, electricity and gas records, rental records from the real-estate office, copies of rent checks from the house on West Fourth all led to dummy companies, fake addresses, disconnected phones. The house had been rented and occupied by phantoms.

Twenty-Eight

Sebastian Ambrose's brownstone on Leroy Street was in a row of similar houses halfway down the block from Greenwich. Cassidy found the address by running Ambrose's phone number against the squad's reverse directory. He needed to find Shaw. Cassidy knew almost nothing about Shaw's habits, except that he worked with Ambrose. Eventually Ambrose and Shaw would come together. When they did, Cassidy would start tracking Shaw.

Cassidy watched the front of Ambrose's house from a deep doorway across the street. There were lights on behind the curtained downstairs windows on the first floor. The top floors were dark.

Occasionally someone moved behind the windows on the first floor, a dark shape against the lighted curtains. Cassidy's feet were cold. His back ached. He began to resent the warmth of the people in the house, the liquor they were drinking, their enjoyment of their evening while he waited out here in the cold for someone to *fucking do something.*

A few minutes after nine the front door opened. A man and a woman came out. They paused at the top of the steps to say something to Ambrose who stood in the lighted doorway. They went down the steps and walked east on Leroy Street. He could not see them well. The man was big, and wore no hat. The woman was small. She had her arm tucked in his and that she talked to him animatedly with her face turned up toward him. Occasionally he nodded. Cassidy caught a fragment of her laughter.

Who were they? Should he follow them? What if Shaw was still in the house and he missed him. Shaw was the important one. He let them go. An hour later the lights went off on the first floor. Shaw never showed. Cassidy walked home, tired and cold, eager for a hot shower and a glass of cognac.

The next night brought the first real freeze of the season.

Orso stamped his feet against the cold. 'They say it's going to be a bitch of a winter. Snow up to our ass. You ever been on a stakeout where it wasn't freezing or hot as hell?'

'Never,' Cassidy said. 'Or raining. It's a natural law.'

They had been in the doorway across from Ambrose's house for two hours. In that time no one had gone in or come out of the house.

'Sorry to have dragged you away from Amy,' Cassidy said.

330

'Forget about it. It's probably a good thing. If I hang around all the time, she's going to take me for granted. Besides, I owe you. I've been fucking up, haven't I? I've been letting everything slide for her.'

'Yes, you have.' They had been partners for four years. There was no reason to shade the truth.

'You've been carrying me. I know. Jesus, Mike, it's just that I can't get her out of my mind. I can't concentrate. We have breakfast, and she has to go off to work, and I think, okay, pull yourself together and go do the job, and then half the time I hang around until I know she's out of class, and we go have lunch or something. I am fucked, man. I am truly fucked.'

'How about I shoot you?' Cassidy said.

'That'd do it. Or I could quit.' He glanced over to see Cassidy's reaction.

That surprised Cassidy. 'Quit? Then what would you do?'

'I don't know. I ought to be able to find something. My cousin Pete keeps telling me I should come work in his wholesale business.'

'Uh-huh. Bathroom fixtures. That sounds exciting. I'm thinking of getting into that myself.'

'I'd be making more money. Amy makes more than I do. That's not right, where the woman makes more than the man. That's going to cause some problems.'

'Are you serious?'

'I don't know what the fuck I am any more. You tell me. Am I serious?'

'I don't know, Tony. Are you?'

'I don't know.'

They were quiet for a while as they thought about the change Orso had proposed and what it might mean to each of them.

Orso pulled his coat tighter. His breath came in plumes. 'What are we going to do with Shaw if we find him? We've got nothing on him.'

'Rhonda can put him with Maxie in the house on West Fourth. The fingertip in Collins puts Collins and Maxie together. The traces of that LSD shit on the broken glass in the refrigerator says they gave the stuff to Collins in that house. It's the same stuff that was in Williger when he went out the window.'

'Circumstantial crap, and you know it. It doesn't prove that Shaw was there when Collins was there. It doesn't prove that Shaw killed Maxie. A good lawyer's going to kick our ass. We could just shoot him, and that would be the end of it. Hey . . .' Orso gestured with his head. The door to Ambrose's house was open. The couple from the other night, the big man and the small woman, were walking down the steps while Ambrose stood in the door and spoke to Spencer Shaw. Shaw said something in turn, nodded in agreement, and then went down the steps to join the couple. Ambrose waved from the top of the steps and then went inside and closed the door.

'If they split up, you take the couple. I'll take Shaw,' Cassidy said.

'You going to clip him?'

'No.'

'Want me to?'

'No.'

Orso shrugged at Cassidy's short-sightedness. They waited until Shaw and the couple were well down the block before following. Neither Shaw nor the couple looked around. When they turned the corner onto Hudson and disappeared, Cassidy and Orso sped up.

Shaw and the couple stopped halfway up the block. Cassidy and Orso watched from the cover of a newsstand in front of a convenience store. The big man was bare-headed and he did not wear gloves. Maybe he was impervious to the cold. A breeze ruffled his thick hair, and he used one hand to stroke it back in place while he held the other up to catch a cruising cab. Shaw talked with the woman. She was small and vital, a woman whose hands were always in motion, gesturing, stabbing the air for emphasis, touching Shaw's arm to massage home a point. Her back was turned, the collar of her coat was up, and she wore a hat that covered her hair, and Cassidy could tell nothing about her beyond her size.

The big man held the taxi door open. The woman shook hands with Shaw and got in the cab. The big man nodded to Shaw and followed her in. The parting was no more than polite. They knew each other but they were not friends.

Shaw walked uptown.

Orso darted into the street and hailed a cab. Cassidy saw him lean forward to show his badge to the driver, and then the cab took off.

Cassidy let Shaw get a block lead, and then went after him.

Shaw wore a tawny camel's hair coat that stood

out like a beacon on the night streets. He stopped occasionally to look in store windows. He waved off the invitation of a group of drunks standing in front of a bar on the corner of Christopher Street. He stopped in the middle of the block to light a cigarette. Cassidy stepped into a dark doorway across the street. Shaw looked around casually, and then went on. It was too casual. Shaw was checking for tails. Did he sense something, or was it just the precaution of a man who works the shadows? To be safe, Cassidy dropped back half a block. A few blocks farther on he watched Shaw duck down into the subway at 14th Street.

Cassidy counted to fifteen, and then went halfway down the stairs and crouched to the bottom. Shaw was just pushing through the turnstile. Cassidy went down the rest of the stairs fast while he searched his pockets for a subway token. He did not find one.

A train pushed air and noise ahead of it as it approached the station. Cassidy shoved a quarter at the uniformed man in the ticket booth, grabbed the offered token, ignored the man's shout of, 'Your change,' and rushed the turnstile. Where was Shaw? Was he headed uptown or downtown? A downtown train stopped in a squeal of metal. There were only a few people waiting on the platform, and Cassidy did not see Shaw among them. The train pulled out. The platform was empty.

Cassidy moved until he could see the uptown platform. Shaw leaned against a pillar and smoked a cigarette. A puff of stale air tinged with the smell of burned electricity announced a train coming along the track. The rattle and squeal of its wheels grew louder. People shuffled toward the platform edge in anticipation of its arrival. Shaw dropped his cigarette and mashed it out with his shoe and moved to stand with a group of people just back from the edge of the platform. The engine and the first cars of the train howled into the station, brakes and wheels grinding. It slowed and stopped with a lurch and a banging of couplings. The doors hissed open. Behind Cassidy a group of college students, boys and girls together came whooping through the turnstiles and running for the train. They stampeded down the stairs. Cassidy went with them. When they got to the bottom, they all tried to crowd through the same door, forcing the conductor to hold the train. Cassidy ducked low, peeled off, ran to the car behind, and jumped in through the forward door just as it started to close.

The couplings jerked tight and the cars banged into motion. Cassidy looked over the shoulders of the two men who stood between him and the end doors to the next car. He could see past the scrum of college students to where Shaw stood in the middle of the car holding on to a pole and swaying with the movement of the train. 23rd Street, Penn Station, then 42nd Street. People got on and off. Shaw did not change positions. At Seventh Avenue and 53rd, the train turned east. As it pulled into Lexington and 53rd, Shaw looked up. When the doors opened, he was the first off the car. Cassidy waited and followed people out of the car and up the stairs.

Cassidy held back for a moment at the top of the stairs, and then went out onto the street. He checked downtown and then uptown and spotted the brightness of Shaw's coat heading north. He dodged across traffic to the other side of the street and followed half a block behind. At 56th Street Shaw turned the corner and walked toward Park Avenue. He went in under the awning of a large brick apartment building on the north side of the street. The doorman greeted him cheerfully, 'Good evening, Mr Shaw, getting cold,' and pulled open the big brass-bound door.

Cassidy found Orso leaning against the bar at Toots Shor's. Orso saw Cassidy come in and raised a hand to the bartender and pointed at Cassidy. A martini arrived just as Cassidy did. 'Thanks, Al.' Cassidy raised his glass to Orso. He took a sip. 'God, that's good. What'd you find out about Ambrose's friends?'

'They live at 23 West 63rd Street. A brownstone. Mr and Mrs Brandt. Karl and Magda. They've been there about three years. Very nice people, according to the neighbor who's out walking his dog. He thinks they're doctors of some kind. He's impressed by that. Very tidy. No garbage cans left on the street. Flowers in the window boxes. Good morning, good evening, when they meet on the street. Very proper. Very orderly. It's the best thing about Germans, he says. They're orderly.'

'They're German?' Cassidy put his glass down and stared at his partner.

'What about it?'

'Leon Dudek is looking for Nazis in New York. He gets killed about four blocks from where two Germans live.'

'Could be a thousand Germans living on the West Side near the park.'

'How many are working for the CIA doing something weird with mind-control chemicals?'

'It's a reach, Mike.'

'Is it?' Cassidy dug in his pocket and found the copy he had made from the photograph in Freddy's hideaway. He put it on the table and touched the small woman sitting among the men on the picnic. 'Is that her, what's her name, Brandt?'

Orso studied it. 'Yeah, that's her.'

'Do you see the husband?'

'Yeah. The big guy in the middle, smiling. That's him. Where'd you get this?'

'It came out of Leon Dudek's room.'

'What's the connection?'

'The camp. He knew them from the camp.'

Twenty-Nine

Cassidy went into the diner on Hudson Street, and took a seat near the far end of the counter. Queenie brought him a cup of coffee and a discarded copy of the *New York Daily Mirror*. 'Eggs?' Queenie asked.

'Over easy. Rye toast.'

'You got it.'

337

The paper was open to the sports section. The headline yelled, *CANADIENS BOUNCE RANGERS 4 –2*. While he was reading, Cassidy was aware that a woman had taken the stool to his left.

Queenie brought Cassidy his eggs and refilled his coffee cup, and then stopped in front of the woman to take her order.

'Black tea. An English muffin, no butter please. Well toasted, yes?'

Her accent, slight as it was, caught Cassidy's ear. He glanced at her while he turned the paper back to the front page. She was a small woman of indeterminate age wearing a frumpy brown suit and a green hat the color of old pea soup. She smiled at him and nodded, one of those nods that acknowledged your presence but did not invite conversation. Cassidy went back to the paper, holding it in one hand while he ate with the other. He was vaguely aware of Queenie arriving with the woman's order.

'Excuse me,' she said. 'May I have sugar, please.'

'Sure.' He put the paper down and turned away from her to get the sugar bowl from further down the counter. When he turned to hand it to her, he noticed that her eyes were like blue chips of ice, at odds with the dowdiness of her clothes.

'Thank you, most kind.' She jerked her head in a small formal bow, and turned back to her breakfast.

When he finished eating, Cassidy left money for Queenie, and went out onto Hudson Street. The day was crisp. The few puffy clouds scudded

338

across a blue sky just above the tops of the buildings. Just past Perry Street he stopped to light a cigarette and saw his reflection in the window of a hardware store. For some reason it made him grin. He stuck his tongue out at himself, and that made him laugh. A woman pushing a child in a baby carriage looked at him, shook her head, and hurried by. She knew a New York whacko when she saw one. It made him laugh again. God, he felt good this morning.

A few blocks later a wave of dizziness made him stop and lean against the corner of a newsstand until it passed.

He waited on the corner of Horatio Street for the light to change. Waited, and waited, and waited. He checked his watch and studied the slow, slow, slow movement of the second hand, *tick, tick, tick,* as if pushing through some viscous liquid. The iron fence around the triangle of Jackson Square Park across the street began to melt, bend, undulate. The branches of the trees in the park rubbed together slowly and whispered a gray, sandy sound. When he moved his hand, the fingertips trailed tracers of color.

What the hell?

He moved his hand again, and again colors wisped from the fingers. *Wait. This had happened before. Why couldn't he remember where? Why was that important?* The light changed from red to green, piercing green, greener than green. It expanded, loomed out from the light pole, and then the pole itself began to slowly twist. He stepped into the street to see better. A high-pitched scream, a roar like an animal, something dark and large hurtled toward him. Someone grabbed his arm and pulled him back. 'Watch out!' The large thing went by in a rush. It was a car. He knew that much. Interesting – a car.

'Are you all right, fella?' A man held his arm and peered at him. 'Hey, are you okay?' There was a fleck of something dark between the man's two front teeth. Big yellowish teeth with something dark between them. Red lips. 'Hey, you've got to cut out the early morning drinking, pal. It ain't any good.'

Drinking? No. Something else. What was it, a ghost of memory, a pale, flimsy thing he could not grasp.

'You want to go up to St Vincent's? It's a couple of blocks. Let me get you up to St Vincent's. They'll take care of you. Come on. I'll help you.'

Cassidy pulled away from the man's grip. Something was happening here. Something he had done before. What was it? He was in a park. Like the park across the street? No. Bigger. Not here. Where was it? What was it?

'We'll take care of him. That's all right. He's a friend. Come on, Michael. It's okay.' A big man smiling at him. Thick chestnut hair. A friendly smile.

A woman near him. A small woman in a green overcoat and a green hat. Smiling at him. He did not like that smile. Eyes like ice. Fear backed him away from her until he bumped into the solid bulk of the man. The man's arm went around his shoulders. 'It's all right,' the big man said, and squeezed Cassidy's shoulders. 'It's all

340

right, everybody. We'll take care of him. He's a friend. This has happened before. I'm a doctor.'

A car pulled to the curb. The woman opened the back door. 'Get in, Michael,' the man said. 'Get in. Everything will be all right.' The woman scared him. He did not want to go past the woman.

'I don't like her,' Cassidy said, his own voice sounding strange to him.

The man said something to the woman in a language Cassidy found familiar but did not understand. She stepped back from the door. The man led him to the car, and Cassidy got in the back seat. The man slid in next to him. The woman got in the front seat. The driver was a big man who watched him in the rearview mirror. The door shut with a solid *thunk*. The lock clicked.

He closed his eyes and watched the play of colors on the inside of his eyelids. He was safe now.

Thirty

'Hello, Michael. How are you?' He was on a bed in a darkened room. The bed was as soft as, what? As soft as something. A cloud? Yes, a cloud. Where was he? The man who bent over him had food scraps in his beard. Who was he? Someone he knew, but who? Maybe if he closed his eyes for a moment, just closed his eyes.

'Michael, open your eyes, please.'

The voice was persuasive. He wanted to please this man. He opened his eyes.

'Good. Now Michael, we're going to talk. I'm going to ask you some questions, and I want you to answer me the best you can.'

Half an hour later, Sebastian Ambrose went downstairs to where Shaw and the Brandts waited in the big kitchen at the back of the house. When he entered, Karl and Magda were talking quietly in German. Shaw sat across from them and toyed with Cassidy's holster rig on the table in front of him. Ambrose poured a mug of coffee from the big electric percolator and splashed in some fresh goat's milk.

'What have you learned?' Karl Brandt asked.

'He's a wonderful subject,' Ambrose said. 'He does not resist the drug, and he is completely willing to answer questions openly and fully. If we could duplicate this result every time, we would have a great success. It would radically improve the quality and efficiency of interrogations. It would be the kind of truth serum, if I might use the layman's term, we've been looking for. I'm also very interested to see if he is highly suggestible under the drug's influence. After all, if we could control a man's behavior, we would have the perfect undercover weapon.'

'How much does he know about what we've been doing?' Magda asked.

'Too much. He assumes that Williger went out the window at the Astor after being dosed with LSD.'

'How does he know enough about LSD to identify it?'

342

'It was in Williger's blood. It was in Collins's blood. He found a professor of chemistry at NYU who was familiar with it. He knows that Collins was killed in the safe house on West Fourth. He believes we used whores like Maxie to lure subjects for the experiment. He assumes that Shaw killed her to keep her quiet. He is aware that we are a CIA operation.'

'Who else knows?' Shaw asked. 'Who else has he talked to?'

'His partner, Detective Tony Orso. The reporter Rhonda Raskin.'

'His brother?' Shaw asked.

'Yes.'

'They know too much. They are dangerous,' Magda said.

'Kill them all?' Karl asked. 'Is this possible in America? In Germany it was not a problem. *Nacht und Nebel*, night and fog. Many people disappeared without a trace.'

'We can get it done,' Shaw said. 'Cassidy and the woman disappear. Really disappear. No trace. Wait a bit, and the brother has an accident. The cop, Orso works in a dangerous profession. Who's going to be surprised if someone shoots him?'

Cassidy awoke in a room he did not know. The light that came in around the shade on the window glowed, broke into prismatic bands, and hummed. He tried to sit up but could not. His hands were immoveable. He rolled his head to look at them and discovered that there were cloth straps around his wrists that bound them to the rails of the bed's headboard. Anxiety bloomed in his chest. Sweat broke out on his forehead.

The door opened, and a man came in. He trailed a mist of colored light that pulsated as he moved, and there was an aura of light around his head. He pulled up the shade, and daylight flooded the room. He picked up a wooden chair and sat on it near the bed where Cassidy could see him.

'Are you with me here, pal?' He slapped Cassidy lightly back and forth across the face. 'Are you tracking? Do you know who I am?'

'Yes.'

'Who am I?'

'Spencer Shaw.'

'Good boy. I want to ask you a couple of questions. Would that be okay?'

Shaw's voice sounded to Cassidy like it was coming through a long pipe. 'Yes,' Cassidy said, and rolled his head from side to side as the room walls bent and straightened.

Shaw reached over and grabbed his face and held it still. 'Did you kill Russell Crofoot?' Shaw leaned forward to hear the answer.

Something in Cassidy fought against answering.

Shaw dug his fingertips into the muscles of Cassidy's jaw. 'Answer the question. Did you kill Russell Crofoot on Bank Street two years ago?'

Whatever held Cassidy back weakened, breached, and fell apart. 'Yes.'

'Why did you kill him?'

The question floated through Cassidy's mind without sticking.

Shaw slapped him again. 'Why did you kill him?'

Cassidy opened his eyes. 'He was trying to kill me.'

A phone began to ring somewhere in the house.

Shaw said, 'Do you remember that I told you I'm going to kill you?'

'Yes.'

'Today's the day. I get to kill you. You get to die.'

'Now?' It seemed like an important question somehow.

'No. I want you sober. I want you to know it's coming. Don't be impatient. We'll get it done today. We're going to have some fun.'

Ambrose opened the door. 'Phone for you, Shaw.'

Shaw went out to the phone extension from a small table at the top of the stairs. 'Shaw, here.' He listened. 'I'm on my way.'

Rhonda took a drag off the cigarette that smoldered in the Stork Club ashtray on the edge of her desk and went back to banging on the typewriter as if force would add energy to the story she was writing. No matter how often she went back to edit and rewrite, it just lay there. It was going to put more people to sleep than Miltown. Who cared about this crap? She should be digging on the Dudek story.

'Hey, Rhonda,' Stan Nagosy yelled from the sports desk. 'Call on line three.'

She picked up the phone and punched the lighted button. 'Raskin, here.'

'Rhonda, Tony Orso. Cassidy's been hurt.' His

345

voice was strained and slightly muffled, and he was talking fast.

'Hurt? What do you mean hurt? Is he all right? What happened?' Her heart jumped in her chest, and her breathing was suddenly tight.

'I'm sending a car for you. It'll be there in five minutes. I've got to go.'

'Wait. Wait. What happened?'

'The driver will recognize you. Get going. He's on his way.' The phone clicked off, and she was left holding the buzzing receiver. She grabbed her coat and purse and rushed for the elevators.

Her heels clattered on the marble floor of the lobby as she hurried for the exit. *Hurt, he had said. Not dead. Okay. That's good. That's something.* She pushed through the doors to the sidewalk. A car was waiting in front, and a man stood at the back door. He raised his hand to her.

'I'm Rhonda Raskin. Are you waiting for me?'

'Yes.'

He opened the back door as she approached, and she bent to get into the car.

She tried to stop, but it was too late. The man from the house on West Fourth reached over and pulled her in, and the door slammed behind her. She tried to scream, but he punched her hard in the stomach and the breath rushed out of her. He hit her again on the side of her neck, and she blacked out.

Spencer Shaw crammed her into the footwell behind the front seat, covered her with a blanket, and put his feet on top to hold her down if she came to. Stefan slid into the driver's seat. 'Go,'

Shaw said. They pulled into traffic and headed uptown toward the Village. Shaw lit a cigarette. A sweet little operation. Snatched a broad in broad daylight, and no one blinked.

Freddy watched Rhonda come out of the *New York Post* building from across the street. She was in a hurry, and she looked scared. A man was waiting near the door of a car parked at the curb. Another man waited in the back seat. When Rhonda started to get into the car, she suddenly lurched forward as if she had fallen, and then Freddy did not see her again. Had something happened? Who were the men? He pulled his bicycle out of the alley behind him and took off after the car. The traffic was slow moving uptown, and he would have no trouble keeping the car in sight.

Fifteen minutes later the car stopped in front of a house on Leroy Street in the Village. Freddy stood in a shadowed doorway half a block away and watched the driver ring the doorbell. A man came to the door. He had a shaggy beard and too much hair on his head. He wore old corduroy pants, house slippers, a wool shirt, and a baggy sweater. He looked to Freddy like a poor man, but it was not a poor man's house. The driver went back to the car and opened the back door. The other man got out and helped the driver carry Rhonda into the house past the man with the beard. The bearded man looked around once and then closed the door. Who were they? Why had they taken the reporter woman? Should he do something? Call the police? No. The police had never been his friends. He would wait for a while. He would watch.

The light coming in the window had changed as the sun moved west, but it was hard for Cassidy to make sense of the thought. Something to do with time. He had a watch. Could he see his watch? He tried to move his hand and realized his wrist was bound to the rails of the metal headboard. Did he know that before? Maybe. He raised his head and looked down the bed at his feet. They seemed far away. No colors trailed from them when he moved them. Why was that important? The drug. Maybe the drug was weakening.

He heard footsteps in the hall. A door opened. After a while, the door closed and the people passed his door again and went down the stairs. Why didn't they stop and talk to him? He needed to ask questions. He needed to know why. Wait, he knew why, but it skittered away out of reach. Frustration and anger flared in him. He jerked at the bonds that held his wrists and the bedstead rattled, but he could not get loose, and that blew the anger hotter. He jerked again and again. He had to get out. He had to be free. He did not know it, but he began to roar as he slammed back and forth on the bed. Something snapped metallically above his head, out of sight. He craned back to see what it was.

'What the hell's going on up there?' Shaw asked. They could hear Cassidy's roars and the banging of the bed against the wall and floor. Shaw stood up, but Ambrose held up a hand to stop him.

348

'It's all right,' Ambrose said. 'He's in a different stage of the drug. This sometimes happens when it begins to weaken in the system. The mood changes radically. It often brings feelings to the surface that the subject normally suppresses. It seems that Detective Cassidy is a very angry man underneath. I'll give him a sedative, and that way when you remove him, he'll be calm.' He went to a black doctor's bag on the counter near the refrigerator and prepared a hypodermic.

'Do you need us any more today?' Magda asked.

Ambrose looked at Shaw, who shrugged. 'We've got it covered.'

'Then we will go. We have things to do if we are going to leave New York.'

Magda and Karl left through the front door as Ambrose started up the stairs.

Freddy watched a man and a woman come out of the house across the street. They turned east toward Hudson Street. The woman took a cigarette from her purse and said something to the man, and they stopped opposite where Freddy sat in the shadows while the man lit her cigarette. When she raised her head from the match, the sun was on her face and he knew who she was – *Eis.* The man was her husband. He remembered his hair. The doctors from the medical unit where no one got healthy. What did the prisoners say? *You could be cured of anything there, you just wouldn't be alive to enjoy it.*

Leon had been right. They were here in New York.

The woman took her husband's arm, and they

349

went on toward Hudson Street. He said something to her, and Freddy heard her laugh. He retrieved his bicycle from where he had hidden it behind a row of garbage cans and trailed after them.

Ambrose unlocked the door and went into Cassidy's room. Cassidy lay on his back with his head turned toward the window. He no longer thrashed on the bed, but the sedative would make him more docile for what Ambrose told himself was 'the removal.' It was too bad, because Cassidy would have been a good subject for extended experimentation. His hostility would be useful. The ideal use of the drug was to control people who were not well disposed toward their interrogators. The more they knew of the drug's ability to control and change hostility the more efficient it would be.

'Hello, Michael. I've brought you something to help you sleep.'

Cassidy watched Ambrose approach the bed. He knew he had planned to do something when someone came back into the room, but he could not sort out what it was. Ambrose put the hypodermic down on the bedside table and started to pull down Cassidy's sleeve. Ambrose's eyes widened as he noticed something. Oh, yes, Cassidy remembered, his thrashing had broken the weld at the top of the metal slat that held his right hand. As Ambrose began to straighten in alarm, Cassidy yanked his hand free and grabbed Ambrose by the beard. Ambrose bleated in surprise. Cassidy jerked his head down by his beard and lunged up to head butt him hard. He could hear and feel the crunch as the man's nose broke. Ambrose went over backward, and Cassidy was left with a handful of hair. He sat up and untied his other hand quickly. He swung his feet to the floor and stood up.

A mistake.

His head spun, and he had to sit down again. Ambrose moaned and twitched. Cassidy took the hypodermic from the bedside table, lowered himself to the floor, and crawled to Ambrose. He drove the needle into the man's neck and pushed the plunger and left the hypodermic hanging there. He patted the unconscious man's clothes, hoping for a weapon, but found nothing useful. He pushed himself back up to sit on the bed.

He stood and steadied himself for a moment with a hand on the headboard and then went to the door. He went out into the hall and locked the door behind him and put the key in his pocket. The stairs were to his left. He moved to them trailing a hand along the wall for support. Indistinct voices rose from below. Could he make it out the front door before they heard him? His legs and body felt weak and insubstantial and he was not sure he could run. He turned away. Maybe there was another way out.

There was a door down the hall past the room where he had been held. It was locked, so he moved on. Another door revealed a bathroom. Its window looked out on a two-story drop to the street. He ran cold water and splashed his face to try to banish the lingering effects of the drug. Out in the hall again. Another staircase climbed to the third floor. He needed to go down, not up.

Footsteps on the stairs. Two men talked as they walked up.

For the first time he noticed the key in the door of the locked room. It was only a few steps away. Cassidy unlocked it, stepped into the darkened room, and shut and locked the door from the inside. He started toward the window, but a noise made his heart jump, and he realized there was someone on the bed. He turned on the bedside light and looked down into Rhonda's terrified eyes. Her hands and feet were tied to the bed, and she was gagged. He fumbled at the knot of the gag until it gave, and pulled the cloth from her mouth. Her mouth was swollen, and there was a livid bruise the side of her neck. She tried to speak, but her voice caught in her throat and choked off. He leaned down and whispered in her ear, 'Don't talk. Someone's coming upstairs.' He freed her feet and hands, and she grabbed his shirtfront and pulled him down and whispered harshly, 'Where are we? Michael, what's happening?'

'Shhhh. It's going to be all right.'

He went quickly to the window and pulled up the shade and looked down into the backyard. Again a two-story drop, and the backyard was walled. It did not look like there was a gate or other way out except back through the house. When he turned, Rhonda was sitting up on the bed massaging her wrists. He went to the door and pressed his ear against it. The two men sounded like they were at the top of the stairs, but he could not hear what they were saying. 'Turn off the light,' he said. Rhonda turned it off and came to stand next to him. The two men stopped down the hall. They could hear the rattle as one of them tried the doorknob of the room where Cassidy had been held.

In the hall Spencer Shaw tried the door again. 'What the hell?'

'What is it?' Stefan asked.

'It's locked.'

'Yes? So?'

'So where's the key?'

'The doc must have taken it.'

'What the hell for?'

'How do I know?'

Cassidy and Rhonda heard the two men walk down the hall. They stopped on the other side of the door. Cassidy watched the knob turn on the inside. It turned back the other way. A fist slammed against the other side of the door with a bang that made Rhonda jump. Cassidy put a reassuring hand on her arm.

'He took this one too.' The door muted Shaw's voice, but they could hear his annoyance. 'Where is he? Hey, Ambrose,' he shouted. 'Ambrose . . .' He kicked the door. 'Goddamn it. Okay, let's find him. He's got to be somewhere. You take upstairs. I'll go down. Maybe he's outside fucking the goat.' Their footsteps went along the hall in either direction.

'Michael, what are we going to do?'

'Let's see if we can find a weapon. We'll take them one at a time while they're separated. One

353

of them is Shaw. I don't know who the other one is.'

'He must be the driver.' She told him about the ruse that took her downstairs and out to the kidnap car while they searched the room. The only thing they found was the wooden bar in the closet for hanging clothes. It was about three feet long and two inches in diameter and had a good solid heft for a club.

Suddenly Cassidy's head was as light as a balloon, and he had to lean against the wall for support. Rhonda put a hand on his arm. 'What's wrong? Are you all right?'

'Yes. Sure. I'm fine.'

Cassidy unlocked the door. They went quickly along the hall and went into the room where Cassidy had been held. Ambrose snored gently on the floor. 'Who is he?'

'His name is Sebastian Ambrose. He's a doctor. He was running drug experiments in the house on West Fourth for the CIA. We got too close, and now we're here.'

'The CIA? Christ, I wish I had a camera.' Her reporter's instinct knocked her fear down a few notches.

'Right. I'd much rather have a camera than a gun too.'

They heard Stefan clatter down the stairs from the third floor. 'He's not upstairs,' he yelled as he came down the hall.

When he passed the door, Cassidy eased it open and went out. He was a couple of yards behind Stefan, but he closed fast and raised the wooden bar.

354

Cassidy felt a bright flare behind his eyes, and something went sideways in his head. He lurched to the left, and thumped the wall. Stefan whirled and came at him. Cassidy swung the club, but Stefan blocked it, and the club flew from Cassidy's hand. Stefan bulled him back against the wall. Cassidy tried to knee him in the balls, but Stefan turned enough so he missed and caught his thigh. He hammered overhand punches at the big man's head, but he was crowded and could get no leverage. Stefan hit him with a short punch under the ribs, and his breath whistled out of him. He heard a shout from below as Shaw heard the noise of the fight. Cassidy grabbed one of Stefan's ears and tried to tear it off. He butted the big man in the face. The blow slowed him and drove him back a step, and Cassidy hit him in the mouth with two jabs, tried for a right hook that missed, and then kicked him in the knee. Stefan grunted in pain, shifted his weight to the other leg, and threw a straight right. Cassidy tried to duck and took the blow on his forehead. It drove him back and turned the world misty. There was another shout from Shaw that sounded like it came from the bottom of the stairs. He knew that when Shaw got to the second floor he was done. He hooked Stefan in the groin, drawing another grunt, but the man wrapped him in a bear hug and pinned his arms. Cassidy kneed him ineffectually and tried to head butt him again.

Footsteps pounded up the stairs.

Over Stefan's shoulder Cassidy saw Rhonda come out into the hall. She picked up the wooden

355

bar and hit Stefan in the back of the head as hard as she could. His grip loosened, and Cassidy broke free. Cassidy hit him with a jab and crossed with his right, and Stefan staggered back toward the head of the stairs. Rhonda hit him across the face with the club, and when he put his hands up, Cassidy kicked him in the balls. Stefan teetered for a moment at the top of the stairs. His arms windmilled for balance, and then he toppled over backward.

Shaw, gun in hand, was halfway up the stairs when Stefan fell. The dead weight of the falling man slammed into him and drove them both down, tumbling and banging. Stefan was unconscious when they hit the floor in the front hall, and Shaw was stunned.

'Come on,' Cassidy said. He led Rhonda down the stairs in a rush. Shaw was trying to push Stefan off him with one hand while he scrabbled for the gun he had dropped with the other. Cassidy wrenched at the door, but it was locked from the inside. He twisted the bolt free, yanked open the door, and shoved Rhonda out. As she went, Shaw fired, and the bullet blew splinters off the doorframe. Then Cassidy was out and pulling the door shut. Another shot and the bullet slammed into the closed door.

Cassidy found Rhonda at the bottom of the stoop, and they ran. Halfway up the block he looked back. The door to the house was still shut. No one came after them.

On Hudson Street Cassidy hailed a cab. 'The first thing is to get you someplace safe,' he said to Rhonda.

'I could go to my mother's.'

'If they've done their research, they'll know where she lives. Don't go to your apartment. Don't go to mine. A hotel or a friend. Call me at the precinct when you're settled. Leave a message, but only there. Don't leave any addresses or phone numbers with my answering service. It's just a precaution. These guys are going to be too busy to think about you.'

'What about you?'

'I've got some things to take care of.'

She hugged him tight before she got into the cab. 'Be careful, Michael.'

He used a telephone booth on the corner to call the Ninth Precinct, identified himself to the desk sergeant who passed him on to Lt Blandon, who said, 'Cassidy, you're spending more time in my precinct than some of my detectives. Why don't you put in for a transfer? What's up?'

'I've got a situation in a house over on Leroy. Kidnapping. Unlawful restraint.'

'Who's the victim?'

'Rhonda Raskin, the reporter from the *Post*.'

'Jesus, she ought to stay home more, stay out of trouble.'

'And me.'

'What?'

'I left one of the perps unconscious upstairs in a room, but there are two others. They're armed.'

'Where are you?'

'I'm on Hudson near Christopher.'

'Meet my guys at the scene. What's the address?'

Cassidy gave Blandon the address and hung up as Blandon began to talk again. Blandon would be pissed off when he didn't show up, but he had other things to do.

He flagged a cab and told the driver, 'Central Park West and Sixty-third.' He lit a cigarette and took stock as the city night went by out his window. There were some bumps and bruises from the fight. His ribs hurt on his right side if he took a deep breath, and there was a place below his left ear that was tender to the touch. He could not remember how that had happened. His right thigh ached from where the man kneed him, and the knuckles of his left hand were skinned and swollen from hitting the man's head. The lights that went by outside the cab were normal and unremarkable. No street lamps bent and melted. The effects of the drug seemed to have dissipated. Maybe he was going to be all right.

The Germans lived in a brownstone on 63rd Street a few houses in from Central Park West. Cassidy watched from the across the street. The sidewalks were empty except for a man and two women who walked arm in arm toward Columbus Avenue. Somewhere down the block a radio played jazz near an open window. Traffic ran like a river on Central Park West, but no cars moved on 63rd. There were lights on behind the windows in the Brandts' house. No one crossed in front of a window. No one threw a shadow on a curtain as he passed through a room. Maybe they were in the back rooms. Or maybe they had already taken off. That worried him.

Cassidy retreated to the phone booth on the

corner to call the Ninth Precinct. He watched the Brandts' house through the glass panels smudged with city grime while he dialed. The desk sergeant put him through to Lieutenant Blandon.

'They weren't there,' Blandon said. 'There was blood on the floor in the front hall, but they were gone.' Cassidy said nothing. 'We found the guy locked in the room upstairs. He was unconscious. Someone stuck a needle in his neck. His driver's license gives the house on Leroy as his address, so we figure he owns it or rents. We didn't know if he was part of the deal, locked up like that, the needle and everything. He's over at St Vincent's till he wakes up. So, what the fuck, Cassidy? What's going on here?'

'The guy in the upstairs room is Dr Sebastian Ambrose. He's part of the deal. Better put someone on his room in the hospital.'

'Yeah, I already thought of that, being a cop and all.' Blandon's displeasure was coming through loud and clear.

'I'll come in tomorrow and give you a full report.'

'Yeah, you do that.' Blandon banged the phone down.

Cassidy opened the booth door and lit a cigarette. There had been no movement from the house. Shaw would want to clean up the operation quickly. The first thing would be to get everyone clear of New York. Maybe he had already called the Brandts. Maybe they were already gone. Time was not on his side. He had to make a move.

He walked to the brownstone and rang the doorbell. No response. He jabbed the button again and held it down for thirty seconds. He could hear the bell shrill in the house. No one came to the door. Maybe they were gone, out in such a hurry they left all the lights on. If they had, there might be something left behind to indicate their destination. He needed to get into the house. He studied the locks on the front door and then took picks and tension bars from the leather roll in his pocket and went to work. They were good locks, and it took a while before the top one clicked open. The bottom took five minutes more. He put the picks away, drew his gun, and opened the door.

Magda Brandt lay in the front hall in a pool of blood. Her throat had been cut. It gaped like a scream.

Thirty-One

Cassidy could picture what had happened. Magda answered the door, and the killer had her before she could turn. He grabbed her and cut her. She would not have made a sound. She lay on her back just inside the inner door with one arm across her stomach and the other flung wide. One leg was straight, and the other was bent at the knee. She had kicked off one of her shoes as she died. Her blouse, white when she put it on, was now dark with blood. The blood left a sweet coppery fume in the air you did not want to smell or taste.

Karl Brandt was in the living room at the end of the hall. He was sprawled on a rug near an overturned table. He must have been sitting in an armchair near the fireplace reading a book, which now lay open on the floor. The heavy bottom of a highball glass, jagged where it shattered, lay near the table. Brandt's throat was cut like his wife's, and there were deep slashes on his cheek and chin, and one of his hands was ripped across the palm. Two cuts through the jacket sleeves of the other arm were soaked with blood. The sound of Magda's body hitting the floor must have alarmed him, and he had risen and started to turn, and by that time his killer was in the room. The slashes on Brandt's face and hands were defensive wounds, but he was too late to avoid the attack. From the shape and depth of the cuts Cassidy had a good idea of the weapon used. Brandt had gone down on his back, with his legs splayed and his arms awkwardly stretched out. The killer had dipped a finger in blood and drawn a swastika on his forehead.

Was the killer still in the house? Cassidy went up the stairs with his gun in his hand. It took him half an hour to satisfy himself that he was alone with the bodies.

Cassidy had hoped to use the Brandts to break open the Collins and Maxie killings. Threat of deportation to Germany and trial for war crimes might have been enough leverage to get them to testify against Shaw and Ambrose in return for a deal to stay in the States. An ugly deal, but he

361

would have done it to get Shaw and Ambrose. That was before he understood the Brandts had killed Leon Dudek. Would he have offered them the same deal now? The killer took care of that problem, and left him with another. He could arrest Shaw and Ambrose for kidnapping him and Rhonda, but there was no real evidence that they had killed Collins or Maxie unless they testified against each other. That wasn't going to happen. The CIA would defend them. They had lawyers, money, power, and they could make the problem of Michael Cassidy go away.

He went to the phone to call the murders into the precinct. Something flicked across his mind trying to get his attention. He waited. He did not know what brought it into sight, maybe some residual effect of the drug they had given him. He looked it over, examined it from all sides, and decided it was workable. If it blew up in his face, it would end his career, and he would probably go to jail. Was it justice, or was it revenge? Sometimes those two were twins. He left the house without making the call.

Cassidy found Benny the Dip and his sister Candy eating chopped liver on toast tips and drinking soda water mixed with lemonade in Jack Dempsey's restaurant on Broadway. No booze while working was one of the family rules. Benny and Candy exchanged a look when Cassidy slid into their booth. 'Hey, Cassidy, what's up? You hungry? Let me get the waiter over here.' Benny raised his hand for attention, but Cassidy stopped him.

'That's okay, Benny. I've got a business proposition.'

Benny and Candy looked at each other again. Candy raised a skeptical eyebrow. 'What've you got?' Benny asked.

Cassidy told them.

'Who's the guy?' Candy asked.

'You don't want to know,' Cassidy said. 'And you're going to have to be really careful. This guy isn't some boozed-up tourist gawking at the lights while you dip him. He's dangerous.'

'Are you going to be there in case something slips?' Benny asked.

'You won't see me, but I'll be there.'

Benny raised his eyebrows. Candy shrugged. Sibling communication. 'Fifty bucks each, right?' Candy said. 'What if he doesn't show?'

'You still get the money.'

'And a week's free pass on the Stem,' Benny suggested.

'No.'

'Just thought I'd ask.'

'You better get going.'

Benny raised his hand for the waiter and mimicked signing a check. 'You got this?' Benny asked.

'Sure,' Cassidy said. 'Go. I'll be right behind you.'

Spencer Shaw came out of his building on 65th Street a few minutes after nine carrying an overnight bag. Shaw lit a cigarette and checked the block out of habit, but he was not worried. If the cops knew where he lived, they would have

363

been on him by now. A man and a woman were walking two small white poodles toward him from Park Avenue, frisky little dogs who roved at the ends of their leashes following interesting smells while their masters flirted the way married couples sometimes do after cocktails and dinner wine. A good-looking blond. He wouldn't mind jumping that.

One of the dogs dodged across Shaw's path, and for a moment the man and the dogs and the couple were tangled up in a dance of leashes, dogs and feet. They disentangled. The man berated the dogs while the woman apologized. 'Hey, no harm, no foul. Don't worry about it,' Shaw said, and the couple went on toward Lexington. The woman looked over her shoulder once and smiled. Nice ass. He wondered if she lived in the neighborhood. Maybe he'd see her around some time. If he ever got back here. Now it was time to move.

Stefan was in a private clinic off Gramercy Park with a broken arm and broken jaw. They had just made it out of the house as the cops turned onto Leroy Street, lights and sirens. He'd hung around long enough to see them bring Ambrose out on a gurney. He'd left a message for the Brandts, and they would get it whenever they came in from wherever they were having dinner. No panic, just time to lay low till things passed. Cassidy watched from a shadowed doorway as Shaw crossed Park and hailed a cab headed downtown. When the cab disappeared, he walked to Lexington to meet Benny and Candy.

*   *   *

364

Bonner and Newly had the frayed look of men who had recently started the night watch and were not yet used to it. Too much coffee, too little sleep, bodies out of whack. 'What the hell are you doing here, Cassidy?' Bonner said when Cassidy appeared in the squad room stairs just before ten o'clock. 'You look like someone's been beating on you with a stick.'

'Someone has.' He slumped into a chair, accepted a cigarette from Newly with a nod of thanks and took them through the story of his day. He did not lie, but he did not tell them everything.

At the end of it Bonner stood up. 'These Krauts live on Sixty-third? Let's go get them.'

'Warrant,' Cassidy suggested, but he knew his man.

'Warrant, my ass. Exigent circumstances. Probable cause. Let's go kick down their fucking door.'

The house on 63rd Street still showed light in all the windows. Bonner stomped up the steps like a man killing cockroaches. Cassidy and Newly trailed. Bonner stabbed the bell push with a thick finger and unbuttoned his coat and jacket to clear his gun. After a minute he rang the bell again. They waited. Lacy curtains hung for privacy over the beveled glass panels of the door. 'Can you see anything?' Cassidy asked. One of the curtains was slightly askew.

Bonner put his eye to the gap. 'Ahh, shit. We've got a dead one in there in the front hall. A broad. Jesus, there's a lot of blood. I guess we're going in.' He stepped back to give himself room to kick the door in, but Newly reached by him and tried the knob with a gloved hand, and the door swung open.

Magda Brandt lay as Cassidy had left her. Newly and Bonner had seen too many corpses to bother looking for signs of life. Newly pulled his gun and headed for the living room. 'Is she one of them?' Bonner asked.

'Yes. Magda Brandt.'

'A cut that deep, whoever did it really didn't like her.' Bonner bent down and touched the pool of blood with a fingertip. 'Skimming over,' he said, 'she's been dead a couple of hours.'

'Another one in here,' Newly called from the living room.

They found him crouched down near Karl Brandt's body. 'Defensive wounds on the hands and arms. The killer probably took off, but I guess we'd better check it out.'

When they were sure the house was secure Bonner used a handkerchief to pick up the phone in the front hall to call the murders in to the precinct. The medical examiner's team arrived twenty minutes later.

Cassidy did not know the team leader. He was a burly, taciturn, black-haired man named Tolliver who was no longer surprised by what his fellow citizens did to each other in the dark hours. He greeted the detectives, listened to their report without comment, nodded, and went to work.

Cassidy, Newly, and Bonner sat at the kitchen table smoking and talking until Tolliver rapped knuckles on the doorjamb. 'You might want to come see this.'

They followed him to the living room. Karl

Brandt's shrouded corpse was on a gurney. A manila envelope holding the contents of his pockets rested on his chest. Tolliver pointed to a blood-soaked leather wallet that lay on the dead man's stomach. 'We found this under him when we rolled him. Jack got photos before we moved it.'

'So his wallet fell out when he went down. So what?' Cassidy said.

'Uh-uh. His wallet's in the envelope. This is someone else's.'

'Did you check it?'

'Yeah. To make sure he didn't carry two for some reason.' He poked the wallet open with the point of a pencil. A Maryland driver's license behind a plastic window identified the owner as Spencer W. Shaw and gave an address in Chevy Chase.

'Do you know him?' Bonner asked Cassidy.

'Yes.'

'And he knew these people, the Brandts?'

'Yes. The Brandts were the ones who picked me up. Shaw and another guy got Rhonda. They were all in the house on Leroy.'

'Came to shut them up, I guess.'

'Did you find a weapon?' Newly asked Tolliver.

'No. From the wounds, it was a thin blade, a really sharp knife, or a straight razor. By now it's probably in a storm drain somewhere.'

'Dropped his wallet in the struggle with Brandt, I guess,' Newly said. 'I wish all our killers were that considerate.'

'What do you think?' Bonner asked Cassidy.

'I'm with Newly.'

367

'Yeah. The guy's going to shit a brick when he reaches for his wallet to buy a drink. I'd love to see that moment.'

By the time Cassidy got home the temperature had dropped hard. Sleet hissed against the cab roof. He paid the driver and made a dash for the door and the sleet blew against his face like cold, wet sand while he unlocked the door. Upstairs he poured bourbon over ice and carried his drink to a window. The sleet rattled the panes and turned the pier lights to soft halos. He sipped the whiskey and thought about what he had done. He had crossed a line. He had crossed it in small ways before, but never like this. Did it bother him? Not if it worked. He finished the drink and went to bed and slept hard.

In the morning he walked to St Vincent's to talk to Ambrose. The skies were clear; the air was still, and cold enough to crackle.

Ambrose was gone. He had made a call to his lawyer after he regained consciousness. Around three in the morning the cop on guard went to take a leak. When he got back to the room, Ambrose had disappeared. The handcuffs that had held him were still attached to the bed rail.

From where he stood near the stripped car body under the elevated roadway to the Williamsburg Bridge, Cassidy could see the front door of Freddy's shack. The padlock was through the hasp. It took Cassidy less than a minute to pick the lock, and he left the door open wide to let light into the room and to warn Freddy off if he came back while Cassidy was there. He did not want a confrontation with the young man before he did what he had come to do. Three straight razors were on the shelf near the door when Cassidy was here before. Now there were four. The fourth had a yellowing ivory handle smeared with blood. Dried blood caked around the blade and sealed it shut.

He put the razors in a brown paper bag he found near the stove, locked the door again, and walked to the river. He threw the bag as far out as he could. The current caught it and swirled it downstream, and he walked along the bank watching it until the water soaked through the paper and it sank out of sight.

Thirty-Two

CIA headquarters in Washington, DC was set back from E Street on a semicircular driveway north of The Lincoln Memorial. Some of the buildings had been thrown up as temporary offices during World War II, but the main building, which had housed the OSS during the war, was a solid work of cut stone with imposing Ionic columns supporting a heavy, unadorned cornice above the front entrance. A sign on a fence near the gate admitted that this was CIA headquarters. It was said that the sign had been put up at the request of President Eisenhower after an aide was sent for a meeting there and

369

could not find the building. Ike suggested that most people in Washington knew where the CIA hung out, and so they might as well do something for the few who did not.

Just after ten o'clock a gray Ford sedan pulled into the driveway and parked at the apex of the curve. Cassidy watched Spencer Shaw get out of the car and enter the building.

Cassidy watched through binoculars on a tripod at a window in a building a block away. He had spent three days watching the CIA's front entrance from this unused office on the sixth floor. Every day he filled the tin ashtray on the desk to overflowing. Occasionally he emptied it into the tin wastebasket that held the paper wrappings and empty bottles from his lunches. He used the phone on the desk to make three calls after Shaw went into the building. Finished, he looked around the office to make sure he had left nothing important, then left without locking the door behind him.

Just after eleven Spencer Shaw came out of CIA Headquarters. He got into the Ford and ran it down the driveway. A Washington, DC police car pulled across the gate to block it before Shaw reached the street. Another police car went in through the other gate and ran around the drive's curve until it blocked the Ford from behind. A detective and a uniformed cop got out of the car blocking the front of the Ford. The cops behind opened their doors in case they were needed but stayed in the car. Cassidy dodged through the cars on E Street that had slowed to see what was happening and joined the detective at the gate.

'Mike, is that the guy?' Sam Watkins asked. Watkins was a tall, thin man with a bony face and dark eyes that women found trustworthy, sometimes to their regret. He had a calm, unruffled way of going about his business.

'That's him.' Shaw stared at them through the windshield of the car. Both his hands were on the steering wheel, and his shoulders were hunched forward with tension. He returned Cassidy's look without blinking.

'Okay. Let's go get him.'

'Hold on a second.'

A car pulled up to the curb just down the block. Brian Cassidy got out of the front seat. He opened the rear door, and Rhonda Raskin got out and smoothed her skirt down. She nodded and started toward the waiting men. She carried a reporter's notebook and a pen in one hand. She lifted the other slightly in greeting to Cassidy. He nodded back but made no move to join her. She moved to where she could see Shaw in the car and began to make notes. Another man got out of Brian's car. He reached back in to retrieve a sixteen-millimeter movie camera, and then he and Brian walked up toward where Cassidy waited with the DC cops. Behind him another car parked, and Dan O'Malley, the reporter from the *Washington Post*, got out with a photographer.

'Are you sure you want to do all this?' Watkins asked, nodding toward the reporters. He had a cop's shyness about the public witnessing an arrest.

'TV, New York and DC newspapers, a

371

righteous arrest, you're going to be a hero cop,' Cassidy said.

'The dream comes true. Let's do it.'

As Brian approached, he was speaking into a small microphone clipped to the lapel of his jacket. A portable voice recorder about the size of a hardback book was slung from his shoulder. The cameraman had moved out into the street so that he could film from an angle that included Brian, the police, and the car in the driveway. Cassidy heard Brian say, 'This is Brian Cassidy. We are outside the headquarters of the CIA in Washington, DC. Washington police officers, accompanied by a detective from the New York City Police Department, are approaching the car you see parked in the driveway . . .' Cassidy stopped listening. He walked around the blocking cop car and stood in front of the Ford. Shaw looked at him through the windshield with angry eyes.

Watkins tapped on the driver's window. Shaw kept looking at Cassidy. Watkins rapped hard with his knuckles. Shaw turned his head. Watkins signaled for him to roll down the window. Shaw shifted in his seat. Watkins put his hand on his gun. Shaw rolled the window down about a foot.

'Mr Shaw,' Watkins said, 'I'd like you to step out of the car. You're under arrest.'

'What for?' Shaw did not look at Watkins. He looked at Cassidy.

'The kidnapping of Miss Rhonda Raskin, and the murder of Karl Brandt and Magda Brandt.'

Cassidy watched Shaw's eyes widen in surprise. 'What are you talking about?'

'Mr Shaw, please get out of the car.' This was

372

the moment when it could crack. Watkins took a couple of steps back to clear the door. The uniformed cop who had driven Watkins's car put his hand on his holstered gun and moved away from Watkins to widen the angle in case Shaw came out shooting.

Shaw turned off the car and got out. He looked only at Cassidy while the uniformed cop cuffed his hands behind his back and Watkins relieved him of the .38 under his arm. Brian's cameraman had moved around to keep Shaw centered in the frame. Brian spoke quietly into his microphone. Rhonda looked up from writing in her notebook and noticed O'Malley and his photographer. She looked at Cassidy and mouthed a sarcastic, 'Thanks.' He shrugged. This was O'Malley's town, and Cassidy needed the story in tomorrow's paper to give it weight. He needed as much public heat on this as he could get, otherwise it could go out the back door and never be heard of again.

A crowd of people had gathered outside the headquarters building. A man in a gray wool suit broke away from the group and hurried down the driveway. 'Hello. Excuse me. Hello,' he called as he came, demanding attention. Watkins said something to the uniformed cop, and the officer took Shaw by the arm and steered him toward the police car in the street. The man in the gray suit asked, 'What's going on here?'

He tried to go around Watkins, but Watkins blocked him. 'Who are you?'

'Assistant Deputy Director Wickersham. Where are you taking that man? Why is he handcuffed?'

373

'He's under arrest for murder and kidnapping.'

Wickersham stopped as if slapped. Watkins put a hand on his arm and turned him away from the watching crowd. He talked to him in a low voice. Wickersham looked over once toward Shaw and shook his head in disbelief.

When they reached Cassidy, Shaw jerked his arm free of the cop's grip and stopped. The cop reached for him, but Cassidy waved him off. 'It's okay.'

'I didn't kill them,' Shaw said. 'I didn't even know they were dead.'

'The evidence says you did.'

'Uh-uh. How did you make this happen?'

'I didn't.'

Shaw snorted at the lie. 'I'll be out in a couple of hours, maybe a couple of days, a week. It doesn't matter. What then? You're going to spend the rest of your life looking over your shoulder. The good news for you is it's not going to last long.' He nodded to the cop and walked to the back door of the patrol car and waited for the cop to open it. When he did, Shaw ducked inside without help and settled himself on the seat. He did not look at Cassidy again.

Thirty-Three

Rhonda's story ran on the front page of the *New York Post*. She revisited her encounter with Spencer Shaw in the house on West 4th Street, the murder of Maxie Lively, her own kidnapping, and the escape from Ambrose's house on Leroy Street. She identified Karl and Magda Brandt as suspected Nazi war criminals. She quoted NYU Professor Junius Morgan on the history of LSD and its possible uses in mind control and interrogations, and the paper ran a sidebar on Chinese brainwashing of American POWs captured during the Korean War. At the end of the article she asked the question: how many other Nazi war criminals were now working for the US Government?

Nobody answered the question. Six congressmen who were veterans of World War Two called for an investigation, but it never got traction. The Nazis were the past. The new threat was Communism.

The arrest of a CIA officer for murder was news in Washington, and Dan O'Malley's story ran on the front page of the *Washington Post*. Dulles dismissed the charges as inconsequential compared to the good fight the CIA was leading against the enemies of Democracy. Partisans of the FBI's J. Edgar Hoover, who had always been jealous of the CIA's rise in power, sharpened their knives and went after the agency's reputation, pointing out its failure to predict the Suez Crisis, and its failure in Hungary during the recent uprising, but it changed nothing.

ABC, after seeing Brian's exclusive footage of Shaw's arrest and hearing his report tying the CIA, Gallien Medical, and Nazi war criminals together, decided his suspension had been hasty. A full hour of *Behind the Headlines* was

375

devoted to the report. The following day three Democratic Senators and two Republicans called for a special prosecutor to investigate the allegations against the CIA.

The CIA released a statement that suggested that Dr Sebastian Ambrose and Spencer Shaw had been running a rogue operation. Their masters were shocked; shocked that they might have contravened the laws of United States in pursuit of their goals. Sebastian Ambrose, the statement said, had suffered a nervous breakdown and had been hospitalized. He would be made available to the media when and if he recovered.

Stefan Horvath, Shaw's driver in New York, who was wanted for his part in the kidnapping of Rhonda Raskin, was described as a local hire with no prior connection to the CIA. The Agency had no information as to his whereabouts.

The story moved off the front pages. Christmas came, then the New Year. The story disappeared.

Spencer Shaw's attorneys waived extradition and he was moved to the Tombs in lower Manhattan to await trial.

Thirty-Four

Cassidy went back to the daily grind of police work: hopped-up drug store robbers, muggers, teenage gang bangers armed with chains and knives and overheated hormones, a guy who threw a hated cat out of the sixth-floor living room window and then threw his wife after it when she complained, rapists, assaults, burglaries, car theft, the underlife of the city.

The hideout was in a five-story brownstone between Ninth Avenue and Tenth in Hell's Kitchen. It was in the middle of the block, which presented problems. Too many routes for escape: up over the roofs, out the back and through the building behind to the next street, down to the cellar and out into the alley. Uniformed patrolmen were stationed to block those exits. They all hoped the primary team did its job, because they had heard the tales of Connor Finn's size and strength, and if anyone was going to bleed making the arrest, it might as well be the better-paid detectives.

The primary team was Cassidy and Orso, Bonner and the Newly, and a big patrolman named Pensikov, who carried a heavy steel ram. Orso picked the street door lock. The stairs were dimly lit and smelled of mildew, dust, and coal smoke. Footsteps clattered above them on the stairs. They flattened against the wall. Orso, in the lead, slipped his gun from its holster. Someone appeared on the landing, saw them, and stopped. He was a mean-faced little man in a gangster suit that was too much of everything – the chalk stripes were too wide, the cloth too blue, the shoulders too padded, the waist too cinched, the lapels like wings, and the pants legs too long so they bunched over his shoes. His shirt collar was too loose and his tie was as gaudy as a tropical sunset. The shoes had two-inch heels but they weren't enough to give him stature. He was a mouse masquerading as a rat on his way out to the evening grift. He read them as cops and took a step back as if to turn and go away.

'Uh-uh,' Orso said and jerked his head to show him the way down. As the man squeezed by him on the stairs, Orso marked him with a look. If they didn't find what they were looking for upstairs, it would be because the mouse made a call, and Orso would remember him. They heard the front door open and close, and they went on up.

The third floor, a dim hallway with a window at the end. There were four apartment doors. The one they wanted was number 44. It was a heavy wood door painted black. Someone had tacked a plastic red rose to the panel under the peephole.

Cassidy and Orso took one side of the doorway. Bonner and Newly took the other. Pensikov stood in front of the door holding the ram in his big hands. He looked to Cassidy for instruction. 'Knock?' he whispered.

'Yeah,' Cassidy said, 'with that.'

The four detectives drew their guns. Cassidy nodded to Pensikov. The big cop hefted the ram, eyed the door, took a deep breath, and then swung the ram back and slammed it into the door close to the lock. The wood shredded under the blow, and the door exploded inward. The cops went in hard and fast.

Bridey Halloran, Connor Finn's girlfriend, sat in a worn armchair in a corner near the window.

378

A cigarette burned in the ashtray next to her while she brushed her hair with long, firm strokes. There were spots of blood on her face and arms. She looked at the detectives calmly. 'How're you doing, boys? He's in there.' She nodded toward the bedroom.

Cassidy and Orso stood in the doorway and looked at the dead man on the bed.

'It is him, right?' Orso asked.

'Oh, yeah. Fucking guy's the biggest thing I ever saw outside the zoo.'

The only way they knew the man was by his size. His face had been pulped to an unrecognizable mess by the cast-iron skillet that lay on the floor near the bed. A coffee cup and a broken plate lay nearby. The plate was covered with hardening egg yolk. A carving knife stuck up from up from the man's groin. It must have hit an artery, because the bedclothes were soaked with blood.

'Connor Finn,' Orso said. 'I guess he wishes he hadn't sharpened that knife so well now.'

Cassidy turned back into the living room. 'How are you, Bridey?'

'I'm okay. How are you?' She was calm, except for the metronomic strokes of the brush.

'What happened here, Bridey?'

'I don't know.' Her hair crackled with static electricity under the brush.

'You don't know?'

She shrugged and stopped brushing long enough to drag on the cigarette. She blew smoke and asked Orso, 'You got a girlfriend?'

'Me? Yeah,' Orso said.

'Are you nice to her?'

'Yeah. Sure. Most of the time.'

'Fucking Finn there wasn't nice to me. He was always giving me the needle. "Bridey, do you have to wear your hair like that? Bridey, you overcooked the fucking steak. Bridey, you do that again, I'm going to slap you hard." He did that a couple of times, and he could hit. Today it was the eggs. He asks for them over easy. I give them to him over easy like always. He says they're too hard. He says I can't do a fucking thing right. I go back to the kitchen and I'm thinking about it. Bitch, bitch, bitch. Never satisfied. Always picking at me. I think, okay, it's going to keep on going like this, ain't never going to stop. I hear him snoring in there. So I go in with the frying pan and give him a couple of whacks to keep him down. Then I think, what the hell, he's going to wake up sometime, and that ain't going to be good. So I go back in the kitchen and get the knife.'

'You've got to come in with us, Bridey.'

'Yeah, yeah. I know.' She put the brush down. 'Let me get my purse.'

Councilman John Franzi arrived at the stationhouse the next afternoon. He was a tall, portly middle-aged man in an expensive suit and a black cashmere overcoat, a survivor of countless political skirmishes. He carried his fedora in his left hand to leave his right hand free for handshakes, back slaps, and shoulder rubs which he dispensed to every cop he could reach along with his automatic smile. He brought a photographer

380

and a press aide with him to make sure his time in the squad room was properly memorialized. There was a group picture with John Franzi in the middle of the four arresting officers, and then shots of the councilman and the individual cops shaking hands, the councilman grinning while the cops stood stolidly looking down the lens with distaste. Lieutenant Tanner was summoned from the sanctuary of his office for a photo and to hear Franzi's blessing.

'A great piece of police work today. The city and the department should be proud of these men for getting a piece of scum like Connor Finn off the streets.' No mention of Bridey's helpful handiwork with a frying pan and a carving knife. 'These drug dealers are poisoning our children, and we will not tolerate it any longer. They will discover they are no match for New York's finest, and they will regret the day they took up their filthy commerce. I am going to recommend honors for the participating officers here, and you can be sure that when we take up the needs of the various precincts in committee that the Nineteenth will have its champion in me.' He stood still for one more photograph at the top of the stairs, blessed them with one more smile, and with a wave, was gone. The squad appreciated the effort he made to lie to them, but they knew that in the end the silk-stocking precincts would get the gravy and they would get the gristle.

Thirty-Five

Three days before Spencer Shaw went to trial, the DA's office discovered that his bloodstained wallet was no longer in the evidence locker. Without the wallet, any case against Shaw was circumstantial. The doorman at his apartment building told the police that Shaw had left the building around nine o'clock, which gave him time to get to the Brandts' house and kill them. But no weapon had been found, no bloody clothes. A canvass of the neighborhood around the Brandts' had produced no witnesses who could put Shaw at the scene. The DA decided to drop the murder charges and prosecute the kidnappings of Cassidy and Rhonda Raskin.

The lead prosecutor was a crackling-smart, perpetually pissed-off Brooklyn-born lawyer named Ted Lombardi who hated to lose. His round head was prematurely bald. It topped narrow shoulders and a long neck and made him look like an angry turtle. Lombardi had handled the prosecution of six or seven of Cassidy's arrests over the years, and they had developed an easy friendship.

The defense team came from Sullivan and Cromwell. They arrived each day in a phalanx, armored in beautifully hand-tailored suits. They had a rich, elegant glow as if they were polished each morning with soft wads of old money.

The prosecution was built on Cassidy's and Rhonda's testimony. The defense countered with witnesses who swore that Cassidy had been drunk and disoriented on Hudson Street the morning in question, that the Brandts had publicly identified themselves as doctors and had volunteered to help him, that Cassidy had entered the car willingly. Shaw testified that Dr Ambrose suggested Cassidy be restrained on the bed in the house on Leroy Street until his disorientation passed. Ambrose, still suffering from his nervous breakdown, was not available to testify. The defense lawyers were not as successful with Rhonda, though they tried their best. They painted her as a promiscuous slut who drank too much and slept around, as an overly ambitious woman who would do anything for a story. Under the cover of national security considerations and the restrictions of classified information, they managed to exclude all testimony that pertained to the house on West 4th Street and to any experiments that might have been going on inside the house on Leroy Street. In the end, the jury found Spencer Shaw not guilty of kidnapping but guilty of the lesser charge of unlawful restraint. The judge took a moment to praise Shaw's war record before sentencing him to three years in a medium-security facility in upstate New York.

Cassidy stood near the prosecution table and watched the bailiffs come to escort Shaw back to the holding cells. The defense lawyers shook hands and patted each other on the shoulder in congratulations while Ted Lombardi looked on sourly.

'Kicked your ass around the courtroom,' Cassidy said.

'Yeah. National security, my ass,' Lombardi said. 'Of course it would have been nice if the fucking police department could hold onto the key evidence.'

'Not the first time something grew legs in the evidence locker and walked away.'

'Well, at least he's off the street for a couple of years.'

'Doesn't seem like much,' Cassidy said. 'He killed two people we know about and at least one we suspect.'

'You know what?' Lombardi said. 'I'm thinking maybe I'm on the wrong side. I've got a good mind to give up all this shit and join Sullivan and Cromwell. I love those suits.'

'Great suits. Do you think they'd have you?'

'Sure. Once I got the transplant – cut out the wop, put in the wasp.'

Before leaving the courtroom, Shaw looked back at Cassidy. He smiled and winked and then allowed the bailiffs to take him away.

Thirty-Six

Rhonda and Cassidy began to slip by each other: missed phone calls, canceled dinner dates, work obligations that pulled them in different directions. The affair was running on fumes, and neither one of them wanted to admit it.

* * *

The dream came back for the third time in a week, a dark, thick, suffocating menace that yanked Cassidy out of sleep, his heart pounding. He lurched out of bed, knocked the bedside lamp to the floor, banged against the wall, clutched the doorjamb to the bathroom to keep from falling, and stood gasping as his heart raced. He fumbled along the bathroom wall until he located the light switch and flipped it up. The sudden light pushed away some of the dream's darkness. He turned on the shower and, while it warmed up, studied himself in the mirror. His face was drawn and pale. He thought about the dream. When had it first started? When had it gone away? What made it come back? The dream had begun in early September, not long before Leon Dudek's murder and Paul Williger's jump from the Hotel Astor window, not long before Cassidy met Spencer Shaw for the first time. The dream came with greater frequency during the next weeks. It stopped when Shaw told him he was going to kill him.

Cassidy lit another cigarette and stared out the window. Could that be it? The dream was of a coming threat. The threat turned out to be Shaw. Once he knew that, the dream disappeared. So why was it back? Shaw was in prison. But Shaw had friends, and the CIA had a long reach. He could have found someone to carry out the threat. Would killing Cassidy by remote control give Shaw the same pleasure? Maybe his arrest had pushed him to the point of just wanting Cassidy dead. He could think of no other reason for the dream to have come back so intensely. Why not

385

ask Shaw? The guy loved telling Cassidy he was going to kill him. He'd probably get a kick out of telling him it was still going to happen. And if it wasn't Shaw? If the dream was about something else that was coming? *Fuck it. Don't worry about that yet. Shaw first.*

Cassidy called the Tombs from his desk in the squad room. A woman named Gail in the records office who thought it was her job to be helpful put him on hold while she went to look up the file. When she came back she reported that Spencer Shaw had been transported to Wallkill, a medium-security facility in Ulster County. She gave him the central number at the prison. The operator at Wallkill passed Cassidy to Deputy Herb Carter in the intake office.

'What'd you say the name is, Detective?' Carter's voice had a country twang.

'Spencer Shaw. Transported from the Tombs on the fourteenth.'

Cassidy could hear the rustle as Carter turned pages. 'The fourteenth? He didn't make it to us. You sure you got the right facility?'

'Wallkill's what they told me down here at the Tombs.'

'I can't speak for them. All I can do is speak for us. He did not come here.'

'Are you sure? Maybe the fifteenth.'

'No, sir. I've checked three days both sides of the fourteenth. I'm looking at the receiving ledgers and the blotters. We've got no Spencer Shaw on any of our books. I'm looking at cell assignments – no Shaw.'

Cassidy called the Tombs again. Gail in the records office told him, 'Detective Cassidy, our records show that Shaw, Spencer, left our facility at ten o'clock the morning of the fourteenth for Wallkill.'

'Did the bus stop at any other prisons?'

'Yes, sir, it did. It had one other scheduled stop. If you'll hold on I'll give you the phone number.'

'Maybe they put him off somewhere by mistake.'

'Detective Cassidy, I'm not going to tell you that has never happened, 'cause it has. They usually catch it in a day or two. I've never heard of someone staying in the wrong facility for more than two weeks. Could happen, I guess.'

'Was Shaw sent out in regular Department of Corrections transport?'

'Let me check.' She was back in a minute. 'No. We were swamped that day. Just about every facility in the system was getting intake that day. Shaw went out in one of the private companies we use on occasion.'

'What's the company?'

'Security Transport. It's over in Queens. I'll get you the number.'

'And the address.'

'Of course.' She read it to him.

Orso came up the stairs carrying two coffees. 'Hey, what's with you? You look like you want to bite someone.' He shoved one of the coffees to Cassidy.

Cassidy told him about the missing Spencer Shaw.

'What the fuck, man? He's got to be someplace.'

They got a list of every prison in the state and called each one. By lunch they knew that Shaw might be someplace, but he wasn't in any facility operated by the New York Department of Corrections.

They checked a car out of the garage, and drove to Queens. Security Transport, was in a three-story, dirty, yellow-brick building a block back from the river.

The manager wore a blue denim mechanic's jumpsuit with a brass zipper that closed it to the throat. 'Rocco Negroponte. What can I do for youse guys?' A gravelly voice and a Brooklyn accent. He waved them to chairs in front of the desk. When they introduced themselves, Rocco grinned at Orso and said, '*Paisan.*'

'We need to know if you guys did a run out of the Tombs on the fourteenth,' Cassidy said.

'The fourteenth of this month? Let me look.' He pulled a big ledger from the desk drawer and leafed through the pages. 'Yeah, here we go. Pick up at ten. Fourteen prisoners, two guards. Up the river to Sing Sing. Then up to Wallkill. What about it?'

'Did it go on to Wallkill?'

'The ledger says that was the run. So, yeah, I guess it went up to Wallkill after Sing Sing. This only shows bookings. The driver's log will show you details of the run.'

'We need to speak to the driver.'

'Let me go check, see if he's here. Be right back.' He left the room leaving the door open.

Rocco came back trailed by a tall, thin man in a gray uniform that said *Security Transport* in gold letters over the pocket. 'This is Howie Kaplan. He drove that run. I told him what youse were looking for.'

Cassidy and Orso stood and shook hands with the driver. 'Mr Kaplan, the guy we're after is thirty-six years old, about six one, a hundred-eighty pounds, and has very light blond hair. His eyebrows are much darker, almost red. He was supposed to go up to Wallkill.'

'We didn't go up to Wallkill that day, 'cause the guy never showed. I go back to dispatch, tell them I'm ready to roll. They check the paperwork and tell me to go. The guy's gone, been transported another way. Good for me. That's a long day, Sing Sing, then Wallkill and back.'

'You're sure? Maybe he got off at Sing Sing.'

'Absolutely sure. Only three white guys in the load. Two wops like Rocco, and an old guy about sixty, killed his wife. Mean-looking fucker, bald as a cue ball. The rest were schwartzes. No blonds in the group.'

'Okay. Thanks.'

'You ever been down there when they're moving guys out?' Kaplan asked. 'On one of the real busy days it looks like someone kicked over an anthill. If you had the balls, you could probably walk in there in some sort of uniform and walk a guy out. Hey Rocco, remember that guy a few years ago wanted to pay me a hundred bucks to use the uniform for a day? A guy like that, who the hell knows what he was going to do?'

389

They drove back into Manhattan against the rush hour traffic.

'What do you think?' Orso asked. 'You think they were lying?'

'No.'

'Weird, huh, first Shaw's wallet disappears from the evidence locker. Then he disappears on moving day.'

'Shaw told me a couple of times, the agency takes care of its own. It was like the Code, no bodies left on the battlefield.'

'They'd do that? Bust a guy out?'

'I don't know. They seem to do pretty much what they want.'

'So Shaw's in the wind. And that's that.'

'Uh-uh. I think he's here in New York,' Cassidy said.

'Why the hell would he come back here?' Orso asked.

'So he can kill me.'

Thirty-Seven

Cassidy and Orso dropped the car back at the garage and walked to the Shamrock on Eighth Avenue and ordered drinks. Orso scooped a bowl of popcorn from the machine near the bar and carried it to a booth. 'Why would he take the chance?' he asked. 'He already got away with murder. It's too much risk.'

'What risk? We think he's in prison upstate.

That's what he's counting on. Nobody's looking for him.'

'He's free. He can do anything he wants. Why go after you?'

'He could have killed me any time a couple of months ago. The night he shot up the front of my building, he could have put a bullet in my head. But he wanted me to know. He wanted to make me sweat, make me wait for it. It's still what he wants.'

'That's nuts.'

'Yes.'

'Let's say you're right. What are we going to do?'

'Nothing.'

'Bullshit. We get Bonner and Newly and a few other guys, and we put a detail on you. He shows up, and we grab him.'

'He's a trained spook. If you put a tight guard on me, he'll spot it immediately. If you run a loose cover, he'll be through it before you know it, and you'll be too far away to do any good.'

'So we'll run it tight. Once he sees he can't get to you, he'll give it up.'

'For how long? If he sees I'm covered, he'll go away for a while, maybe six months, maybe a year, maybe two. Then when we've forgotten about him, he'll come back.'

'Call the agency. Tell them what you suspect. Put them on notice that we know what's going on.'

'The same thing happens. They ship him off to Italy, or someplace. I begin to forget he exists. He takes a week of leave, comes back here, and hits me. Right now I know he's out there. He doesn't know I know. That's my edge.'

'You're using yourself as bait.'

'What are my choices? If this doesn't end now, I'll spend the rest of my life waiting for him.'

'There's got to be something we can do. Let me talk to Bonner and Newly. We'll come up with something.'

'No.'

'Mike.'

'Tony, no.'

'So why'd you tell me?'

'In case I'm not as good as I think I am. If he gets me, you'll know who to look for.'

'This is fucked.'

'Yeah, I know. We better have another martini. I want to be nice and relaxed when the bullet hits.'

'You're an asshole, you know that?' Orso raised a hand for the waitress.

Cassidy wasn't quite as easy with the situation as he made out to his partner. He left Orso in Times Square and went down into the subway station. He did not go through the turnstiles. He hesitated as if changing his mind about something, and then went across the lobby past the token booth and up the stairs on the other side. He grabbed a cruising cab and watched through the back window to see if any car suddenly pulled out of a parking spot to follow. The cab stopped right in front of his building, and he went up the stoop fast with the key in his hand. He opened the door, stepped inside, and closed it quickly. The muscles in his back clenched against bullet impact until he closed the door.

Cassidy paused in front of his apartment door and examined the two locks. Shaw was trained to get through most doors. Picking a lock left minute scratches. Cassidy saw none. He crouched down and looked at the toothpick he had wedged in the jamb to fall out if someone opened the door. It was still there. Did Shaw know that trick? Probably. He drew his gun before he unlocked the door, and he went in fast, ducked to the side, and flipped the light switch.

The empty apartment mocked him.

He drew the curtains across the living room windows, double locked the door, and drove the heavy steel security bolt into its socket. He made a drink, and carried it to the sink in the bathroom where it was handy for an occasional sip while he was in the shower.

He tried to put himself in Shaw's mind. If killing Cassidy were his problem, how would he go about it? First he'd have to know Cassidy's routine. Shaw could not risk being seen, so he would need a place to watch from. Was the routine the same as before, or had Cassidy been moved to a new assignment? Was he still working days, or was he back on night watch? When he was home, was someone else with him? Was Rhonda still in the picture? A good question. Was she?

Rhonda. It was almost eleven. Too late to call her? He wrapped a towel around his waist and used the phone on the bedside table. She answered on the third ring.

'Hello?' Her voice was expectant.

'It's me.'

'Oh.' The tone changed. She may have been expecting someone to call, but it wasn't him.

'Too late to call?'

'No. I was up.'

'We need to talk.'

'What about?' Her tone was flat now.

'Let's have breakfast.'

'We can't do it on the phone?'

'It would be better in person.'

She thought about it for a while. 'All right. It will have to be early. I've got an appointment.'

'Seven thirty. The place on Bleecker.'

'Fine.' She hung up.

A cold morning with a sky like gray steel. At seven fifteen the streets near Cassidy's building were nearly deserted. A few bundled figures hurried, heads down, toward the subway, a bus, a taxi, a coffee shop, someplace warm. Cassidy used the cold as an excuse to push his pace. If someone followed him, he would have to move fast to keep up. Just before Bleecker Street Cassidy stopped to light a cigarette behind cupped hands. He ducked his head to the match and used the movement to check the block. No one on the street slowed or took a sudden interest in a store window. He was not worried about Shaw following him. Shaw would not risk being spotted, but Cassidy did not know if he had helpers. If there was someone, he was not out this morning.

He needed Rhonda to stay away from him until

this thing with Shaw was settled. If she were with him, she would be in the blast area for whatever happened. It was going to be hard enough to protect himself. But if he told her that Shaw had escaped and was looking for him, she would not go. She wasn't a woman who would desert someone in danger. And, of course, there was the story: CIA agent escapes prison to kill arresting officer. She couldn't resist that.

Rhonda was already in the diner when Cassidy arrived. He could feel the coolness of her look as he approached the booth. 'Hi. Sorry if I'm late.' He bent to kiss her, and she moved just enough so he missed her mouth.

Uh-oh.

He shrugged out of his coat, hung it on the hook above the booth, and slid in opposite her. The waitress poured Cassidy a cup of coffee and took his breakfast order.

'How are you?'

'I'm fine,' she said.

'I haven't seen you in over a week.'

'I've been busy.'

'I've missed you.'

'Have you?' She examined him over the rim of her coffee cup.

Uh-oh, again.

'I have,' he said. 'But something's come up on the job, and I think we better not see each other for a little bit.'

'What's come up?'

'I can't really talk about it.' He hoped she would not push, because he did not have a plausible lie prepared.

'Michael, if you want to break it off, break it off. Don't give me some lame crap about work.'

He wasn't expecting that. 'I don't want to break it off.' Did he?

Her smile said she knew better. She reached across the table and patted his hand. 'Let me make it easier for you. I've met someone.'

'What?'

'I was going to tell you.'

'Who is he?' *What? What?*

'It's nobody you know. He's really nice. I really like him, and he likes me. You and I were great for a while, but we both knew it wasn't going anywhere. The last few weeks . . . I mean how many times have we even had dinner together? Twice? I should have said something before. I'm sorry.' She stood, picked up her coat, touched him on the shoulder, and left.

The waitress put down Cassidy's eggs and bacon. 'You all right, honey?'

'Yes. Sure. I'm fine.'

'She'll be back.'

'I don't think so.'

She patted his hand, and went away.

Cassidy stood behind a wooden fence on Bethune Street. He stamped his feet against the cold and pulled his coat collar high. His breath smoked. A new building was going up behind him. The foundation excavation had been dug, and pilings had been driven, but no one was working the site today. He could see through the fence slats to the building on the south side of the street. It had been abandoned more than a year ago.

Demolition work began. Then it stopped. Development money dried up, and the owners struggled to find new loans. At least that was the word in the neighborhood. The first-floor windows were boarded shut. Like a lot of light manufacturing businesses the first floor had been built big enough to allow trucks to enter so loading could be done out of the weather. A padlock secured the big double front door. The lock looked too new to have been on the door long. It could mean that the demolition was about to begin again and that the owners were storing equipment. Maybe a couple of bums were camping out in there and had invested in a good lock to keep their place secure. Maybe local scavengers were stripping the place of copper pipe and scrap metal and wanted to preserve the site from other lowlifes with the same good idea.

Or maybe Spencer Shaw had set up again in the room on the fifth floor where he had fired the rifle that blew out the fanlights above Cassidy's entry door.

Right now the padlock meant there was no one in the building.

Cassidy crossed Bethune and went down the alley between the abandoned building and the warehouse next to it. All the first-floor windows along the alley were heavily boarded, and someone had taken the trouble to gouge the screw heads so they could not be unscrewed. It was the same at the back of the building.

He returned to the alley. Halfway back to the street, metal doors slanted out from low on the brick wall. They closed the chute that delivered coal to the basement furnace. The doors were bolted and the bolt was rusted shut, but no one had bothered to attach a lock. Cassidy crossed to the construction site and found a three-foot-long piece of rebar in a pile of scrap. He used the rebar to hammer the bolt that held the two halves of the coal chute door. Flakes of rust flew off it from the blows. He hammered the end of the bolt and slowly it began to work its way back through the staples. One more smash, and the bolt moved an inch back and no longer held the doors shut. Cassidy grabbed one of the door handles and pulled. It did not move. One of the doors had a metal lip that fit over the other. Rust sealed its length.

Cassidy found a place where he could get the end of the rebar under the lip. He leaned hard on the rebar. The door suddenly ripped free of the rust seal. Cassidy, unprepared for it, found himself on his hands and knees on the alley concrete. 'Shit!' He stood up. His right knee burned. His pants were torn, and the knee was scraped raw. 'Goddamn it.' That was a good pair of pants.

He went back to the door, gripped the handle, and pulled. The hinges squealed in protest as the door opened. A wave of cold, damp air came up from the cellar carrying the mingled smells of coal dust and mold. He could see the coal chute on the cellar floor ten feet down. Its upper end had rusted free, letting the chute fall. An iron ladder was fixed to the concrete wall at one side of the cellar opening. The top rung was rusted thin. Cassidy looked down into the gloom of the cellar. Some light fell through the door opening, but the rest of the cellar would be dark, and so would the first floor of the building where the windows were blocked. He wasn't dressed for this. He was dressed for the office, not for exploration through a crapped-out building. He needed a flashlight. How the hell was he going to see anything down there? It had been a spur of the moment idea to go into the building, and now that he was there, he was going in before whoever put the padlock on the front came back. Clothes could be cleaned and mended. He had matches in his pocket. He needed to know if he was right about Shaw.

He slung a leg over the sill and put his foot on the top rung of the ladder. It bent under his shoe. He took more weight on his hands and moved his foot down a rung. It seemed more solid. He went down a few more rungs, testing each before giving it weight, and then reached up and pulled the doors closed. Now he was in darkness. A rung near the bottom gave way under his foot, but he caught himself. He eased himself down, taking his weight on his hands, until his right foot touched the cellar floor. He let go of the ladder and turned away from it. At his first step his left foot came down awkwardly on something, and he rolled his ankle and went down hard.

He lay on the concrete floor of the basement and took stock. A bruised elbow, a scraped knee, and the ankle. He tested the ankle. Tender, still useful if he was careful, but not good. He found matches in his coat pocket and lit one. It made a small circle of warm light in the darkness. He used the bottom of the ladder to pull himself up. The match burned out. He lit another match. There was enough light to see the floor in front of him was strewn with junk, pieces of coal, bricks, scrap wood. He limped toward where he thought the stairs up might be and used his good foot to kick things out of his path. When a match burned low, he lit another. Claws scraped on the concrete as something skittered away from him. Rats. He didn't like rats. He found the bottom of a flight of rough wooden stairs. At the top of the stairs a line of dim light showed through the bad join at the bottom of the door. He lit another match and went up step by step. He could not afford another fall. The door at the top of the stairs opened to a broad hall. Light filtered down the stairs from the windows above, and he no longer needed the matches. The front door was twenty feet down to his right. The floor was made of concrete to support the weight of trucks. Oil stains showed where they had parked.

The stairs to the floors above were near the front of the hall. On the way to them, Cassidy passed a freight elevator. The doors were open a couple of feet. The elevator had come to rest on its last ride with its roof four feet below floor level.

The second floor was made up of big rooms fronted by a corridor. The ceilings were made of patterned pressed tin. There was nothing in the rooms that hinted at what the building had been used for. The elevator doors were closed. The third floor was identical, a big, empty echoing

400

space. The doors to the elevator shaft were closed there too. Cassidy limped up the stairs to the next floor.

Building demolition starts at the top and works down. Gravity speeds the process. The wrecking crew had been at work on the fourth floor. They had torn the floors up from the south wall to the closed elevator, leaving the big joists and cross beams. Cassidy could see the pressed tin of the third-floor ceiling still nailed below. They had ripped down many of the walls, and there was a big pile of broken plaster and wood near the elevator. The destruction was even greater on the fifth floor. The rooms here were smaller and had probably been used as offices. The walls had been stripped to their studs, and Cassidy could see through, room to room to room, all the way to the front of the building.

One room remained intact. It was at the back of the building, and it looked south over low roofs to the front of Cassidy's building a block away. A mattress covered by a couple of wool blankets was pushed against one wall. A squat propane tank held a big heating element. Near it were three one-gallon jugs of water. Two were full; the other was half empty. Blackout curtains were pinned back from the window. A Garand M-1 rifle was propped in a corner. Its butt rested on a green canvas beanbag. There was nothing personal in the room. Shaw was living somewhere else. This was his observation post.

Cassidy went over the room to make sure he had left no trace of his visit. He could be at the Ninth Precinct in fifteen minutes. All he would need is a couple of cops to throw a loose surveil-lance net on the building. As soon as the padlock came off the front door, they would know Shaw was inside. Then they could tighten the net. Teams front and back. They could wait him out until he left the building and take him on the street, or they could take him in the building. Better to take him on the street. Surprise and overwhelming force. If they tried to take him in the building and he didn't go easily, they'd have to fight their way up five floors. Shaw had the rifle. Maybe he had other weapons. People could get hurt. Cassidy thought about jamming the M-1, but if Shaw was meticulous about his weapons, he might check it. If he found it jammed, he would know someone had been there. *Be patient. Go get some cops. Take him outside.*

Cassidy went down the stairs favoring his sprained ankle. He had just reached the third floor when he heard a car stop on the street in front of the building. Moments later he heard the rattle of the padlock and hasp, and then the creaking as someone shoved the big doors open. He hobbled to the window at the end of the hall. A four-year-old Studebaker was parked outside the double doors. As he watched, a man came out of the building and got back in the car. For a moment Cassidy did not recognize him, and then he realized that Shaw had dyed his bright, distinctive hair dark brown. Shaw pulled out, swung the car around, and then backed into the building. Cassidy went back to the stairs. He heard the car door open as Shaw got out to

402

close the garage doors, then the thump as they slammed together, and the rattle as Shaw bolted the doors shut.

Take him now.

Cassidy pulled the .38 from under his arm and went down the stairs. He reached the second floor and limped into a room opposite the stairway. When Shaw started up toward the third floor, his back would be turned for a moment. Cassidy would take a couple of steps into the hall. Speed wasn't necessary. The ankle would not matter. Shaw would be no more than ten feet away, back turned, surprised. What happened next would be up to Shaw. He heard the car door slam two floors below. Footsteps on the stairs, and then Shaw's voice.

'You've got a great ass, honey. I'd be happy to follow that ass anywhere.'

'This is stupid. He won't come for me. We broke up.' Rhonda's voice, angry and scared.

'He'll come for you. He won't be able to resist.'

'He'll bring cops. You'll either end up dead or back in prison.'

'You know what? Women never know who the fuck their men really are. They make up who they want them to be, and then try to squeeze the guy into the mold. You think Cassidy's some sort of pragmatic guy? Bullshit. He wants to be the hero. Why else would a rich guy's son become a street cop?'

Cassidy found a crack in the wall where a piece of plaster had been knocked off. Through it he could see the stair landing fifteen feet away.

He was confident of putting a bullet in a two-inch circle at that distance. All he needed was a clean shot. Rhonda rose into view on the stairs. Shaw was close to her, shielded from him by her body. She stopped on the landing.

'Keep going,' Shaw said. 'We're going all the way to the top.'

When they turned, Shaw would be exposed. Cassidy would take the shot then.

Rhonda turned to go up the next flight. Shaw went with her. When he turned, Cassidy saw the gun Shaw held. It was pointed at Rhonda's back. The muzzle wandered with Shaw's movements. Sometimes it pointed at her spine, sometimes at her leg. Once it wandered off to the side. Cassidy took up the trigger slack and let his breath out slowly. Now.

Rhonda stopped on the stairs, and Shaw bumped into her. They were too close together now to risk the shot. 'Move it.'

'No.'

He jabbed her hard in the back with the pistol. 'Don't be a pain in the ass. I'll shoot you and send him your ear. He'll come running. Move.' He poked her with the gun again, and they went up the stairs together and disappeared.

Cassidy pulled the gun back from the crack and eased the hammer down. He could be out the door and at the Ninth Precinct in minutes, even walking on a bad ankle. They could have the building covered and sealed off in half an hour. Then what? Wait Shaw out. There was no electricity in the building. He would have to leave to call Cassidy. There'd be no reason to risk taking Rhonda with him. He could leave her tied down upstairs. He'd go alone, and they'd take him in the street. Cassidy looked it over from a couple of angles. He did not want to leave her here, but it was the smart move.

Cassidy listened for a moment. No footsteps on the stairs. Shaw and Rhonda must have reached the top floor. Cassidy left the shelter of the room on the second floor and headed for the stairs.

In the room at the top of the building, Rhonda screamed.

Thirty-Eight

Cassidy climbed the stairs as fast as his bad ankle let him. Rhonda screamed again. The sound was muffled. Shaw must have closed the door to the room. Cassidy stopped on the fourth floor. A thumping, banging came from the floor above. Shaw yelled something Cassidy did not understand, and then Rhonda cried out in pain.

Walls of the fourth floor had been ripped out and was little cover. The fifth floor was worse. Only Shaw's room had walls. There was no cover up there. He could go up quietly, and kick open the door to the room, but he did not know where Rhonda was. Close to Shaw? He could not risk gunplay without knowing that.

He had to get Shaw out of the room.

Metal garbage cans filled with broken plaster

and wood scraps stood near the closed elevator doors. He carried them to the stair landing and threw one down toward the third floor. It crashed and banged down the stairs and clattered out into the hall. Cassidy heard Shaw shout on the floor above. He threw the second can to follow the first, and then limped as fast he could down the hall, his footsteps covered by the crash of the garbage can. He went into a room where a partial wall would give him cover.

Shaw's footsteps pounded across what was left of the fifth floor and stopped at the head of the stairs. From his angle, Cassidy could see part way up the stairs. Shaw's feet showed. They came down another step and then stopped. A hand carrying a black automatic appeared, followed by Shaw's torso as he crouched to look down toward the landing. Cassidy drew back behind the wall. A footstep on the stairs. The brush of Shaw's jacket back against the wall as he moved down slowly. Cassidy needed Shaw on the landing. If he tried to take him while he was on the stairs, he might miss, might hit the banister or one of the newel posts, and he could not let Shaw get back upstairs to Rhonda.

The quality of the footsteps changed. He was on the landing. Cassidy risked a quick glimpse and jerked back. Shaw was crouched at the top of the stairs looking down toward the third floor.

Cassidy stepped out of the room, gun up. 'Freeze, Shaw.'

Shaw was snake quick. He twisted and fired two shots toward where he thought Cassidy might be. One of them blew chips of plaster into Cassidy's face as he fired. Shaw went over backward and clattered down the stair. Did he hit him? Cassidy hobbled to the stair landing. Shaw was crawling for the doorway at the bottom of the flight. Cassidy fired once as he disappeared, but he knew he had missed.

If he went down, he'd be walking into Shaw's gun. He went up. As he reached the top of the stairs, a shot blasted wood out of the wall, and then he was through and in cover. He went flat on the floor, rolled over, peeked around the doorframe. Shaw fired two quick shots that went high. Cassidy fired once, and missed, and Shaw was gone.

Cassidy rolled over on his back and reloaded his gun. Then he pushed himself up against the wall and limped to the room at the end of the hall. When he opened the door, Rhonda stared at him wide-eyed from the mattress against one wall. Her hands were tied to the radiator behind her. Her skirt was bunched around her waist, and her blouse was torn.

'Michael?' Disbelief. 'Michael. Michael.'

'It's okay. Everything's going to be okay.' He holstered his gun and crouched down to work on the knots.

'How did you get here? How did you know?' Her voice rasped with shock and fear.

'I was here when he brought you. I was looking for him.' He found his pocketknife and sawed through the clothesline Shaw had used to tie her.

'He's supposed to be in prison.'

'I know. Hold on for a second.'

407

'Where are you going? Don't go.' She pulled at his sleeve.

'I'll be right back.' He got up and went out in the hall and listened. The stairs were covered with grit and dirt, and he did not think Shaw could sneak up quietly. He heard nothing. He went back into the room. Rhonda had straightened her skirt and had done the best she could with her blouse. 'How do we get out of here?' she asked.

'I'm working on it.' He grabbed the M-1 and went back into the hall. He took a quick peek around the doorway to the stairs. Shaw was out of sight two flights down. Cassidy checked the safety at the front of the trigger guard and then fired three shots spaced along the wall where Shaw might be hiding. The .30 caliber ammunition was powerful enough to blow through the plaster. Maybe he'd get a lucky hit, but at least it would remind Shaw that they had more fire power than just his .38. He went back into the room and propped the rifle near the door.

'He was in prison,' Rhonda said. 'I didn't have to think about him anymore. I ran across the street to get some cigarettes, and he grabbed me when I came out of the store. He had a gun.' She took a deep breath and let it out. 'He was going to rape me. He acted like he was going to do me a favor.'

'Stay here. I'm going to talk to him.'

'I'm not staying here. I'm going with you.'

'Rhonda—'

'I'm going with you. I'm not going to stay here alone.'

She followed him back out into the ruined hall. Cassidy stood where he could be heard but not seen and called down the stairway. 'Shaw. Hey, Shaw.'

'Yeah?' From his voice, he was somewhere near the third-floor door.

'The best thing you can do is get in your car and take off. With a little lead time, you might get away.'

'Don't worry about me getting away. I'll be out of the country by this evening. I can't leave yet. I built a whole plan to get you here, and here you are.'

'It's a stalemate. You can't come up, and we can't come down. I told my partner what I was doing. He knows you're out of prison. When I don't show up for my shift, he'll come looking.' Rhonda looked at him with hope.

Silence while Shaw thought it over.

'I don't think so. If you'd told him, he would have come with you. No, no. You came looking for me alone. That's how you want it to end – you and me. Nobody to interfere.'

The hope went out of Rhonda's eyes.

'Hey, Cassidy, how'd you do the thing with my wallet?'

'I don't know what you're talking about.'

'Yeah, yeah, yeah. I figure it was that couple with the dogs. The blond with great ass.'

'What couple?'

'Sure. Sure. I didn't kill the Brandts. Did you? This is the time for truth telling, Cassidy. You're not getting out of here.'

'I didn't kill them.'

'Maybe, but you know I didn't. You set me up. You framed me.' There was a shuffling, scraping below, and Cassidy fired two more shots through the wall hoping to get lucky.

Shaw laughed. 'Hey, Cassidy, I'll tell you what. If you come down, I'll let the woman go.'

Rhonda shook her head violently. She knew the lie.

'She says, no,' Cassidy yelled.

'All right. She's on your head. I gave you the chance. I have a solution. It's not perfect. I wanted to watch you die. But this'll work for me. At least I'll hear you scream.'

Rhonda touched him, her face tight with alarm. 'What does he mean?'

'I don't know. Nothing. He's making a noise.' He wished he believed it. He led her back into the room and inventoried what was there – the mattress, the propane tank with the heater attached. Was there something he could do with that? If there was, it escaped him. The jugs of water, useful for a long siege. Could they wait Shaw out? Maybe. He could not think of another choice.

'Michael,' Rhonda was standing in the open door. 'He's doing something.'

They could hear scraping sounds and occasional thumps and clatter rising from the stairwell. Cassidy, carrying the rifle, edged around the stair door and looked down. A pile of demolition debris was growing on the third-floor landing. As Cassidy watched, pieces of broken wood flew through the doorway and landed on the pile. A moment later, a large wad of torn wallpaper followed. Cassidy leveled the rifle at the wall near the doorway and fired two shots. For a moment it was quiet below, and then Shaw threw more wood on the pile from a different angle.

'What's he doing?' Rhonda asked. 'Is he trying to block us from getting down there?'

She had her answer a moment later. A line of fire crept along a ribbon of wallpaper and disappeared into the pile. For a few seconds Cassidy thought the pile had smothered the flame, but then fire began to flicker deep in the pile. Something dry and volatile caught, and a tongue of flame rose and licked the wall of the landing. The material that covered the plaster began to burn.

'What do we do?' She was scared, but her voice was steady.

'There has to be another way out.'

'The roof?'

'There's an alley between us and the next building. It's too far to jump.'

'Maybe we'll find something on the roof, a plank or something. Maybe we can make a bridge.'

It did not take them long to search the fifth floor. There was no trapdoor to the roof.

By the time they got back to the stairs, the fire was raging. The stairwell acted like a chimney, and the blast of heat coming up the stairs drove them back from the door.

'Well, at least we don't have to worry about him sneaking up,' Cassidy said.

It got no smile from Rhonda. 'Someone on the block has to have noticed. Someone will call the Fire Department.'

411

'They don't know we're in here. The firemen'll try to keep the fire from spreading to the next building. That won't do us any good.'

He led her out around the heat that blew up the stairwell to the elevator doors. Like all the other doors to the shaft except at the first floor, they were closed. He tried to fit his fingers into the seam where they came together, but there was no room. He stepped back and shouldered the rifle. 'Better stand back. We might get a ricochet.' She crossed to the other side of the hall. Cassidy aimed the rifle at the join between the two elevator doors. He fired. A hole appeared at the door seam. He shifted his aim and fired again. The second shot caught the right edge of the hole. The third caught the left. The clip popped out with a *ping*. The rifle was empty.

He went to look at his work. He could get two fingers into the hole, but it was not enough to move the doors. He jammed the tip of the rifle barrel in and levered. The doors creaked open a few inches and stopped.

'Wait,' Rhonda said, 'I'll find something bigger.' She went to one of the demolition piles and came back with a five-foot piece of two by four and pushed it into the gap between the two doors. They both put hands on it. 'Ready?'

'Yes,' Cassidy said, and they leaned into it. The doors scraped open a few more feet.

Cassidy stepped into the gap between the two doors. The interior walls were burning on the third and fourth floors, and the brick walls of the shaft were beginning to heat up. The air from the shaft was warm, but not yet hot. The shaft was dark. Only the doors on the first floor were open, but the windows on that floor were blocked. Cassidy put his back against one door and shoved hard on the other, and that one gave another foot and then stopped and would not move again.

'How do we get down?' Rhonda asked.

Cassidy lit a match and leaned into the shaft. There was enough light to show him the steel rungs of a maintenance ladder fixed to the wall to the left of the doors.

He pulled back out of the gap. 'There's a ladder. The ledge leading to it isn't very wide, but we can get to it if we're careful.'

'What happens if he looks up?'

'I shoot him, or he shoots us.'

'This is why my mother didn't want me going out with a cop.'

There was a roar from the stairwell, and a tongue of flame reached out into the fifth floor and then withdrew again.

'We've got to get off this floor,' Cassidy said. 'Stay here. I'll be right back.'

'Michael,' she protested.

'Right back.' He hobbled fast to the room, grabbed the blanket off the bed and the two full jugs of water and hobbled back to where Rhonda waited. The fire roared in the stairwell, and somewhere below them a ceiling collapsed with a crash. Cassidy gave Rhonda the blanket.

'Put it over your head and shoulders.' When she did, he poured a jug of water on the blanket. She gasped with shock from the cold as it soaked the blanket and her clothes. He handed her the other bottle, and she soaked his head and coat with what was left.

A piece of the wall at the top of the stairs blew out, and flames surged into the fifth-floor hall.

'We have to go.' Cassidy turned his back on the shaft, held the edges of the doors and felt for the ledge with his foot. It was narrow and his heel hung over the drop. He released the door edge with one hand and groped to his left until he found a metal brace on the door he could grab. He shuffled left, holding onto the brace with his chest pressed against the door. 'Rhonda, come on.' He watched while she backed through the door the way he had. Her high heel caught on the door track, and for a moment he thought she was going to topple backward down the shaft. She caught herself and he could hear her breath blow out in relief. 'Rhonda, get rid of the shoes.'

'Goddamn it, they cost me fifty bucks.' She stepped back into the hall and out of sight, and then reappeared crouched down in the door gap. She wedged the heel of one shoe in the slot where the door ran, and levered until the heel broke off. She did the same thing with the second one, stood to put the heelless shoes on, and stepped back into the gap. 'Someone is going to pay for those.' She felt gingerly for the ledge, found it, and brought the other foot out to join it.

'Reach out. There's a metal brace about three feet to your left at shoulder height.' She reached for it and missed. 'A little higher. There. There. Come on. No problem now.'

She edged slowly away from the door. Cassidy

414

shuffled out of her way toward the end of the ledge. He stretched out for the ladder, got a grip on a vertical, reached out with his left foot and found a rung, and pulled himself over. 'Okay,' he said to Rhonda, 'come on.' The wall in front of him was warm. The longer they waited the hotter the shaft would become. She shuffled toward him on the narrow ledge.

'I'm not scared. I'm not scared. I'm not scared.' She said it over and over again as she came. Then she stopped. 'I can't reach. Cassidy?'

'I'll get you. It's all right. I'll get you.' He reached toward her. 'Don't take my hand. Go up a little and lock on my wrist. It's a stronger grip.' Her hand was too small to go all the way around his wrist, but his went easily around hers. 'When I say, go, push off and I'll pull you over. Grab for the ladder with your other hand.'

'I'm not scared. I'm not scared. I'm not scared.'

'Come on.'

'Oh, Christ . . .'

When she pushed off, the leather sole of her shoe slipped on the metal of the ledge. She flailed for the ladder with her free hand, but missed and swung like a pendulum over the drop held only by their locked wrists. She let out a cry of fear.

'Grab for the ladder.' He could feel their hands slipping. 'Grab it.' The swing had turned her free hand away, and when she twisted for the ladder, he felt her grip on his wrist slip more. He squeezed hard and swung her toward him and heard her gasp as she banged into the ladder below him, and then the weight on his arm slackened as she got a foot on a rung.

415

'Okay. Okay. Let me go. I've got it.' For a moment her head rested against his leg, and he could hear her breath rush in and out. She moved lower on the ladder. He leaned his head against the steel rung and tried to banish the vision of her falling.

'Are you all right?' he asked.

'I don't know. I think so. Jesus Christ, I don't want to do that again.' On the other side of the wall, something went off like a bomb. The propane tank for the heater.

'We can't stay here. We have to go down. Can you do that?'

'Yes.'

When Cassidy felt her move down, he followed.

'The wall is much hotter down here. Ow.'

'What?'

'It burned me.'

'Don't touch it.'

'Good advice, Michael. Thanks.' She kept going.

The fire roared outside the fourth-floor elevator doors. Smoke wisped in around the edges, and there was a line of red where the doors did not quite join. The brick wall they passed grumbled and crackled in the heat. The air smelled of burned metal and brick, of wood smoke, and the stench of burning plaster.

'Michael,' said Rhonda, halfway down to the third floor. 'I don't know if I can go any further. The rungs are really hot here. Ow, shit.' She climbed back up until her head was at Cassidy's knees. 'I burned my hand.'

'It'll be cooler once we're past the third floor.'

416

'It was burning through my shoes, too.'

'Hold on.' Cassidy found his pocketknife. He looped one arm around an iron vertical for support, and opened the knife. 'I'm going to cut strips off the blanket. We'll wrap our hands.' The wet cloth resisted the knife. He had to work the tip of the blade through and saw it until he cut a long strip free. He cut it in shorter lengths. They wrapped their hands and went down.

The elevator doors at the third floor bulged inward. The fire on the other side had burned a cherry-red patch of metal in the middle of one door. The rungs under their shoes were hot enough to burn their feet through their soles, and the wet blanket strips on their hands steamed. A brick exploded from the wall above the third-floor elevator doors, then another one, and another. Flames snaked out through the hole into the shaft and then retreated.

'Michael, the whole place is coming down.' Her voice was harsh with strain.

The rungs of the ladder were cooler, and the air seemed less dense as they went below the third floor. Rhonda stopped below him opposite the second-floor elevator doors. 'It's better here,' she said. They could see the top of the elevator twenty feet below. 'Why don't we go down to the bottom?' she asked.

'We don't know where Shaw is. If he thinks we could use the shaft to get down, he may be set up to see into the gap at the top of the elevator. He'd have us before we had a chance at him.'

'He'll be gone by now. He must think we're dead. He wouldn't risk staying.'

'Are you sure?'

'No.'

'We're okay here for a while. The firemen are going to show up any minute. People were working up the street. Someone will have called in the alarm. When we hear them, we go. Shaw's not going to do anything in front of a bunch of firemen.'

Just under the fourth floor a section of shaft wall blew out. Shards of brick, plaster, and burning wood rained down on them. Cassidy leaned out to shelter Rhonda below him. A piece of flaming wood landed on his shoulder. He brushed it off as another part of the shaft wall exploded above them. Cinders and flaming bits of wood rained down on them. They burned through Cassidy's wet hair and coat before he could slap them off.

Thirty-Nine

Spencer Shaw stood at the bottom of the stairway on the first floor and listened to the roar of the fire and the explosion of bricks as the building destroyed itself above him. Goddamn, he liked this. He'd never done anything as goddamn much fun as this. He'd done a lot of fun shit in his life, but he'd never burned a whole goddamn building down. Flaming debris blocked the stairs from the second floor up, and the walls along the stairs were burning. A few minutes earlier he had gone part way up the stairs in time to watch sections of the third-floor ceiling collapse. When the second floor caught fire, he retreated to the first floor. It would not be long before the ceiling above him collapsed. The first floor was concrete, but the walls would catch. Cassidy and the broad had to be dead. It pissed him off that he had not seen Cassidy die, but what the fuck? Into each life a little rain must fall. It was time to go.

He started the Studebaker and then went to unbolt the big front doors. He could hear fire engine sirens as they crowded into the street. When he shoved the doors wide, cold wind rushed in. The staircase acted like a chimney, and the new air fed the fire to a higher rage. Shaw got into the car, put it in reverse, and rolled it toward the door. Idlewild Airport in an hour. TWA to Los Angeles. Pan Am tomorrow out to Hawaii and then Guam, Hong Kong, and then finally Saigon. Saigon was going to be fun. Shit was happening there.

A tornado of fresh air swirled up the elevator shaft sandblasting Cassidy and Rhonda with dust and dirt from below. The air was almost too thick to breath, but the wind drove the rain of flaming embers back up the shaft. That was the good part, but the new air fueled the fire higher and hotter. Parts of the walls at the top of the shaft collapsed inwards, and pieces of the shaft ceiling crashed down in flames to the top of the elevator.

'Go. Go,' Cassidy shouted over the roar. 'He opened the doors. He's gone.'

419

Rhonda climbed quickly down the last twenty feet to the roof of the elevator. Cassidy was right behind her. He kicked flaming pieces of wood out of the way and led her to the gap between the elevator roof and the first floor. He stirrupped his hands. She put a foot in and scrambled out onto the floor. He levered himself up and rolled out after her. Shaw's car was gone, and the doors were open. A piece of the ceiling at the back of the first-floor hall fell in a shower of sparks. They ran for the open door and out onto the street that was now flickering with the red lights of fire engines and alive with the shouts of firemen dragging hoses toward the building.

'Where the hell did you come from?' one of them yelled in surprise. He did not wait for an answer. His hose bucked tight with water. He unblocked the nozzle and walked the stream up the wall and into a second-floor window. Flames bannered from all the windows from the second floor to the top of the building.

Cassidy pulled Rhonda out of the way of the firemen. She limped alongside him. 'I've got to sit down, Michael. My feet are burned.'

'Hey,' Cassidy called to a fireman, 'we need a medic. She's got some burns.'

'Jesus, you sure do. There's an ambulance on the other side of that pumper,' the man said.

Cassidy realized what they looked like – black with soot, singed, limping.

'Come on.' He put an arm around Rhonda's waist and walked her around the back of a fire truck. A paramedic saw them and left the ambulance to put an arm around Rhonda from the other side to guide her to sit on the back bumper under the open doors. 'Her feet are burned,' Cassidy said.

'That's not all of it,' the medic said. 'She's got a couple of nasty burns on her arm, and one on her cheek.'

'I didn't feel those,' Rhonda said.

'Let's get those shoes off,' the medic said, and went down on one knee to help her. He glanced up at Cassidy. 'What about you? You're limping.'

'Just a sprain. I'll be okay.'

'You've got burns that need attention.'

'Take care of her. I'll be right back.'

The Studebaker was fifty feet away. It was blocked by a fire engine. Spencer Shaw stood next to the open door arguing with a fireman. Cassidy took his gun out from under his arm.

'Hey,' the medic said in alarm.

'I'm a cop,' Cassidy said. He limped away. As he got closer he could hear Shaw arguing with the fireman. Their voices were thin under the racket of the fire, the shouts of the firemen, and the liquid hiss of the hoses.

'I'm on government business,' Shaw said. 'I'm going to miss my plane.'

'Sorry,' the fireman said. 'I can't help you. I can't move the truck till my captain gives me the okay.' The fireman walked away.

'Shaw,' Cassidy said to Shaw's back.

Shaw stiffened without turning. 'Jesus Christ,' he said, 'what do I have to do, put a stake through your heart?' He turned slowly. His right hand was under his jacket.

'Don't,' Cassidy said.

421

Shaw smiled like a wolf and fired through his jacket. The bullet hit Cassidy low in the side and rocked him back a step. Cassidy shot Shaw in the chest. Shaw banged back against the Studebaker and brought his gun up. Cassidy shot him again. Shaw's legs gave way and he slid down the car and sat with his legs sprawled out and his back against the door. He tried to raise the gun but didn't have the strength. He looked down at the blood on his chest and then up at Cassidy. 'Shit,' he said. 'This wasn't supposed to happen.' He toppled over sideways, dead before his head hit the street.

Cassidy touched his side. His hand came away sticky with blood. The gun was heavy in his other hand, and it took an effort to get it back in the holster. He started back toward Rhonda and the medic. After a few steps, it seemed too far. One knee crumpled, and he sank to the street. He managed to break his fall with one hand and as he lay there on his back, he saw the building give up and cascade in on itself with a crackling roar. Flames and sparks flared into the sky.

Cassidy blacked out.

Forty

Cassidy swam up through layers of drugs to a vague understanding that he was in a hospital room. His sister, Leah, leaned over him and asked, 'Are you awake?'

'No,' he said, and swam back down.

When he awoke again, she was sitting in a chair by the window reading a book. 'Still here?' he asked.

'That was yesterday.' She put the book aside and came to the bed.

'How long have I been here?'

'Three days.' She leaned over and kissed him on the forehead. 'I'm going to go tell the doctor you're awake.'

The doctor arrived with a nurse named Valerie. Doctor Farrow was a short, harried man in his forties with the distracted air of someone with many things to do and not enough time. 'How are you, Mr Cassidy?' He picked up the clipboard at the end of the bed and checked the nurses' notations.

'I was going to ask you that.'

'Not too bad, I think, considering. Valerie's going to help you and we'll take a look.'

The nurse helped Cassidy roll to his side.

Farrow cut the bandage with scissors and peeled it from the wound. He had gentle hands. 'The bullet hit a rib and came out your back, just missing the spine. Lucky that,' Farrow said. 'You had some internal bleeding and lost a good bit of blood, but nothing vital damaged. Except for your left shoulder, the burns aren't too bad. We'll keep an eye on that one for the rest of the week. You have a sprained ankle, but that's going to take care of itself. All and all not too bad, I'd say.' He straightened up. 'Nurse, let's get a fresh dressing on the wound.'

'What about Miss Raskin?' Cassidy asked.

'We saw to the burns, kept her overnight for observation, and discharged her in the morning. Her feet will be tender for a while. I've asked her to stay off them as much as possible, but it's up to her what that means.' He patted Cassidy on the shoulder and left the room.

Cassidy was sitting up against the elevated head of the bed when his brother, Brian, came into the room. Leah had gone home. Brian pulled a chair up next to the bed. 'Are you all right? You look like crap.'

'Nothing better than family sympathy.'

'Dad was here, but he had to go to rehearsal. He wants you to come stay with him and Megan when they let you out. He insists.'

Brian stayed for a few more minutes. 'The papers' stories are pretty much all the same: rogue CIA officer escapes from prison, returns to New York for revenge. Hero cop saves the newspaper reporter. A wild west finish with gunplay in the street.'

'Uh-huh.'

'I think there's more to it than that. Am I right?'

'Not much.'

'Bull. Why'd Shaw risk his life to revenge a three-year sentence that would have seen him on the street in two? Why'd he want you so badly?'

'I don't know.'

'You're not going to tell me.' He watched Cassidy for a moment and then nodded in acceptance. 'Okay. But I'd like to get you on film when you feel up to it. Whatever details you want to

424

give. How you knew where he was. What happened in the building. How you got out. It'll be a good follow up to the program we did on Shaw's arrest and the experiments they were running. Will you do that?'

'Yes.'

'Are you ever going to tell me the rest of it?'

'Maybe when we're old and gray.'

'Deal.' Brian patted him on the shoulder and left.

Rhonda came the next day. She knocked tentatively on the door frame, because his head was turned away, and she was not sure if he was asleep.

He wasn't. 'Hey, come in.'

'Hi. How are you?' She seemed nervous.

'I'm okay. A little tender in places, but they keep me doped up.'

She bent down to kiss him on the cheek. When she straightened, she touched the dark red-and-blue scarf she wore on her head. 'Want to see?'

'Sure.'

She pulled the scarf off. Her skull was bare of hair and patched with small, white dressings. 'They shaved parts to get at the burns. I figured, what the hell, we might as well do the whole thing and let it all grow in together. What do you think?'

'Only you could pull it off.'

'Liar.' She stole a cigarette from the pack on the bedside table. 'Did you see my story?'

'No. I haven't seen a paper.'

'It tells how I carried you down the ladder in the elevator shaft and out onto the street. I

425

decided to let you have the credit for shooting Shaw.'

'It's the kind of accuracy in reporting we expect of the *Post*.'

'They moved me to the Metro desk.'

'Congratulations. And it's about time.'

She smiled. 'Thanks.' She stubbed out the cigarette she had just lit. The nervousness was back. 'I want you to meet someone.'

'Sure.'

She went out into the hall and came back trailed by a tall, thin man with curly dark hair. 'Michael, this is Bill Long. I told you about him.'

What had she told him? She said she met someone, but that was all. Maybe there was no need to say any more after that. The rest was just details. 'Bill, good to meet you.'

Long shook his hand and then stepped back from the bed. 'Good to meet you. You're a hero in my book, what you did for her. Thank you.'

'You're welcome.'

Long smiled. 'Rhonda, I'll wait for you out in the hall. Take your time.' He nodded to Cassidy, and left the room.

'Michael,' Rhonda said. 'I . . .' She trailed off.

'Rhonda, it's okay. He seems like a nice guy. I'm happy for you.'

'Thanks.' She kissed him on the cheek, looked back once as she left the room, and then she was gone.

Shit. Well, that's that – leaving Cassidy sad and just a little relieved.

Orso came by and brought a box of chocolates and a police stenographer to take Cassidy's report

426

of what happened in the building on Bethune Street. He ate half the chocolates while he listened with a hint of a smile to Cassidy's truths and half-truths. When they were finished, he patted Cassidy on the shoulder and said, 'Good story,' and followed the stenographer out of the room.

Dr Farrow decided he was well enough to get out at the end of the week. Cassidy, without much reluctance, allowed himself to be chivvied by his family into accepting his father's invitation to stay for a while in the apartment in the St Moritz with its stunning view north over the length of Central Park. His father's play was days from opening, and he was rarely there. His stepmother, Megan, understood instinctively that Cassidy did not want company. She taught him some dancer's exercises that would strengthen the areas the bullet had pierced and left him to his own devices.

Kay Lockridge came by one day. She had meetings with money people on Wall Street and then an appointment with Mayor Robert Wagner in the afternoon. She brought him an expensive bottle of single malt Scotch. They talked mostly about family the way people do when they've been worried and need to feel close. When it was time for her to go, Cassidy walked her to the door. While they waited for the elevator, Kay said, 'I saw Allen Dulles the other day. He wanted me to give you a message.'

'What?'

'He said, "Tell him the offer still stands. Tell him, I like winners." What does that mean?'

427

'He offered me a job with the CIA when I met him at your house. I said, no. I killed Shaw, so now I look like a useful replacement.'

'Are you going to take it?'

'Will you give him a message from me?'

'Of course.'

'Tell him to go fuck himself.'

She smiled. 'I'll do that.' The elevator arrived. She kissed him on the cheek, and went away.

After a week the apartment closed in on him, and he had to get out.

It was a cold, clear day. High clouds drifted through the blue sky above the city. Cassidy waited for a break in traffic to cross Central Park South. He went into the park and found the place where Leon Dudek's body had lain on the first cold night of fall. There were a few discolored patches on the pavement. Maybe they were Leon's blood and piss, but probably not. In the past months tens of thousands of people had walked across this spot without knowing what had happened here. He walked out to Fifth Avenue and caught a cab going downtown. He had the driver drop him on Delancey Street and walked the last couple of blocks to Freddy's shack under the Williamsburg Bridge. The door was open. The bed was gone. The clothes were gone. The stove was gone, and so was the shelf that held the straight razors. There was no more evidence of Freddy's presence here than there was of Leon's in the park.

Cassidy walked to Houston Street and caught a cab back uptown. He settled back in the seat and watched the city pass by. His wound ached.

His legs were tired. He felt kind of – what? – used up. The thought jerked a bark of laughter out of him that made the driver check him in the rearview mirror.

He paid off the cab at the Plaza Hotel and walked the last long block. As he approached the St Moritz, he saw Orso walking toward him from the west. He raised a hand, and Orso nodded in response and waited for him at the entrance.

'How are you doing?' Orso asked.

'Fine.'

'Yeah, I can see that.'

'How are you?'

'Not so hot. Amy gave me my walking papers.' He tried to throw it away, but his pain was clear.

'How come?'

'She said she met someone.' He shrugged.

'Huh. I've heard that song recently.'

'I thought we could go have a drink.'

'Maybe have couple,' Cassidy said. 'Let's walk down and see if Toots Shor is still selling booze.'

Historical Note

At the end of World War Two in 1945, a covert operation originally dubbed Overcast and later renamed Operation Paperclip brought roughly sixteen hundred German scientists to the United States to work for America during the Cold War. The program was run by the newly formed Joint Intelligence Objectives Agency (JIOA). The goal was to harness German scientific resources to help develop America's arsenal of rockets, and biological and chemical weapons, and to make sure those same scientists did not end up working in the Soviet Union. President Harry Truman sanctioned the operation but forbade the agency from recruiting any Nazi members who might be suspected of war crimes. Officials within the JIOA and the Office of Strategic Services (OSS), the forerunner of the CIA, feeling the scientists' knowledge was crucial to the country's Cold War efforts, often ignored this directive by rewriting or eliminating incriminating evidence of war crimes from the scientists' records.

After World War Two, the CIA, and the US Army Biological Laboratories at Fort Detrick, Maryland, did work with industrial partners such as the pharmaceutical concern Merck & Co. to develop bioweapons.

*   *   *

430

The MK-Ultra project, known also as Project Artichoke, and earlier as Project Bluebird, was started on the order of CIA Director Allen Dulles in April 1953. It was a program to develop mind-controlling drugs for possible espionage and military uses in response to Soviet, Chinese, and North Korean use of mind-control techniques on US prisoners of war in Korea. One of the major aims of its research was to determine the efficacy of LSD as an interrogation tool. It was hoped that it would be a useful 'truth serum' for the interrogation of suspected Soviet spies during the Cold War. It was additionally hoped that the drug would induce amnesia in the subjects questioned so that the spies would have no memory of the interrogation and would, therefore, have no reason to warn their masters about the secrets betrayed. Dulles approved MK-Ultra with an initial budget of $300,000. Under its auspices LSD was administered to CIA and other government employees, doctors, prison inmates, mental patients, and prostitutes and their clients, often without their permission or knowledge. The program was reduced in scope in the 1960s, and was terminated in 1973. That year, Richard Helms, then Director of the CIA, ordered the records on MK-Ultra and similar projects destroyed.

In the mid-fifties an American biological warfare scientist working for the CIA went out a window of a New York City hotel after being covertly dosed with LSD by a CIA superior. It was not the Astor Hotel.

431

The CIA's MK-Ultra project did set up safe houses in Greenwich Village and later San Francisco where prostitutes brought their johns and covertly fed them LSD while operatives watched through one-way windows.

The rest of the story is fiction.

Author's Note

Night Watch is the third novel in the Michael Cassidy series. While the story works by itself, there are references in it to events and people from the first novel, *Night Life*. Spencer Shaw's half brother, Russell Crofoot, was a CIA agent killed near Cassidy's apartment two years before the events of *Night Watch*. Dylan McCue, Cassidy's lost love, was also a significant actor in *Night Life*.

Night Life was followed by *Night Work*, whose story takes place two years after the events of *Night Watch*, so the strict chronology of the books would be *Night Life*, which takes place in New York City in 1954, *Night Watch* – New York City and Washington, DC in 1956, and *Night Work* – Havana Cuba, in 1959, at the time of Fidel Castro's successful revolution and his first visit to New York.

Each book stands alone, but there may be some advantage to reading them in this chronological order. It was the author's own peculiarities that led him to write them out of the proper order, and the characters in the books should not be penalized for his failings.

433